AS MASLOV LOCKED HIMSELF INTO the ski-lift-like seat, the cable that led to the iceberg rocked from side to side. The seat slid swiftly along the cable taking Maslov out over the churning frigid water. From the deck of the ship, Sally followed his progress anxiously, wishing she had her mini-cam with her.

The cable's midpoint was perilously close to the sea. The rolling and pitching of the ship was transmitted to the cable, and its vibrations set Maslov bobbing up and down like a yo-yo. He inched his way forward with great effort, and out of the corner of his eye he caught sight of an enormous, freak wave rising directly to his starboard side. Grasping the line as tightly as he could, he braced himself for the onslaught. Higher and higher the gigantic wall of water rose, eventually curling itself and smashing down upon him in a raging, freezing, gray-green deluge.

Helpless, Sally watched the assault of the giant wave in horror. When it subsided, she saw the cable was empty. Yuri Maslov was nowhere in sight. . . .

THE AQUARIUS TRANSFER

by

Robert F. Joseph

FAWCETT GOLD MEDAL • NEW YORK

THE AQUARIUS TRANSFER

Published by Fawcett Gold Medal Books, CBS Educational and Professional Publishing, a division of CBS Inc.

ISBN: 0-449-14467-4

Printed in the United States of America

First Fawcett Gold Medal printing: May 1982

10 9 8 7 6 5 4 3 2 1

This book is dedicated to
Richard Pine

The author wishes to express his deep appreciation to the following for their generous help and technical assistance in putting together this book.

Dez Fretz
Roger Dudnick
David Bond
Tom Hardison
Fred Gorel
Phil Sotel
Mike Peterson
Jim Ordner
Lt. Mel Sundin, U.S.N., and the many other men of the U.S. Naval Support Force, Antarctica
and
Celeste Mitchell

CALIFORNIA
1983

1

Beneath the ice her mouth gasped desperately for bubbles of trapped air while her fingers clawed frantically at the frozen layer above that entombed her. Whatever sounds she might have uttered to signal her distress could not penetrate the icy sheet. Even if they could have, they would have been drowned out by the relentless howling of the savage wind. He, too, heard that frightful wind and felt the vicious, stunning cold that could freeze human eyes hard as marbles and make every breath a searing, stabbing agony. But he had to ignore it, ignore the shock, the pain, the wind, the numbing cold. He had to go on. He had to reach her. Save her. He had to. But his legs refused to move, refused to carry him to where she was trapped. He felt as though he were running in place, moving his legs up and down, pumping hard but getting nowhere. No matter how fast he pumped his limbs, he remained stuck in the same place. And it was growing late. Too late. He had to move quickly. He had to. . . .

"Neal . . ." Ingrid said softly, not wanting to startle him, as she gently laid her hand on his shoulder.

"Huh? What? . . ." Neal Haverson awakened with such a violent start that his wife instinctively backed off. He shook his head as if he were clearing his brain and stared at his wife in the light of the desk lamp, his clear blue eyes bewildered, questioning. "What's the matter?" he mumbled, although he already knew the answer from her troubled expression.

"I think you'd better come to bed," she replied quietly, her tone almost maternal. Her pale green negligee hung loosely about her tall, slender, slightly angular body. Her blond hair

7

was tangled, indicating that she had been in bed, probably asleep.

Haverson gazed around the room, struggling to orient himself. "Did I wake you?" he asked. In his head the polar wind was still howling. Outside, beyond the sliding glass windows leading to the patio, not a single breeze stirred; the night air was stifling and close. Slowly, the den began once again to be familiar, cluttered and comfortable with all the things that made it his room: shelves of technical books and manuals on all aspects of ships; his drafting table; papers and monographs he had published. The walls were filled with framed photographs, diplomas, and other personal mementoes: their wedding picture taken just outside the chapel at Annapolis, Ingrid in veil and train, he in his crisp white uniform, gloves, scabbard, a shot of the training ship on which he had spent one of the most exciting summers of his undergraduate days; the gunboat riddled with Viet Cong sniper fire on which he had patrolled the Mekong River; his diploma in physics from graduate school; the cover of *Scientific American* in which his first article had appeared.

"I wasn't asleep very long," she replied.

He squinted at the brass ship's clock on the mantel over the fireplace. "I didn't realize it was so late," he said, rising and gathering up a group of drawings and papers.

Glancing at one of the sketches, Ingrid asked, "What's this?"

"This? Oh, just an idea for some equipment to apply insulation," he answered, slipping it into a folder.

"Insulation?"

"Underwater insulation. It's a special method." His blue eyes met her hazel ones, and his voice dropped its casual tone and became grave. "I was having that dream again, wasn't I?"

"Yes," she nodded.

He looked at her anxiously. "Was I making a lot of noise?"

"No. You were muttering. Moaning."

"Did I wake the girls?"

"I doubt it. Nothing wakes them once they're asleep."

"It was so vivid," he said, shaking his head. "I kept seeing her under the ice. I wanted to get to her so bad, to help her, but I couldn't move. I was powerless."

Ingrid sighed. "Maybe you'd better make an appointment with Dr. Miller," she suggested.

8

"What for? Miller said he can't do anything more for me. He said the nightmares will start tapering off eventually."

"Maybe you should see another doctor."

"Those shrinks are all the same," he said, reaching across the desk and snapping off the light. He put his arm around her smooth, cool shoulders and pulled her close, inhaling the fresh scent of her hair, kissing the top of her head.

"Let's go to bed, Neal. It's late and we're both tired."

"Got a big day tomorrow?"

"No bigger than usual."

"I think forty kids in one classroom is too many for one teacher," he declared.

"Tell the schoolboard that," she said. "And the voters."

"You don't have to work," he reminded her.

"I like teaching," she said. "It took me long enough to get my credentials. I want to use them."

"It took you a long time because you were busy raising two kids."

"And taking care of you," she added, sliding her fingers through his and giving them a squeeze. "That is, when you were home—which wasn't often."

"You could quit," he reiterated. "We don't need the money. After years in the navy, I admit that this cruise ship isn't much, but the pay is okay. That's the only good thing about it."

"What about all those lonely, horny widows that are always throwing themselves at you?" she teased, cheerfully aware that even at forty-two her husband was still devastatingly attractive.

"I let them know right off that I'm happily married."

"When has *that* ever stopped you?"

"Hey, what do you mean?"

"Let's face it, Neal, dear, fidelity has never been your long suit."

"It is now," he insisted.

Smiling in the darkness, she said, "We'll see."

The air in the bedroom was hot and dry and the bedclothes snapped and crackled with static electricity. Side by side they lay outside the covers, Haverson in only a pair of undershorts.

"Neal, are you still upset about what happened in New York last week?" Ingrid asked.

"I'm not 'upset,' just disappointed," he replied. "I didn't expect Rudd International to turn down my proposal flat like

9

that—not after the way their Hydrolliance division keeps dishing out all that propaganda about how dedicated they are to bringing water to the arid areas of the world. Hell, you've seen their commercials on TV. At least, I got in to see Jeremiah Gaines."

"I've forgotten who he is."

"He used to be old Howard Rudd's right-hand man," Haverson replied. "For a guy his age he's sharp as hell."

"Then why'd he turn you down?"

"Rudd's widow got into the act. She said the company is committed to an entirely different kind of approach to the water problem, a whole different technology, grandiose schemes—like changing the course of big rivers."

"What's she got to do with it?"

"She's running the company now," he explained. "Gaines complimented me on my work. It was a case of 'thanks-but-no-thanks.'"

Resting her head against his bare chest, she said, "Well, somebody will wake up and take an interest in your idea one of these days."

Pleased by her encouragement and by having her close, he said, "I'll tell you one thing, I'm going to push like hell until I get this thing off the ground."

"I know."

"The trouble is nobody takes water seriously in this country," he complained.

His statement shook Ingrid out of a momentary reverie. "What are you talking about?" Beyond the windows she could see the silhouette of her favorite Indian laurel tree and remembered how brown and withered it was. "We're in the middle of one of the most severe droughts in history," she said. "We haven't been able to water the lawn or our so-called 'ornamental shrubs' for over a year. Every plant, every blade of grass on this property is dead or dying, for God's sake! How can you say that nobody takes water seriously when things are so bad it's got to be rationed? Every house in Los Angeles County gets water for only two hours a day. People are so uptight that if anybody dared to turn on a sprinkler, they'd find the cops at their door—to say nothing to what their neighbors might do to them."

"Honey, you're talking about *California*," he reminded her.

"I *know* I'm talking about California."

"Yes, but some of the country is being plagued by floods and torrential rains. The rest of the United States, including

10

the Congress, couldn't care less about what is happening to us. What people don't realize is that what's happening here in California could happen all over the world. And fast. Before anybody knows it. I'll tell you one thing, a water shortage will make the oil shortage look like a piece of cake. Nobody can drink oil."

"Enough," Ingrid said, snuggling closer. Glad to feel her near him in spite of the oppressive heat, he enclosed her in his arms, enjoying the faint traces of cologne in the nape of her neck. Their lips touched, gently at first, then more forcefully, hungrily. Ingrid pressed against him, warm and demanding, her soft hands traveling lightly and deftly over his shoulders, back, and chest and finally inside the elastic waistband of his shorts, producing a strong surge of sexual excitement. As he slowly lifted the hem of her negligee, she moaned softly, encouragingly, and, in moments, the drought, the heatwave, the terrible nightmare were all forgotten, dissolved in the pleasure and passion of the night.

The next morning Haverson appeared for breakfast in his uniform, which consisted of a short-sleeved shirt with gold epaulets, white bermuda-length shorts, and white knee socks, an outfit well suited to the sweltering weather.

"Well, Captain Haverson, you look very dashing," she said. "Hairy knees and all."

Approaching her from behind as she stood at the stove, he kissed her and playfully pinched her bottom at the same time. "You look pretty good yourself."

"Thanks," she said, "considering I haven't had a morning shower."

"Jesus, I hate getting dressed without a morning shower," he complained.

"Well, you'd better get used to it," she said, turning off the coffee. "From all indications, this drought is going to be around for a long time."

"Not if I have anything to do with it," he said. "By the way, thanks for drawing a basin of water last night so I could shave."

"Foresight," she grinned.

"The cologne industry must be making a fortune in California since water rationing started," he said, pulling out a kitchen chair and sitting down. The kitchen was Ingrid's domain, a bright, cheerful room, mostly yellow with red hearts and blue flowers decorating the cabinets, designs reflecting her Swedish ancestry.

"I wish they'd invent something for kids—a kiddie cologne. I dread the thought of facing forty little unwashed bodies every day," she said. "How do you want your eggs?"

"Do you have to talk about unwashed bodies and my eggs in the same breath?" He made a face. "Over easy." He reached for the *Los Angeles Times* and scanned the front page. "Hey, there's one helluva fire in the west Valley," he remarked.

She nodded. "There are a lot of fires these days."

"Yeah, but this is a really big one."

"I thought I detected the faint odor of smoke this morning when I went in to wake the girls for school," she said, cracking a pair of eggs on the edge of the frying pan.

"Here's an article on the World Weather Symposium coming up in Washington," he noted. "That reminds me, I still have to answer their letter."

"Are you going?"

"I was planning to. Why?"

Ingrid sighed. "I wish you weren't."

"What?" He scowled.

"You just got back from New York. And you're off to Acapulco . . ."

"That's my job. . . ." he protested.

"When you get back from there, you'll be off right away to Washington," she continued. "You're always away. It's just like it was when you were in the navy. You're never here."

"What can I say, honey?" he replied. "It's my work. It's what puts food on the table, clothes on our backs, gas in the tanks."

"I'm not talking about your job. I'm used to that. It's all this other stuff you're involved in. When you're supposed to be home between voyages, you're either away in connection with this project of yours or else you're holed up in the den with all your books and papers and . . ."

Haverson interrupted. "I thought you understood how important this project is?"

"I do, but still . . ."

Haverson's face brightened. "I've got an idea. Why don't you go to Washington with me?"

Ingrid frowned thoughtfully. "The principal doesn't like it when we take off without a good reason."

"I suppose that going to Washington with your husband isn't a good reason?" he challenged.

"Not in the principal's eyes. But let me see what I can do about it."

"That's what I like to hear," he said, reaching out and pulling her toward him.

"Be careful, Neal," she warned, waving the spatula. "I'll overcook your eggs."

"Screw the damned eggs!" he said, giving her a loud smacking kiss. She kissed him back, but returned to the eggs.

Haverson picked up the newspaper again. "Oh, by the way, did I tell you that Terhune wants me to deliver a paper at the symposium in Washington?"

"Are you talking about *the* Dr. Thurston Terhune?"

"Right."

"He's such a radical. I mean, politically."

"I'll admit he and I don't see eye to eye on much, but he is one of the world's foremost climatologists."

"He also hates nuclear power and anything remotely related to it."

"As a climatologist, he hates anything that he thinks might—in his words—'alter the earth's delicate systems that determine climate patterns.' "

"Tell Dr. Terhune that I'm sorry, but I wish somebody would do something to alter *our* climate pattern," said Ingrid, flipping the eggs onto his plate.

2

Paul Fernandez Kirkwood, Governor of California, planted his wing-tip oxfords firmly in the open doorway of the helicopter, shook his neatly barbered head, and pounded his fist against the side of the aircraft. "Goddam!" he swore as he surveyed the vast stretches of charred and smoldering acreage below. "Jesus, will you look at that?" he said, nudging his youthful, modishly bearded press secretary, Wally Weisswasser.

"I see it, sir," Weisswasser replied, trying to sound appropriately concerned.

"What a goddam shame!" Kirkwood exclaimed. "What a goddam crying shame."

"It's devastated the whole western sector of the San Fernando Valley." Jane Garcia, the governor's attractive special assistant, said, struggling to be heard above the roar of the motor. "Homes, barns, stables, businesses. Everything. There's nothing left. Thank God it's not an area of dense population."

"It's dense enough," Kirkwood said, turning to Weisswasser. "Where is it heading now?"

"The latest reports have it sweeping across the Santa Monica mountains toward the Pacific," Weisswasser answered.

Alarmed at the news, Kirkwood paused, then asked, "Toward Malibu?"

"Yes, sir," Weisswasser affirmed. "The sheriff's department is diverting all traffic away from Pacific Coast Highway. They don't want anybody coming into the Malibu area. You always get a lot of damned curiosity-seekers with any big fire."

"We'd better head over that way," Kirkwood said, beckon-

14

ing to his chief aide, Drew Ramsdale, who was conferring with the pilot.

"What's up, Paul?" The chief advisor, a well-groomed, smartly tailored but slightly pudgy man responded immediately. Ramsdale had gone to school with Kirkwood, and he was the only one on the staff permitted to call the governor by his first name.

"Drew, tell the pilot to head out to Malibu," Kirkwood directed.

"We were just discussing that," Ramsdale said. "There's a lot of heavy air traffic out that way right now—spotter planes, fire and police choppers. The pilot's got serious reservations about entering the area with you aboard."

"Bullshit, Drew," Kirkwood snapped.

"There is a certain risk."

"Every time I go out in public there's a certain risk," Kirkwood said. Then in a more amicable tone he continued, "Look, how many years have we known each other?"

Ramsdale's round, affable face broke into a baffled smile. "What the hell kind of question is that?" At Stanford Ramsdale had managed the first campaign Kirkwood ever won. It had made him the youngest student body president in the university's history.

"You know when I make up my mind about something it's made up. Right?"

"Right, Paul."

"Then you go tell the pilot I don't care how much goddam air traffic there is over Malibu. That's where we're going."

"All right, Paul," Ramsdale agreed reluctantly and went to relay the instructions to the pilot.

The aircraft climbed higher, heading west toward the sea. In the distance great clouds of dense smoke could be seen rising into the sky, obliterating the sun.

Jane Garcia gasped. "This is the worst fire I've ever seen," she said. "It's almost as if there were some evil force raging inside it, thirsting for revenge."

Kirkwood smiled at Jane, feeling a special kinship with the bright, energetic young Chicana. His mother's family had come from Mexico with Padre Junípero Serra.

"It's unbelievable what two years without a drop of rain have done to this state," Weisswasser said. "To top it off we've been having the hottest weather ever recorded, not just in the south, but all over."

15

"I get the reports, Wally," Kirkwood said. "Daily. I don't need you to remind me."

"I know that, sir. Sorry."

"What a term this has been," Kirkwood sighed.

"It's been rough all right, sir," Weisswasser said.

"I wouldn't wish a term like this on my worst enemy—not even Preston Farleigh," Kirkwood said. "These last two years in Sacramento make my first term seem like a picnic by comparison."

"But you've been doing a great job, sir," Jane Garcia said. "Everybody says so. You were complimented on your handling of the rent control crisis. . . ."

"I know I was," Kirkwood said, looking pleased to be reminded of a success.

"You paved the way for rapid transit in Los Angeles finally," Weisswasser added. "To say nothing of the way you mediated the strike by . . ."

"That stuff is nothing compared to what's facing us now," Kirkwood interrupted, refusing to be assuaged for long.

"You mean the drought?" Jane Garcia asked.

"What else?" Kirkwood replied sharply.

As the Pacific came into view, Kirkwood left the doorway and took a seat next to Ramsdale, who was going over a sheaf of notes on a clipboard.

"Listen, Drew, I'm worried," Kirkwood confided. "Have you been able to contact Bonnie yet?"

"Not yet," Ramsdale replied. "We've been getting her answering service."

"Shit!" Kirkwood muttered. "Her goddam ranch is in a helluva bad spot, you know."

"Yes, I've been thinking about that."

"I told her not to buy out there," Kirkwood said. "But you know Bonnie. She wanted to get as far away as possible from the frenetic Hollywood scene. She's a pretty stubborn woman."

"We just got word that the sheriff's department is evacuating everybody from the area," Ramsdale said. "I contacted them and informed them that you have a personal interest in seeing that Bonnie Breit is evacuated quickly."

"Thanks, Drew. If anything happened to Bonnie, I don't know what I'd do. I'd feel like a goddam widower all over again. Once was enough.

"*Señora! Señora!*" the maid called out as she pounded frantically on the bedroom door.

Opening her eyes, Bonnie Breit strained to focus on the luminous dial of the clock on the nightstand. It was nearly noon. Despite the insistent knocking, she crawled out of bed very slowly, searched around for her robe and a pair of rubber thongs, and shuffled to the door.

"What the hell's the matter, Modesta?" Bonnie demanded, opening the door. "Why are you making such a fuss?"

"*Policía, señora,*" the short, squat Guatemalan maid, whose English was somewhat limited, replied.

"Police?" Bonnie repeated with a puzzled frown. "What the devil do they want?" She was about to reach for a cigarette, when she suddenly realized that the hall was already permeated with smoke, thicker and more irritating than cigarette smoke. "Did you leave something on the stove?"

"*No, señora.*"

"Then what's burning? Is there a fire someplace?" Bonnie asked impatiently.

"*Sí, señora,* fire." Modesta nodded and pointed toward the window.

"Fire?! My God! . . ." Bonnie's ranch extended over several brush-covered acres in the isolated hills and canyons. Running to the window, she parted the tightly drawn drapes and peered outside. The air looked hazy and gray, but the fire did not seem to be in the immediate vicinity. As she gazed out, she heard the drone of an engine overhead and, looking up, spotted a helicopter. "I think they're trying to broadcast something over a loudspeaker," she said. Throwing open the window, she poked her head out and strained to make out the message. But sensing impending danger, she promptly closed the window and decided to find out what was going on from the police.

Bonnie pulled on a pair of jeans, T-shirt and riding boots, ran her fingers through the mass of bright red curls crowning her head, and dashed downstairs.

A rather concerned-looking sheriff's deputy stood in the hall waiting for her. "Oh, hello, Miss Breit," he said. "My name is Watkins. I'm sorry to burst in on you like this, but we have orders to evacuate all residents of the area at once, you in particular."

"Evacuate?" Bonnie repeated. "How come?"

"A big fire started out near Agoura some time last night," he answered. "For a while they thought they had it under control, but it flared up again. It's heading this way. And fast. For your own safety you have to vacate the premises at once."

"What about my horses?" she said, making an excited gesture toward the stables at the rear of the property where her two mounts, Pepper and Salty, were housed.

"I'm afraid there's no time to worry about horses now," the deputy replied. "If the wind shifts, that fire could sweep through here in seconds. We can't take any chances. Round up all persons in the house and come with me."

"There's only Modesta, my maid, and myself."

"I volunteered to come here personally because I'm a big fan of yours, Miss Breit. I've seen all your movies," Watkins said, blushing slightly. "I wouldn't want anything to happen to you."

"That's very nice of you," Bonnie said, "but what about my car? I have a new Mercedes 450SEL in the garage." She was not nearly as concerned about the car as she was about the horses, but hoped she could use it as an excuse to stall for time to try and get them out. "Look, Officer Watson . . ."

"Watkins," he corrected.

"Officer Watkins, I'll tell you what. You take Modesta with you, and I'll follow in my own car. Okay?"

The deputy shook his head regretfully. "I'm sorry, but we can't tie up the highway with a lot of private cars. We have to keep it clear for emergency vehicles, like fire trucks and ambulances."

"Please," she coaxed, touching the sleeve of his uniform and looking at him pleadingly. "At least let me get my car out of here."

"I'm afraid I can't do that."

"I promise I won't tie up the highway. Listen, if you let me take it, you can come to dinner next week. How's that? Modesta is a terrific cook. She makes fabulous guacamole and tamales. I'll even screen one of my films for you. I have my own private projection room here. Which one is your favorite?"

"I like all your films, Miss Breit. My girlfriend and I saw *A Time for Loving* four times."

"Then that's what I'll screen for you. Just between you and me, that's my favorite, too. I think the dance numbers in it are terrific."

"Oh, yeah, me, too," he nodded enthusiastically. The offer proved too tempting for the young deputy, a highly suscepti-ble fan, to resist. "All right," he capitulated. "I'll go along

18

with you and make an exception. But only this one time. Go get your car. But you'd better hurry."

"Oh, I will, officer," she vowed, breathing a secret sigh of relief. "I swear I will."

The deputy moved on out of the house with an apprehensive and bewildered Modesta in tow.

The area of the crowded Malibu fire station where media personnel were assigned was noisy and filled with the irritating, acrid odor of smoke. Sally Brennan, a reporter for television station KHOT, suppressed a cough as she whipped a hairbrush out of her handbag and attacked her thick, strawberry-blond hair. In an atmosphere of jangling phones, radios, sirens, and much shouting, things would be tough and she was understandably nervous.

Once she finished with her hair, she proceeded to apply mascara, keeping her eye on the little red light on the side of the minicam. When it flashed she had to be ready to go on the air live. As she raked her lashes with the tiny brush, she was suddenly struck with the frivolousness and irrelevancy of such preparations in view of what she was about to report. "Screw it," she said, snapping closed the makeup case in disgust.

While fire captains barked orders to their crews on the line over shortwave radios and planes roared noisily overhead, the red light flashed and Sally reached for her microphone. Stepping in front of the minicam, she announced, "This is Sally Brennan coming to you live from the Malibu emergency command post. I'm going to try and keep you abreast of the gigantic fire raging out here. Fire officials assure us that the flames, which have thus far blackened more than twenty-thousand acres on both sides of the Santa Monica mountains, are rapidly being brought under control and should be safely contained by dark. Let me see if I can get one of the men in charge to say a few words." Turning to a rugged-looking fire captain, she said, "Captain Garrity, I wonder, sir, would you say something to our viewers about your progress in fighting this fire?"

Scowling at the microphone Sally shoved at him, he muttered, "What do you have in mind, ma'am?"

"I understand fire fighters are battling this blaze on several different fronts at once," she said. "Is that right?"

"That's correct," he affirmed.

"Both on the ground and from the air?"

"Yes, ma'am. We've got the Super Scoopers in operation as well as the choppers."

"Would you mind telling us what a 'Super Scooper' is, Captain?"

"They're special planes that can scoop up water from the ocean or other large body and drop it on the fire while they are still airborne," he replied.

"I understand, too, that special units have been brought in from all over the country?"

"That's right. From all over the U.S."

"Is there anything else you'd like to say to our viewers?"

"Yes, ma'am," he replied eagerly. The formerly laconic fireman seemed suddenly to spring to life. "I want to say that if we could get adequate pressure in our lines, we could have this fire under control in no time. We have the best damned firefighters in the world. What we don't have is the goddam water. We're doing the best we can with what we've got, but it's not nearly enough. Not by a longshot. Because of the low pressure in our lines, we have to depend almost entirely on our air support, mainly the choppers and the Super Scoopers."

"Would you say that many homes in the area are threatened at the present time?"

"I wouldn't want to hazard a guess," he replied. "The big problem is that we can't draw water off the main lines in order to wet down the homes that are in danger. In the past that's been an important protective measure. These homeowners are going to have to take their chances. We just can't spare the water. Let me say right here and now that if California expects to survive another fire like this one, this state had better damned well get some water. And quick! Otherwise, it's going to go up in flames from Eureka to Calexico, and the best fire companies in the world won't be able to put out the blaze."

As soon as the deputy's car started down the long driveway toward the electronic gates, Bonnie raced out the back door to the stables. At the moment the horses seemed far more important to her than her Mercedes, her antique doll collection, or even her Oscar on the shelf in the den.

The stables were a modified U-shape ringed by a semicircle of gentle hills covered with dry, brittle grass and weeds. A double row of stalls opened, not to the outside, as was characteristic of most California stables, but to a central straw-strewn passageway.

Approaching the corral, Bonnie glanced up at the surrounding hills and was filled with fear and apprehension as she watched great clouds of thick, yellow-brown smoke rolling over the crests. Hot, gusting winds, generated by the sheer heat of the approaching fire, assaulted her, making her aware of how fast it was traveling. From inside the stables she heard the panicky cries of the horses and the frantic hammering of their hooves as they attempted to kick out the sides of the stalls and burst free, reacting to the fire with an animal's instinctive fear.

Just after Bonnie entered the stable door, a bundle of flaming tumbleweeds, propelled by the hot, driving winds, bounced over the crest of the hills and landed on top of the stable, instantly igniting the shingles.

Unaware that the roof above her was burning, Bonnie dashed toward Salty's stall, coughing and choking from smoke. Salty, a white mare and the calmer of the two horses, would be easier to handle than the more excitable Pepper. Through the dense smoke she could see that Pepper's stall door was already badly battered by his furious kicking. Attempting to calm the mare with soothing words, she stripped off her T-shirt, ripped it in two and tied one of the pieces over Salty's eyes. Then, gripping Salty's bridle, she led her out of the stall and went after Pepper. At her approach the great gelding reared, and neighed hysterically as Bonnie prepared to blindfold him with the remaining half of the torn T-shirt. As she reached for his bridle, her skin prickled from the heat, and beads of sweat streamed down her forehead and back. Her eyes smarted and watered, as smoke, even more dense, began to fill the stable. Calling out reassurances to the horses, she tugged on the bridles, urging the blindfolded and terrified animals toward the open door, now only a faint rectangle of light at the end of the smoke-filled passage. Managing to coax the panic-stricken mounts to within a few yards of escape, she noticed the support beams overhead swaying back and forth, groaning and creaking loudly. Salty balked, frozen with fear, and Pepper reared, his hooves wildly thrashing the air.

"Come on, damn it!" Bonnie yelled, yanking on the bridles with all the strength her slender arms could muster.

The groaning and swaying of the overhead beams escalated steadily until the entire structure shuddered violently.

"Come on, Pepper, Salty!" she begged the petrified mounts,

knowing that any moment the whole stable might collapse. "For God's sake! Please!" But the horses refused to budge.

Suddenly, without warning, smoke and flames seemed to engulf the entire wooden building at once, transforming it into a holocaust. Covering her head protectively with her arms, Bonnie screamed in terror. With a deafening roar, an avalanche of flaming timbers came crashing down.

At producer Ken Wilson's behest, Sally set about interviewing fire victims who had been brought into the first aid station for treatment. Just as she was about to talk to a well-known movie director and his wife, whose Malibu home had burned to the ground, the KHOT cameraman intervened. "I just got word," he said. "The governor's chopper has landed outside."

Sensing some commotion behind her, Sally repeated, "The governor?" and turned to see Paul Kirkwood, in a dusty three-piece tan gabardine suit, looking somewhat disheveled, but still determined and forceful, striding into the fire station. He was flanked by his retinue of aides, press people, and bodyguards.

The moment Drew Ramsdale spotted Sally, microphone in hand, he left Kirkwood and took her aside. "The governor would like to say a few words on the air. Do you think that's possible? Could you do us that favor?" he asked earnestly, though he knew very well what her answer would be.

"Certainly," she agreed, grateful for the opportunity to interview the state's chief executive on camera.

Signaling her crew, Sally faced the minicam once again. "We now have Govenor Paul Kirkwood with us here in the emergency command post at Malibu." Concealing her nervousness, she turned to him. "Good afternoon, Governor."

Looking appropriately grave, Kirkwood stepped in front of the minicam. "I'm afraid it's not a very good afternoon for the residents of the Malibu area."

"No, sir, it certainly isn't," Sally agreed.

"I have just been in touch with the president, and he assures me that federal disaster loans will be available to the victims of this tragic fire."

"I'm sure that they'll be glad to hear that," Sally interjected.

"While I have the opportunity, I would like to pay tribute to our excellent firefighters who, as we all know, have been tirelessly battling this blaze for hours on end. I think these men deserve a big vote of thanks from all of us for the magnificent job they've been doing.

"I also want to personally congratulate the Los Angeles Sheriff's Department for the smooth and efficient way in which they evacuated residents of the fire area. I am proud to announce that, as far as can be determined, there has been no loss of life directly attributable to this fire," he asserted. "I think that is something we can all be proud of."

"Señor Kirkwood! Señor Kirkwood!" A short, plump Latin woman cried as she headed for the governor. Instantly alert, members of the California Protective Services Bureau, a division of the state police assigned to guard the chief executive, closed ranks around their charge. Two men stopped the nearly hysterical woman.

"Ay! Señor Kirkwood!" she wailed, struggling against the men who restrained her.

"Modesta!" Kirkwood looked surprised. "It's all right. I know her. Let her go. She's okay," Kirkwood assured his bodyguards. In the same flawless Spanish that had won him the votes of the state's large Hispanic population, he calmly advised the maid to relax and tell him what was wrong.

Sobbing, Modesta began to recount her story, and the more Kirkwood heard the more alarmed he became. It was the maid's contention that all the residents of the fire area had *not* been safely evacuated as he had just assured the television public.

"Señora Bonnie is still in there!" she insisted.

"Oh, my God, no! ..." Kirkwood groaned, his face suddenly ashen.

3

A buzzer in Room 424 of the Russell Senate Office Building alerted the senators assembled in the green and marble conference room that they had fifteen minutes to get to the floor of the Senate for a roll-call vote. Sheridan Eubanks, chairman of the International Finance Subcommittee, a portly man with a florid complexion, slack, bulldoglike jowls, and tiny eyes that squinted behind wire-framed trifocals, perhaps from many years of gazing over Kansas wheat fields, quickly recessed the meeting, and the senators, accompanied by their various aides and legislative assistants, filed out.

Preston Farleigh led the way down the hall, walking at a brisk pace, even though his colleague Eubanks was well into his seventies. The elder statesman from Kansas had difficulty keeping up with the junior senator from California. Some might have thought Farleigh's pace inconsiderate in view of Eubanks's puffing and flushed face, not that the California senator was any model of physical fitness with his sallow complexion, stooped shoulders, and paunchy stomach. Farleigh with his slicked-down salt-and-pepper hair, puffy eyes, and tight, thin-lipped, slightly bitter mouth was the kind of man people usually described as "colorless."

"I've got to tell you, Farleigh, I am amazed at the way you've been kicking your governor's ass these days," Eubanks chuckled, breathing in wheezing gasps.

"Well, goddam it, Sheridan, he has it coming," Farleigh snapped. "I refuse to sit back and watch him run the state I love into the ground."

"It's a crying shame you lost to him back in '76," Eubanks lamented. "You could have sure run the state a helluva lot better. Yes, sir, a crying shame."

24

Farleigh's defeat by Paul Kirkwood, whom he considered beneath contempt, in the California gubernatorial race had been a severe blow, causing him to withdraw from political life for a short time. He was coaxed out of retirement only when Howard Rudd, head of the rich and powerful Rudd International, urged him to run for the Senate and promised him generous support in his campaign. Both Rudd and Farleigh had known it was going to be a tough race against the popular senatorial candidate, Tony Rincon, but Farleigh viewed the contest as a chance to once again redeem his political fortunes, a desperate, last ditch effort, but a chance nevertheless. Rudd, on the other hand, was determined to bring his massive desalination project to California despite the governor's stiff opposition and, therefore, wanted to place as many sympathetic supporters in positions where they could be useful to him as he could possibly recruit. The embittered Farleigh seemed an ideal choice. Rudd was certain he would do all in his power to turn the California electorate against Kirkwood, and Rudd needed this kind of man in the U.S. Senate.

"I can't let the responsible citizens of California—the ones who get out and work for a living every day and pay taxes—suffer. It wouldn't be right," Farleigh said. "And I wouldn't feel right."

"Well, something's sure as hell got to be done about that drought," Eubanks said. "That's for damned sure. We're keeping a good eye on it back in Kansas. I'd hate like hell for something like that to happen in our state."

"It could, you know, Sheridan," Farleigh warned. "It could happen anywhere. It's nothing special to California. The bad part is that we've got a helluva lot more people than any other state. That's why it's important for all of us in the Senate, and especially those of us on the International Finance Subcommittee, to back Hydrolliance all the way. I don't care what it is—whether it's to build a string of desalination plants up and down the California coast or to reroute major rivers all over the world."

Eubanks considered a moment. "I don't know if I like the idea of them rerouting rivers," he said. "I mean, hell, they've been talking about the *Mississippi,* for chrissake. And the Colorado and the Missouri and the Columbia. . . ." he said, ticking them off on his fingers.

"Look at it this way, Sheridan," Farleigh interrupted, "if

Hydrolliance were to reroute the Missouri, Kansas would be a major benefactor."

"I don't know," Eubanks said, shaking his head doubtfully. "There's no doubt that we could use the water, but folks back there don't much care for the notion of using nuclear energy to blast out new river channels."

"It would be carefully controlled—you can bet your boots on that," Farleigh assured his colleague. "All the appropriate agencies, both state and federal, would be keeping a sharp eye on things. All radiation would be monitored. There'd be no danger from fallout or anything like that. You people in Kansas can't be like Kirkwood and try and stop progress. There's no way. It can't be done." Shifting his briefcase from one hand to the other and glancing over his shoulder to see if his aides and legislative assistants were still following, Farleigh continued. "Howard Rudd's plan was a good one—damned good. I supported it when he proposed it and I support it now. Hell, I even made it part of my platform when I was running for governor. If I had been elected instead of Kirkwood, I'll tell you one thing: California wouldn't be in the bind we're in now. If I were governor, we would have had those desalination plants in operation by now."

"Yes, too bad about old Howard Rudd," Eubanks said, shaking his head. "I knew him before you were born. We were old friends. He started Rudd International from scratch, just a few thousand his old granddaddy left him. He parlayed it into a fortune in no time, built a goddam empire. You got to hand it to a man like that. The Rudd name is known in just about every corner of the world, I suppose. Oil, gas, shipping, chemicals, electronics, you name it—he was one of the few men I know who really understood the power of the dollar and how to use it."

"Very few men had the power Rudd had," Farleigh said. "Power's not hard to use once you've got it. Getting it is what's difficult."

"I guess one of the old man's biggest disappointments came when Kirkwood managed to block his desalination project. That was his special baby."

"If you want to know the truth, I think that's what killed him," Farleigh said, recalling bitterly the way Kirkwood had invoked the old argument of nuclear power being inappropriate in fault-ridden, earthquake-prone California. "I really do."

"Rudd managed to get his LNG terminals in California,

though," Eubanks continued. "That's one thing. His lobbyists managed to whip up enough support in the legislature to override Kirkwood's veto on that, but they just couldn't muster the support for his desalination plants in spite of all the green stuff they spread around."

"I know, I know, Sheridan," Farleigh said. "It's that same old buzz-word 'nuclear.' It'll kill anything. There are just enough horses' asses in Sacramento who are scared of the mere mention of the word and its effect on the voter to turn down anything connected with it."

"How come he insisted on nuclear power to run his desalination plants?" Eubanks asked. "I understand there are other ways to fuel them, aren't there?"

"Oil's out of the question. Coal pollutes too much," Farleigh replied. "Besides, Rudd had a big interest in those uranium mines in Utah. He planned to channel the uranium directly from Utah to the West Coast."

When they reached the bank of elevators, one of Farleigh's aides stepped ahead and pressed the call button.

"Say, Farleigh, you're still in solid with the Rudd organization people, aren't you?" Eubanks asked.

"Yes. Why?"

"Tell me, is it true that Howard's wife is running the show now that he's passed on?" Eubanks asked. "What was her name? I forget; he had so many wives. I think she was German. . . ."

"Annalise," Farleigh supplied. "She's a very capable woman. Yes, I'm sure it would be safe to say that she has a definite hand in running things now."

"Boy, that must rile old Jeremiah Gaines," Eubanks said. "He was just waiting for old Rudd to kick off for years so he could take over and run things the way he thought they should be run. He was Rudd's right-hand man for years. Old Rudd didn't do a thing without consulting Jeremiah. Not a damned thing. That old coot's older than I am. Hell, he's even older than God."

"As far as I know, Jeremiah Gaines is still very much involved with everything Rudd International does," Farleigh answered.

When the elevator doors opened, the two senators stepped inside, leaving their aides and staff to wait for the next car, and joined a third colleague, Senator Edward Newquist from South Dakota, another member of the International Finance Subcommittee.

"Hey, Ed," Farleigh greeted his colleague.

"Edward," Eubanks nodded genially.

"Gentlemen," Newquist replied as the doors closed and the car descended.

"I understand you're looking favorably on the Brazilian issue I brought up today," Farleigh said, his thin lips spread into a smile of forced friendliness.

"There are some more things I'd like to know before I make up my mind," Newquist replied.

"I intend to put it all out there in front of the committee," Farleigh promised.

"We're waiting," Eubanks said, giving Farleigh a comradely nudge in the ribs.

"On another issue of prime concern to your state, Preston," Newquist said, "I think we've got to start getting tough with your governor right here in Washington."

"Don't go calling that bastard Kirkwood 'my' governor," Farleigh protested. "I didn't vote for him."

"We can't keep on bailing him out all the time," Newquist continued. "It's all right for him to be against nuclear energy in California, but he's got to offer an acceptable alternative."

"He hasn't offered a damned thing so far," Eubanks snorted.

"Well, he'd better come up with something fast or he's going to find himself in a lot of hot water," Newquist said, quickly adding, "if you'll forgive the word."

"I think right now Kirkwood would like to find himself in any kind of water," Eubanks laughed.

"I hear he aspires to run for president in '84," Newquist said. "The way I see it, as things stand now, there's no way in hell he'll ever get the nomination."

"Fat chance," Eubanks agreed. "By the way, Ed, I think you're right about putting the squeeze on him here in Washington. Maybe if we cut off some of the funds we've been so generous with, he'll get off his high horse and start to see things in a new light."

"Doesn't he realize how desperate the water situation is?" Newquist asked, looking from Eubanks to Farleigh. "Or is he too wrapped up with what's-her-name?"

"Bonnie Breit," Farleigh supplied.

"That's the one," Newquist said. "How did those two ever get together anyway?"

"I think they met at one of those fund-raising dinners some big Hollywood agent gave during Kirkwood's last campaign. He was still getting over the death of his wife, and she was

28

trying to recover from her last divorce," Farleigh explained. "I think they used each other's shoulder to cry on."

"I can't picture the star of *Shoot* as our First Lady somehow," Newquist mused.

"Hell, why not?" Eubanks chuckled. "Any damned thing goes these days."

"Politically speaking, as far as I'm concerned, Kirkwood's been wrong-headed since the day he got into office," Newquist declared. "Somebody needs to straighten him out."

After the roll-call vote, Farleigh returned to his headquarters in the Dirkson Senate Office Building, a virtual warren of cubbyhole office spaces divided by plywood partitions where a staff of twenty labored in his behalf. The moment he arrived, his secretary informed him that Annalise Rudd had been phoning all afternoon. Farleigh went into his personal office, which, in contrast to the Spartan accommodations of his staff, was spacious, quiet, and tastefully furnished, designed purposely to give an impression of power and stability with its rich, dark colors, massive furniture, and highly polished brass. He closed the door, and dialed her number.

"Annalise, how are you?" he said, trying to sound as amiable as possible. He hated the obligation he felt toward the Rudd organization, and somehow Annalise's steely voice with its faint trace of a German accent seemed to underscore his feelings of humiliation and resentment when he spoke to her. Despite the facade of friendship he and his wife, Sarajane, had striven to maintain with the Rudds, neither ever felt completely at ease with them.

"I'm fine, thank you, Preston," Annalise replied crisply. "I was calling to remind you about the party at the Brazilian embassy tonight. You and Sarajane will be there, won't you?"

"Yes, of course," he answered. "Sarajane's been looking forward to it all week. You know how crazy she is about bossa nova music."

"Good. Mr. Pinhiero is very important to our Amazon project. We need him. It's important that he knows Hydrolliance has your support in the Senate. I want him to be aware that the United States government is backing us in this."

"I understand perfectly," Farleigh assured her.

"I'm glad you do," she said. "Then, I'll see you there. I'm flying to Washington later in my jet. Please, Preston, tell Sarajane not to try out her 'Tex-Mex' Spanish tonight. Remind her that Brazilians speak Portuguese. I don't want her offending anyone. Pinhiero's too important."

"I will," Farleigh said with a forced, good-natured chuckle, despite the fact that he was angered by the remark.

"Oh, and Preston, one last thing—see that she doesn't drink too much." Annalise clicked off the line.

4

In the spacious suite of offices furnished with the finest of Spanish colonial antiques from Lima, Bogotá, and Quito, thick vicuña carpets on the floor, and a huge beaten-gold altar plate depicting Incan priests making human sacrifices to their gods on the wall behind her massive desk, Annalise von Lachen Rudd gazed out the vast expanse of floor-to-ceiling windows at the Manhattan skyline. She buzzed her British secretary. "Margaret, will you please send for my car?" said the deep, commanding voice. "Have it brought to the Fifth Avenue entrance."

"Yes, Mrs. Rudd," the secretary replied, adding: "You haven't forgotten that Mr. Gaines is waiting to see you, have you?"

"No, I haven't forgotten," Annalise answered, curling her lip slightly in unconscious contempt for the elderly assistant. She lifted her carefully manicured finger from the intercom, then rose from her desk, and strolled to a mirror framed in finely wrought solid silver, which had once belonged to an early viceroy of Bolivia, to inspect her face. The mirror hung above an ebony display case housing onyx, obsidian, and jade Incan ceremonial objects, including a knife which purportedly still had traces of a sacrificial victim's blood. At forty-five, Annalise was a coldly attractive woman with short, frosted silver-blond hair and steely gray eyes. Gently, she ran her finger under her eyes, beneath her chin, over her smooth, unlined cheeks. Not a sign of a wrinkle, nothing resembling the crepe of some of her contemporaries. That clinic in Switzerland had done a magnificent job, and it was holding up well—not just the face but the breasts, buttocks, and thighs as well. She was truly youthful, and that was

31

important. If one wanted to attract the young, one had to look young. All young people are basically narcissistic, she thought with a sigh.

On the floor below, in an office far less opulent than that of his employer, Jeremiah Gaines, distinguished in his gray pinstriped suit, gold watch and chain in the vest, and snow-white hair, paced impatiently. He still wasn't used to waiting for permission to enter the summit of the Rudd Building. When Howard Rudd was alive, they had shared the top floor, and Gaines had had free access to Howard any time he wished; but things were different now. All entrances were locked at all times and security was formidable; in order to be admitted to Annalise's offices he had to call and request permission. For a long time Gaines had known that Annalise exerted great influence over her late husband and that she undoubtedly had been involved in some of his decisions. But when the old man died, Gaines had, perhaps naively, expected her simply to sit back and let him run things. Although Gaines was well into his seventies he was blessed with an almost youthful vigor, keen mind, and a physical appearance belying his age by a couple of decades. The members of the board of directors of Rudd International knew that he was fully capable of assuming leadership, having been closely associated with Howard for more than forty years—all except Annalise, that is. When she announced that she was taking over the reins of the corporation and relegating Gaines to an "advisory" capacity, it had been difficult for him to accept. He had contemplated resigning, but big business, with all its machinations, was his life's blood, what kept him going. Despite his valuable connections all over the world and impeccable reputation within the business community, he knew that no other organization wanted a man almost eighty, not even if that man were Jeremiah Gaines. He knew that if he were to stop working, he would die. It was Rudd International or nothing. Besides, he was far too sentimentally attached to the vast organization that he and Rudd had built to quit. And so, on the theory that if Annalise were given enough rope, she would eventually hang herself, he had decided to tough it out.

As he was summoned to enter her private office, he heard Annalise ask, "Well, Gaines, what is it this time?"

Ignoring her condescending tone, he said, "About the stock you were planning to use as collateral in the Neptunus Limited deal . . ."

"Well, what about it?"

"I would say it's a very unwise move," he ventured. "It's a very speculative, highly risky venture."

"Really?" She raised a carefully shaped eyebrow skeptically.

"Our legal department still isn't clear on just who has jurisdiction over the area where Neptunus plans to harvest those manganese nodules. They want to investigate the company's claim that the nodules are simply lying on the ocean floor waiting for some enterprising soul to come along, snap them up, and get rich," Gaines explained.

"I don't care what our legal department or anybody else thinks—including you," she said. "I intend to go ahead on the Neptunus deal."

"I just wanted to be sure you were fully aware of the situation," Gaines replied.

At that moment Margaret buzzed and announced that Annalise's car was now waiting.

"I'm leaving early today," she announced. "I plan to attend the Pinhiero party in Washington this evening. It's vital to the Amazon project."

"It might be useful for me to attend, too," he suggested. "I've known Pinhiero a long time."

"You've known everybody a long time," she said testily.

Once inside her elegant, five-story brownstone townhouse on East Sixty-fifth Street, Annalise handed her mink to her butler and proceeded up the stairs to the second floor. Encountering one of the maids dusting a carved white jade incense burner from the Ming dynasty, Annalise asked, "Is Rico in?"

"Yes, Mrs. Rudd," the maid replied and pointed toward the master bedroom suite with her feather duster.

The moment Annalise opened the door her nostrils were assailed by the pungent odor of burning hashish mingled with *Carciofo*, the Italian artichoke liqueur Rico adored. The boy's principal occupation in the afternoon seemed to be lying on Annalise's bed, which was built in the shape of a golden swan and had once belonged to Ludwig, the mad king of Bavaria, and watching two soap operas simultaneously on adjacent television sets, sipping the disgusting liqueur and puffing on his hash pipe. He was the model of indolent repose, wearing a short silk robe, half open and exposing his nut-brown, long, slender legs. Rico's absorption with American soap operas amused Annalise especially when his large, velvety brown eyes would fill with tears over the tribulations of their characters. It was especially amusing because Rico's English was still somewhat limited.

Annalise "discovered" Rico on her last trip to South America to visit her father, Helmut von Lachen, an ex-Nazi who had successfully evaded Israeli pursuers for many years in Paraguay. While she was on a side trip to Rio de Janeiro to discuss the Amazon project with Pinhiero, the boy had tried to snatch her purse. From the Rio police she had learned that he was an orphan from the *favelas,* hillside shantytowns of the poor that ringed the city. His exact age was uncertain; even Rico himself was not sure. The only thing that mattered to Annalise was that he was past puberty, and that hadn't taken her very long to find out. Once he was assured that she was not going to have the police arrest him, he willingly accompanied her to her hotel suite and performed tirelessly in bed with a zeal and skill that amazed and overwhelmed her. Recognizing a good thing when she saw it, Annalise quickly made arrangements to "adopt" Rico and bring him back to the United States with her. On the immigration forms she had his age listed as "fourteen," which was as good a guess as any.

When she first installed Rico in her townhouse it aroused considerable interest and speculation on the part of friends and neighbors. Delighted by their curiosity, she loved to watch their expressions when she introduced the former Brazilian street-urchin-purse-snatcher as her newly adopted "son." Naturally, she was aware of the comments circulating behind her back, most of the more ribald relating to such matters as the dimensions of the youth's organ or his ability to perform with priapic zest. Much to Annalise's great amusement and satisfaction, nearly all of her friends' speculations were correct. It had been a long time since she had made love and even longer since she had been satisfied by the act. Rico filled the bill—and then some. Somehow in the past, despite his obvious youth, he had acquired a few special abilities that enhanced her already exquisite pleasure.

Her marriage to Rudd had been nearly celibate. Her late husband was more than thirty years her senior, and by the time he had gotten around to her, after three previous wives, he was pretty well burned out. On several occasions she had tried to have affairs with other men, but Rudd inevitably got suspicious and put detectives on her. Knowing how much was at stake if she got caught, Annalise stifled her lust and satisfied herself with a vibrator she had especially designed for her in Copenhagen. It gave her some measure of temporary relief, but was a poor substitute for what she really craved.

As Annalise moved across the thickly carpeted bedroom, Rico kept his eyes glued to the television screens. Annoyed by his lack of attention, she flicked a master switch that turned off both television sets. Immediately, he reacted, protesting loudly in a combination of English and Portuguese.

"I don't want to have to listen to that garbage while I'm dressing," she said. "Go and watch the television in your own room, if you must."

Rico did not stir. Instead, he folded his arms on his chest and formed his mouth into a sullen pout. Ignoring his reaction, Annalise casually ran her fingers through his wiry mop of thick, curly black hair, undressed, and headed for the adjoining bath.

When she finished and returned to the bedroom wrapped in a towel, Rico was gone. Annalise shrugged indifferently; he would soon get over his sulk. Then she settled down on the golden swan bed for a brief nap.

She had scarcely dozed for more than a few minutes when she was aware of Rico's presence in the room once more and smiled, admiring the boy's uncanny awareness that she needed him.

Slowly Rico lowered the towel covering her and gently caressed her breasts, playing with her nipples until they grew hard and erect, his fingertips as smooth as silk. Annalise simply allowed herself to flow with the sensations she was experiencing, drifting into the rosy haze that Rico always seemed able to evoke. When she felt his smooth, beardless cheek against the inner curve of her thigh, she moaned and gyrated her hips ever so slightly to let him know he was on the right track. The gentle probing of his soft, warm tongue sent tiny shivers of joy coursing through her entire body. Taking his curly head in her hands, she pressed it into the vortex of her now overwhelming desire.

Finally in one swift but graceful move, Rico raised himself above her on his elbows, separated her legs, and inched ever so slowly, ever so teasingly into her, withdrawing just enough every so often to cause her a temporary moment of panic. It seemed to amuse him to hear her gasp, fearful that the incredible ecstasy he brought her might suddenly be wrenched away.

As she writhed in joy beneath his steady, rhythmic thrusts,

35

Annalise reveled in the knowledge that this was only the beginning. The real *pièce de résistance* was yet to come. With other men she had known, there had been nothing further, no heightening of an already exquisite pleasure. Revealing his strong, gleaming white teeth, Rico smiled, slowly encircled her throat with his hands and began to squeeze, ever so gently at first, yet with steadily increasing pressure. Tiny pinpoints of light burst in showers upon the rosy haze as the outline of his beautiful face faded into a blur, his sensual voice growing ever more distant. With sublime anticipation Annalise welcomed the approaching blackness soon to engulf her.

Neal Haverson kissed Ingrid goodbye, slid behind the wheel of the family station wagon, and headed down the Palos Verdes peninsula toward San Pedro where the cruise ship was docked and waiting. It was very hot, and the smell of smoke hung heavily in the air. Glancing north, he observed dense clouds of dark smoke from the Malibu fire pouring into the sky.

Goddam drought, he cursed. Goddam stupid people in this country. Goddam stupid politicians. If somebody would just listen to me—take me seriously—I could show them the way out of this thing.

At one time the drive to the harbor had been pleasant, the road winding past banks of succulent flowering ice plant, well-maintained suburban lawns, and vast fields of gladiolas, daisies, and stock, lovingly tended by conscientious Japanese commercial flower-growers. But all that had vanished with the drought. The hardy ice plant had succumbed, the lawns withered, the flowers gone. It was frightening. And depressing.

To take his mind off the immediate effects of the drought, Haverson tried thinking about the upcoming weather symposium. He felt honored that Terhune, dean of the world's climatologists, had asked him to deliver his paper on the effects of the polar ice pack on surrounding air and water temperatures. He was looking forward to the trip to Washington, to talking about the work he loved so much and from which he had been cut off so abruptly. He hoped that Ingrid would be able to go with him. She had complained about his being away from home too much and was right, of course; he *was* away too much and at a time when his daughters needed him. His work had always taken him away from home, but Ingrid had begun to object so strongly only recently—ever since the trouble in Antarctica and his resignation from the navy.

As he approached the sleek, glamorous cruise ship, he could hear the happy Dixieland music of the band pulsating through the air and the excited voices of the passengers on deck.

As quickly as he could, Neal made his way through the riot of balloons, showers of confetti, and explosions of champagne corks, according the jubilant voyagers only the most perfunctory greetings, and headed for his office. There, he found a message on his desk asking him to call Dr. Thurston Terhune as soon as possible.

He dialed the number on the paper and asked for Terhune. "Good morning, sir," he said. "This is Neal Haverson."

"Oh, yes, Haverson," the cultured, well-modulated voice on the other end of the phone responded. "You haven't given us an answer yet about delivering your paper in Washington next week. Today's the deadline. The program has to go to the printer this afternoon. I had to go east for a protest rally last week and, as a result, I'm late putting things together. Are you going to honor us with your presence?"

"Yes, I'd like to be part of the program," Haverson responded.

"Then you shall be!" Terhune confirmed. "I'm going to schedule your paper for Tuesday at ten. How's that? I admire the work you were doing in Antarctica very much, you know."

"Thank you, sir."

"Too bad it had to come to an end."

"It couldn't be helped, sir."

"I like the way you got the government to subsidize you, even though they didn't know it." Terhune chuckled. "And without going through a lot of bureaucratic red tape. I wish more military men were like you and would use their spare time doing something useful, instead of playing golf or drinking all day at taxpayers' expense. There should be some way for you to go on with your research. You were on to something really important; but that's your business. Antarctica is a fascinating place. Fascinating! It's going to play a large part in the future of the world—" he said and paused. "Of course, I don't agree with everybody on what part it should play—including you, Haverson. My own work indicates it is a leading factor—if not *the* leading factor—in determining the world's weather. I'd hate to see it disturbed even in the slightest way."

"I understand your feelings, sir."

"I hope you do, Haverson," Terhune said. "Well, we'll schedule your talk for Tuesday then."

When Haverson put down the phone, he sat back and mused about Antarctica and the time he spent there. In many ways it had been one of the most interesting and rewarding periods of his life. His assignment had been challenging, and he had had plenty of time in which to indulge his scientific curiosity. How could something that seemed so ideal, so perfect, end in such tragedy? His life, his naval career, even his marriage had been damaged, his dreams haunted ever afterward. At times, he wondered if he would ever overcome the anguish of the whole thing. If only there were some way to prove that his negligence had not been the cause of what had occurred, some way to clear his name. He felt that somewhere there must be evidence, some clue to Elizabeth Nagy's state of mind on that fateful day. Knowing her as he had, he held the firm conviction that her death had not been accidental, as it had been ruled as a result of the investigation. To prove it, he would have to go back, and that was something he had no wish to do. The pain was still too strong.

5

The Guatemalan maid's insistence that Bonnie had been trapped at the ranch as the fire went raging through it obviously shocked and upset Kirkwood, and his staff attempted to shield him from curious reporters and the merciless eye of television cameras. At Drew Ramsdale's request, a Spanish-speaking volunteer nurse tried to calm Modesta and had almost succeeded when Sheriff's Deputy Watkins came staggering into the Malibu fire station, uniform in tatters, arms and face scratched, bloody and blackened with soot, and hair, eyebrows and moustache singed. His sudden appearance triggered a resurgence of the woman's hysteria.

Kirkwood was not so stunned by Modesta's story that he failed to observe her reaction to the deputy's entrance.

"What's the matter? What is it, Modesta?" he asked in Spanish.

"He is the one!" Modesta replied, pointing toward the officer who seemed to be having great trouble breathing. "He's the one who came to the house to take the señora and me away!" she cried, her plump body wracked with sobs. "But the señora would not go. She sent me alone with him."

"Are you sure he's the one?" Kirkwood asked, gripping her firmly by the shoulders.

"Yes. I'm sure," she affirmed, wiping her tear-streaked face with the hem of her sooty apron.

Quickly regaining his composure, Kirkwood turned to Ramsdale. "I must talk to that officer," he said.

"I don't think now is the time," Ramsdale cautioned. "He doesn't look like he's in very good shape."

"I have to ask him about Bonnie," Kirkwood insisted. "I have to find out . . ."

39

While Ramsdale and the rest of the staff looked on, Kirkwood approached the deputy, much to the consternation of the paramedic who was trying to administer oxygen to Watkins.

Kirkwood spoke to the paramedic. "I have to have a word with this officer. It's very important."

"I'm sorry, but you can't now," the paramedic said brusquely, either unaware or not caring that he was addressing the governor of the state. "This officer was overcome by smoke."

Ignoring the paramedic, Kirkwood knelt beside the stretcher on which the deputy lay. "I'm Governor Kirkwood," he said. "Can you tell me anything about Bonnie Breit?"

Despite his obvious respiratory distress, a look of both surprise and recognition crossed the lawman's face. "Bonnie Breit?" the stricken officer repeated hoarsely, raising the oxygen mask.

"Yes. Do you know where she is or what's happened to her?" Kirkwood asked anxiously.

Watkins shook his head. "Don't know," he wheezed. ". . . Went back . . . Maid told me . . . Look in stable . . . Burning bad . . . Horses trapped . . . Found her . . ."

"Then what?" Kirkwood demanded.

". . . Ambulance was there . . ."

"You put her in an ambulance?"

The deputy nodded affirmatively.

"Where did the ambulance take her?"

"Don't know . . ." Watkins shrugged, setting loose a flurry of gray ashes.

Some of the tension eased out of Kirkwood's face at the mention of putting Bonnie in an ambulance. "What kind of shape was she in?" he asked.

"Don't know," the deputy said once again.

"Was she breathing?"

". . . Think so . . ."

"Was she conscious?"

The officer shook his head from side to side. "No," he muttered.

"But you say she *was* breathing?" Kirkwood repeated.

"Yes," Watkins answered.

Kirkwood sighed. "Thank God for that." Turning to the paramedic, he said, "Take good care of this officer." He called to his aides, "Drew, Wally, Jane, I want you to get on the phones and call every damned hospital until you find Bonnie."

*   *   *

40

One of the KHOT crewmen informed Sally that her boss was on the phone and wanted to talk to her. "He says it's important."

"I want you to leave Malibu and get in here for the five o'clock newscast," Ken Wilson ordered.

"What?!" Sally protested. "I thought I was supposed to cover this fire? What the hell is this, Ken? What's going on?"

"I need you here at the station," Wilson said. "I'm sending Jesse Sandoval out to take your place. There's a great human interest story that's just developed, and it needs your special touch."

"Yeah? What is it?" Sally asked skeptically.

"We got a kid here from out in Thousand Oaks who lost her pony in the fire," Wilson replied. "A really dynamite little kid."

"Oh, great!" Sally groaned. "What's the rest?"

"You're going to interview her."

"What the hell am I supposed to do? Ask her how it feels to have her pony roasted? Jesus, Ken . . ."

"You didn't let me finish," Wilson said. "A pony club down in Rolling Hills heard about this kid in Thousand Oaks and took up a collection to buy her a new pony. That's terrific, isn't it? A great human interest angle, you know, kids helping kids. We're going to have the pony in the studio, too."

"Shit," Sally muttered. "Pony shit."

"Look, Sally, one of the choppers will be bringing Jesse out there. I want you to come back in on it," Wilson went on. "Linda can get you made up and dressed by air time. She's got a fantastic outfit for you from Bullocks'. Western. Great for the pony story. We've agreed to give Bullocks' a plug in the credits."

Still fuming from Wilson's call, Sally rejoined the news team and said, "If I didn't have a big, fat mortgage on my condo in the Marina and those payments on my Porsche, I'd tell Wilson where to shove it."

"Sally, listen," the cameraman said, sounding excited. "I just overheard one of Kirkwood's staff saying that they finally located Bonnie Breit at UCLA Medical Center."

"Bonnie Breit in the hospital?"

"Yeah. She was caught in the fire."

Sally bit her lip thoughtfully a moment. "Jesus, if I could just get Kirkwood to talk about it on camera . . ." she speculated. Observing Kirkwood and his entourage hurrying out of the fire station, she said, "I've got an idea, guys. Grab your stuff and follow me."

Racing after the governor and his staff, who were heading for the waiting helicopter, she called out, "Governor! Governor Kirkwood!"

Wally Weisswasser, who was used to dealing with the aggressive media, attempted to fend her off. "We're sorry but the governor can't give any further information at this time. We'll issue a statement later today."

"I don't care about any statement. . . ." she said.

"If you have further questions, the governor will be holding a press conference later today."

"I just want to ask him about Bonnie Breit," she blurted out.

Hearing Bonnie's name, Kirkwood paused just as he was about to board the aircraft. "What about Miss Breit?" he said.

"I just heard she's in UCLA Medical Center," Sally said. "I wanted to find out more . . ."

"We're not issuing *any* statements now," Weisswasser snapped emphatically.

Continuing to direct her pleas to Kirkwood, Sally said, "Look, I did you a favor earlier and turned my whole segment over to you. Now you can do one for me. All I want to know is how Miss Breit is."

"If you'd like to talk, climb aboard," Kirkwood invited, much to the displeasure of his staff, who found the KHOT crew with their cameras, microphones, and other equipment disconcerting. "We can talk on the way to UCLA."

"Thanks," she said, overjoyed. The invitation was more than she had bargained for.

Weisswasser felt obliged to warn, "The governor's remarks will be strictly off the record. Is that clear, Ms. Brennan?"

"Depends on what I happen to say," Kirkwood said as he helped Sally on board.

Sally was aware that she had to take advantage of every moment of the brief flight from Malibu to Westwood. While the hand-held camera whirred away with Kirkwood's generous permission (and his staff's chagrin), he talked with surprising candor. Sally thought that perhaps the shock of Bonnie's current plight accounted for his sudden and unexpected openness.

"Governor, we're all very concerned about Bonnie Breit, who is a close friend of yours," Sally began, her palms sweating as she gripped the microphone.

"Yes, she is," Kirkwood affirmed.

"We've just heard that she was apparently injured in this terrible fire today."

Kirkwood took a deep, anxious breath before replying. "Yes. I understand from a member of the sheriff's department that Bonnie was trapped by the fire at her ranch while trying to rescue her horses. Both Bonnie and I love horses," he replied, as the wind from the open doorway whipped his striped tie out of his vest and about his neck.

"Have you had any news of her condition yet?" Sally asked.

"We've been in touch with the doctors at the UCLA Medical Center," Kirkwood answered. "And they informed us that her condition is listed as 'critical.'" His voice cracked on the word "critical." Reaching into his hip pocket, he extracted a monogrammed white linen handkerchief and blew his nose. During his years in public life he had faced many tough situations, but this was one from which he could not remain emotionally detached. Once before, at his wife's funeral, the public had seen him with tears in his eyes. He loved Bonnie very much, and her present plight affected him deeply. "Excuse me," he said.

Sally debated whether or not to go on with the questioning, in light of the man's emotional state. She had no desire to embarrass anyone, especially the governor. But he put his handkerchief away and indicated that he was sufficiently composed to go on.

"And you're heading there to see her now?" Sally asked.

"That's correct," Kirkwood replied. "To see Bonnie and other victims of this devastating and tragic fire as well. It's a terrible thing—this fire. And the drought—what it's doing to our state."

6

Senator and Mrs. Preston Farleigh had purchased their stately brick Georgian colonial home on 30th Place in Forest Hills, one of Washington's finest residential areas, for a ridiculously low price despite the inflated market. The house had originally been acquired for speculation by a real estate firm largely controlled by Rudd International. When Farleigh was elected to the Senate, Rudd arranged for him to buy the residence at a fraction of its actual value. It was one of the many fringe benefits the junior senator realized from his association with the Rudd organization.

Sarajane Farleigh, the senator's petite, curly-haired wife, paced nervously between the blue chintz and white organdy bedroom and the adjoining bathroom where she took secret nips of vodka from a Givenchy perfume bottle while her friend Dottie Calhoun lounged in a chaise sipping coffee.

"Oh, dear, I do hope Preston isn't late tonight," Sarajane fretted in her thick Texas drawl. "When some of those senators get to talking, there's no way of shutting them off. Some of those sessions can last way into evening. When your husband's a senator, you never know when he's likely to come walking in the door."

"The only husband I ever had owned a honky-tonk," Dottie remarked. "Shoot, he *never* came home."

"I declare, it's no wonder there's so much hanky-panky going on in this town. Everything is just so crazy," Sarajane went on.

"Listen, Sarajane, honey, if a man wants to fool around, he's going to do it and nobody's going to stop him no matter where he happens to live," Dottie said. The two women had grown up together in a small town outside Dallas and were the closest of friends. One of the advantages of that friendship was that Preston Farleigh always seemed able to find a place on his payroll for Dottie Calhoun. Officially listed as his receptionist, Dottie spent more time with Sarajane than she did in Farleigh's office. Sarajane would have found it nearly impossible to get ready for an occasion such as the evening's reception at the Brazilian embassy without Dottie's help. But Dottie's main asset was the skillful way she helped hide the senator's wife's greatest weakness. She knew better than anyone how to sober Sarajane up, and when her friend had been on a long drinking bout and was past the point of sobering up, the Texas ranch Dottie had inherited from her late husband proved a very useful hideaway.

"Golly, Dottie, I wish you were coming with us tonight," Sarajane lamented. "I'd feel so much better."

"Now, listen, you all go on and have yourselves a good time and don't worry," Dottie said, well acquainted with her friend's almost pathological shyness and anxiety over attending large gatherings. Everyone had assumed that after a few years in public life, Sarajane would become acclimated and lose her fears, but she never had. Instead, she just drank more.

"I am excited about tonight," Sarajane said, more apprehension than enthusiasm in her voice. "You know I just love anything Brazilian. Remember how you and I used to go see all those Carmen Miranda movies back home? The last time Preston and I went to Brazil, we had us the best time. We really did. He went on a fact-finding tour to learn why coffee prices were so high."

"I remember," Dottie mused.

"We were wined and dined by all the most important people in Brazil," Sarajane went on. "I danced the bossa nova all night with this very nice gentleman who has something to do with the Amazon River."

Sarajane paused. She heard the front door below close and voices in the vestibule. "Oh, dear, that must be Preston now," she said.

"In that case, I'm going to scoot," Dottie aid, rising from the ruffled chaise.

"Thanks ever so much for coming to help me out—again," Sarajane said. "I don't know what I'd do without you."

After exchanging a few words with Dottie on the stairs, Farleigh headed straight to the master bedroom where he greeted his tiny, fluttery wife with a perfunctory kiss. "My, don't you look pretty!"

"Careful, honey, don't mess up my hair," she cautioned with a giggle, backing away from him. "It took Dottie hours to get it just right."

"Well, it looks real nice."

"Thank you," Sarajane smiled.

"And so does that dress," he said, referring to her floor-length pink chiffon gown.

"My, my, aren't we full of compliments tonight," Sarajane giggled coquettishly.

"Only because you deserve them, doll-baby."

"How did things go on the hill today, honey?"

"Real fine," he answered, starting to undress. Glancing at the clothes neatly laid out on the bed, he said, "I see it's black tie tonight."

"You know how formal these South Americans are," Sarajane replied. "Of course, I do like formality once in a while. I think it's good for people to dress up, if you ask me."

As he unbuttoned his shirt, Farleigh said with a grin, "Well, I think the old noose is finally starting to tighten around Kirkwood's neck. The heat's on him now, and I think he's going to start to sizzle very soon."

"Good!" Sarajane said. "The sooner he's through, the better. He deserves whatever he gets after the way he talked about us during the campaign—trying to make us out to be fools. Well, if you ask me, he's the fool."

"He's starting to catch hell all around," Farleigh said, stepping out of his trousers. "He's been arrogant with too many people too long. A lot of them have been looking for a chance to sock it to him, and now it looks like they're going to get it. There's a move afoot to start tightening the strings on the federal purse as far as he's concerned. A lot of folks in this town are tired of bailing him out of this drought mess. Kirkwood's about to feel the pinch real soon, and when he does, it's going to hurt, and hurt good."

Sarajane looked perplexed. "If Kirkwood gets hurt, California gets hurt, too, and that's our state," she said. "If we lose federal funds, isn't that going to be bad for us, too?—you and me?"

"Not if we play our cards right," Farleigh said. "In politics, if you're clever enough, you can turn any situation around to your advantage. Haven't I proved that often enough?"

"Yes, you have, dear," Sarajane agreed.

"I'm going to make it look like I'm fighting like hell for California here in Washington but can't get anywhere because of Kirkwood. Do you follow?"

"I think so, dear."

"Oh, I tell you, Sarajane, he signed his death warrant when he blocked that desalination plants bill," Farleigh said.

"But couldn't somebody reintroduce it?" she questioned. "I mean, with the terrible drought and all? . . ."

Farleigh grinned. "That's what I'm going to push for on our next trip to California," he said.

"Good for you, darlin'," Sarajane said, clapping her tiny hands together in a childlike fashion which delighted her husband.

"And when the bill is reintroduced in the California legislature, Kirkwood won't dare to oppose it this time," Farleigh asserted.

"But if they do build the desalination plants and the drought ends, it will only help him, won't it?" Sarajane pondered. "And we both know that anything that helps him surely doesn't help us."

"Right," Farleigh praised, kissing the tip of her turned-up nose. "The people aren't going to forget the way he fought the Hydrolliance proposal. They're already blaming him for the drought on account of it. They're going to say the whole goddam drought could have been avoided if he had just let Hydrolliance come in and build those desalination plants like they wanted to, instead of fighting them. It will take some people years to get over their losses. Some will never recover. Some are finished. They've lost millions. In any case, they're all going to hold Kirkwood responsible."

"I would surely think so," Sarajane said. "But suppose he does a flip-flop and decides to back the desalination plants project the second time around?"

"There's no way he can do that without looking like a complete fool and a hypocrite besides. Even his famous charisma couldn't get him out of that. Unless he pulls some kind of a rabbit out of the hat, he's as good as washed up right now. He doesn't have a snowball's chance in hell of getting the presidential nomination no matter how much he wants it. And he wants it bad."

"I should hope not," Sarajane said. "There's only one person who belongs in that White House and you know who that is."

Farleigh smiled and put his arm around his wife. "And who might that be, sugar?"

"Senator Preston Farleigh," she replied staunchly.

"You want me to tell you something, honey?" he said. "I want to get inside that White House so bad I can almost taste it."

"Me, too," Sarajane said, but there was far less enthusiasm in her voice.

7

Sally Brennan's exclusive interview with Governor Kirkwood at the Malibu fire station and later, in the helicopter, had been part of an incredible streak of luck, but to be included in the official party crowded into the special VIP elevator at UCLA Medical Center topped everything. Sally could scarcely believe what was happening.

In the corridor outside Bonnie Breit's room, Kirkwood was greeted by a group of doctors. From their grave expressions, Sally feared that the news was not good. The governor was the only one permitted to enter the room.

As he stepped through the door, the first thing that struck Paul Kirkwood was the odor. The heavy, all-pervading smell so characteristic of hospitals could not mask the scent of charred flesh. He felt an immediate, sickening feeling in the pit of his stomach—because he realized that the charred flesh was Bonnie's own.

Behind the screens surrounding the bed, a platoon of interns, residents, and nurses were working feverishly.

Sensing Kirkwood's anguish, the surgeon in charge of the case laid a reassuring hand on his shoulder.

"How is she?" Kirkwood asked.

"We consider her condition critical," the surgeon replied. "If she makes it through the next twenty-four to forty-eight hours, she has a very good chance of pulling through."

"Can I see her?" Kirkwood asked. The screens obscured his view.

"There's not much to see, I'm afraid," the surgeon said. "We've got her pretty well covered up." He moved aside one of the screens.

The surgeon was right. Bonnie was swathed in various

kinds of dressings from head to toe. "How badly burned is she?" Kirkwood asked anxiously.

"We haven't determined the exact percentage yet," the surgeon replied. "It's her face we're most concerned about."

"Her face?" Kirkwood repeated with a nearly audible gasp.

"Somehow it got burned pretty badly," the surgeon said. "But don't worry. We've got excellent reconstructive techniques these days. Restoring her looks is the least of our worries right now. Our primary concern is to get her out of shock and stabilize her physical condition. Aesthetic considerations can come later."

When Kirkwood emerged from the room he appeared badly shaken.

"There's a lounge at the end of the corridor, Governor," Sally suggested. "I mean, if you'd like to sit down . . ."

"That sounds good," Kirkwood said.

Sally tagged along as the governor led his retinue down the hall.

"You should see her," Kirkwood said. "Poor Bonnie! She's lying there wrapped like a mummy from head to toe, tubes coming in and going out everywhere."

"I'm sure she'll pull through," Sally said encouragingly.

"I wish I felt as confident as you do, but thank you anyway," Kirkwood said, unexpectedly taking her hand and giving it a squeeze.

When Sally and the KHOT crew arrived back at the station, both the Five and Six O'Clock News had long been over, and Ken Wilson was in a rage. "Where in the hell have you been?" he stormed, his heavy-bearded face flushed with anger.

"On assignment," she answered casually, as if nothing were amiss, deciding to try and avoid an out-and-out confrontation if at all possible.

"Where the fuck were you for the five o'clock interview with the goddam pony kid?" he went on. "Hank had to do it."

"So what?"

"He was hired to cover sports, not pony stories."

"I thought ponies were the sport of kings," she quipped as she headed for her office. Once inside, she tried to close the door before Ken could force his way in, but she wasn't fast enough.

"Look, I've had it up to here with you today," he said,

50

slicing his open hand across his throat to give his words added emphasis.

"Really?" she said indifferently.

Pounding his fist on the desk, he said, "Goddam it, you're fired! Clean out your desk and get out."

Sally frowned as though she didn't quite understand what he had just said. "Fired?" she repeated. *"Now?"*

"Now," he affirmed.

"What about the eleven o'clock newscast?"

"Forget it."

"You mean you aren't going to let me do it?"

"You did your last broadcast at KHOT."

"Well, that's too bad," Sally sighed. "I guess I'll just have to take the interview I did with the governor after his visit to Bonnie Breit at UCLA Hospital to one of the other channels. I'm sure somebody'll be interested."

Wilson was skeptical. "You don't have any interview like that," he said, but a tentative note had entered his voice.

"Want to bet?"

"You'd better not take it to another channel," he warned.

"Try and stop me," she smiled slyly.

"You're bullshitting and you know it," he scoffed. "You don't have any goddam interview. What do you take me for, a fool? Everybody knows Kirkwood is like a fucking clam when it comes to talking about his relationship with Bonnie Breit."

"He didn't seem to mind talking to me about it," Sally replied casually as she opened the top drawer of her desk and began to remove personal articles. "As a matter of fact, he spoke pretty freely. There are a lot of people who might be very interested in what he had to say. If it were plugged right—say, with spot announcements inserted every half hour during prime time that an exclusive interview was coming up at eleven—the Eleven O'Clock News might generate some pretty big numbers in the ratings." Sally knew that ratings were Wilson's lifeblood.

"Well, listen, Sally," Wilson said, attempting to sound genial once again. "Maybe neither one of us should do anything rash. You know . . . like anything we might regret later on."

"I'm not going to regret anything, Ken," she said, starting to empty a second drawer. Wilson reached out and slammed the drawer shut.

"Maybe we should sit down and talk," he suggested.

Pretending to mull over his suggestion a few moments, she

said, "No harm in that." Kicking off her shoes, she plopped in a chair, folded her arms, and looked at him expectantly. "Go ahead and talk."

Sally's exclusive interview with Kirkwood on the late news proved to be the ratings grabber she had thought it would. In a lounge at the UCLA Hospital the governor had spoken openly and freely with Sally about his relationship with Bonnie Breit.

"It seems to be working well for both of us," he had said candidly. "I have great respect and affection for Bonnie and I think I'm safe in saying that she feels the same way about me. She's a wonderful and very talented actress. We both have careers that demand a great deal and carry with them considerable responsibilities. Our personal relationship has to take this into consideration. It's not a conventional relationship, and one that might not work for other people, but it works well for us. This fire today has been a terrible blow, not just for me personally, but for many other people as well. You saw that when you were out on the fire-lines in Malibu with us."

"It's been one of the worst disasters I've ever covered," Sally had agreed.

Tears beginning to well in his eyes for the second time that day, Kirkwood struggled to maintain his composure. "Today's tragic fire pointed up to me—as it never has before—just how imperative it is to end this drought as soon as possible. We in California can't depend on Washington to bail us out. Two years have gone by and nothing's been done. We can't wait any longer. We've got to get busy and do something on our own. We've got to show the rest of the country that we can and will do it."

"Do you have any specific measures in mind, Governor?"

"The only thing I have in mind is the firm conviction that we're going to get water for California if it's the last thing we do!"

The next day, Ken Wilson stood in the doorway of Sally's office scratching his bald head. "Goddamit, Sally," he said, "I'm proud as hell of you. You've been doing a first-rate job."

Scarcely looking up from the script of the evening's newscast, she mumbled, "Thanks, Ken."

"Because you've been doing such a great job," he went on, "I've decided to give you a special assignment."

Putting the script aside, she looked directly at him, wondering just what he had in mind. "Oh? What's that, Ken?"

"I've decided to turn the drought over to you," he announced. "Exclusively."

"Really?" Her reaction was a combination of surprise and skepticism.

"I want you to cover anything and everything related to it, including the governor's efforts to end it," Wilson said. "After last night's broadcast, I'm convinced it's our most important story. This could be a big opportunity for you."

Unfazed, Sally asked, "What's the rest?"

"What 'rest'?"

"Why me?"

"I told you. Because you're doing such a great job."

"I thought one of the guys would get this assignment."

"What do you think I am, some kind of a chauvinist?" Wilson said indignantly. "I give the job to the best qualified man on my staff—or in your case, woman."

"I appreciate that," Sally said.

"Go wherever you feel you need to—spend whatever you have to—within reason, of course," he said. "Just give me exciting, hard-hitting stories, the way you have been. That's all."

"Okay," Sally agreed.

Wilson stared at her, looking disappointed. "Is that all you're going to say?"

"What do you want me to say? I feel the same way you do," she replied. "The drought *is* a big, important story. I'll try and do just what I've been doing all along—my best."

8

"**Hello, Sally, how are you?**" the genial yet authoritative voice on the end of the line said. "This is Paul Kirkwood. I'm flying to Los Angeles today to see Bonnie. I wonder if you and I might get together? I have an announcement I'd like to make on the air. But it's something I'd like to keep as informal as possible. Do you think you could help me out?"

Sally tried to play it cool, realizing that he was subtly offering her an exclusive. She glanced at the lineup for the Eleven O'Clock News to see what could be eliminated. "Sure," she said. "I'll be glad to."

"What I want to announce is that I've decided to go to Washington and attend the World Weather Symposium," he continued. "I'm hoping that with so many experts in one place at one time, we might get some ideas, perhaps some workable suggestions on how to combat this drought. I feel that this problem is so serious, so grave that it demands my *personal* attention."

Kirkwood's on-the-air announcement of his intention to attend the weather conference was picked up for broadcast on the national news. After the interview, Kirkwood told Sally, "I've been extremely pleased with the way you've handled these interviews."

"Well, thank you, sir."

"I like the way you never badger me, never try to put me on the spot or embarrass me the way some of your colleagues try to," he said, adding, "not that they succeed very often."

"I don't happen to feel that those tactics help much in getting a good, in-depth interview."

"Don't get me wrong, Sally. I think that oftentimes your questions are hard-hitting, but I have no objection to that."

Smiling, she said, "Thanks again."

At that point Wally Weisswasser interrupted. "Will you also be going to Washington, Ms. Brennan?" he inquired.

"If the governor feels this trip is important to the drought situation, then I think it's important enough for me to cover," she replied.

"Good. We'd like to have you there," Kirkwood said. "I'll tell you one thing, if I do find a workable solution to the drought at this conference, you'll be the first to know."

Turning to his press secretary, Kirkwood said, "Wally, do you happen to have one of those programs for the symposium on you?"

"Yes, sir. Right here." Weisswasser produced a folder from the breast pocket of his three-piece suit.

Kirkwood unfolded and scanned the program. "I think nearly every country in the world is represented at this symposium."

"That's only natural," Weisswasser replied, stroking his neatly trimmed beard. "Weather is no respecter of political boundaries or ideologies."

"Do you know this man Terhune who's heading up the conference?" Kirkwood asked Sally.

"Yes," she replied. "I've interviewed him several times. The last time was during the protests over the proposed desalination plants along the coast."

"Fortunately he was with us on that one," Weisswasser said.

"That isn't always the case with Terhune," Kirkwood added.

"I think he's getting more radical as he gets older," Weisswasser said. "He started out way back in the late forties battling against the use of nuclear power and attempted to spearhead a worldwide ban," Weisswasser recounted. "When that didn't work out, he became bitter. Maybe that's why he's allied himself with so many dubious groups lately."

"The title of his paper is 'Insidious Effects of Radiation on World Weather Patterns.'"

"That sounds like something you'd expect from him," Weisswasser remarked.

Running his finger down the list of participants, Kirkwood said, "There's one name here that particularly interests me. Ah, yes, here it is—Neal Haverson." Turning to Sally, he asked, "Ever come across him?"

Sally frowned thoughtfully a moment. "As a matter of fact I have. The name sounds definitely familiar. For some crazy reason the thought of champagne popped into my head when you mentioned his name."

"Really?" Kirkwood smiled, looking bemused. "Why champagne?"

"I was at a party celebrating the maiden voyage of a new cruise ship, and there was a lot of champagne flowing that day," Sally explained, adding: "That's the sort of story they used to have me covering."

"Sounds like fun," Kirkwood quipped, "but what does it have to do with this Haverson man?"

"Haverson was the only thing appealing about the whole assignment," Sally recalled. "He's tall and sturdy and somewhat intense and looks super in his captain's uniform."

"He doesn't sound like the sort to be at a serious scientific conference—a cruise ship captain. Sounds more like a sea-going gigolo than a scientist," Kirkwood remarked.

"Actually, despite his attractiveness, Haverson is quite a serious person, from what I remember," Sally said. "Very knowledgeable, very well informed. He's more than just a pretty face."

"He'd have to be with a paper titled, 'Effects of the Polar Ice Mass on Surrounding Air and Water Temperatures,'" Weisswasser said.

"Why does he interest you so much, Governor?" Sally asked.

"It's not only this particular paper of his," Kirkwood replied. "He's called the office repeatedly requesting an appointment to see me. He claims to have a method for ending the drought."

Weisswasser groaned. "Oh, one of those," he said disparagingly. "We've had a million cranks calling the office with all kinds of crazy schemes."

"Yes, but somehow I think this fellow might be worth looking into," Kirkwood speculated. "I'd like to learn a little more about him."

"Maybe you'll get a chance in Washington," Sally said.

"Maybe we both will, Sally," Kirkwood smiled and handed the program back to his press secretary.

Lulled by the steady hum of the jet engines, Neal Haverson fought the tendency to sleep, afraid that if he did, he might have the recurrent nightmare and frighten the other passengers, as well as embarrass himself. In order to keep awake, he tried perusing the notes he had made to use when he addressed the symposium, but he wasn't able to keep his mind on them for long. He was far more interested in something else he had written which was *not* going to be delivered at the conference, a thick, bound monograph with pictures and diagrams. When he learned that Governor Kirkwood planned to attend the symposium, Haverson planned to find an opportunity to bring his monograph to the governor's attention. Just how he would go about it, he didn't know, but he was determined to succeed. For months he had tried to get an appointment with the chief executive in Sacramento only to be put off by one officious secretary after another. A lot of time and effort had gone into preparing the proposal, and Haverson sincerely believed that it would solve the California water crisis. The problem was that he hadn't been able to enlist anyone else to his cause, at least not so far. In fact the only person who had expressed any interest at all was a Saudi Arabian prince he had never met.

The vacant seat beside Haverson was a reminder that at the last moment Ingrid had decided not to accompany him. She had had a whole list of reasons to back up her decision—her job, the lack of a dependable sitter for the children, the fire danger. He had made no attempt to hide his disappointment. They had even had a small tiff before he left. No doubt her presence would have made the trip more enjoyable. They needed time away together. They had spent too much time apart in their marriage, and with the passing years, Ingrid had become more resentful of his absences, less willing to accept them as she had for so many years in the past. He worried about her change in attitude and felt alternately sad, guilty, and bewildered. The marriage had been strong. It had to be to have withstood the trouble in Antarctica. But he was beginning to have doubts that it could survive another such crisis.

During the last voyage to Acapulco, he had resolved to spend more time at home and yet, here he was flying off to Washington and the conference. Alone. He tried to console himself with the thought that sometimes a man had to make sacrifices in his personal life in order to achieve larger goals.

9

As Sally Brennan stood on the corner of M and 15th streets waiting for the light to change, a few snowflakes brushed her cheek and she smiled. How ironic, she thought, drought and heat in California and a freak spring snowfall in Washington, D.C.

She entered the fourteen-story, glass-and-brick Madison Hotel with its sleek and attractive blend of marble and rosewood and headed for the elevators, clutching a briefcase beneath her arm.

At Kirkwood's suite she was admitted by none other than the governor himself, after a credential check outside the door. He immediately led her to a sitting room away from the jangling phones and his staff. Inviting her to sit on one of the two sofas in the room, he offered her a drink. Sally looked around the attractive suite, a grandfather's clock, standing beside an antique breakfront filled with rare Chinese porcelains, chimed the hour.

"A martini, please," she said, and settled back on the couch, opening her briefcase.

"Got something you want to show me?" he asked.

"As a matter of fact, I do," she replied, extracting a sheaf of papers. "One of the researchers at the station came up with some information on that guy you asked about—Neal Haverson. Remember?"

"Ah, yes!" Kirkwood said. "The mysterious cruise ship captain."

Taking a manila envelope from the case, Sally sifted through the papers it contained. "It seems that Neal Haverson was a naval officer at one time and commander of the support force at McMurdo station in the Antarctic. There, he acquired a considerable reputation for his scientific endeavors, studying icebergs and glaciers and their effects on the surrounding environment in conjunction with the scientists working at the station under the auspices of the National Science Foundation."

"That's pretty unusual for a commanding officer," Kirkwood remarked. "This interest in science, I mean."

"It certainly is," Sally agreed, "but that's the kind of man this Haverson seems to be. Unusual."

Kirkwood looked at Sally expectantly. "Is that it? Is that all you've got on him?" he asked.

"Oh, no, there's lots more," Sally assured him. "While he was in charge at McMurdo, a controversial Russian ship designer and adventurer, Yuri Maslov, defected after a daring attempt to completely circle the Antarctic continent alone in a small craft of his own design. This feat of his endeded unsuccessfully, and he had to put in at the American station. When he did, he begged for political asylum. The story drew a lot of attention."

"I thought only ballet dancers did things like that," Kirkwood quipped. "Why didn't I read about him?"

"Maslov's defection was overshadowed by another event," Sally continued. "A lot more tragic."

Kirkwood frowned. "Oh? What was that?"

"An eminent biologist and nun, Dr. Elizabeth Nagy, one of very few women ever permitted to 'winter over' at the antarctic station, was found, apparently frozen to death, under the ice. She had failed to stay in contact with headquarters while she was out on a research expedition," Sally related. "There were rumors that she was involved in a romance and had committed suicide from guilt, despair, and frustration. Very soon after the nun-scientist's death Haverson suddenly resigned his navy commission and returned to civilian life."

"What does that mean?" Kirkwood mused.

"I'm not going to speculate on that one," Sally said. "Rumors circulated at the time that he was at least indirectly responsible for Dr. Nagy's death. But his resignation seems to have been voluntary."

Kirkwood sighed. "Well, that's quite a story."

"There's a little more," Sally said, referring once again to her notes. "After his resignation from the navy, Haverson did not abandon his interest in science. In fact, he wrote a number of papers based on data he compiled while at McMurdo."

"One of which he's delivering tomorrow," Kirkwood concluded, anticipating her.

"Correct," she said.

"Well, dry as it sounds from the title, it's one paper I'm not going to miss," Kirkwood said.

"Me neither," Sally replied.

Kirkwood's presence at the symposium drew considerable attention from the media, and after Haverson's talk, the governor was confronted by a barrage of reporters as he emerged from the auditorium.

"What's your purpose here, Governor?" one reporter asked, shoving a microphone at Kirkwood.

"Looking for ideas on how we might get some water for our state," he replied.

"Come across any leads yet?" another reporter called out.

"Not yet, but we're hopeful," Kirkwood answered, amid the popping of flashbulbs.

"How important do you consider ending California's drought to your future as a possible presidential candidate?"

"I'm not concerned with my possible candidacy at the moment. That's far in the future," Kirkwood replied. "Our immediate concerns are ending the drought. That's where we intend to concentrate all our efforts. Thank you, gentlemen . . ."

Escorted by his security force, Paul Kirkwood exited through a special side door and climbed into a waiting car.

"Get in touch with Neal Haverson and set up a meeting," he directed Drew Ramsdale. "I was impressed as hell by both him and his paper, weren't you?"

"Yes, I was, Paul," Ramsdale agreed.

"And include Sally Brennan in that meeting, if you can."

Ramsdale consulted a small notebook. "You're invited to a reception at the White House tonight with the president,"

"To hell with that," Kirkwood said brusquely. "This is a helluva lot more important."

Ramsdale arranged a dinner meeting with Neal Haverson and Sally Brennan at the exclusive Cosmos Club. The subdued lighting and dark wood interior of the club's dining room created a sedate atmosphere enhanced by vases of freshly cut flowers atop the white linen tablecloths.

Kirkwood had picked up Sally at her hotel in his official car, and when they arrived at the club, Haverson, quietly handsome in a dark blue suit and striped, regimental tie, was already waiting.

"Captain Haverson?" Kirkwood said.

The former naval officer rose and shook hands with the governor. "How do you do, sir?"

Introducing Sally, Kirkwood said, "I'd like you to meet Sally Brennan."

For a moment Neal Haverson stared at her as if her face might be familiar. But "Pleased to meet you," was all he said.

"I think we've already met," Sally replied and recounted the circumstances.

"I thought you looked familiar," Haverson said. "I remember the reporting job you did. It was very good."

"At least you didn't say, 'I never forget a pretty face,'" Sally quipped. "That's what I usually get."

"Congratulations on the excellent paper you delivered today," Kirkwood said.

"Yes, even I found it interesting," Sally added.

Pleased, Haverson asked, "You didn't find it too technical?"

"Somewhat," Kirkwood admitted.

"Let's just say I got the general idea," Sally added.

"Sally's been assigned by KHOT in Los Angeles to cover progress in the drought situation," Kirkwood explained.

"I'm still waiting for a really big story," Sally said.

"Maybe I can do something about that," Haverson replied.

"I understand that you've been trying to contact our Sacramento office?" Kirkwood said, perusing the menu.

"Yes, I have," Haverson confirmed. "And without much luck."

"What did you want to talk about?" Kirkwood inquired.

"At the risk of sounding immodest, Governor, I think I may have a workable solution to the drought," Haverson replied. His matter-of-fact tone made the statement sound perfectly routine. "As you may have gathered from my paper, it's a known fact that ninety percent of the fresh water on earth is trapped as ice in the glaciers of Antarctica."

"So I understand," Kirkwood nodded, indicating that he wished to hear more.

"That's enough water to meet the world's demand for the next five thousand years or so."

"Wow!" Sally murmured.

"What's more, I firmly believe that right now we possess the technology and necessary know-how to transport this frozen fresh water to anywhere it's needed," Haverson went on, his intense blue eyes fired with enthusiasm for his subject.

"You mean to California, for example?" Kirkwood asked.

"To just about anywhere," Haverson assured him.

Kirkwood was intrigued. "Do I understand you correctly that California's drought could be relieved by icebergs from Antarctica?" he asked.

"Yes," Haverson affirmed without hesitation. "As a matter of fact, I've written up a proposal for just such a pilot program."

"Do you have a copy here?" Kirkwood inquired.

"Yes, I do," Haverson replied.

"Funny you should ask . . ." Sally joked.

"It's in my hotel room," Haverson said, with a smile at Sally's teasing.

"May I have a look at it?" Kirkwood asked.

"Certainly," Haverson agreed, managing to restrain himself from adding that he had been trying to bring it to the governor's attention for months.

10

The next day when Drew Ramsdale appeared at the governor's suite, freshly shaved and attired in a crisply pressed dark pinstriped suit, ready to begin work, he was shocked to find the chief executive still in bed. Kirkwood was usually up and working by six A.M.

"In case you're wondering, this is what kept me up half the night," Kirkwood explained, patting a thick volume beside him.

"What is it?" Ramsdale asked, putting down the stack of newspapers from all over the country, in which he had circled in red articles he considered worthy of Kirkwood's attention.

"Captain Haverson's monograph on the transport of antarctic icebergs," Kirkwood revealed. "Frankly, I'm pretty impressed with it. *Damned* impressed."

"You don't think the guy's a nut?" Ramsdale questioned.

"If he can get water for California, he can be the biggest nut in the world and I don't care," Kirkwood said.

Surprised by the chief executive's enthusiasm, Ramsdale said, "Are you really serious?"

"Sure I'm serious," Kirkwood replied. "So serious, in fact, that I intend to get some expert opinions about the feasibility of this whole thing as soon as possible."

"And then what?"

"And then try and find some way to come up with twenty million," Kirkwood said.

"Twenty million?"

"That's what Haverson estimates a pilot run will cost."

"Where are we going to get that kind of money for something like this?" Ramsdale asked. "There are a lot of people who would call his idea harebrained."

"Haverson mentioned some Saudi Arabian prince."

Ramsdale frowned a moment. "It wasn't Prince Rashid al-Akbar, was it?"

"How the hell did you know?"

Ramsdale grinned. "I came across an article on him in *Fortune*," he replied. "He's exploring ways of bringing water to Saudi Arabia."

"Can you get hold of him?"

"I could try calling his London office," Ramsdale suggested. "That is, if you're really serious . . ."

"Hell, yes, I'm serious!" Kirkwood said, bounding out of bed.

Several transatlantic calls were necessary to arrange a meeting between Prince Akbar and the governor, which the Arab entrepreneur insisted take place in London, much to Kirkwood's displeasure.

"Since he's holding the moneybags, I suppose we don't have much choice," Kirkwood admitted, finally consenting to the London meeting site. "Be sure to notify Sally Brennan and Haverson. I want them to go with us."

"Are you sure you want Sally Brennan along on this junket?" the chief aide questioned.

"That's right," Kirkwood affirmed. "I want to make sure we get the right kind of coverage."

"Whatever you say, Paul," Ramsdale agreed.

By telephone Ramsdale informed Sally, "The governor would like you to accompany him to London."

"London!?" she repeated, her tone somewhat incredulous.

"Right. He's meeting with Prince Akbar of Saudi Arabia."

"Really?" she said, obviously delighted to be included in such a development. "How long do I have to get ready?"

"The chartered jet will be leaving tonight at seven. We'll send a car for you at six. Please be ready."

After the call from Ramsdale, Neal Haverson paced the floor, downed several Scotch-and-sodas, and practiced what he was going to say before he worked up the courage to call Ingrid.

"How are things going, honey?" he asked, trying to sound nonchalant.

"It's been an awful day," she sighed.

"I'm sorry . . ."

"I decided to take my kids to the beach today—it was so hot

64

in the classroom and they were so restless. They love the tidepools and I thought it would be a good opportunity to give them an informal lesson in marine biology."

"That sounds good."

"Well, it wasn't. There was a flasher hiding behind some rocks. Whenever I happened to look in his direction, he sneaked out and flashed."

Haverson chuckled. "How did he measure up?"

"That's not funny, Neal," she reproached.

"Sorry . . ."

"When are you coming home? Soon, I hope. We've got a couple of serious problems here. I smelled marijuana in Cathy's room last night. I think she swallowed the roach when she heard me coming."

"Just stay cool and don't make a big issue out of it. It's a phase. She'll get over it."

"I want you to have a talk with her when you come home."

"Okay. I will," he promised.

"And another thing, Jill's refusing to wear her helmet when she rides and you know the Sheldons' daughter fractured her skull last year when she fell off a horse."

"Tell Jill, no helmet, no riding."

"It's easier said than done. She leaves the house with it on and then takes it off later."

There was a momentary pause before Haverson said, "You're pretty wound up, aren't you?"

"Well, I told you it was a bad day. When the girls were little, I could handle them. But now they need a firmer hand. I need a good, strong, masculine presence to back me up. When are you coming home, Neal? You haven't said."

"That's what I called to tell you," he said as he reached for the glass of Scotch on the nightstand and took a big swallow. "I'm going to be here a little longer than I expected."

"Oh, Neal . . ." she groaned.

"I'm sorry, honey, but something's come up. I'm leaving for London this evening."

"London!?"

"The governor is interested in my iceberg plan. There's the possibility of financing in London. I'll explain when I see you."

"When will *that* be?"

"Is that all you can say, Ingrid? Can't you say, 'Gosh, Neal, I'm happy for you' or something like that? You know how important this is to me."

"Yes, I know," she conceded. "London today, the Antarctic tomorrow."

"Once I help to get this thing set up, my involvement is over. I'll be more than willing to turn it over to anybody that wants to take charge."

"You'll never let go."

"Want to bet?" he challenged, irritated by her unwillingness to share his enthusiasm.

"I know you."

"There's no way in hell I'd ever go back to Antarctica," he declared. "You know how I feel about that place and what happened there," he declared staunchly.

Early in his political career, Paul Kirkwood learned to conserve his energies by sleeping whenever and wherever the opportunity arose. Airplanes, he had found, were ideal. Throughout the flight to London, he stretched out across two seats and snoozed, leaving the others in the plane to make small talk among themselves.

Sally Brennan was fairly well accepted by the governor's staff, though some of them still displayed traces of distrust politicians and their associates traditionally reserve for media people. Sensing this coolness, she chose to devote her attention to Haverson.

"How are you doing, Captain?" she asked as she kicked off her shoes and made herself comfortable in the adjoining seat.

"Okay," he responded, pleased by the attention of a bright, attractive woman and still smarting a little from Ingrid's attitude on the phone. "How about yourself?"

"Hanging in," she smiled. "I guess you must be pretty excited about meeting with Prince Akbar? Or don't you get excited?"

"I don't want to count on anything. . . ." he said. "There's still a helluva lot of groundwork to do before we start hauling icebergs."

"It'll be a sensational story if it really works," she said.

"I have all the confidence in the world in this project," he asserted, "but I've been working on it so long I can hardly believe that I might get the backing at last."

Shortly after they landed at London's Heathrow airport, Sally Brennan asked Ramsdale to brief her on the Arab prince.

"Prince Rashid al-Akbar is reputed to be one of the most

intelligent, progressive, and ambitious of the many princes in the royal family," he told her, looking at his notes on the man. "He was educated in the United States with an undergraduate degree in petroleum engineering from the University of Southern California and an MBA from Harvard Business School. Through shrewd investments and clever business acumen, he has been able to parlay the income he receives as a member of the royal family into a personal fortune estimated in excess of three hundred million."

"That's a lot of bucks," Sally said.

Ramsdale continued, "In recent years he is reported to have concentrated his investments in real estate, mostly American."

"Does he have any holdings in California?" Kirkwood asked.

"We're not certain, Paul," Ramsdale replied.

"If he does have land in California, that automatically gives him a vested interest in our water crisis and could make him a lot more sympathtic to our proposal. Sometimes it helps to know what the stakes are in a game before you start to play."

From Heathrow, a car took the party directly to the Dorchester Hotel where they changed clothes and freshened up from the flight before the meeting with the prince.

Akbar's firm was located in a modern building in the Knightsbridge section. Most of the employees seemed to be British, and only after a male secretary had ushered the Kirkwood party into an elegantly appointed conference room did they encounter an Arab. A sallow complected man with a carefully trimmed black beard and soulful, alert dark eyes, he wore a beautifully tailored dark suit, obviously from the best of Savile Row.

"Governor, ladies and gentlemen," the secretary said, "may I present His Highness, Prince Rashid al-Akbar."

"I am honored by your presence," the prince said. His speech had a slight Near Eastern accent.

Drew Ramsdale performed the introductions for the group.

Immediately warm and friendly, Akbar took Kirkwood by the arm and steered him toward the conference table, signaling to the secretary to serve tiny cups of highly aromatic Arabic coffee.

"I have been looking forward to this meeting, Governor," Akbar said.

"Not half as much as I have, Your Highness," Kirkwood replied.

"I find your proposal most interesting," Akbar said.

"Perhaps we should begin by having Captain Haverson briefly outline his scheme," Kirkwood proposed.

At the head of the table Akbar nodded. "Very well," he agreed, fingering a tassled string of black worry-beads.

Pleased at the opportunity to present his material so soon, Haverson rose and, with the aid of a portable blackboard, explained his plan. Akbar listened attentively, but Haverson could not determine from his expression whether or not the prince was favorably impressed by what he heard.

When Haverson finished, everyone at the table automatically looked to Akbar for a reaction. Before he spoke, the Arab prince seemed to be considering his words.

"Thank you very much for this presentation," he said. "Please forgive me, sir, when I say that this idea in itself is not a new one. It has been proposed before but never with the kind of impressive detail that you have given us."

"Does that mean he liked it?" Sally whispered to Haverson.

"As I am sure you all know," Akbar continued, "that although we have plenty of oil, water is scarce and very precious in my country. In the future it is my dream to provide every one of our subjects with as high a standard of living as possible. That includes sufficient water to meet all needs. As you know, we have built desalination plants at several locations in our country, but the water these plants provide is not yet enough to meet the needs of the country. So as a result, we have been looking for other sources of water for a long time. The transporting of icebergs from Antarctica has been brought to our attention in the past, but we have not seen fit to proceed with this method because too many factors, such as the currents in the Indian Ocean, for example, are unknown or have been insufficiently studied. On the other hand, Captain Haverson has just pointed out that the South Pacific has been thoroughly studied and charted. I think that if we can arrive at an agreement to our mutual satisfaction, I might very well be interested in participating in the pilot project you have devised. Much could be learned from such a project which would benefit both California and Saudi Arabia."

"What conditions would such an agreement entail?" Kirkwood asked.

"California has some very rich agricultural land, does it not?" Akbar asked.

"When there's water, it's rich," Kirkwood said.

"As a student at USC I used to admire all those acres and acres of wonderful grapes and apricots and plums and almonds. We Arabs are people of the desert. We delight when we see land that is lush and fruitful," Akbar said.

"I'll tell you what, Your Highness," Kirkwood said, impulsively playing a hunch. "How would you like some of that wonderful California land you admire so much?"

"How is that possible?" Akbar questioned. "The United States Congress has recently passed laws prohibiting the sale of agricultural land to foreigners. Drought or not, I would like very much to possess California farmland, but that is now out of the question, is it not?"

"Do you realize that you just indirectly expressed confidence that the drought will end?" Kirkwood said.

"So it will," Akbar affirmed. "I have no doubt of that. California cannot be permitted to become a desert. That would offend Allah."

"Tell me this, Your Highness," Kirkwood said. "Do you think that Captain Haverson's plan could be the will of Allah?"

"It's possible," Akbar conceded.

Haverson and Sally exchanged puzzled glances. Neither of them, nor anyone else around the conference table, had any idea what the governor was getting at.

"I'll tell you what, Your Highness," Kirkwood continued. "My mother's family has many thousands of acres of land, most of it granted to them years ago by the king of Spain. They never sold their land to the Anglos when they arrived in California as most of the other Spanish families did. Those original acres of the land-grant are still in the Fernandez family. If you agree to finance the iceberg project, I will personally see that you acquire this California land you so strongly desire."

Neal Haverson could scarcely believe what he was hearing. Was Kirkwood really willing to exchange his family's own land for Akbar's funding of *his* project? It seemed incredible. Haverson had never known a politician to make that kind of personal sacrifice before. Didn't he realize how risky it was? How easily such an offer could be twisted to seem like a bribe? Was it an indication of Kirkwood's tremendous faith in Haverson's idea, or was it a sign of his political desperation? Or was it merely some kind of trick?

The prince, who was also astonished by such an unorthodox offer, said, "But, Governor, how can you? I don't understand. . . . It is not possible. You have laws against this. . . ."

"We have laws against foreigners purchasing farmland," Kirkwood agreed, "but the law says nothing about *gifts*."

11

Rico's lovemaking had been more zealous than usual, and it had left Annalise with a cluster of red blotches on her graceful neck. The high, collarlike choker of pearls and diamonds she wore to the party at the Brazilian embassy successfully hid them, but the next morning the red marks evolved into purplish splotches which persisted, forcing her to attempt to conceal them at the office beneath a turtleneck cashmere sweater.

When she stepped off her private elevator, escorted by a security guard, into her top-floor suite, Annalise was greeted by Margaret with the news that Gaines was in his office on the floor below awaiting permission to ascend.

"Let him wait," she said, removing her jaguar coat, a gift from her father in Paraguay. She had had to pay dearly to have the coat smuggled into the United States.

"He says it's urgent, Mrs. Rudd," Margaret said.

"Everything is always 'urgent' with that old fuddy-duddy," Annalise remarked contemptuously, taking her place behind the carved teak desk.

Eventually she got around to summoning Gaines to what the employees referred to as the "forbidden city" but did not invite him to sit. She kept him standing, more or less at attention, before her desk. "Things went well in Washington last night," she announced proudly. "It looks like we are finally going to get the go-ahead from Pinhiero on the Amazon project. All that's left is the matter of the loan from the Import-Export Bank. If we can get approval on that, we're on our way."

"Mr. Rudd would be most gratified if he were alive. The

Amazon project was very dear to his heart. He and I worked together very hard and very long on it," Gaines reminisced.

"Yes, I'm sure you did," she said brusquely. She hated Gaines to remind her of how close he and her late husband were.

"There shouldn't be any difficulties with the Import-Export Bank," Gaines speculated, "not with Senator Farleigh on the International Finance Subcommittee. He's very clever and persuasive. That's why Mr. Rudd rescued him from oblivion and offered him the chance to run for the Senate."

"One dumb thing Farleigh did was to marry Sarajane," Annalise said.

"Oh, I think Senator Farleigh knew what he was doing when he married Mrs. Farleigh," Gaines asserted. "I'll admit, she does become a bit garrulous at times."

"Her tongue gets loose because she can't hold her liquor," Annalise said. "That's a dangerous liability in the wife of a man in public life."

"Still, she does set a certain tone with her gracious manner and quiet southern voice," Gaines remarked.

"When she's sober," Annalise snapped.

"She helps to soothe those whom Farleigh has ruffled with his abrasive ways," Gaines continued. "You know how he can be. I think that Sarajane will prove to be an asset to him if they get into the White House."

Annalise glanced up. "Do you think he has a chance?" she asked in a somewhat incredulous tone. She had known for a long time that Farleigh had presidential aspirations, but never really took them seriously.

"Yes, I think Senator Farleigh has a very good chance," Gaines replied. "As I see it, Governor Kirkwood of California is his only serious threat."

Brushing that line of conversation aside for a moment, Annalise said, "Margaret said you had something urgent you wanted to see me about?"

"Yes," Gaines affirmed. "As a matter of fact, it's about Governor Kirkwood, strangely enough."

"What about him?"

"I thought that perhaps you might be interested in knowing that he is at present in London conferring with the Saudi prince, Rashid al-Akbar."

Annalise frowned. "Who is he?" she asked. Gaines's habit of doling out important information piecemeal fashion exasperated her.

"A member of the Saudi royal family," Gaines replied. "He's actively involved with the Central Planning Organization, among other things, including a search for possible sources of water."

"What are you getting at, Gaines?"

"Simply that Governor Kirkwood is obviously looking for financing."

"For what?"

"For that scheme of Captain Haverson's, that former naval officer," he answered. "You know, towing icebergs from Antarctica to the arid areas of the world."

"Oh, *him*. Now, I remember. He was tall and good-looking—the strong silent type," she recalled with a smile. "He came to us with that crazy scheme of his."

"You practically threw him out," Gaines reminded her.

"His plan was totally insane."

"At the time—if I recall correctly—you said it sounded feasible but that Rudd International already had too much invested in desalination and river rechanneling to get involved in a third method of water redistribution."

"I was just being kind," she said defensively. "The scheme was ridiculous. It would never work."

"Apparently Governor Kirkwood doesn't agree with you," Gaines contended. "According to our information, he believes in Haverson enough to go begging to Akbar for twenty million."

"Kirkwood is desperate," she replied. "At this point he'll clutch at any straw."

"If his plan is successful and results in water for California, any chance of reviving our plan for a chain of desalination plants on the California coast is in trouble," Gaines warned. "You realize that, don't you?"

"The iceberg is a ridiculous idea," she reiterated. "It will never work."

"For the sake of Rudd International, I hope you're right," he said.

Annalise looked the elderly man squarely in the eye. "*You* don't think it will work, do you, Gaines?"

"Are you asking my opinion, Mrs. Rudd?"

"Yes."

"I studied Haverson's proposal carefully at the time," he said. "I think that there is a possibility that it just might work—a very remote possibility."

73

Annalise considered what he had just said a few moments. "Well, what do you think we should do?" she asked.

"Stop him, of course," Gaines answered.

"How?"

Gaines smiled, displaying his pale, shriveled gums. "I leave that to you. After all, you're in charge now," he said. "Besides, you're far more clever than I."

"Yes, I am," she agreed, annoyed. "And I *will* handle the matter." With an impatient wave of her hand, she dismissed him.

When Gaines was gone, she directed Margaret to get Preston Farleigh on the phone at once. The secretary came back with the announcement that Senator Farleigh was engaged in a debate on the Senate floor and could not take any calls.

"This is an emergency, damn it," Annalise declared. "I *must* speak to him. *Now*."

"Very well, Mrs. Rudd," the conscientious secretary agreed.

In a few moments, Farleigh, sounding stressed and short of breath, was on the other end of the line. "What is it, Annalise?" he inquired anxiously. "They told me it was an emergency."

"Kirkwood is in London," she said.

"Is that the 'emergency'?" he replied, sounding incredulous.

"I'll explain," she said and proceeded to relate what Gaines had told her. "We've got to stop him," she said. "If we don't and this crazy scheme of his is successful, Hydrolliance will be finished. There won't be a prayer of getting our desalination plan through the California legislature when it's reintroduced. Our foreign commitments are in jeopardy as well. As you might well imagine, countries like Brazil and Argentina and Paraguay aren't going to want to go to the expense of rerouting the Amazon and the Plata rivers if they can just haul in icebergs. I tell you, it could mean real trouble."

"Maybe," Farleigh concluded.

"There are no 'maybes' about it," she went on. "This affects you, too, Preston. If Kirkwood does manage to end the California drought, he'll not only be the Golden State's golden boy again, he'll be the nation's as well. Your chances for the presidency will be over, believe me. If one single iceberg makes it to California, there'll be no stopping him. We both know what an opportunist he is. He'll use it to propel himself from Sacramento straight to the White House. He nearly ruined you once. You don't want him to ruin you again, do you? And this time Rudd International won't be there to pick you up and dust you off. It'll be the end, Preston."

12

"**Look, Drew, I don't like** giving our best land to foreigners any more than you do—especially when it's my own family's land, which we've managed to hang onto for over two hundred years," Kirkwood confided to his chief aide, when they returned to his suite at the Dorchester after meeting with Akbar. "What I did today was merely expedient."

"Some people would call it rash," Ramsdale said in a slightly reproachful tone.

"If you knew the reasoning behind it, you'd understand why I made Akbar what you just called such a 'rash' offer today," Kirkwood said, removing his jacket and throwing it over the back of a chair.

Exhausted from the flight, the meeting, and the general tension surrounding the events of the past twenty-four hours, Ramsdale plopped onto the sofa. "I'd be anxious to hear your reasoning," the aide said.

"Realistically, the best farmland in the world isn't worth a damn without water," Kirkwood said. "You could say the same thing about my political future, too. You and I both know that I'm out of the running in the presidential sweepstakes unless I come up with a successful solution to this drought." He gestured toward the window, which was, ironically, streaked with rain from a London downpour. "I believe Haverson has come up with the genuine answer. If this iceberg business works out, I'll consider it a bargain."

"That's a helluva big 'if,' " Ramsdale said, reaching for the bottle of Irish whiskey on the coffee table and pouring himself a generous slug. "Do you realize the scandal that could erupt if our opponents found out you were, in essence, bribing a foreigner with California land? For one thing, it's illegal . . ."

"George will find some way around the law," Kirkwood said with an indifferent shrug, referring to his legal advisor, George Bashore. "He always does. That's why I retain him as chief counsel."

"Just remember, there are a helluva lot of people out to get you. It's been open season since the drought started—even before, since the desalination business," Ramsdale reminded him. "You're providing our enemies with the kind of ammunition that could knock you right out of the political arena."

Kirkwood refused to be ruffled by any of his chief aide's arguments. "The way I look at it, by the time our enemies find out about the deal with Akbar, antarctic water will be flowing through California aqueducts. When people can start turning on their taps twenty-four hours a day and watering their lawns and filling their swimming pools again, they won't give a damn what kind of deal we made. We'll be home free."

Taking a big swallow of whiskey, Ramsdale said, "Yes, but suppose the iceberg thing is a flop?"

"That's the gamble," Kirkwood shrugged. "I'm betting my political fortunes as well as several thousand acres of Fernandez land that Haverson's scheme will succeed. The only thing on my mind now is closing the deal with Akbar. I'd like to conclude it in the next twenty-four hours. I don't want to waste time hanging around here playing games."

"You know, Paul, there's one big question you haven't touched on yet," Ramsdale said.

Surprised, Kirkwood asked, "What's that?"

"Who the hell we're going to get to head up the project," the chief aide replied.

"I don't see that that's a problem," Kirkwood said. "There is only one logical choice and that's Haverson."

"So one might think," Ramsdale said.

"Well, who the hell knows more about this whole thing than the guy who thought it up in the first place?" Kirkwood said.

"Have you discussed it with him?"

"Not in so many words," Kirkwood replied. "But this project is his baby. I can't imagine his not wanting to see it through. Unless you know something I don't?" The governor stared at his chief aide expectantly.

"It's just a feeling I have," Ramsdale said. "Nothing definite. On the flight over, I tried to sound him out and perceived a certain reluctance on his part."

"In that case, I think we should lay it all out right now," Kirkwood said. "Get a definite commitment from him."

Reaching for the phone, Ramsdale said, "Shall I invite him down for a drink?"

"I think we'd better do that," Kirkwood agreed. "Now."

When Haverson arrived at Kirkwood's suite, there was already a slight air of tension in the room despite the governor's attempts to look relaxed.

Handing Haverson a Scotch and soda, Kirkwood said, "What a massive undertaking that must have been to get this whole iceberg hauling scheme down on paper."

"And in such precise detail," Ramsdale added. "When in the hell did you get time?"

' I put my spare time to good use," Haverson replied.

"What does your wife say about that?" Kirkwood said.

"She doesn't like it much," Haverson admitted, wondering what the reason for summoning him was, certain it wasn't to make small talk.

"Now that it looks like we're going to get a firm commitment from Prince Akbar on the financing, I'd like to get this project under way just as soon as possible," Kirkwood said. "I assume you'll be able to work things out with your employer—a leave of absence or something—so that you'll be free to take command. I want you to have the opportunity to carry out this plan you've so ingeniously and painstakingly devised."

"When that ship arrives in port with the iceberg in tow, we want you to be standing proudly at the helm," Ramsdale added.

"As far as we're concerned, it's your baby," Kirkwood said. "You'll have full authority all the way. The only thing we want is the water."

"You'll retain the rights to the process and whatever patents are involved," Ramsdale assured him.

"My counsel, George Bashore, will see that your interests are fully protected from a financial standpoint," Kirkwood said.

"I appreciate the offer and your confidence in me," Haverson said. "I feel flattered and honored and all that. And I am willing to stick with this project and help get it off the ground, but when we reach the point where the ship is ready to sail, I have to bow out."

"Bow out?" Kirkwood got up and began pacing around the room. "How can you bow out of the most important phase?"

"You aren't serious, are you?" Ramsdale said.

"Yes, I am," Haverson said.

"But why on earth?" Kirkwood questioned.

"I have my reasons," Haverson replied.

"What kind of reasons could you possibly have?" Ramsdale said.

"Personal reasons," Haverson said quietly.

Wondering if perhaps the reasons had anything to do with the matters Sally Brennan had mentioned in Washington, Kirkwood said, "Well, I hope this isn't your final answer, Captain."

"I'm afraid it is, sir," Haverson said.

"Promise me you'll think it over some more and not arrive at such a hasty decision," Kirkwood urged.

"It's not a hasty decision," Haverson assured him.

"Good God, man, we need you in command of that ship," Ramsdale asserted.

"At least say you'll think it over," Kirkwood persisted.

"I'll think it over," Haverson reluctantly agreed. "But I doubt if I'll change my mind."

The next day George Bashore, a sharp-featured lawyer with a luxuriant black moustache, arrived in London to confer with Kirkwood. He handed Kirkwood a rough draft of the proposed agreement with Akbar written out in longhand on a yellow legal-sized pad.

"I wrote it up on the way over according to what we discussed on the phone," Bashore said.

When he had read over the copy, the governor complimented his chief counsel. "Nice job, George," he said.

"I tried to stick to your guidelines as much as possible," Bashore replied. "The way I set it up, the land goes to Akbar in such a roundabout fashion that anybody would be a fool to challenge it. I think it could stand up to any kind of test. Besides, just to cover our asses, I've learned that one of Akbar's kids was born in a New York hospital. If worst comes to worst, the land could be put in the kid's name. They'd have a helluva time disqualifying him as a citizen if it went to court."

"We'll let Akbar and his lawyers haggle for a while just to massage their egos, but I'm not about to deviate from the terms you've outlined in this agreement."

"How can you be so sure Akbar will accept these terms as is?" Bashore questioned.

"Money isn't an issue here," Kirkwood replied. "After all twenty million is a pittance to Akbar. He has more American dollars than he knows what to do with. This agreement enables him to acquire American land, something none of his rivals could do. I'm sure he sees it as a prestige thing, a status symbol. He wants water for Arabia, to be hailed as a true hero of his people, a faithful servant of Allah, worthy of His blessing. That's what Akbar is really getting off on."

The negotiations were concluded after some relatively brief haggling by the two sides, but Kirkwood insisted that the agreement be signed in the strictest secrecy. Akbar had no objection to such a condition, nor to any other conditions agreed upon. In essence, upon successful completion of the iceberg project, Akbar would receive parcels of land belonging to the Fernandez family in exchange for underwriting the mission.

To soothe Sally Brennan, who complained that the secrecy surrounding the signing of the agreement robbed her of a major scoop, Kirkwood took her aside and promised, "When I feel the time is right, I'll release the whole story, and when I do, you'll have an exclusive on it. Fair enough?"

"I'm going to hold you to it, Governor," Sally replied, temporarily placated.

Still baffled and disappointed by Haverson's refusal to head the project, Kirkwood decided to take up the matter with Sally, hoping that perhaps she might be able to shed some light on the subject.

"Your friend, the captain, handed me a surprise," he said. "He declined to head up this iceberg project of his. What do you make of that?"

"I don't know," Sally said with a puzzled frown. "He's always seemed gung ho about it to me."

"Got any ideas why he might have turned it down?" Kirkwood asked.

"No, not really," Sally replied. "Unless his wife had something to do with it. He did mention a couple of times that she doesn't like him being away from home so much. Can't say that I blame her. He'd be pretty nice to have around the house."

"Do you know Haverson's wife?"

"No," Sally said, "but he said he'd like me to meet her some time. He said we were pretty different but that we'd get along fine—whatever that means."

"Why don't you do just that—get to know her?" Kirkwood

suggested. "Maybe she can give us some clue. And, maybe, if we're lucky, she might even help change his mind."

Weary from negotiating with the Akbar team, George Bashore returned to his London hotel room after seeing Kirkwood and the rest of his party off at the airport, threw his attaché case containing a copy of the secret agreement on the dresser, and flopped across the bed.

Having fallen asleep almost instantly, Bashore had no idea how long he had slept nor what time it was when he awoke; jet travel always seemed to obliterate his sense of time. Outside, beyond the closed drapes, he could still hear the sound of rain. He wasn't certain what had awakened him except for the vague feeling of someone else in the room, which he reasoned was hardly possible, since he distinctly recalled having locked the door. Sitting up in bed in the darkened room, he reached out to turn on the bedside lamp, and as he did so, a figure suddenly lunged at him. Before he could cry out, a blunt, heavy instrument came down hard against his skull, and the warm, salty taste of blood filled his sleep-dry mouth.

Waiting in front of the Los Angeles air terminal for Ingrid to pick him up, Neal Haverson watched Sally Brennan climb into the governor's car. He was almost sorry that the London trip was over, that they had to part. He liked Sally. She was a bit aggressive and more outspoken than most women he knew, but he found her more appealing than he liked to admit. He would even have liked to see her again, share her sense of humor and open attitudes about life, but he knew it would be better if he didn't, especially since his marriage seemed to be on somewhat unsteady ground lately. As Kirkwood's security men closed the car door behind Sally, she turned and waved, looking slightly wistful.

The chief executive's car had just pulled away from the curb, when Ingrid drove up and honked the horn. She greeted him with a perfunctory kiss and slid out from behind the steering wheel, allowing him to take over.

"How was the trip?" she asked.

"Okay," he answered. "We got a lot accomplished. Akbar formally agreed to fund the iceberg project."

"Oh, wonderful. That's really great, Neal."

"The governor asked me to head up the whole thing," he

said, easing into the heavily congested traffic surrounding the airport.

"What did you tell him?"

"I turned it down."

Ingrid seemed surprised. "You did?"

"Yeah. The real excitement for me was dreaming up the whole thing. As far as I'm concerned, the rest is nothing. The 'blueprints' are all there. Anybody can follow them," Haverson said. "Everything's spelled out like a cookbook. You just follow the recipe."

"You don't mean that and you know it."

"Sure I do."

"Besides, not just anybody could carry out your plan," she disagreed.

"There are a lot of people capable of carrying out the project," he insisted, although not very convincingly.

"I hope you didn't turn it down because of me and the kids?"

His voice taking on a more serious tone, he said, "You know why I turned it down as well as I do." He followed the governor's car in the distance until it turned onto the freeway on-ramp and finally disappeared.

13

When Neal Haverson returned from his next voyage to Acapulco, he received a message from Kirkwood asking him to come to Sacramento as soon as possible.

In his office, Kirkwood greeted Haverson with a friendly smile. "You haven't changed your mind, have you?" he asked.

"No, sir," Haverson replied.

"Damn, that's too bad," Kirkwood said, shaking his head. "I can't think of anyone better qualified for the job. In any case, you said you'd stick with us until we found someone else, isn't that so?"

"Yes, sir."

"Good," Kirkwood said. "We'd like to get moving on this right away. What do you see as our first step at this point?"

"As I see it, sir, the first step is securing a ship or ships capable of towing an iceberg sufficiently large to provide a significant amount of water."

"Is such a ship available?" Kirkwood asked.

"Ocean-going tugs with a capacity to tow an iceberg the size of the one I'm speaking of—say, roughly one hundred billion kilograms—do exist, but approximately six or seven of them would be required. It would be very difficult to coordinate the movements of that many vessels, especially in antarctic waters, which are the most dangerous and treacherous in the world. The first thing you know, they'll be ramming each other."

"Then obviously you think it's best to go with a single ship?"

"Yes, if possible," Haverson confirmed. "But it would have to be designed and built especially for this project."

Kirkwood frowned. "How long would it take?"

"Maybe a year," Haverson guessed.

"A year's too long," Kirkwood objected. "I want water in California sooner than that. In fact, the sooner the better."

"Perhaps an existing supertanker or other very large ship could be converted for our purposes," Haverson speculated. "It would be a matter of finding a ship designer with the skill and imagination to do the job."

"Can you help us find him?" Kirkwood asked.

"I'll try," Haverson agreed.

"Good," Kirkwood said. "I appreciate your willingness to help out—at least at this stage of the game. I just wish you were going to be with us every step of the way, damn it."

Rising from his chair, Haverson said, "Is that all, sir?"

"Not quite," Kirkwood replied. "Before you leave, there's another matter I want to take up with you. It's about the floating aqueduct you describe in your monograph. I was looking it over again last night. It might not be a bad idea to get started on it soon. What do you think? It sounded to me as if its construction could get pretty involved."

"That's a good point, sir," Haverson agreed.

"If you don't mind, then, I'm going to start talking to some contractors?"

"I don't mind at all, Governor," Haverson said, and they began discussing possible sites and ship builders.

Sally Brennan had promised the governor to have a talk with Ingrid Haverson. And so, she found herself pulling up in front of their comfortable home on the Palos Verdes peninsula in her yellow Porsche.

"Come in, won't you?" Ingrid invited, friendly but reserved in her manner, sizing Sally up. "Neal's told me so much about you that I feel I already know you. Besides, we see you on television all the time. Why don't we sit outside? It's a little cooler."

"Great," Sally said, following Ingrid down a flagstone path to a latticed arbor at one end of the empty swimming pool. On a table beneath the arbor, which supported a withered fuchsia vine, a frosty pitcher of lemonade with ice seemed a curious luxury amid such bleak and desiccated surroundings.

"It's devastating what a lack of water can do to a place, isn't it?" Sally remarked, surveying the scene.

"Yes, it certainly is," Ingrid concurred.

"I think it's just great that your husband has a plan to end this drought," Sally said.

"He's certainly worked long and hard on it," Ingrid said, pouring a glass of lemonade and handing it to Sally.

"By the way, did you know that Governor Kirkwood asked him to head the project?"

"So Neal told me," Ingrid replied.

"And I guess you also know he refused?"

Ingrid traced her finger around the rim of the pitcher. "I suppose he must have his reasons," she said.

"Why on earth would he refuse such a fantastic opportunity?" Sally asked.

"Well, to be perfectly honest, one of the reasons is that it would entail going to Antarctica. He feels a certain bitterness about that place and about some things that happened there. It's a long and complicated story that resulted in Neal's resigning his commission in the navy. It was especially hard on him because he was a truly dedicated officer, but at the time he felt he had no other choice," Ingrid said.

"Doesn't he realize that if his iceberg plan is a success, whatever happened in the past will be totally forgotten?" Sally said. "He'll be hailed as a hero."

"But suppose—just suppose it should fail?" Ingrid said. "I don't mean to sound negative or imply that I don't have faith in my husband's work—it's just that one has to consider such a possibility. I don't want Neal to go through another major trauma—which the failure of this iceberg project could be. Frankly, I doubt if either of us could survive it."

Looking her straight in the eye, Sally said, "But you don't really believe it's going to fail, do you?"

"Of course, I don't," Ingrid responded staunchly.

"Then maybe you should encourage him to take the job," Sally urged.

"I'm not the one that's stopping him," Ingrid said.

"That wasn't my understanding from some of the conversations he and I had on the London junket," Sally said.

Ingrid arched one of her eyebrows. "Really?" she asked.

Well, here goes, Sally thought. Might as well jump in with both feet. "In fact, I know he feels that it would be wrong for him to suggest leaving you when the project is ready to set out for the Antarctic. But if you were to talk to him and let him know that it would be okay with you if he accepted the position, I know he'd be less resistive. I'm convinced he wants to follow it all the way through."

Ingrid looked at her directly, but didn't answer. Finally, she said, "More lemonade?"

* * *

A pale and badly shaken Drew Ramsdale dashed into Kirkwood's office and closed the door. "George is in the hospital," he announced.

"George Bashore?" Kirkwood said.

"Yes," Ramsdale nodded.

"In London?"

"Yes."

"What's wrong with him?"

"A skull fracture—among other things."

"Oh, God." Dreading the answer, Kirkwood asked, "How did it happen?"

"He was struck with a large, blunt instrument while asleep in his hotel room."

"What about the copy of our agreement with Akbar?" the governor asked, apprehensively. "Is it safe?"

"His attaché case was missing at first," Ramsdale replied. "But it turned up later in the Thames."

"Empty, of course," Kirkwood concluded. "If the contents of that agreement get out . . ."

"We might as well consider them as out," Ramsdale said. "I'm sorry, Paul, but it's true."

"I know," Kirkwood agreed. "What do we do at this point?"

"The only thing we can do is sit tight and wait for whoever broke into George's room to make the next move."

Kirkwood contemplated the situation a moment. "I suppose that's all we can do," he conceded. "I don't suppose I have to tell you, it could be a very sticky situation."

"Hardly," Ramsdale said.

Pressing the buzzer on his intercom, Kirkwood said, "Well, I guess the first thing I'd better do is call a staff meeting right away and develop some contingency plans for when the shit hits the fan."

When Haverson got in from Sacramento, Ingrid picked him up at the airport once again, and as they headed around the Palos Verdes peninsula, he recounted his meeting with the governor.

"I promised him I'd try to find a naval architect capable of understanding the peculiar needs of the project," he said. "It's got to be somebody with a lot of imagination, ingenuity, and a good solid knowledge of the sea in that area of the world."

"You'll come up with somebody," Ingrid said.

"Anything exciting happen while I was gone?" he asked.

"I had an interesting visitor," Ingrid said.

"Oh? Not *too* interesting, I hope?"

"Sally Brennan."

Surprised, he asked, "What did she want?"

"She came to tell me what a wicked man you are, Neal Haverson," Ingrid teased. "Actually, I'm not sure why she came. I think she was trying to get me to persuade you to take charge of the iceberg project for the governor."

"And?" he asked expectantly.

"I promised her I'd talk to you about it," she said. "She's a very attractive girl, more so in person than on TV."

"Do you really think so?"

"Don't you?"

"She's okay," he conceded with an indifferent shrug of his broad shoulders.

"You know, Neal, I've always tried to stay out of your work," she said.

"Yes, you have," he agreed, adding, "and I appreciate it."

"But I do think that you should seriously reconsider your decision," she continued. "I mean it. I want you to get the credit for something you've spent years working on, something that was your idea from the very beginning."

"This is a new tack for you, isn't it?" he questioned, surprised by her complete change of attitude.

"I suppose it is," she admitted.

"You do realize, don't you, that if I head up this iceberg project, it's going to mean I'll be away for a long time—maybe as long as a year. I want to be sure you understand that."

"I know," she assured him. "That's not saying I'm going to like it or that I'm not going to have my hands full with Cathy and Jill, but I feel it's something really important to you—maybe the most important thing in your life."

"Could be," he said thoughtfully. "It just could be."

That night while Neal was sleeping, Ingrid got out of bed and went to the kitchen. Once again, as it had been for weeks, a hot, dry wind was blowing from off the inland deserts. She could scarcely remember the last time they had enjoyed an ocean breeze. The drought had begun two years before, and since then the climate seemed to change completely—and with a vengeance.

Sensing his wife's absence, Haverson awoke and got out of bed to look for her. He found her sitting cross-legged on the kitchen floor, sorting through a pile of old newspapers.

"What the hell are you doing?" he demanded.

"Looking for something," she replied casually.

"At this hour?"

"I'm trying to find an article I read in the *Times Book Review*," she said, referring to the *New York Times*. Pointing to an article as he stooped to look over her shoulder, she said, "Here, read this."

Almost immediately Neal was struck by a familiar photograph, which accompanied the text, the picture of a man with a lock of dark, unruly hair tumbling over a wide Slavic forehead, prominent, almost Asiatic, cheekbones, and a generally intense, moody demeanor.

"That looks like Yuri Maslov," he said.

"It *is* Yuri Maslov," she assured him.

Grabbing the paper, Haverson began to read the article, which noted that Yuri Maslov had been given a large advance by a leading New York publisher to write his life's story, the climax of which would be his daring attempt to sail alone around Antarctica in a small craft and his dramatic defection from the Soviet Union. The article concluded with the statement that, at present, Mr. Maslov was living in seclusion outside the small Maine coastal town of Winter Harbor.

"What made you think of Maslov?" he asked.

"Well, I was lying there contemplating what you said about finding someone to design a boat and this article just popped into my head," she said. "I remember how you used to talk about him, how eccentric and innovative he was and what a brilliant ship designer."

"He's all those things all right—and a few others not as admirable," Haverson concurred. "When he was assigned to the Russian Antarctic station at Mirny, which is about 1,500 miles from McMurdo by land, he spent all his time designing and building that boat he tried to circle the continent in until the Soviets lost their patience with him and ordered him back to Moscow. That's when he decided to fly the coop. At least that's *his* story. When he landed at McMurdo he was suffering from extreme exposure and frostbite, so we put him in the base hospital. When he recovered, we made arrangements to return him to the Soviets, but he suddenly pleaded for asylum. I would have probably sent him back if it hadn't been for Elizabeth Nagy. She intervened in his behalf and prevailed on me to change my mind."

Ingrid was surprised to hear him mention Dr. Nagy's

name. It was the first time since her tragic death and the subsequent investigation that Neal had said it in her presence.

"Maslov eventually got the asylum he wanted, which stirred up a lot of trouble between us and the Russians."

"I remember your telling me," Ingrid said.

"Frankly, I never trusted him—but I respected his talent and ability when it came to ships. We used to discuss his ideas for improvements in the design of various navy vessels. I couldn't believe how much he knew about our ships—little, intimate details. His ideas were brilliant. There's no denying that."

"You said he was a genius."

"When Maslov fled the Soviet research station at Mirny, he took a lot of stuff with him—blueprints and drawings for unique and startlingly original ships. I was really impressed with his work. From a certain standpoint I could sympathize with his frustration at the Soviet bureaucracy. His ideas were far too radical, too unconventional, and too daring for them—exactly the kind of ideas we need now."

The stillness of the stifling night was suddenly shattered by the blast of a single shot, accompanied by the shattering of glass and a childish scream.

"My God! The girls!" Ingrid cried.

The two of them scrambled to their feet and raced down the long hall to the room shared by their two daughters, Cathy and Jill. Neal flung open the door and switched on the light. Cathy flew out of her bed, her nubile young breasts bouncing beneath the thin fabric of her nightgown, and threw herself into her father's arms.

"Dad! Oh, Dad!" she sobbed.

Ingrid started toward Jill, sitting up on her own bed, strangely silent and grave, and suddenly halted. "Neal! Look at her!" she cried out. "She's bleeding!"

"Somebody shot a bullet through the window," Cathy said, indicating a jagged circle of glass in the aluminum window frame. The floor was covered with fragments of glass.

Cradling Jill in her arms, not caring that the girl's blood was staining her own nightdress, Ingrid said, "She's been shot! My baby's been shot!"

"It's just glass, Mama," Jill said, starting to cry as the full impact of what had happened became clear to her. "It flew at me when the window got shot."

"We've got to get her to the emergency room," Haverson said.

Turning to Cathy, who was still clinging to him, trembling, he said, "Are you okay, honey?"

"Yes, Dad, I'm okay," the teenager assured him. "Just scared, that's all."

Quickly pulling herself together, Ingrid gathered a bunch of towels from the adjoining bathroom and plastered them over the cuts the flying glass had inflicted on Jill. "You'll have to carry her to the car, Neal," she said.

"I can walk, Mama," Jill announced and started to get out of bed.

On the way to the hospital, Cathy asked, "Why did somebody shoot a bullet through our bedroom window, Dad?"

"I don't know," Haverson said, shaking his head. "It must have been an accident—a stray shot or something."

"If it was an accident, what were they really shooting at, Daddy?" Jill asked from the back seat where she lay wrapped in a quilt.

"Who knows?" Haverson said with a shrug.

"This drought is making people crazy," Ingrid said. "I swear it is."

During the next few days, Maslov's name kept recurring in conversation.

"How did Maslov react to Elizabeth Nagy after she helped him get his asylum in the United States?" Ingrid asked one evening as she and Haverson sat in the dark on the verandah. Inside, Jill was studying, her long, straight blond hair touching her slim shoulders. Fortunately the wounds from the flying glass caused by the shot were only superficial and were healing nicely. Haverson had dug a .22 rifle bullet out of the plaster in the ceiling of the girls' room and turned it over to the police who received it rather indifferently.

"Strangely enough, once he got what he wanted, he seemed to turn on Elizabeth," Haverson replied.

"Turn on her?" Ingrid repeated, surprised.

"Yeah. He began to hassle her."

"Why did he do that?"

"Who knows? He's an odd bird," Haverson said. "When he wasn't criticizing her for burying her head in the sand of science and religion, he was accusing her of being a secret Soviet agent. She was a sensitive woman. Things like that got to her after a while. In some ways, I blame him for contributing to her death. In fact, the very night she disappeared Maslov was causing a terrible ruckus, insisting he be evacuated at once to the United States because of a supposed plot to assassinate him. He tried to implicate her in the plot. It was one of his periodic attacks of paranoia. I was so involved in trying to calm him down that I neglected to pay serious attention to reports of Elizabeth Nagy's failure to keep in touch with the base while she was out on a research trip. When I finally realized she had not been heard from for more than twenty-four hours, I went out to look for her, but it was too late. You know the rest—the way I found her under the ice. God, it was awful. The expression on her face . . ." At this point his voice became suddenly hoarse and quavery. He stopped talking and covered his face with his hands.

Sensing his anguish even in the darkness, Ingrid tried to comfort him. "It's all right, Neal. Don't upset yourself."

"It's *not* all right," he blurted, rising abruptly and heading into the house.

14

As Neal Haverson went over the lists of naval architects, he could not get Yuri Maslov out of his mind. He knew that if the Russian were presented with the problem at hand, he would come up with a solution that was both unique and practical.

"If someone asked Maslov to transform a birchbark canoe into a battleship, he would find a way," he remarked to Ingrid who had come into the den to check on his progress.

"Then why don't you contact him?" she urged.

"I just wish I felt he could be trusted. There was always something about him I was never quite sure about. I guess I never quite bought his reasons for defecting," Haverson said.

"Why don't you at least talk to him?" she suggested.

In a burst of frustration, Neal tore up the lists he had made and stuffed them into a wastebasket. "You're right," he concluded. "There's no use considering anyone else when Maslov's so obviously superior."

Reaching for the phone, he called the publisher mentioned in the *New York Times* article to ascertain Maslov's current address. When he hung up, he declared, "That settles it. I'm going to Maine and have a talk with that sonofabitch Maslov."

From Bangor, Haverson had to take a combination of buses and cabs to the town of Winter Harbor which lay across Frenchman Bay from the well-known resort, Bar Harbor. Spring had not yet arrived in Maine, and Haverson, accustomed to California's unrelenting heat, hugged his gabardine raincoat around him as he gazed over the choppy, white-capped bay. For an instant McMurdo, blindingly white and icy, flashed through his mind, although there was very little resemblance between Maine and the frozen continent at the bottom of the earth. Perhaps it was the fierce wind that stirred the memory.

At this time of year the presence of a stranger in the small town with no ostensible reason for being there, except to ask questions about a Russian defector, aroused considerable curiosity, but Haverson remained undaunted as he strolled up and down the streets, seeking clues to Maslov's whereabouts. Eventually he encountered a young Canadian gas station attendant of Ukranian extraction who was far more communicative than anyone he had met thus far in the Yankee community.

The attendant said, "Yeah, some Russian guy came in here a couple of times. He invited me to play chess with him some time."

"Do you know where he lives?" Haverson asked.

"Outside of town. He gave me directions," the youth replied and proceeded to describe the route to an isolated cabin several miles away.

Haverson rented a car and, following the young Ukranian's directions, located a cabin which matched the attendant's description of the one occupied by Maslov. The primitive dwelling was hidden in a thick grove of pines near a rocky bluff overlooking the bay. Haverson stopped the car, got out, and started toward it, listening to the crunch of snow under his feet. A curl of black smoke rose from the chimney, indicating that someone was inside. As he approached the porch, a pair of ferocious-looking Dobermans dashed out. Barking and snarling viciously, the dogs surrounded him. Haverson stopped and stood motionless in the snow until the cabin door opened and a stocky man of medium height stuck his head, crowned with a thick mop of unruly dark hair, outside to see what the ruckus was all about. His suspicious glance alternated between Haverson, trapped by the dogs, and the strange automobile parked nearby.

Recognizing the cabin's occupant at once, Haverson shouted, "Hey, Maslov! Call off these damned dogs, will you?"

Scowling, Maslov called out, "Who are you? What do you want? How do you know my name?"

"It's Neal Haverson. I was the commander at McMurdo when you defected. Remember?"

Maslov stared at him in astonishment, almost as if he were a ghost. "Haverson?" he repeated incredulously. "What are you doing here?"

"I came to talk to you, if you'll call off your dogs."

Maslov shouted some commands in Russian and the Dobermans retreated instantly. "They won't trouble you any more," he said, patting the dogs who now sat obediently at his side. "Come inside," he invited.

The rustic cabin consisted of a single room heated by a central wood-burning stove, nearly bare of furnishings except for a few scattered chairs and a table piled high with books and papers. Apparently, if Maslov were writing his autobiography, he was doing it in longhand; there was no typewriter in evidence. Sketches of unusual ships were scattered about on the floor and a sleeping bag Haverson assumed he slept in rolled up in a corner.

"I keep the dogs for safety," Maslov said, clearing a pile of books from one of the chairs so that Haverson might sit down. From a battered teakettle boiling on the woodstove he poured hot water into two jelly glasses through a strainer filled with dark tea, passing one to Haverson. "It's been a long time, my friend," Maslov said.

"You haven't changed much, Yuri," Haverson said. "I recognized you the moment I saw you."

"Tell me, my friend, why have you come here?" Maslov asked, a note of uneasiness in his voice, perhaps an overlay of his old paranoia.

"I need somebody to design a ship," Haverson replied.

"But why have you come to me for that?" Maslov said, sounding slightly incredulous. "You have many ship designers in this country. Some of the Americans are very good."

"This is a very special kind of ship with a lot of unusual requirements," Haverson said.

Raising one of his thick eyebrows, Maslov questioned, "How do you mean 'special?' "

Haverson proceeded to relate the entire project in detail and he could soon see that Maslov was intrigued with the idea of hauling antarctic icebergs to California.

"What you are asking, my friend Haverson, is to take an old ship and make a new one from it. Is this correct?" Maslov asked.

"Right," Haverson affirmed.

"This I don't like so much," Maslov said. "I think it is not for me."

"Naturally, we'd prefer a new ship," Haverson admitted, "but as I explained, there isn't time. We have to be underway by the end of August or the beginning of September at the latest. You know as well as I do that the only time a ship can safely enter antarctic waters is during the height of the Austral summer, January or February. Once things begin to freeze, it's too late. Timing is crucial. If we don't move according to a strict schedule, the project will be delayed another year. By that time it might be too late."

"I'll tell you the truth," Maslov said, filling his tea glass, this time adding a shot of vodka. "This project you talk about is not something I like. For a new ship I have many ideas, but to put these new ideas in an old ship . . ." Maslov shook his head. "I am not sure."

"My feeling is to start out with a supertanker and try to convert that," Haverson said, trying to overcome Maslov's lack of enthusiasm.

"Certainly it could not be a smaller ship," Maslov agreed. "The most ideal ship is one between eighty and one hundred thousand tons. Although supertankers have many faults and are often badly constructed, a smaller ship is not satisfactory. For the ice, the hull will have to be made stronger."

"Yes, reinforced," Haverson supplied. "A double hull, in essence."

"Many other structural modifications will be required," Maslov continued, a hint of enthusiasm creeping into his voice as he spoke. "To tow an iceberg weighing one hundred billion kilograms, the ship will have to have at least four synchronized propellers. The entire engine system will have to be electronically controlled and integrated by a common computer. I think the ship must be capable of fifty-thousand horsepower of towing force." Maslov's face brightened. "Such a ship will be expensive, both to purchase and modify."

"Fortunately, money isn't such a problem," Haverson remarked.

"There's another thing," Maslov said, somewhat hesitantly. "I think such a ship will have to be nuclear powered. I don't believe that enough diesel fuel can be stored for such a journey as you describe," Maslov said. "There are some in this country who will not like that."

"We aren't the ones who have to worry about them," Haverson said. "That's somebody else's job."

"Good," Maslov grinned, taking a generous swallow of vodka-laced tea. "Tell me, Haverson, why have you come here to see me? In the past we were not always such good friends."

"True," Haverson conceded. "The reason I want you for the

job is because you know more about ships and sailing the Antarctic than just about anybody I know."

"You flatter me, my friend."

"I admit we've had our differences and our problems in the past, but I'm willing to overlook them for the sake of the project," Haverson said, wanting to add: And I hope you will too.

Reaching for the bottle of vodka, Maslov offered it to Haverson. "You are very frank, my friend," he said.

"Can you give me a decision?" Haverson said.

"Decision?" Maslov echoed.

"On whether or not you are willing to design the ship we need?"

Glass in hand, Maslov rose and glanced at the stack of pages written in Russian longhand. "You know I am writing a book?" he inquired.

"So I've heard," Haverson said.

"It is the story of my life," he said. "I have to do much thinking to write it. Writing is difficult for me. I need much time. Now it seems I have time only for my book. My answer, my friend, is *nyet*."

"That means no," Haverson concluded, somewhat disappointed.

Maslov grinned. "That means no."

15

As far as Kirkwood was concerned, Gabriel Rincon was the only contractor for the aqueduct. Flying back from UCLA Hospital where he had paid a call on Bonnie, who was continuing to hold her own, the governor decided to stop in Oxnard where the Rincon Brothers Construction Company was headquartered and discuss the project with Rincon himself.

"Gabe Rincon has a reputation for handling difficult and unusual projects well," Kirkwood said to Drew Ramsdale, raising his voice in order to be heard above the roar of the helicopter engines as they neared the Oxnard airport. "His company is responsible for most of the equipment involved in the irrigation systems around here," he said, pointing to the barren, caked and cracked fields of the once fertile and highly productive Oxnard plain directly below them, adding: "Not that all that equipment is doing much good now without any water."

"I'm glad you're giving Gabe Rincon first crack at the job," Ramsdale said. "Not just because his outfit's good but because his brother Tony was one of our staunchest political allies."

"He certainly was," Kirkwood concurred, shaking his head sadly. "It's hard to believe he's gone."

"Yeah," Ramsdale agreed. "Just when he was on the verge of winning the Senate seat. I'm sure he would have beaten Farleigh in spite of the other's high-powered campaign and the money Rudd International was pouring into it. The polls all showed Rincon the favorite. I don't know why the hell he ever decided to take that single-engine plane. Everybody knows how risky they are, especially flying over mountains."

"I've never been convinced that Tony Rincon's death was

an accident," Kirkwood said as the helicopter began its descent.

Surprised, Ramsdale said, "What are you implying, Paul?"

"I don't know," Kirkwood replied. "It's just that I feel the whole story of that crash hasn't come out yet. The real version."

The sudden death of his brother had dealt Gabriel Rincon a severe blow and had resulted in a profound depression. Kirkwood hoped that on this occasion he would find him in better spirits, but knowing the depths of his grief, he was not optimistic.

"The word is that Gabe Rincon let the business languish after Tony's death," Ramsdale remarked as he and the governor were enroute to the company offices from the helipad.

"They were very close," Kirkwood said.

"Too bad . . ."

"Maybe the challenge of constructing the aqueduct will help get him going again," Kirkwood said. "At least I hope so."

Gabriel Rincon, a stocky, olive-complexioned man in tan cotton work clothes with the Rincon Brothers Construction Company written in red letters over the breast pocket of the shirt, met them at the office door and greeted Kirkwood with an embrace which gave the governor's security men pause for a moment.

"Hermano," Rincon said, using the Spanish word for "brother" to address the governor. "How have you been?"

"Fine thanks, Gabe," Kirkwood replied. "How are you and the family?"

Rincon shrugged. "So so," he said. "You know how it is. None of us can get Tony out of our heads. We still miss him like hell."

"How's Adriana getting along?" Kirkwood asked, referring to Tony Rincon's widow.

"She's doing okay," Rincon answered. "It's been the roughest on her and the kids. She tried to take over where Tony left off in politics, but it was too much for her. At least right now. But maybe in a few years . . ."

"It's been rough on all of us who knew and loved Tony," Kirkwood said.

After some shared reminisces about Tony Rincon, the three men eventually got down to the matter of building the aqueduct. He and Ramsdale explained the iceberg project, first in general, overall terms, and then specifically described the need for a floating aqueduct and Gabe Rincon's possible participation. They concluded by showing him sketches of the proposed structure taken from Haverson's monograph.

"Well, Gabe, do you think you can build it for us?" Kirkwood asked.

"I don't know," the Mexican-American contractor said, shaking his head discouragingly. "It looks like a pretty big job."

"You've handled big jobs before," Kirkwood reminded him.

"Probably a lot bigger than this," Ramsdale added.

"Yeah, but not for a long time," Rincon said. "This area has been hit pretty hard by the drought. There isn't much going on these days around here. Things have been real quiet for us."

"This aqueduct is going to liven things up and help end the drought," Ramsdale said.

Sounding skeptical, Rincon questioned, "Are you sure it's going to do that?"

"We're sure," Ramsdale affirmed.

"So sure I'm staking my political future on it," Kirkwood said.

"In that case it would be hard to say no but still . . ." Rincon said, hesitant to commit himself.

"You know damned well that if Tony were alive he'd want you to take on this job," Kirkwood urged, deciding it was time to apply a little subtle pressure.

"My brother loved this state. He would be sick if he could see what's happening to it on account of this drought," Rincon said.

"We intend to turn things around as fast as possible," Kirkwood declared. "That's why I'm giving top priority to this project."

Glancing at the sketches with more interest, Rincon said, "It's pretty damned big from these dimensions, if you ask me. But I suppose if we build it in sections, we could haul it to wherever it's supposed to go and assemble it there."

"Sure," Ramsdale nodded encouragingly. "Right on the water."

Pleased by this first positive sign of interest, Kirkwood ventured, "Then you're interested in taking on the job, Gabe?"

Rincon hesitated. "When would you want it completed?"

"As soon as possible," Kirkwood replied. "I'd rather have you get started on it now and pay storage fees to keep it

98

around than not have it ready when we need it," Kirkwood said.

After thinking it over for a moment or two, Rincon said, "Maybe I could get a team started on it this week. You know, draw up some plans. Sort of get things rolling."

"Great," Ramsdale said.

"But I'm not making any definite promises," Rincon cautioned.

"Now you're talking, *amigo*," Kirkwood said, clasping Rincon in a strong and affectionate farewell embrace.

16

It was not yet light when Neal Haverson was awakened by the insistent ringing of the telephone in his Maine motel room. Sleepily he reached out and took the receiver off the hook, hoping that nothing was wrong at home. Since the mysterious shot through the girls' bedroom window—and the subsequent police investigation which had revealed nothing— he had been extremely apprehensive. He was not entirely convinced that it had been an accidental, stray shot, as the police report concluded. He was surprised and perhaps even a little relieved to hear Maslov's voice on the other end of the line.

"What the hell are you doing calling me at this hour?"

"Can you come out here right away?" the Russian asked. There was a note of urgency in his voice.

"Now? You've got to be kidding. . . ."

"Please. It's important."

"What the hell's so urgent?"

"You will see when you arrive here," Maslov said and hung up before Haverson could question him further.

The sun was rising over the bay as Haverson pulled up in front of Maslov's cabin—or, rather, what was left of it. During the night the wooden structure had been reduced to a smoking rubble.

Staring at Maslov, Haverson asked, "What happened?"

"The place caught fire while I was sleeping," Maslov replied, shivering with the morning cold, his two Dobermans obediently at his side. "I don't know how it happened. Perhaps the stove . . . The dogs were very nervous all evening while I was writing my book. They were barking very much. I went outside and looked around, but I saw nothing unusual. I went

100

to sleep, but the dogs woke me. The cabin was full of smoke. I almost didn't get out of my sleeping bag in time. In minutes, it was completely burned." Maslov kicked at the rubble. "All is lost—everything. Months of work. My memories—lost. Now I have nothing. Nothing . . ."

Haverson sympathized with the Russian, and told him he was sorry about the manuscript. Putting his hand on Yuri's shoulder, Haverson said, "I guess you'll just have to start all over again."

"Impossible," Maslov snapped. "I cannot do that. I cannot start from the beginning again. I must forget the book."

"What about your publisher?"

"I will return the money," he said. "I don't want to write the book. What good is writing about the past? The past is over. Besides, I am a man of the sea, not a writer. I want now only to go to sea again. I need the peace of the sea."

"My offer still stands, you know," Haverson said.

Maslov sifted the blackened ashes of his former home a few moments, staring at the ground. Suddenly he raised his head and looked straight at Haverson. "I think I will take it," he said.

When Haverson informed Kirkwood that he had engaged Maslov as the ship's designer, the governor was less than enthusiastic.

"I'm not sure I like the idea of Yuri Maslov being connected with this project," he said. "His involvement will only add more controversy to an already controversial undertaking. There are a lot of people just waiting for the first chance to pounce on us and I don't want to give them an excuse by hiring a Russian defector."

"Frankly, Governor," Haverson replied, "we don't have much choice. The designer of this particular ship has to have special knowledge and expertise. Very few, if any, individuals can match Maslov."

"Still, I would think somewhere there's got to be an American capable of designing the ship we need," Kirkwood insisted. "I can't believe it takes a Russian."

"I've considered others," Haverson replied. "There's nobody with Maslov's knowledge of both shipbuilding and antarctic conditions. He's made it his life's work. It's almost an obsession with him."

"But he's still a Russian defector. We mustn't lose sight of that," Kirkwood said. "Russian ballet dancers, writers, and musicians are one thing—somehow people in the arts aren't nearly as suspect or as politically controversial. But a ship designer—a technical person—that's something else again. Nobody ever completely trusts a defector. Frankly, Captain, I wish you'd get somebody else. If we should, by any chance, fail or, God forbid, some unforeseen disaster should occur, a lot of people are going to point a finger at Maslov and accuse him of sabotage, and they're going to hold us responsible for engaging him in the first place. In the end, we're the ones who'll take the heat."

"I wouldn't have confidence in anybody else for this job," Haverson insisted. "And he realizes he'll be taking a risk, too."

"Well, I'm going to have to take it up with my staff," Kirkwood said. "I'll get back to you later."

"Very well, sir," Haverson said. "But as far as Maslov is concerned, my decision stands."

At Kirkwood's staff meeting, Jane Garcia reported on Yuri Maslov's status from a security standpoint, as the governor had directed her to do.

"As far as the State Department, CIA, and FBI are concerned, Yuri Maslov is not regarded as an enemy agent, although they have had him under surveillance since his defection," she said. "I would say that their overall evaluation of him is that he was kind of a square peg that couldn't fit into the round hole of Soviet bureaucracy. On the other hand, they don't regard him as altogether innocuous either. In short, I'd say that nobody is sure about him."

"Can he be trusted? That's the main thing," Kirkwood said.

"Washington doesn't think anybody can be trusted," Ramsdale said. "You should know that, Paul."

"I know they don't trust me," Kirkwood quipped.

"It sounds as if Maslov would be pretty low on the official list of suspicious characters," Weisswasser said, stroking his wiry beard.

Glancing from face to face around the conference table, Kirkwood said, "In other words, then, if Haverson wants him, we should give him our okay?"

"The one we really want is Haverson," Ramsdale pointed out. "He's the one we need."

"Drew's right," Weisswasser agreed.

Kirkwood contemplated a moment before he spoke. "Maybe, just maybe," he said, "we might be able to use this Maslov character to make a deal with Haverson. Despite certain risks, it might be worth our while to let him have Maslov—but only with certain provisions, of course."

The following day at his Maine motel, Haverson received a call from Kirkwood's office.

"Captain? This is Drew Ramsdale, chief aide to Governor Kirkwood," the smoothly professional voice on the other end of the line said. "The governor has been seriously considering your request for Yuri Maslov on the project. He wonders if you and Mr. Maslov might come to Sacramento to meet with him."

"I'll have to speak to Maslov," Haverson replied.

"Do that," the chief aide directed, "and get back to Governor Kirkwood's appointment secretary."

Reluctantly, Maslov boarded the two Dobermans, whose names were Russlan and Ludmilla, in a local kennel and accompanied Haverson aboard a plane for California. It had not taken much effort to persuade him to agree to meet with the governor. Since the fire, Maslov, who was staying at the motel with Haverson, had shown increasing interest in the iceberg project, poring over the monograph, trying to absorb its technical points in detail, even making notes and drawings based on its contents.

As the "Fasten Seatbelts" sign flashed, Maslov turned to Haverson in the adjacent seat. "I have decided that you are perfectly correct," he announced. "If we must convert an already existing ship, then it must be a supertanker." From his battered briefcase, he extracted some sketches and passed them to Haverson. "Here is my preliminary design for the ship's propeller," he explained, indicating the appropriate drawing.

"I see," Haverson nodded, observing at once that it was quite different from the ordinary propeller.

"I have not accurately determined the exact pitch yet, but obviously it must be one that produces a maximum speed-to-power ratio. I don't think that even with four propellers of the dimensions of this one, we can achieve a speed of more than one or two knots when towing a huge iceberg. I think that is the most we can expect, although I would prefer three or four knots if possible."

When he arrived in Sacramento, Maslov was shocked to see the effects of the protracted water shortage. Walking down the drought-ravaged Capital Mall with Haverson, he shook his head in dismay. "This is terrible," he muttered, "terrible. What has happened to this city? Is nothing green any longer? Is there not a single leaf on a tree? Are there no flowers? Is everything dead? In Russia we have also had droughts—severe ones—but never like this. The city looks as though it has been the victim of a great fire."

"The entire state looks this way—or worse—from north to south," Haverson said.

"My God, it's terrible, terrible," Maslov repeated. "Awful. Someone must do something. And quickly."

"That's what this meeting is all about," Haverson reminded him, as they turned down the walkway toward the governor's office.

After quick introductions all around, Haverson, Kirkwood and Maslov got down to business.

"Let me be frank with you, Maslov, and say that when Captain Haverson proposed you as the designer of the ship, we weren't very happy with his choice," Kirkwood said. "But since then, my staff and I have had several meetings to discuss this matter, and we've decided to reconsider and go ahead with you."

"I regard this project as a great challenge and a great opportunity, a chance to repay this nation, which was so kind to me and took me in when I escaped from the Soviet Union," Maslov said. "For that reason I am anxious to begin work on it."

"No more anxious than we are to have you start," Kirkwood replied. "It looks like our first step is to acquire one slightly used supertanker. Is that right?"

"Got any suggestions where we might get one, sir?" Haverson asked.

"I have a suggestion where *not* to get one," Kirkwood said. "Stay away from any ship belonging to the Rudd International organization. In fact, don't get involved with them in any way despite the fact that they've got a big fleet of supertankers hauling LNG from Indonesia."

"I know. Before I came to you with the project," Haverson said, "I tried to sell Rudd International on it, but they weren't interested."

"I'm not surprised," Kirkwood said. "Their Hydrolliance division is going a whole other route—far more grandiose and ambitious. They're talking about rerouting the Amazon and the Mississippi and crazy schemes like that.

"There's nothing Rudd International would probably like better than to see this project fail," Kirkwood said. "But getting back to your original question, I think that the one person who might be most helpful in solving the problem of a ship is none other than our old friend, Prince Akbar. After all, he owns a fleet of supertankers. He decided a few years ago to cut out the middleman's profits and transport Arabian crude in his own ships."

A subsequent call to Akbar in London yielded an offer of a supertanker currently in a San Diego shipyard for repairs.

"How does that sound to you?" Kirkwood asked.

"Maslov and I would have to inspect the ship in question before we could make a decision on it," Haverson said.

"Yes, absolutely," Maslov concurred.

"Let me have my secretary make arrangements to fly you to San Diego," Kirkwood said, buzzing the intercom.

17

At approximately eighty thousand tons Prince Akbar's vessel, the *Princess Mouna,* was neither the largest nor the smallest of the supertankers currently afloat; neither was it the oldest or the newest. In fact, it was quite average. Aesthetically it was pleasing to the eye, its bow tilting slightly upward for cutting through the seas, its hull, a wide, solid, very straight piece of pure steel, extending to the stern where it flattened abruptly, almost as if sheared at that point. Its large, slightly raked funnel, far more attractive than the usual and purely functional pipelike engine room uptake, added a nice touch.

Its overall impression was thoroughly shiplike, perhaps as much a result of its superiorly designed superstructure as of its hull. The superstructure displayed an excellent sense of proportion and seemed to evolve gracefully from the overall plan instead of sitting like a multistory, characterless block atop a long steel pier, as in the case of many other ships of this type.

The many-windowed superstructure, fifty feet high, contained five decks connected by wide stairways painted in diagonal yellow and black stripes; an elevator ran from the engine rooms at the lowest level to the bridge. Like the rest of the ship, the bridge, with wings extending beyond its door, reaching out in long promenades, the ends of which extended over the water, gave a feeling of spaciousness. Large, angled windows in the bridgehouse overlooked the vast, red-painted main deck above which a catwalk stretched so far in the distance that it seemed to fade into infinity as it approached the bow. Atop the bridge, a steel tower served as a base for radio antennae and radar scanners.

Maslov, accustomed to the rather spartan nature of Soviet vessels, was struck by such luxurious details as teak rails surrounding the bridge deck, spacious alleyways running across the ship and, perhaps most of all, by the facilities of the lower bridge deck—the movie theater, gameroom, hospital, officers' wardroom, library, and dining room. More importantly, he was impressed by the excellent condition of the working parts of the ship such as the boilers, turbines, and propellers. As he and Haverson inspected the supertanker, he was quick to note that the storage areas which were formerly filled with crude oil, would provide sufficient space in which to install the drive systems for the two additional propellers he planned to install.

All in all, Akbar's ship proved neither worse nor better than expected. But after talking it over, Haverson and Maslov concluded that the ship might well be converted into the sort of vessel they envisioned.

"It'll take a lot of ingenuity and effort," Haverson pointed out.

"That is what we will bring to the project," Maslov said.

"True," Haverson said. "Well, what do you say? Do we give Kirkwood an okay on this baby or not?"

"Da," the Russian nodded. "Tell him okay."

When Haverson informed the governor that he and Maslov approved of the ship, Kirkwood insisted he come to Sacramento once again. "There's an urgent matter I must discuss with you in person," he said. "I'll send a chopper to San Diego to pick you up. Leave Maslov there. This matter is strictly between you and me."

Arriving at the state capitol, Haverson was whisked immediately to the governor's office.

"So you and Maslov like Akbar's ship, do you?" Kirkwood asked. The two men were alone in the governor's office.

"It's well constructed and looks like it will be able to do the job," Haverson replied. "Serve as a suitable framework for the ship we have in mind."

"Good," Kirkwood smiled. "And what about Maslov? You're sure he's going to work out?"

"He's come up with some excellent ideas for the conversion."

"You realize, of course, that his job doesn't end when the ship sails out of San Diego," Kirkwood said. "He'll be aboard all the way. At least that's my understanding. Correct me, Captain, if I'm wrong."

"You're right," Haverson confirmed. "There'll be a lot of experimental equipment aboard, some of it my design, some Maslov's. If something malfunctions, he'll have to be around to fix it. No one else would be capable—except possibly me."

"And you won't be around?"

"That's correct, sir."

"Then he'll definitely have to sail?"

"Yes, sir."

Kirkwood perched on the corner of his desk, folded his arms on his chest and looked Haverson squarely in the eye. "Tell me, Captain, how do you rate Maslov as a possible security risk?"

"I don't have the proper information to make such a judgment," Haverson replied.

"Can he be trusted?" Kirkwood persisted. "Do you think there's any possibility of this project failing because of something he might do?"

"You mean sabotage?"

"Yes."

Haverson frowned. "There's always that possibility, I suppose," he admitted. "But it seems unlikely."

"But you agree with me that Maslov *could* be a security risk?"

Hesitating a moment, Haverson said, "It is possible."

"As I explained at the very beginning, this project must be free from any kind of outside interference. I am the only person in an official government capacity who is to be connected with it," Kirkwood said. "As far as the world is concerned, the 'Aquarius Transfer' is strictly a private enterprise."

"The 'Aquarius Transfer,' sir?" Haverson questioned.

"Yes. That's the name for the project. A friend of yours suggested it," the governor said. "Sally Brennan."

"I might have guessed," Haverson said. "One of the first things she asked me on the way to London is what my 'sign' was."

"It's an unusually serious matter," Kirkwood continued. "I don't want any outsiders sticking their noses in this project—especially agents or agencies connected with the federal government. That's of the utmost importance. I want the tightest security. Above all, I want Maslov closely watched, just in case he should try anything. But I don't want him to be aware that he's under surveillance. There's only one person for that job as far as I'm concerned and that's you, Captain."

"Why me?" Haverson asked.

"Because it's got to be someone working very closely with him, someone whose presence would not make him suspicious."

"That could be any captain."

"No, it's got to be you."

"I don't understand . . ."

"Because you need this mission to succeed as much as I do," Kirkwood said. "And you know what I mean."

When Haverson got home from Sacramento Ingrid was still at school. He was beginning to get a headache, so he took two aspirins and lay on the chaise in the verandah. Kirkwood had put him in a difficult spot earlier, and he needed a clear head in order to think through his decision.

He had only been asleep a short time when a piercing shriek that seemed to come from the front of the house awakened him. Leaping to his feet, he dashed to the front door and was stunned to find Cathy lying motionless on the lawn, her schoolbooks scattered around her on the dry grass. Her boyfriend was bending over her.

"What's wrong?" Haverson demanded. "What happened?"

"I don't know, Mr. Haverson," the youth replied, looking frightened and concerned. "I just dropped Cathy off from cheerleading practice. She was running up the walk to your front door, when all of a sudden she let out a yell and said a bee stung her. Then she just sort of passed out."

Grabbing his teenaged daughter's wrist, he took her pulse, which was weak and rapid. "She's going into shock. I'll have to give her mouth-to-mouth resuscitation."

Haverson worked over his daughter until Cathy's color returned to normal, her pulse grew stronger, and she was breathing normally on her own. He bundled her in a blanket and her boyfriend David drove her to the emergency hospital in his beercan-littered van.

By the time they returned home, Ingrid had arrived from school and was surprised to see Neal carrying Cathy into the house. Recalling the recent incident with Jill, she was alarmed. "Neal, what is it? What happened to Cathy?"

"Nothing. She'll be okay," he assured his wife as he laid the girl on the sofa. She was still wearing her pert cheerleading outfit. "The doctor said she'd been stung by a bee and is apparently allergic to bee stings. She had what he called an anaphylactic reaction."

"My God!" Ingrid gasped. "We could have lost her." Falling to her knees beside the sofa, she put her arms around her older daughter and hugged her tight.

"Come on, Mom," Cathy protested, embarrassed by Ingrid's display of emotion.

"You could have died," Ingrid said.

"I don't understand it," Cathy mused. "I've had bee stings before and nothing like this ever happened."

"The doctor says people just get sensitized for no apparent reason," Haverson explained.

"Poor Cathy," Ingrid said, brushing the girl's light brown hair out of her eyes. "First Jill with the glass and now this. That emergency room is going to get tired of seeing us."

A little later when Jill came home from her riding lesson and heard her sister's story, she offered Cathy a tiny dartlike object with bright green and yellow feathers.

"What's this?" Cathy demanded, indignant at such a gift.

"I don't know," Jill shrugged with a chuckle. "I just found it out by the front walk."

"Throw it away, Jill," Ingrid commanded.

"Wait a minute," Haverson said suspiciously. "Give it to me."

"For heaven's sake, Neal, it's just some old thing from a kid's game or something," Ingrid said and before he could stop her, she threw it into the toilet of the adjoining guest bathroom.

That night when they were in bed, Ingrid turned suddenly to Neal and said, "You know, with all that excitement about Cathy and the bee sting today, I forgot to ask you about the governor and what went on at your meeting."

"He laid something pretty heavy on me today," he said.

"Oh? What was that?" she asked.

"You might not like what I'm going to say," he warned her.

"You're probably right," she agreed, "but tell me anyway."

"He wants me to take complete charge of the project."

"That's what you've been doing," she said.

"No. From start to finish," Haverson went on. "In other words, he wants me to take charge of the voyage—you know, captain the vessel."

"That's nothing new. That's what he's wanted since the beginning. What did you tell him?"

"I told him I'd have to think about it."

"What new ploy did he use this time to make you come around?" she asked.

"I haven't 'come around,' as you put it," he replied, slightly resentful of her remark. "At least not yet."

"But you will."

"Yeah, probably," he conceded.

"What's the new wrinkle he came up with?"

"He doesn't trust Maslov."

"Neither do you," she reminded him.

"He wants me to be a watchdog," Haverson said and went on to relate his meeting with the state's chief executive in its entirety.

When he concluded, Ingrid sighed. "Well, as I said before, Neal, it's your decision. Whatever you decided to do is up to you. You know that whatever your decision is, I'll stand behind you, just the way I always have," she said.

"Do you really mean that?"

"Yes, I do," she affirmed. "The only condition I'm going to make is that I don't have to live with a lot of bad dreams from you when you get back."

"That's another reason I'm going," he said.

"Then you've made up your mind?"

"I figure it might be a way to get rid of a lot of bad dreams, and finally clear my name."

To facilitate the transfer of the supertanker, the *Princess Mouna* was renamed the *Aquarius* and a company called Aquarius Limited was formed in London. In keeping with the ship's new name honoring the water carrier of the zodiac, the iceberg project was to be known officially as the "Aquarius Transfer" in all transactions. In the organizational plan of Aquarius Ltd. Prince Akbar was listed as head with Haverson as "Chief of Operations," Maslov as "Chief Engineer," and Kirkwood as "Special Consultant."

It was decided that the conversion of the supertanker to iceberg hauler would take place in the San Diego shipyard where the ship was already docked. Hence, office space close to the yard was acquired and a secretary hired. Maslov would remain in San Diego and oversee the work at the shipyard, but Haverson would stay in Los Angeles, commuting between the two cities by company helicopter when necessary.

Both men, despite whatever misgivings they might have had about one another, shared an enthusiasm for the project that made them anxious for the conversion to proceed as rapidly as possible. They spent long hours at their respective drawing boards, often working late into the night. In Ingrid's opinion, both men were working too hard, but she decided that it was better not to express such thoughts. Neal had had more than a few moments of anxiety since he had decided to take charge of the voyage, and she didn't want to add to his stress. At least he was home now.

In addition to the conversion of the ship itself, many other considerations had to be worked out, such as provisions for a hangar in which to house the small helicopter on board, equipment with which to insulate the iceberg once it was attached to the ship, space for a two-man underwater bathyscaph, electronic devices to monitor the physical state of the iceberg, and storage of spare parts, not the least of which included gigantic extra propellers. Despite occasional differences, the two men got along remarkably well.

Several times a week Kirkwood himself or one of his staff called to check on the progress of the project and to relay pertinent information.

"I don't want to interfere with your end of things, Captain, and I know how busy you are," the governor said, "but don't you think you'd better start thinking about a crew? Akbar's people want an actual breakdown of the various crew positions and the corresponding salary scales. He's giving us carte blanche, more or less, but he obviously intends to keep a close check on how and where his money is being spent."

"Can't say that I blame him," Haverson replied.

A few days later, Haverson began placing advertisements for crew positions in various international maritime journals, navy periodicals, and newspapers in all the major cities. For security reasons, the wording of these ads was deliberately vague, and as a result of this vagueness, some of the respondents lacked qualifications Haverson felt were essential. When the conversion was completed, the *Aquarius* would be one of the most technically advanced and complex ships afloat, and as captain, he needed a crew equal to the challenge of running it.

In the evening, Haverson would often take a break from the drawing board, and he and Ingrid would sort through the responses that had arrived in the day's mail. Both of them appreciated this shared activity, knowing that they would soon be separated. They did not voice their apprehension, but both wondered what the effects of that long separation would be.

When the conversion plans were past the drawing board stage and it was time to implement them, it was decided to engage three shifts of workers around the clock to speed up the project as much as possible.

"I've notified the shipyard head that I want this job given top priority," Kirkwood informed Haverson.

Once the actual work began, it progressed at a rapid rate. Whenever problems or snags arose—and there were many, as might be expected in such an innovative undertaking—Maslov seemed to have a gift for solving them in such a way that work was seldom delayed for long. So far he appeared to be a definite asset to the project, and Haverson was pleased with his decision to engage him. In addition, he had observed nothing to create even the slightest suspicion that the Russian was anything except completely loyal.

"If the *Aquarius* sails earlier than our projected departure date," Haverson told the governor, obviously pleased by the project's progress, "so much the better. And if it arrives at its destination before the sea ice is sufficiently thawed, it can wait out the thawing. Nothing will be lost by being early, but everything could be lost if we're late. Keep that in mind."

After some weeks of interviewing in Los Angeles, Haverson temporarily transferred operations to San Diego and interviewed applicants for the crew in that city. Although Maslov was occupied most of the time at the shipyard, he made it a point to drop by the Aquarius Limited offices whenever possible while Haverson was in town so that he could discuss various matters and keep abreast of what was happening with regard to the hiring of the crew.

"The men of this ship must be the best," Maslov insisted. "I have given everything I had to this ship—my knowledge, my experience, my sweat, my blood."

"You forgot 'tears,' " Haverson said wryly.

Ignoring the comment, Maslov continued, "It is very important to me that this project is a success."

"It's important to all of us," Haverson reminded him, somewhat wary of the Russian's zeal. "Do you think you're the only one with anything at stake?"

"It *must* be a success," Maslov reiterated, almost as if he hadn't been listening to Haverson.

"It *will* be," Haverson assured him firmly, reminded of Shakespeare's line from *Hamlet* about the lady protesting too much.

"But only if the crew is the best," Maslov continued.

"It'll be the best goddamn crew you ever sailed with," Haverson asserted, bristling slightly. "I guarantee you that."

"I hope you're right," Maslov said and left the office.

18

As simmering spring blazed into broiling summer, the drought continued, wreaking further devastation on stricken California. Governor Kirkwood called a special meeting of his staff to discuss ways of handling the crisis during the especially sensitive summer months.

Ramsdale, Weisswasser, and Jane Garcia gathered around the conference table in Kirkwood's office. The chair usually occupied by George Bashore was still vacant.

"People are packing up and leaving in droves," Jane Garcia reported glumly. "Tensions and anxiety are soaring. People are having trouble coping with the heat, the dust, water rationing, astronomical food prices, and unemployment."

"The economic ravages of this drought are far greater than our estimates, Paul," Ramsdale said, taking up where the pretty brunette Chicana left off. "Every industry is affected. We've got layoffs, slowdowns, and out-and-out closures all over the state. I know I don't have to tell you that agriculture, our number one, ten-billion-dollar-a-year industry is in a shambles because of its obvious dependence on water, but so are the industries closely allied to it such as food processing, transportation, and marketing, which account for another eighteen billion dollars a year. Even such industries as steel, automobile manufacture, and aircraft are tumbling."

"Thanks, you two. You've just made my day," Kirkwood said. "Seriously, I realize that the pressure on all of us is fast becoming unbearable. We've got to find ways to get the people to give us more time. I believe very strongly that the Aquarius Transfer project *will* succeed. It'll be the salvation of us all if we can just persuade the public to be patient a little longer."

"Then why keep it a secret?" Weisswasser asked, stroking his beard. "If it's security you're worried about, we'll just have to make provisions to provide for more."

"Haverson already has twenty-four-hour guards at the shipyard," Ramsdale pointed out.

"Wally's right," Jane Garcia agreed. "Why not come out and tell the public all about it? Security doesn't present that great a problem, does it?"

"That's not what I'm worried about, Jane," Kirkwood said.

"Listen, if we break this story right, it could be dynamite from a public relations standpoint," Weisswasser said.

"We're just kidding ourselves if we think it's a secret any longer," Ramsdale said, referring to the fact that whoever attacked George Bashore in London did it to get a copy of the agreement with Akbar.

"I think we should let it all hang out," Weisswasser advised. "We've got to show people that we're determined to lick this drought and we've got a new and solid plan to do just that. We should go public with this story in a big way. That's my advice."

"Yes, but I wonder just how much we should reveal," Kirkwood mused, pensively chewing on the end of his pen.

"What are you worried about?" Jane Garcia asked.

"After what happened to George, I'm worried about everything," Krikwood replied.

"The way I see it," Weisswasser continued, "the best way to go would be to let somebody we trust break the story—you know, as an exclusive. That way we can retain some control."

Kirkwood raised a single dark eyebrow. "You mean somebody like Sally Brennan?" he asked.

"Why not? Sally's given us a pretty fair shake in the past," Weisswasser said.

Remembering his promise to Sally in London, Kirkwood concurred. "Sally Brennan sounds good to me."

At the end of the week Kirkwood paid a visit to Bonnie at UCLA Medical Center. Sitting at her side, silently holding her hand, he listened uneasily to the oxygen hissing as it passed through the tracheostomy tube in her neck. Although she couldn't speak, he knew she was aware of his presence and was glad he was with her.

From the hospital he called Sally at KHOT and arranged a meeting with her in the plush new office Ken Wilson had bestowed on her. When he arrived there with his aides

Kirkwood lost no time coming to the point, informing her that they had decided to break the whole Aquarius Transfer story.

"We're giving you first crack at it," he said.

"Wow! This is a real coup," Sally responded, delighted and surprised. "You're the rarest of creatures, Governor—a man of his word."

"I try to be," Kirkwood said. "Before we make the announcement, there are a couple of things we ought to discuss."

"Yes, of course," Sally nodded, looking attentive.

"Do you think there's any way we could make it more than just another routine news story on the Six or Eleven O'Clock News?" he asked.

"I agree that it ought to be presented in a very special way," Sally concurred.

"Got any suggestions?"

"Well, I was thinking of *Open Forum*," Sally answered. "That's our most prestigious show with regard to current events. A member of the KHOT news staff moderates and questions a panel of experts, usually on some political or relevant topic."

"Well, this is certainly a relevant topic," Weisswasser chimed in. "Who would you suggest for the panel in our case—besides Governor Kirkwood, of course?"

"I'd like to have Captain Haverson," she said. His was the first name to pop into her head.

"Yes, of course," Ramsdale agreed.

"How about Prince Akbar?" she proposed, keeping in mind the show biz appeal of an "exotic" like Akbar for the program.

"No. Let's leave him out for the time being," Kirkwood said.

"Okay," she agreed. "How about Yuri Maslov?"

"We don't want to slight Maslov or downgrade his role in the project, but for now at least, I think it's best not to include him," Kirkwood said.

"Too controversial," Ramsdale added.

"All right," Sally said, somewhat reluctantly. "Strike Maslov."

"Don't worry, we'll come up with somebody else," Ramsdale assured her.

",Yeah, somebody good," Weisswasser promised.

"You guys better because if you don't, Ken Wilson will," she warned.

* * *

When Kirkwood's office suggested the head of the Department of Water Resources as the third member of the *Open Forum* panel, Ken Wilson was not pleased.

"The head of the Department of Water Resources is a nobody as far as the viewing public is concerned. We need names. We need controversy. We need conflict if we're going to get ratings," he complained loudly as he paced back and forth in Sally's office, nervously scratching his bald head. "The show already has a reputation for being highbrow and stuffy, and I want to get away from that image."

"It's important to Kirkwood and his staff that we attract a large audience, too," Sally said. "They've reiterated that several times."

Wilson's face brightened. "Maybe if we could spark a little controversy in advance . . ." he contemplated aloud.

Sally glanced at him suspiciously. "What did you have in mind?"

"I don't know," Wilson replied. "Tell me more about this so-called 'solution' of Kirkwood's. Maybe it'll give me an idea."

Sally did not realize when she revealed the plan which Haverson and Kirkwood had formulated to end the drought that its more controversial aspects—the fact that the ship was nuclear-powered and that it would tow a gigantic iceberg across thousands of miles of ocean—would appear in a television column devoted to *Open Forum* in the *Los Angeles Times*. As a result of the column the station was barraged with letters and telephone calls. The loudest protests and strongest demands for equal time came from a group calling themselves the "Sea Vigilantes."

Indicating the pile of mail and telegrams on his desk, Ken Wilson shook his head. "What do you think of this?" he said to Sally. "It's something, isn't it? I tell you . . ."

Sally was not amused. "I think it was pretty low of you, Ken," she said.

Feigning surprise, Wilson said, "What do you mean?"

"You know what I mean. You couldn't wait to leak that information as soon as you got it out of me," she said.

"Oh, come on, Sally," he chided.

"You know you did," she reproached.

Wilson shrugged indifferently. "So I told a couple of columnists. So what? It's no big deal. And, besides, it'll generate interest in the show. I mean, *Open Forum* isn't exactly a blockbuster in the ratings, you know."

"Public information shows aren't supposed to be," she reminded him. "If I knew you were going to leak it, I would never have told you some of those details."

"What difference does it make if it comes out today or Sunday?"

"It might make a lot of difference to the governor," she said. "And it makes a lot of difference to me. The reason he picked me to break the story on *Open Forum* is because he trusts me."

"Look, Sally, nobody in politics trusts anybody," Wilson said. "Believe me, I know."

"Sure you do," she muttered, shoving the newspaper with the offending column aside.

"You know, we're going to have to let the other side air their views," Wilson said, watching carefully for her reaction.

"What?!" Sally said.

"We don't have any choice," Wilson replied. "In the interest of fairness . . ."

"What the hell do you know about fairness?"

"It's station policy," he asserted.

Sally sighed. "Okay. But how do you plan to work it? Let the opponents have a couple of minutes at the end of the show to air their viewpoint or what?" she asked.

"Oh, no. I've got a much better idea," Wilson replied proudly. "This Sunday we're going to extend the show to sixty minutes and enlarge the panel. Kirkwood and Haverson will represent the 'pro' side and the two spokespersons from the Sea Vigilantes, the 'cons.'"

"Have you informed Kirkwood's office about this switch yet?" she asked.

"Yes. They were quite enthusiastic," he replied.

Sally looked at him skeptically. "I don't believe you."

"So don't believe me," Wilson said. "But it's true. The governor himself agrees with me that a little controversy might be a good thing to pull in the viewers."

"What about Captain Haverson? Did you tell him, too?"

"I figured you could do that."

When Sally called and informed the former naval officer that he would be facing representatives of the Sea Vigilantes, he sounded puzzled and asked, "Would you mind filling me in on who they are? I only have a vague idea."

"Well, they're an organization supposedly dedicated to protecting the oceans of the world," Sally replied. "They were highly supportive of Kirkwood's opposition to the LNG terminals on the California coast."

"Oh, yes, now I remember," Haverson said.

"This time, however, I'm afraid they're on the opposite side of the fence, at least as far as the Aquarius Transfer project is concerned," she said.

"Who heads up the organization?" he asked.

"Their current spokesperson seems to be a young law student named Amy Armistad," Sally replied.

"How big are they in terms of numbers?"

"I'm not sure. They seem to be growing fast—at least in terms of numbers and influence."

"Where's their money come from?"

"That's anybody's guess," Sally said. "In any case, Ken Wilson is insisting we have them on the show. I don't have any choice in the matter—at least not at this time," she said with a note of regret in her voice. "I haven't called Governor Kirkwood yet."

"I don't know how the governor will take this news, but it's okay with me. I feel secure enough about the project to stand up to any critics," he said. "Maybe if we know their specific gripes, we can reach some kind of compromise. After all, I'm not unreasonable. I'm always willing to listen to new input."

"If I know Amy Armistad," Sally said, "you'll get a lot of it."

On the day of the broadcast, Amy Armistad appeared at the KHOT studios at the appointed time. Although she was well into her twenties, she appeared almost adolescent with her lithe, slender body, thick mane of long black hair, fiery dark eyes, and full, ripe breasts, unfettered by a brassiere, which quivered beneath the thin fabric of her T-shirt emblazoned with the Sea Vigilantes' logo. She was accompanied by none other than the world famous climatologist, Dr. Thurston Terhune, white-haired, aged and bespectacled, attired in a conservative blue-and-white-striped seersucker suit. While Amy displayed an almost surly attitude toward studio personnel, Terhune was far more cordial, greeting those about him with a friendly smile. Together they seemed an odd combination—the patrician, cultivated, intellectual liberal and the angry street radical—but as a team, Sally could see, they might give Haverson and Kirkwood some difficult moments.

Kirkwood arrived with Haverson later than their opponents from the Sea Vigilantes and were immediately ushered into separate quarters where Kirkwood's security could be maintained. A few minutes before air time Haverson encountered Terhune with whom he had not communicated since the World Weather Symposium in Washington. Their greeting was reasonably amicable, considering they were on opposite sides as far as the issue to be discussed on the show was concerned.

"Damn it, Haverson, I wish we could see eye to eye on this iceberg thing," Terhune lamented, shaking his head.

"We could, if you'd show a little flexibility, sir," Haverson replied with a playful grin.

When the program got under way, Haverson and Kirkwood were seated at one table facing Amy Armistad and Dr. Terhune at another with Sally moderating from behind a desk placed between the two tables. She opened the program, giving a brief introductory sketch of each participant and his or her accomplishments and then called on Haverson to discuss the background on the proposed Aquarius Transfer.

He outlined the project with the aid of graphs, charts, and drawings. "With the population of this planet almost doubling every decade or so, water consumption will increase sharply. More people means more water. The demand for water is already tremendous, and it's going to get even greater. The big question is, Where is all this water going to come from? Only nine percent of the water on earth is fresh water, and most of that—as high as ninety percent—is bound up as ice, most of it in the Antarctic—which brings me to why we're here today. It's my firm belief that this antarctic ice will eventually supply a large part of the world's demand for water—pure, safe, and inexpensive water, free from dangerous pollution or the risk of nuclear accident. Although we tend to take it for granted—or we did before the drought—water is the most vital resource on our planet. We've learned from our various probes into space that where there's no water, there's no life. As far as we know, life can't exist without water. It's time for us to stop taking this precious resource for granted and to stop assuming that we have an unending supply at our disposal. The past two years have taught us a hard, painful, but very important lesson, and it's forced us to come up with a workable solution to the problem. That solution is the Aquarius Transfer."

When Haverson concluded his portion, Sally called on Kirkwood, who had graciously relinquished the opening spot to his colleague in the interest of a smoothly developed program. Rising, he said, "I firmly believe that this unique and important project developed by Captain Haverson deserves the full support of not only the people of this great state of California, but of the entire world. Before we go on, let me just point out that this project will not cost the taxpayers one cent. It is being funded privately by concerned individuals whom we believe are among the most forward-looking on the planet. They have full confidence in the Aquarius Transfer and believe that it will lick this drought, come hell or high water—and in this case, you can be sure that we hope it's high water."

When Haverson and Kirkwood had finished, Sally called on Amy Armistad and Dr. Terhune. Amy spoke first.

"Governor Kirkwood has shown himself to be a self-serving hypocrite as far as this drought is concerned," she accused, her dark eyes blazing. "We all remember how vigorously he opposed the nuclear-fueled desalination plants, and we of the Sea Vigilantes still applaud him for his stand. Now, however, he does a complete turnaround and endorses a nuclear-powered ship with an even greater capacity for disaster and deadly pollution of the oceans. All nuclear power is dangerous, expensive, and unnecessary. All of us must stand firm in our opposition to it, no matter how or where its use is proposed—whether on land or at sea, as is the case of the Aquarius Transfer."

When she finished, Terhune began. "There are other serious considerations apart from the dangers of nuclear energy of which we must be aware," he said. "As Captain Haverson has just made clear, this nuclear-powered ship will tow an iceberg of immense proportions from Antarctica to California. I doubt if most of you out there can conceive how big a one hundred kilogram iceberg really is. It's huge. Vast. As large as some counties in this state. It's also very, very cold. Nothing like what Captain Haverson proposes has ever been attempted before. God only knows, I certainly recognize the need for water in California. But I also recognize the governor's political ambitions and his present desperation. I am aware, too, of his, 'water-at-any-cost' attitude. Today I want to remind all of you that we must not ignore the dangers involved. Towing a great block of ice along the coasts of South and North America will markedly cool the surrounding atmosphere. That is a generally accepted fact. It will also cool the surrounding water as well. What will happen as a result of this cooled air and cooled water no one can predict. It is possible that it may adversely affect the weather to a great extent, producing other droughts as severe—or more severe—than the one we are currently experiencing in California, tropical storms of a magnitude and intensity that we may not have witnessed before, and other potentially dangerous meteorological phenomena. At this time, there's no way of knowing what effect that iceberg will have on the weather and climate of the regions through which it passes, on the ocean currents, on fish and fishing, on birds and other wildlife. It could cause immeasurable harm. We simply will not know until it's too late. I say the risks of the Aquarius Transfer project are not worth the possible benefits—if, indeed, there will be any benefits. I say we must all ban together and stop this Aquarius Transfer before it's too late!"

In spite of Sally's efforts to maintain a cool unemotional tone to the program and turn the discussion back to Haverson once again, Amy Armistad, apparently fired by Terhune's words, leaped up. "It's all a lie to deceive the people of the United States," she declared. "This project isn't going to produce any significant amount of water. I agree with my colleague, Dr. Terhune, that the Aquarius Transfer must be stopped. If we of the Sea Vigilantes can't shut it down by peaceful means, we will not hesitate to resort to other methods."

Sally was appalled to see her discussion program transformed into a political rally and knew that she was going to have to come down fast and hard in order to retain control, but before she could interrupt Amy, Terhune, roused by his companion's call to arms, raised his bony, white fist high in the air. "Right on!" he cried, "By God, right on!"

19

Because of Amy Armistad's on-the-air threat followed by the sudden appearance of vociferous and hostile protesters outside the shipyard, Haverson tripled the security around the *Aquarius*. But when sabotage struck the project it was not at the San Diego shipyard.

Drew Ramsdale was awakened from sleep in the middle of the night by a phonecall from a highly emotional Adriana Rincon, widow of Tony Rincon, sister-in-law of Gabe, and one time candidate for the U.S. Senate, herself.

"They wouldn't put me through to the governor," she complained, sounding upset.

"I know and I apologize, Adriana," Ramsdale replied sleepily. "But that's the official policy. I'm sure you understand. How can I help you?"

"I've got to get through to the governor. It's urgent."

"What's wrong?"

"There's been a big explosion and fire at Gabe's construction company in Oxnard," she said.

"My God! . . ." Ramsdale gasped.

"They cut through the steel chain-link fence and knocked out the dogs and the security man with some kind of drugged darts," she recounted. "Then they blew up the aqueduct."

"Jesus . . ." Ramsdale muttered. "Listen, Adriana, let me get in touch with the governor. I'll get back to you as soon as I can."

When Ramsdale reached Kirkwood, he had already heard the news about the aqueduct.

"I don't understand it," Kirkwood said. "I didn't think anybody was paying attention to the goddam aqueduct."

"Got any idea who might be behind it?" Ramsdale questioned.

"Sure. I've got a lot of ideas," Kirkwood said. "I've been informed that immediately following the blast, a female voice telephoned KHOT and credited the Sea Vigilantes with the deed. They taped the caller and turned the tape over to the FBI for voice analysis."

"Did it sound like anybody familiar?" Ramsdale asked.

"Yes. *Too* familiar," Kirkwood said.

In her New York townhouse Annalise Rudd was frantic. After pacing the floor for a long time, she finally picked up the phone, checked the electronic equipment to be certain the line was not tapped, and called Farleigh in Washington.

"It's been three days since the Oxnard explosion and I still haven't heard from Rico," she said.

"Have you heard the news?" Farleigh asked. "The FBI took Amy Armistad into custody. They've charged her with the destruction of the aqueduct based on voice analysis of a tape that that TV station made."

"I know. I've heard." Annalise impatiently dismissed the news. "I'm reasonably certain they haven't got Rico and aren't saying anything. I'm also sure he hasn't been killed. They couldn't keep something like that secret even if they wanted to. Where the hell can he be? Why didn't he follow instructions this time? He's got to learn to follow instructions; that's all there is to it. I can't have him disobeying me when I send him out on a mission. My God, I had him trained by the best terrorists in South America. You'd think he'd have learned something."

"Yes, you would think so," Farleigh agreed.

"Every time my phone rings I jump, thinking it's him. I haven't slept for two nights."

"Take something," he advised. "Sarajane always takes some Valiums when she's upset. She swears by them."

"I just took two," Annalise replied. As she was speaking, another line rang and she jumped, startled. "Maybe that's him. I'll get back to you later, Preston."

Annalise was truly stunned to pick up the phone and hear Rico's voice on the other end. "Why haven't you phoned me before this?" she demanded.

"I was not able," he answered. "I am too sick."

His answer took her by surprise. "What do you mean 'sick'?" she asked.

"I am hurt. Very bad. Everywhere."

"What are you talking about?"

125

"The explosion, you know? . . ." He paused.

"Well, what about it?"

"It was not so good."

"I don't understand. I saw it on TV. It looked fine to me. That damned aqueduct was demolished," she said. "The FBI is holding Armistad."

"Sure. That part went okay," Rico conceded. "It was after . . ."

"What do you mean 'after'?"

"I was hurt. Bad." His voice sounded as though it were about to crack. Rico's prime weakness as a saboteur was his inability to tolerate the slightest physical injury or illness. He would become upset over a sore throat, pimple, or minor cut.

"What happened? I don't understand . . ."

"You know when the thing blew up? Well, a lot of little pieces went flying around."

"I thought they taught you how to handle explosives when I sent you to South America."

"They did, but something went wrong," he replied. "Some of the pieces hit me. They cut me and went inside my skin. Hurt me bad."

Annalise was growing extremely apprehensive. When Rico felt his physical health was endangered, he could become irrational. This was something she had always feared. "What did you do?" she asked anxiously.

"That man, you know, the one who met me at the airport? Took me to Oxnard? The same one who took me to Palos Verdes a couple of weeks ago?"

"Yes. Gunther. What about him?"

"I called him and told him I needed to see a doctor. He took me to Tijuana and they fixed me up."

"Who fixed you up?"

"This Mexican doctor."

"Did he ask a lot of questions? About how you got hurt?"

"Not so many."

"You didn't talk, did you?"

"Do you think I'm crazy?" Rico answered indignantly. "I didn't tell him nothing."

Annalise breathed a sigh of relief. "Is that why you didn't call? Because you were in Mexico?"

"Yes."

"Listen to me carefully, Rico. I want you to come home

immediately, do you understand?" she directed. "I'm sending a plane to pick you up just as we arranged. You do remember, don't you?"

"Yes."

"Good." She smiled into the receiver. "I'll see you this evening."

"When I get home, don't expect too much," he cautioned. "I have much pain."

Over and over Annalise told herself that she must be stern with Rico when he arrived home. After all, he had disobeyed her instructions and caused her a great deal of anguish. However, when he came limping slowly up the stairs of the townhouse, she could not restrain herself from embracing him. Rico responded to her affectionate greeting with a loud cry of pain.

"I'm sorry," she apologized, releasing him at once. "Forgive me, my darling."

Brushing aside her apologies, Rico went to his room in the rear of the house and began to undress. Annalise followed him and gasped in horror when she saw him nearly naked. She could scarcely believe her eyes. His lithe, slender body with its satiny, caramel-hued skin appeared ravaged by some bizarre affliction. From head to toe his entire body was peppered with tiny metal fragments. Some of the fragments had obviously been removed by the doctor in Mexico and the wounds dressed, but others had either been too deeply embedded or too small to remove and apparently left to work their way out on their own.

Rico instantly sensed her shock and revulsion, although she did her best to try and conceal it. Throwing himself across the bed, he furiously pounded his fists into the pillow. "I am ruined!" he wailed. "Look at me, I am ruined. Nobody will ever want to make love with me again. I am a—what do you say?—freak!"

"Don't be silly," she assured him. "We'll get you fixed up. I know a wonderful plastic surgeon in Switzerland. He'll make you good as new again. Don't worry, dearest."

"Everywhere is hurt. Even here is hurt," he whined, indicating the generous bulge in his brief undershorts.

Annalise laid her hand lightly on his shoulder, wanting desperately to assure him of his desirability, but he winced and shrank away from her. She shook her head, thinking,

127

Rico was exciting, daring, impulsive, and, at times, even courageous, but he would require a lot more training and discipline if he were ever to become a truly successful terrorist.

20

Despite Annalise's assurances that he would eventually be all right, Rico grew increasingly anxious about his wounds, and when several of the embedded fragments began to fester, draining foul-smelling pus, he went into hysterics—crying, thrashing about on the floor, wailing that he was going to die. Fearful that in such a distraught state he might make damaging disclosures, Annalise hastily arranged to have him admitted to an exclusive clinic in Switzerland as she promised.

Heavily sedated, Rico was put aboard one of Rudd International's jets for Europe. As soon as he was gone, Annalise hopped another jet for Washington.

"What a surprise! I had no idea you were coming," Sarajane cried, clasping Annalise's hands and hoping that the other woman wouldn't detect the odor of liquor beneath the minty aroma of hastily-gargled mouthwash. "Shame on Preston for not telling me."

"Preston didn't know," she replied. "It was a rather sudden decision."

"Nothing wrong, I hope?" Sarajane said apprehensively.

"No. Just a couple of matters I wanted to discuss with him," Annalise replied. "Somehow I thought it might be better to do it in person."

"It's always better to discuss things in person. I don't even like to talk to Dottie Calhoun on the phone, and she and I have been friends ever since we were little bitty girls back home in Texas," Sarajane prattled. "Preston should be here shortly—although I can't guarantee it."

Annalise glanced at the Piaget around her slim wrist. "It's seven o'clock," she announced.

"My goodness! Is it really?" Sarajane gasped. "That Senate is running late again. You'd think none of those senators had wives and children, the hours they keep. Can I offer you a drink or something to nibble on?"

"I'll just use the phone." Annalise began dialing before Sarajane had a chance to reply.

"You just go right ahead. Make yourself at home," Sarajane said, starting to leave the room to allow her guest privacy.

"You can stay," Annalise said. "I'm only calling your husband."

A weary, Preston Farleigh shuffled into the living room a short time later, and dropped his briefcase on the nearest chair. "Hi, doll-baby," he said, greeting Sarajane with a kiss. Then turning to his visitor, he said, "How are you, Annalise?"

Sensing that he might prefer to talk to Annalise alone, Sarajane said, "I'll just go to the kitchen and see how Darlene is coming with dinner," and left the room.

The moment she was gone, Annalise turned to Farleigh. "We've got to take advantage of the arrest of Amy Armistad," she said. "And fast."

Puzzled, Farleigh frowned. "With Armistad taking the rap for the aqueduct, it's an ideal setup. What more could we ask for?"

"From the information I've been able to gather, all they've got on her is a lot of stuff that will never stand up in court," Annalise said.

"I agree that so far they've probably got a pretty weak case against her," Farleigh said. "I'm sure the defense will try to introduce a motion to deny the voice tapes as evidence. It's too bad. The girl we hired to imitate her was a superb mimic. It's amazing what an out-of-work actress will do for money. It's too bad. I'd like to see those tapes make a bunch of jackasses out of those lawyers."

"She's going to get off," Annalise said. "You and I both know that."

"It's quite possible," he agreed.

"That's why we've got to act fast," she continued. "We've got to get the charges against her dismissed and get her released. With our connections—yours and mine—it shouldn't be difficult."

Farleigh was stunned. "Get her released?" he repeated incredulously. "Now why the hell would we want to do that?"

With a sly smile Annalise replied, "To gain her eternal gratitude. And cooperation."

Puzzled, he confessed, "I don't follow you."

"Don't you see? They haven't got enough on her to put her behind bars," Annalise pointed out, "but she doesn't know that."

"You're forgetting, she's a law student," he reminded her.

"What do law students know, for God's sake?" She brushed his question aside impatiently. "If we make it look to her as if we're the ones responsible for getting her out, she just might be grateful enough to come over to our side."

Looking at her skeptically, he said, "You don't really believe that, do you?"

"Of course I do," she said. "Besides, we have the means to generate publicity—lots of it. If we handle things right, we can make it look as though she's an innocent victim being persecuted and oppressed by the cruel and ruthless governor of California and his henchmen. We can promote her into looking like the biggest martyr since Joan of Arc."

Farleigh was astounded by such a proposal. "What makes you think she'd be willing to come over to our side?" he asked.

"A number of things," Annalise replied, as she snapped open her Vuitton attaché case and handed him a manila folder. "This is a dossier I've had prepared on her. You'll soon see that she's not simply the dedicated, committed radical she wants everybody to think she is. Like a lot of others, she's selected a popular and convenient bandwagon to hop aboard and make a name for herself. She's merely using the Sea Vigilantes and that whole movement to gain her own ends. She's in it strictly for the notoriety. Now that she's managed to get herself thrown in jail, she won't want to stay there long. If she remains locked up, the public will forget her fast, and that's the *last* thing a girl like Amy Armistad wants. You can bet your bottom dollar she wants out. And fast. That's where you and I come in."

Weary from a grueling day in the Senate, Farleigh rubbed his eyes. He seemed to have some difficulty following her logic. "You'll have to pardon me if I don't quite follow what you're getting at," he said. "What's Amy's ultimate goal? What the hell does she go through all that radical business for if she's not genuinely committed?"

"Very simple. She wants a political career," Annalise explained. "Just like you, Preston."

* * *

The following day Farleigh directed his press secretary to release the story that he was taking time out from his busy Washington schedule to personally make a trip to California to look into the case of Amy Armistad. He also asked him to schedule as many television appearances as possible while he was in his home state so that he could demonstrate to his constituents that he was laboring energetically in their behalf. Few politicians knew better than Farleigh how critical exposure was in public life.

"You can be sure I'm going to use every television exposure I can to attack Kirkwood," he confided to his press secretary, Jeff Meiner. "It just tickles me to death to jump to the defense of someone the governor is accused of persecuting."

"It'll be a new image for you, Senator—champion of the oppressed," Meiner replied.

Farleigh grinned. "Kirkwood's already stated publicly that he hopes that if she's guilty, Amy Armistad will receive the maximum sentence."

"Yes, sir, and in the same interview he went on to attack the Sea Vigilantes for their continued opposition to the Aquarius project, calling their motives suspect and their actions reprehensible," Meiner added.

"Kirkwood's involvement with that iceberg hauling plan has set him up as a target, and don't think for a minute I'm going to pass up an opportunity to take a few potshots at him," Farleigh chuckled as he left his Senate office to catch a plane for California.

"The governor of this state is doing everything in his power to shove this ridiculous iceberg project of his down the throats of the citizens of this state," Farleigh declared on California television screens. "He is even willing to persecute an innocent young girl who was merely trying to exercise her American right to free speech to prevent him from carrying through his insane scheme to bring water to this stricken land of ours. In my opinion, Governor Kirkwood is so embarrassed and ashamed that he opposed the Hydrolliance desalination plan that he is now trying to save face at any cost. He is so desperate that he is willing to make a scapegoat of a girl who dared to speak out against this dangerous and foolish solution to the drought. I say that it's time for Governor Kirkwood to stand up and admit that he's been wrong. Dead wrong. And abandon his scheme to haul icebergs from the

South Pole. It's time for him to back the Hydrolliance plan when it's reintroduced in the California legislature."

Farleigh's television addresses not only increased the unpopularity of the governor, just as the senator intended, but at the same time stirred up popular sentiment for "innocent" Amy Armistad. The first step in the Farleigh-Rudd master plan had been successfully completed.

The second trap called for a series of strategic calls to those with power over Amy's fate. In these calls, Farleigh emphasized the weakness of the case against the girl and the embarrassment that might be suffered if she were actually brought to trial, only to be ultimately set free.

The third and final step was a meeting with Amy herself, who was fast becoming the government's hot potato.

A prison attendant conducted Farleigh down a long hallway to a dormitorylike room, Spartanly furnished with a cot, small table, and two chairs, where Amy was waiting.

"Amy, how do you do?" he said, extending his hand to her. "I'm Senator Farleigh. I've come to see if I can help you."

Sitting sullenly on the edge of the cot, Amy looked at him skeptically and made no move to accept his hand. "Why should you want to help me?" she challenged suspiciously.

"Because I think you've been unfairly accused," he replied. "As senator of this state, I feel it's my duty to protest the arrest of any citizen whom I believe is unjustly accused."

Amy smirked. "I didn't vote for you in the last election, Senator," she said. "I voted for Adriana Rincon."

Secretly smarting at her nerve, when he had just said he had come to help her, he managed to remain affable. "In any case, let's not waste time on trivialities," he said. "I'd like to get down to business, if you don't mind."

Amy shrugged indifferently. "Go ahead," she said.

"As I mentioned, I think you have been unjustly accused," he repeated.

"I didn't blow up that aqueduct—if that's what you're talking about," she said. "I'm glad somebody did, but I didn't do it."

"I believe you when you say you're innocent," he replied. "What's more, I'd like to try and get the charges against you dropped."

In spite of herself, Amy's face brightened somewhat. Annalise was right. It was suddenly clear that above all,

133

Amy wanted out of jail. "How do you propose to do that?" she asked skeptically.

"There are ways," he replied with deliberate vagueness, adding: "That's if you are willing to cooperate . . ."

Warily she asked, "What do I have to do?"

"Well, for one thing, we would want you to continue with your work for the Sea Vigilantes," he replied. "I happen to think the work of that particular organization is very important and very worthwhile. I'm proud of what you and the Sea Vigilantes stand for and I firmly believe that our seas must be protected from those who would destroy them."

"There's no way I'd cop out on the Sea Vigilantes." Amy assured him.

"Good," Farleigh said. "I would also like you to work for us as a special advisor on ecological issues."

"Who is 'us'?" she questioned.

"My office."

Amy laughed, her smoldering dark eyes sparkling for the first time since he entered her cell. "You're kidding?" she said.

"I'm perfectly serious," he assured her. "I feel your commitment and dedication to ecology makes you especially well qualified for such a post. It's an important field and one in which I'm anxious to be kept well informed."

Cocking her head, she asked, "What do I have to do?"

"Well, you'll have to keep me abreast of the issues—what's happening among the various ecology groups, suggest possible solutions to problems. That sort of thing . . ."

Still not completely trusting, she asked, "What else?"

"From time to time, you'll receive special assignments from me or members of my senatorial staff," he replied. "But most of all, we would want you to remain active in the Sea Vigilantes. How does it sound to you so far?"

"What's the catch?" she asked.

"There's no catch, Amy," he said, forcing a smile on his thin lips. "Perhaps the only thing that might be called a 'catch' is that I would have to have a firm commitment from you to work for us before I try to get the charges against you dropped. Well, what do you say?"

"So you came here to make a deal?" she said, twisting her sensuous mouth into a crooked, slightly contemptuous smile. "Is that it?"

"You could call it a 'deal,' I suppose," he conceded. "Well, what's your answer?"

"I'll have to think it over," she replied.

Farleigh was disappointed by her hesitancy. According to Annalise she was supposed to jump at the chance to get out of jail. "Don't think too long," he cautioned. "We want to get moving right away, before the prosecution has a chance to start building their case against you."

"This whole thing is a frame-up," she protested. "I consider violence only a last resort—when all else fails. I don't consider our efforts against the Aquarius project a failure yet. Therefore, why would I engage in violence?"

"I'm not the one who's saying you did. I happen to believe you. That's why I'm here," he sympathized. "While you're thinking it over, also keep in mind that, as our advisor, you'll probably receive lots of national attention—and of a favorable kind, not like the kind you've been receiving lately. I guarantee you that if you accept this appointment, it'll make news."

"You have all kinds of connections, don't you, Senator?" she said.

"Yes, I do," he acknowledged. "And if you work for us, you'll have a chance to make some valuable connections of your own."

After a moment or two of contemplation, she said, "If I were to give you my answer right away, how soon do you think you could spring me?"

"I can't give you a definite answer, but you can be sure I'll start working on it right away. You have my word," he promised. "But you said you needed time to think. I don't want to rush you."

"I like what you're offering," she decided.

"Good!" Farleigh grinned, pleased to see that she was finally taking the bait. "I knew you were too smart a girl to let an opportunity like this slip through your fingers."

"I'm not a *girl*," she corrected resentfully. "I happen to be a woman."

Admiring her voluptuous body beneath the drab prison garb, he agreed, "Yes, you certainly are, Amy. You certainly are."

21

For each day of the long, hot summer without a major catastrophe, Paul Kirkwood offered a silent prayer of thanks and wondered how much more punishment his beleaguered state could take. In this bleak, sweltering, and strife-ridden season, he could point to two bright spots: Bonnie had begun to improve dramatically, and the work on the *Aquarius* was progressing steadily—so steadily, in fact, that it seemed certain the ship would be ready to sail before the projected target date. Kirkwood marveled at how skillfully Maslov had converted an ordinary supertanker into a truly unique and somewhat spectacular vessel. Many of the Russian's innovations were specifically tailored to the particular mission in the dangerous waters surrounding the Antarctic and for heavy-duty towing on the return trip. Its heavily reinforced hull—a double hull in essence—was especially designed to cope with the dense pack ice around the frozen continent at the bottom of the globe. On one of Kirkwood's official visits to the shipyard, Maslov proudly pointed out a system he had devised whereby a continuous stream of tiny air bubbles forced through minute openings in the hull would "lubricate" the ship's passage through the sea ice.

From all indications, Maslov seemed to be giving it his best efforts. Kirkwood wanted desperately to believe that he was as dedicated to the success of the project as he seemed, but he still could not bring himself to trust the ingenious defector completely and hoped Haverson would continue to keep an eye on him, as he promised.

Despite the outcry voiced by the Sea Vigilantes, the vessel had been converted to nuclear power. The *Aquarius* was capable of carrying nearly three tons of uranium oxide in its reactor, a fuel supply Haverson considered more than adequate for the proposed voyage.

Maslov designed and supervised the installation of an entirely new kind of propeller system for the ship which endowed it with a maximum of power and speed. The four engines which drove the propellers were synchronized, controlled electronically by a sophisticated computer system. Haverson and Maslov estimated that with this four propeller system the *Aquarius* would have a towing capacity equal to approximately eight to ten of the largest tugs in existence.

As the conversion neared the final steps of completion, the ship had to be transferred from the building basin to an outfitting pier where the work would be completed. While the great ship was moored at the outfitting pier, it would be more difficult to protect from sabotage and, therefore, would require more security.

"Cost be damned!" Kirkwood said when Haverson advised him of the matter. "Get all the protection you need. We're too close to completion to allow anything to happen that could set us back."

"Things have progressed far more smoothly than I anticipated," Haverson said. "Maslov and I are anxious to take this baby on a shakedown cruise to see how it handles. We want to eliminate any 'bugs' before setting out to Antarctica."

"So our friend Maslov seems to be working out all right?" Kirkwood asked.

"So far, so good," Haverson replied.

"Just so you keep a good eye on him," Kirkwood advised. "All the security in the world isn't worth a damn if trouble comes from the inside."

"I know, Governor," Haverson said. "Maslov's rarely out of my sight."

"Good," Kirkwood smiled. "Let's keep it that way."

As work on the vessel continued, Sally Brennan kept KHOT viewers up to date with frequent progress reports. The ratings on her "Aquarius Update" segments of the news were very high, and Ken Wilson was anxious to keep it that way. Sally was thoroughly enjoying her success, and glad that she and the ship had captured the public's fancy. But she began to worry about what might happen when the vessel left San Diego and she no longer had the *Aquarius* to report on. Slowly, she decided that she would make the trip to Antarctica and back aboard the ship, and nothing was going to stop her. Unless she could continue to cover the vessel and its progress, she was sure she would be given silly, inconsequential stories to cover again in spite of the fact that Ken Wilson was high on her at the moment and had promised her bigger and better things. Producers' memories were notoriously short, especially when ratings began to slip. Thus, Sally decided it was time to feel out the situation and Neal Haverson seemed the most appropriate place to start.

On the pretext of needing information to prepare another special on the Aquarius Transfer, she called Haverson and invited him to meet her at Madame Wu's Garden in Santa Monica, her favorite Chinese restaurant, for lunch.

"You know, I really feel like I'm a part of this whole Aquarius thing," she remarked, sipping the fragrant, pale tea from the tiny, handleless cup.

"You've been giving the project great coverage," Haverson replied, happy to be with her once again. It reminded him of their time together in London. He enjoyed Sally's company, even though today he felt she might have something up her sleeve.

"Thank you," she smiled. "I've certainly tried to give it my best shot. My dream is to continue to cover the story all the way to Antarctica and back. I'm sure that in this day of sophisticated electronics, it could be easily worked out. From what I understand, the ship is being fitted out with a wide-band transmitter unit that can beam stuff from either videotape or directly from a live-action camera to a synchronous-orbit satellite, so it could transmit programs to ground pickup stations anywhere in the world."

"Well, I had no idea you were so up on all the latest in the communications field." Haverson was impressed.

"There are a lot of things you don't know about me, Captain."

"Maybe so," he conceded.

"Seriously, in my job you have to be up on everything," she said.

"The only problem with your sailing with us is that I'm opposed to having a woman aboard the ship," he said.

"That's a little sexist, don't you think?" she challenged. "Especially when the navy's got women aboard ships in just about any capacity you can name these days. I really didn't expect you to be so chauvinistic."

"Let me explain my reasons," Haverson replied. "There will be an all-male crew of thirty-five. A lone woman

138

among thirty-five men will only be a source of trouble, especially when the woman's ... well ... damned good-looking."

"I don't want compliments," Sally said. "I want aboard the *Aquarius*."

"As long as I'm in charge, you—or any other woman, for that matter—isn't going to sail on my ship."

"Look, I'm not your usual woman. I'm used to working with men. Every story I cover involves working with men—cameramen, soundmen. I know how to handle myself around men," she said.

"Things are a lot different when people are forced to live and work together in relatively close quarters. The situation can get touchy. Believe me, I know." As he spoke he was thinking of that fateful winter at McMurdo when Elizabeth Nagy had attached herself to him, at first as a kind of buffer to demonstrate to the men who outnumbered her hundreds-to-one that she had the commander's protection and, thereby, discourage any of their advances. Later, she became trapped in circumstances of her own making. In spite of the fact that he might have enjoyed Sally's presence aboard the *Aquarius*, he was not willing to risk a repetition of what had happened years before. "My answer is no, and it's going to continue to be," he declared.

"You know, Captain," Sally said, signaling the waiter to bring her the check, "I might be a woman, but I'm not one who takes no for an answer very easily. As a matter of fact, I always regard it as a challenge."

The next few days Sally spent at various newspaper morgues searching for information about the antarctic incident in which Haverson was involved. Once she was satisfied that she was armed with a thorough knowledge of the situation, she arranged a second meeting with Haverson, ostensibly to cover the latest progress on the *Aquarius*.

Although he greeted her in the San Diego shipyard in a friendly manner, he was also somewhat wary, suspecting ulterior motives.

"As far as present technology allows, this ship is nonpolluting," he explained as they toured the ship's sewage treatment plant. "No raw sewage is discharged overboard. All trash will be burned in pollution-free incinerators and the residue held for safe disposal on shore."

"Do the Sea Vigilantes know all this?" Sally asked, referring to the fact that the organization was still picketing the shipyard. She had been forced to cross their picket line to meet Haverson that morning. Amy Armistad, their spokesperson, was now very much in the news as a result of her release from prison through the efforts of Senator Farleigh. She continued to denounce the Aquarius Transfer project with renewed vehemence.

"Those people only hear what they want to hear," Haverson said.

As they returned to his future quarters on the Captain's Bridge Deck she chided, "Surely you don't believe in that old seafaring superstition about a woman on a ship being bad luck, do you?"

"Look, Sally, I have nothing against you personally," he protested. "It's just that . . ."

Before he could finish, she interrupted. "Then why won't you let me go?"

"I explained before," he said, sounding a little annoyed at having to repeat himself. "It's my final word on the subject. "We've been good friends so far. Let's keep it that way."

"Frankly, I thought we might strike a bargain," she said.

"Bargain?" he frowned. "I don't strike bargains on issues like this."

"You might if you were to mention a certain name."

"Whose name?"

"Elizabeth Nagy," she said, carefully watching his face for a reaction. She hated to stoop to this kind of strategy, but she was desperate. She knew that Ken Wilson would not hesitate to demote her if the ratings fell.

Haverson could not conceal his surprise, despite his efforts. "What about Elizabeth Nagy?" he asked.

"Oh, nothing much," she replied, trying to sound as nonchalant as possible. "But on the other hand, maybe too much."

"What are you getting at?" he demanded.

"Some information has come into my possession," she lied. There were no new facts. The ploy was inspired by a newspaper article which noted that the nun-scientist was supposed to have been a prolific letter-writer. "Letters written by Elizabeth Nagy when she was at McMurdo," Sally said. "They're very intersting, especially the parts that mention a certain Captain Neal Haverson . . ."

"Are you trying to blackmail me?" he asked. "My God,

Sally, I can hardly believe my ears. I thought we were friends."

"We are," she assured him, despising her own coyness and the depths to which she was allowing herself to sink in the name of her career.

"Where in the hell did you ever see letters written by Elizabeth Nagy?" he demanded.

"I'm a journalist," she replied. "I know how to investigate a story. I always wondered about your sudden resignation from the navy, especially when it came so soon after the death of Dr. Nagy. I came across names of people who knew her and decided to contact some of them. One of her friends gave me some letters. Do you want me to go on?"

"Okay," Haverson sighed, knowing she had him over a barrel. "What's your price?"

"Price?" she repeated, looking puzzled.

"All blackmailers have a price," he said. "What's yours?"

"I don't have any price," she said. "All I want is to follow through on what I consider an exciting story. But since I'm not allowed to continue my coverage of the Aquarius Transfer once the ship leaves San Diego, I'll have to go after other aspects of the story. I thought that perhaps Elizabeth Nagy with her unique background and tragic death would be a good subject to explore on the air. There are still a lot of unexplained factors surrounding her death. The letters I've seen just might shed some new light on the story."

Haverson was upset by the disclosure of the existence of the letters and wondered whether they might contain information which would help him clear his name. Still, he could not allow Sally to gain the upper hand by openly revealing his interest in the letters.

"On the other hand," she continued, "if I were permitted to sail with the Aquarius, I wouldn't have much interest in pursuing her story. I suppose, Captain, that one might say the choice is up to you."

22

Rico had returned from Switzerland, but his foul, sullen mood had not changed. His multitude of fragment wounds from the blast had been treated successfully and healed, but, unfortunately, had resulted in a mass of small, raised scars all over his body. The plastic surgeon, one of the world's finest, could do little to prevent the scar formation, explaining that in medical terminology Rico was what was known as a "keloid-former," an individual with an inherited tendency to form prominent scars. The boy's skin would never be as sleek and satiny as it had once been.

On his return, Annalise, knowing his almost obsessive love of footwear, presented him with a gift of a pair of ostrich leather shoes, joking that their nubby texture matched his. Rico flew into a rage, heaved the expensive shoes out the window into the carefully tended garden below, and sulked for days. He kept almost exclusively to the bedroom with the drapes drawn both night and day, lying on the bed watching television, and downing large quantities of his favorite artichoke liqueur amid the smoky haze of hashish. As far as Annalise was concerned, Rico was fast becoming both a bore and a liability. The formerly priapic Brazilian seemed to have lost all interest in sex, once his favorite activity. Whenever Annalise subtly suggested that they indulge in their former fun and games, he refused, and when she went further and began to caress him in various erotics spots, hoping to arouse his desire, he cried out in pain. Annalise considered dumping him and importing some fresh, new talent but feared that Rico might retaliate by spilling what he knew to the wrong people; at the moment she could make no changes. She would have to endure his bad moods, indifferences, and sexual apathy a little longer. If, in time, his disposition failed to improve, she would simply contact some of her people who would take care of him for good. Hitmen were all over New York and the price competitive.

Much to Rico's annoyance, his favorite soap opera was preempted by a special covering the departure of the *Aquarius*, and he got up from the bed to turn off the television in disgust.

Normally, Annalise ignored television, even when she and Rico were in the same room, but when she heard the name Aquarius and saw Sally Brennan, microphone in hand, describing the forthcoming voyage of the revolutionary ship, she put aside the special report on the Amazon project that Jeremiah Gaines had given her just before she left the office. "Turn up the sound," she said.

"What?" Rico asked, certain he had not heard correctly. Annalise usually wanted the sound lowered.

"Turn up the sound, I said," she repeated, and Rico obliged, looking at her as if she had suddenly gone mad.

When the words, "FILMED EARLIER FOR BROADCAST AT THIS TIME" appeared on the screen, Annalise realize that the ship had already left San Diego and was probably heading out to sea at that moment.

"That sneaky bastard!" she muttered, startling Rico for the second time.

"Who is a bastard?" he asked.

"Kirkwood," she replied. "I know what he's done. He's had that ship leave earlier than the announced time. Oh! That sneaky sonofabitch! The Sea Vigilantes planned a massive demonstration to coincide with the ship's departure. When they arrive on the scene they'll be too late. The ship's already gone. He's managed to outfox us this time—but not for long."

On the flickering screen, Sally Brennan continued her patter: "This highly unusual ship about to embark on an eight-thousand-mile journey to Antarctica to bring back a gigantic iceberg for thirsty California is a technical marvel, to say the least. I have here with me now on deck the two men who are primarily responsible for getting this whole project off the ground." At that moment the camera pulled back revealing Haverson and Maslov standing beside her. Briefly, she interviewed each. Haverson modestly gave most of the credit for the conversion of the ship and its many technical innovations to Maslov, and Maslov, in turn, praised Haverson for devising the entire project in the first place. As the two men departed to attend to what Sally described as "urgent last minute details," a helicopter, bearing the seal of the state of California, landed on the deck of the converted supertanker and none other than Governor Paul Kirkwood stepped out, looking cheerful and triumphant.

"You must be very, very pleased today, Governor," Sally said, thrusting her microphone in front of him.

"Yes, Sally, I am," he agreed. "I am indeed. This is a proud and happy moment not only for me, but for all of California and, if I may project into the future a bit, the world as well." He went on to extol the project, thank the people involved, and assure viewers that if it were as successful as he hoped it would be, the great drought would not only be at an end, but it was unlikely that California would ever face the risk of another one again. Much to Annalise's annoyance, he went on to say that the *Aquarius* offered hope not just to California but to other arid parts of the world as well, which were watching with avid interest, especially those nations considering other far more costly and ecologically hazardous means of obtaining water.

"That bastard!" Annalise cursed. "You know what he's referring to, don't you?" she asked Rico who could not have been less interested in her business dealings. "He's referring to Hydrolliance's projects—my projects. He's trying to discredit us. He thinks he's being so subtle about it. . . ."

Kirkwood concluded his remarks, waved goodbye to the camera, and flew off again in his helicopter. At that moment, Annalise's private line rang. It was Farleigh from Washington. "Have you heard?" he asked.

"Of course, I've heard," she replied. "Rico and I are watching the television now."

"I told you we should have blown up that goddam ship instead of the aqueduct," Farleigh said.

"We will take appropriate steps against that ship when the time is right. We mustn't be too hasty. It's best to strike when the ship is most vulnerable. Our time will come, but later. We must be patient. By the way, how is Amy working out?"

"Okay, so far," he replied. "She got her first check this week. You should have seen the smile on her greedy little face. At first she insisted on being paid in cash, but when I told her that no employees on my staff would be paid in cash, she was suddenly willing to accept a check. She's still throwing her weight around a little and is going to have to be taken down a peg or two. Not only does she like the money she's earning as special advisor to me and my staff, but she also wallows in the publicity."

"I thought she suffered from a star complex right from the start," Annalise commented.

"Both her and that crazy old coot, Terhune," Farleigh said.

"Don't knock Terhune," Annalise cautioned. "He and his silly idealism have been very useful to us and—unlike Ms. Armistad—we get him for nothing."

"We aren't going to ease up on Kirkwood now that the ship's on its way, are we?" Farleigh asked. No matter what Annalise chose to do, he would never abandon his personal vendetta against his hated political rival.

"Of course not," she said. "You've got to believe me, Preston, when I tell you I have everything worked out—everything. Now stop fretting and trust me."

François Gaspar, the *Aquarius*'s French-born pilot, stood at the rail and, with great enthusiasm, guided the great boat away from the outfitting pier, calling out his commands loud and clear in his appealing French accent.

"Wheel fifteen degrees port," Gaspar called out.

"Port fifteen," Alex MacFergus, the Scottish First Officer, echoed across the bridge.

"All right, stop it," Gaspar said.

"Stop it," MacFergus relayed.

Haverson remained inside the bridgehouse, listening to the orders as they were relayed to him, saying little, glancing from time to time at the Bridge Movement Book.

"Slow ahead," Gaspar called out.

"Slow ahead," MacFergus repeated.

By now the bows were moving faster, the San Diego skyline rapidly fading in the distance.

"Tell them to let go," Haverson said, referring to the tugs surrounding the great ship. MacFergus relayed the order to the crewmen on the bows by means of his VHF radio, the standard means of communication across the vast expanses of the vessel. All officers carried portable VHF radios, and orders and responses cackled continuously, especially when the crew was moving about busily, tossing the lines to the tugs and bringing in those loosened by the shore.

"Port. South, three-six-zero," MacFergus said, and the men on the bows worked the lines feverishly. "That's the port tug gone," he said to Haverson.

"Three-four-five."

"Starboard tug gone."

One by one the tugs were released, and with a friendly, farewell toot, they headed back into the yard. When they were free, Haverson ordered, "All ahead full," and the *Aquarius* was underway, under its own steam.

The ship made its way along a south-southwest course following the coast of California. Haverson, Maslov, Gaspar, MacFergus, and the rest of the crew were delighted with its early performance and handling. All of them realized, of course, that the first leg of the journey was, by far, the easiest. The real challenge would come much later when the ship reached antarctic waters. The turbulent, icy, fog-shrouded Southern ocean surrounding that most forbidding and mysterious of continents was the supreme test of any vessel.

Haverson knew that once the ship reached the vicinity of Clipperton Island, a tiny speck of land about twelve hundred miles directly west of Costa Rica, there were two possible routes they could take. The shorter of the two was naturally more direct, heading south between one-hundred-twenty and one-hundred-fifty degrees west longitude, far from any land throughout the voyage, except for one point near the Tropic of Capricorn where it would pass between Pitcairn and Easter islands. The other, longer route followed the west coast of South America closely, veering sharply westward, however, off the southern coast of Chile and ultimately arriving at the same point—approximately one-hundred-seventy degrees west longitude—as the first route. Before departing, Haverson consulted with his officers and after some discussion decided to take the shorter route going down and the longer returning. If there were trouble, it was far more likely to occur on the return trip when the ship was towing the iceberg and, hence, it might be advantageous to be relatively close to ports along the coast which were within the range of the helicopter the *Aquarius* carried in a special hangar on deck.

The first few days out were relatively smooth. As far as Haverson was concerned, the only fly in the ointment was Sally Brennan, not that he was unaware of her good looks and lively personality that he had often appreciated under different circumstances. Still smoldering over the way she had blackmailed her way aboard, he was determined to make things as difficult as possible for her. Perhaps if conditions got sufficiently unpleasant, she would ask to be put ashore. Haverson would be only too happy to oblige. He had seen to it that Sally was housed in what had once been the owner's suite when the ship was an ordinary supertanker. It was located on the Captain's Bridge Deck between his own suite and that of Chief Engineer Maslov. Her quarters were spacious and comfortable but isolated from the rest of the officers and crew. In addition, he directed her to take her meals alone in the officer's dining room after he and the others had finished. This edict did not sit well with the naturally gregarious Sally. In consideration of their past camaraderie, he did assure her, however, that he would try not to interfere with her work, although she would have his approval on all stories and seek his permission before engaging in any kind of extended contact with the men.

"In other words I'm essentially in isolation. Quarantined, for God's sake!" Sally protested angrily. "You know what you remind me of? A goddam sorority housemother."

Haverson grinned and shrugged indifferently. "I'm just giving you the rules," he said. "As long as I'm running this ship, they're going to be obeyed. Now that we're out at sea your 'letters' aren't going to do you much good."

To add to Sally's annoyance, she had been prevented from bringing along her KHOT camera- and soundmen. Before departing, Haverson informed her that there were well-qualified men and equipment aboard to assist her in the taping and transmission of her reports and, thus, no need for outsiders. When Sally appealed to Kirkwood for help in getting around Haverson's rigid rules, the governor reminded her that the captain was in charge and obliged to maintain security on the voyage, especially when there was an ever-present threat of sabotage. Many of Haverson's rules, Kirkwood felt, were for security purposes and he explained that she might unknowingly make disclosures that would place the ship in jeopardy. Reluctantly she had accepted the conditions Haverson laid down, although she didn't like the situation and was determined not to let him humiliate her further. So far he seemed to be doing a good job of it.

"You know, Captain," she remarked, as she submitted some material for his approval, "I'm not very fond of dining alone. I have no intention of trying to seduce any of your men right there in the dining room—if that's what you're worried about. I mean, I'm tired of being treated like a leper."

"When I agreed to take you aboard, you agreed to abide by the rules. That was the deal," he reminded her. "One of the rules was that you would not mingle with the officers or the crew."

Sally pondered his answer a moment or two. "Isn't it customary for the captain to have guests at his table?" she asked.

"Some do," he conceded, recalling rather unenthusiastically his recent cruise-ship days.

"But not you?"

"I don't dine with blackmailers, if that's what you mean," he said, scrawled his initials on her papers, and handed them back to her.

Considering its huge size, the *Aquarius* handled easily and smoothly. Gaspar swore it was far superior in that respect to many smaller ships. They were just off Punta Eugenia in the center of the Baja California peninsula. Both Haverson and Maslov decided to stick fairly close to shore on this leg of the journey until they were absolutely certain all the complex and highly sophisticated equipment was working to their satisfaction.

"Well, I've stopped crossing my fingers," Haverson said to Maslov one night as they met just outside the bridgehouse. "How about you?"

Maslov frowned. "I'm sorry, but I don't understand," he admitted. Although his English was excellent, he had trouble with certain idiomatic expressions.

"What I mean is, I now have confidence in the ship," Haverson explained.

"Why would you not?" Maslov replied matter-of-factly, preparing to check on the nuclear reactors below. "I have always had confidence."

Immersing herself in her work, Sally planned stories on some aspect of the voyage or the ship every day and, as ordered, submitted all material and requests for interviews with the various personnel for Haverson's approval. He treated her coolly but with reasonable courtesy and rarely censored her efforts or denied her request for camera- and soundmen. In her reports she never failed to present him in an extremely flattering light, hoping to gain some changes in the rigid rules he had imposed on her.

"Look, Captain," she said, "according to the interview you gave me, we might be on this ship together for months, right?"

"It's conceivable," he agreed. "Of course, you might decide you want off the ship earlier."

"I intend to stick it out to the end," Sally assured him.

"Well, that's your decision."

"Why can't we be friends?" she said almost pleadingly.

" 'Friends'?" he repeated, raising his eyebrows. "Friends don't usually blackmail each other."

"I'm sorry," she said, sounding genuinely apologetic. "I admit it was a rotten thing to do, but you've got to understand how desperate I was. I had to follow through on a story that was hot, one that I was with from the beginning. I couldn't let it just slip away from me. You have to admit, I tried every respectable way I knew. The letters bit was the last resort. I'm truly sorry I stooped to something as low as that, but my career—my whole life—was on the line, and I was willing to do anything. Try and understand, will you?"

"The only thing I understand is that I'm stuck with you," Haverson said. "And, frankly, I don't like it."

23

Every day at twelve o'clock Haverson in the longstanding tradition of the sea, met with his men for the noon chat, formally presenting them with such information as the ship's mileage since the previous noon, its speed, and other statistics pertinent to the voyage. Now well south of Mexico, the *Aquarius* was entering the tropics where the heat was damp and intense and the sky and sea seemed to melt together in a single misty union.

"I'm pleased to announce," Haverson said, "that the ship has been making excellent progress so far. In a very short time, if all goes well, we will be crossing the equator."

"And you know what that means, sir," Lew Corbin, the radio operator, his young face full of pleasant anticipation.

MacFergus drew deep on the pipe clenched between his teeth and said, "Aye, we've got to initiate all those crossing the equator for the first time into the realm of Neptune, King of the Deep."

"I doubt if any men aboard this ship are crossing for the first time," Haverson replied.

"Don't limit yourself to one sex, Captain," MacFergus said. "We're an integrated crew."

Maslov, who had seemed uninterested until this point, suddenly sat up straight in his chair. "Are you talking about Sally?" he asked.

"She's our token female," Corbin said.

"She is also not a part of the crew of this ship," Haverson said.

"Maybe not officially," Gaspar said with a shrug.

"Besides, I don't think it would be wise for her to participate in any ceremonies," Haverson said and quickly returned to official business before any of the men could raise any objections.

The moment Sally heard about the approaching equator crossing and the traditional ceremony, she was determined to take part in it no matter what Haverson ruled. She knew that she would not only enjoy the celebration, but it would also be a good human interest story to send back to the station, which would contrast nicely with the more serious material she had been transmitting. In order to overcome Haverson's edict, she decided to enlist Maslov's help. Recently he had managed to pursuade Haverson to allow her to play chess with him in the wardroom, and she hoped he could be equally persuasive in this matter as well. "You've got to help me get around Haverson, Yuri," she said, advancing her knight. "I know he's going to exclude me from that King Neptune business, and it's important to me."

Studying the chessboard intently, contemplating his next move, Maslov replied, "You must be allowed to celebrate your first crossing of the equator. It is a very important event in the life of anyone devoted to the sea."

The next morning at breakfast, the chief engineer appealed to Haverson in Sally's behalf. "You must allow her to participate, Neal," Maslov urged.

First Officer Alex MacFergus stirred his coffee and listening sympathetically. He decided to speak up. "If you don't let her," he said in his soft Scottish burr, "I'm going to hear a lot of moaning and groaning from the crew."

By the time pilot François Gaspar had added his vote for Sally, breakfast was over and Haverson had reluctantly relented. Sally would be permitted to be initiated into Neptune's realm.

The day of the celebration was as bright and balmy as Sally hoped. The men were already lively and boisterous and ribbed her as she gave instructions to the cameramen who were to record the ceremonies for KHOT. Haverson's appearance on deck from time to time kept things from getting out of hand. Sally knew he didn't like her participation in the proceedings, and she hoped he wouldn't interfere, at least not until after she got some good footage. MacFergus persevered on his bagpipes despite the good-natured jeering of the men, and Gaspar played his accordion, giving the festivities a slightly nostalgic Parisian air. Maslov broke out some Russian vodka he had stashed away in his quarters, grabbed Sally by the arm while she was conferring with the soundmen, and forced her to dance a wild Russian *kopak* with him on top of the refreshments table. As they whirled about madly, Sally became giddy and breathless and emitted a loud squeal as Maslov suddenly hoisted her high in the air, twirling her over his head while the men cheered. When he finally set her down, he grabbed her and planted an enthusiastic kiss on her mouth.

Shoving his way through the crowd of men around the refreshments table, Haverson grabbed Sally. "All right, that's enough," he said. "Somebody's going to get hurt."

Sally tried to squirm out of his hold. "Hey, what is this?" she said, still dizzy from the wild dance on the table top. "Can't anybody have any fun around here?"

Haverson looked at her askance and Sally felt suddenly embarrassed and ridiculous, dressed as she was in halter, grass skirt fashioned from old newspapers, and a mop dyed bright red on her head as a wig. "Come on," he said quietly but firmly. "I'll escort you back to your quarters."

"Suppose I'm not ready to go back to my quarters," she challenged. "And, besides, I don't need an escort, thank you." She attempted to shake loose from his hold on her, knocking the golden paper crown atop her head askew.

"You're going," he said, steering her across the deck toward the elevator.

At the door of her suite, situated between his own and Maslov's, she attempted to insert the key in the lock but fumbled badly. Impatient, Haverson snatched it from her, effortlessly slipped it into the lock, and opened the door. "Good night," he said brusquely.

Hands indignantly on hips, Sally said, "Want to know what you are?"

"No, not particularly," he said, about to close the door and leave.

"I'll tell you anyway. You're a goddam party pooper," she said, petulantly. "A festivities fucker. That's what you are."

With an indifferent shrug, Haverson said, "Well, everybody's got to be something," and closed the door after her.

Beyond the equator, the next important crossing was the Tropic of Capricorn, which separated the tropic zone from the Southern Hemisphere's temperate zone. It occurred a few days later when the moist, oppressive heat gradually seemed to dissipate, giving way to fresher air and a more distinct definition between sky and sea.

The voyage was still proceeding smoothly and the ship functioning well with far fewer problems than anticipated. By means of the sophisticated communications system, Kirkwood kept close tabs on the odyssey from his Sacramento office. His total faith in the ultimate success of the mission contributed greatly toward maintaining a high level of morale aboard ship.

At station KHOT Ken Wilson was elated with the reports Sally was sending back. Hopeful California television audiences faithfully tuned in to follow the latest news of the *Aquarius* and ratings soared.

As the ship continued south, leaving the tropics and entering the temperate zone of the Southern Hemisphere, the weather grew progressively cooler, requiring heavier clothing, although not the special fur-lined red nylon parkas designed for the Antarctic. The clear, fresh days soon gave way to rainy ones, and the frigid currents rushing north from the Southern ocean brought with them dense fog and masses of dark, threatening clouds. It was not at all unusual for those aboard the *Aquarius* to find the ship completely engulfed in an impenetrable shroud, the decks wet, the damp chill of seawater pervading everywhere.

"As you can see, folks," Sally said on the television screen, her image fuzzier than usual because of the disturbances in the weather, "things are not always sunny and bright in the South Pacific. Today, I'm going to talk with a man who plays a big part in the life of a ship, radio operator, Lew Corbin."

At that point, Sally led the cameras into the radio room and introduced the viewers to Lew, a tall, lanky, shy youth with a faint trace of an Oklahoma accent.

"Lew works amidst all these glowing dials and banks of communications equipment. This is probably worth hundreds of thousands of dollars. Wouldn't you say, Lew?"

"I'd say easily that much, ma'am," the radio operator agreed from his swivel seat in front of the equipment just mentioned. While they talked, their conversation was punctuated by the steady cacophony of static and the howl of Morse code.

Lew explained to Sally that the third and final major geographic line the ship would cross was the Antarctic Circle, and that by the time it was finally reached, the days of smooth sailing through relatively untroubled waters would

153

be over. More and more the crew would have to depend on the ship's sophisticated electronic system to guide them to their final objective.

As they drew closer to their destination, dense fog often surrounded the *Aquarius* for days at a time, enveloping it in clammy, icy swirls of feathery dampness. For the unaccustomed, it created an ominous feeling of being cut off from the rest of the world, insulated in a chilly, cottony blanket.

When the ship eventually emerged from a particularly thick fog bank, one could see that the formerly clear, azure skies of the more northerly latitudes had become a threatening, foreboding gray. Often, the horizon was difficult to discern, as dull gray merged into dull gray. Both Haverson and Maslov were familiar with the waters surrounding the Antarctic continent and knew that the real test of the ship still lay ahead. The Southern ocean's seas were the most terrible on earth, a region where storm height rose to sixty feet (as opposed to the North Atlantic's dreaded forty feet), and gales could swirl round and round, unimpeded by geographical barriers, free to build in power and size.

As the *Aquarius* sliced across the Antarctic Circle, the wind was fairly steady—about force eight or nine on the Beaufort scale—but in the distant southwest, the gray skies were deepening into a dense, menacing purple, which experienced sailors knew meant trouble.

The ship sailed quietly into the night, falling southwest with the wind, which began to increase markedly, howling eerily over the deck, weird and elemental, stirring up dread among the men. Soon, the air temperature plunged below freezing, and a few tentative flakes of snow began to fall. The waves no longer succeeded one another in an orderly fashion, but degenerated into a confused, haphazard mass of surging water. From the bridge one could smell the crests as they broke against the hull, furiously, one after the other. The light snowfall, which had begun at sunset, quickly became a blizzard, driven over the top of the churning sea by the wind.

Through snow, wind, and raging seas the *Aquarius* had to fight to maintain its southwesterly course, staggering a little from time to time as it plunged into the deep troughs between waves, its bows striking with an almost explosive impact, sending shudders throughout, struggling to right itself before another wall of water struck. Rolling and pitching, the ship valiantly battled its way through the savage sea.

Because of the heavy seas and the severity of the storm, Haverson was forced to order the ship's speed reduced. He also made a special point of instructing Sally to remain in her quarters.

"Stay in my quarters?" she repeated. "What is this?"

"It's an order," he replied. "For your own safety."

"Yes, sir," she said sarcastically as he walked away.

Alone in the confined space while the ship tossed and rolled, she grew increasingly uneasy and claustrophobic as well as nauseated for the first time since leaving San Diego. Sally had prided herself on not succumbing to seasickness and was determined to preserve her record and fight off the dizziness and urge to vomit developing in the pit of her stomach.

If I could just get some air, she told herself, I know I'd feel better.

The driving blizzard almost obscured the windlashed waters, and perhaps, if she had had a better idea of the ferociousness of the weather beyond the windows of her suite, she might not have felt so compelled to disobey Haverson's order and leave.

Earlier when the storm was less severe, she had encountered Maslov, who laughed at the weather and ridiculed her fears. "This is nothing," he said. "You should have seen the storms I had to fight when I attempted to sail around Antarctica alone. They were *real* storms."

Bundled up against the subzero cold in the special red parka designed for the Antarctic, Sally struggled with the door of her cabin. What she did not realize was that, outside, the wind was howling up the stairwell with such force that it created a vacuumlike effect that made the door nearly impossible to open. Never one to give up easily, Sally struggled with it, and finally, after great effort on her part, it gave. Shivering under the sudden impact of the extreme cold, she began to make her way down the five flights of stairs to the main deck, a descent made extremely difficult by the continuous pitching and rolling of the ship.

If I can just get some air, Sally said to herself, clutching her queasy stomach.

The closer she got to the main deck, the more aware she was of the fury of the storm, but Sally was not one to turn back or give up easily.

As the ship heaved and rolled and crashed into, and then

under, the huge troughs, it seemed no match for the raging sea.

At the doorway leading to the main deck, she paused a moment, seriously considering whether or not conditions on the other side just might not be too severe for her to step outside, but her reporter's curiosity won out over her better judgment. She was determined not only to get a breath of fresh air in hopes of calming her churning stomach, but to witness the storm firsthand, experience it as she had so many other things in her news-gathering past, get the impact of nature at its most furious—danger be damned.

Up in the bridge, Haverson was seated near the primary control console, which stretched the full width beneath the huge armored windows, checking the illuminated digital displays which kept him informed on the functioning of the ship. Although the blizzard badly hampered his vision, Haverson, with his keen powers of observation, suddenly spotted a lone figure emerging onto the main deck.

"Who the hell is that?" he exclaimed aloud.

MacFergus, in the navagational area at the rear of the bridge, heard him and rose from the chart table to join him.

"Maybe it's Greg Dunne going to check on the chopper," the Scotsman suggested.

Peering through his binoculars, Haverson replied, "No, that person is far too slight in build to be Dunne."

"Then who is it, sir?" MacFergus asked, puzzled.

"I don't know, but I'm going to find out," Haverson said, leaping to his feet so fast he startled the First Officer.

Racing down the steps, two at a time, Haverson reached the main deck in seconds and threw open the door. Despite the darkness of the storm, he made out the individual he had seen from above. He—or could it be *she?*—was clutching desperately to the railing which surrounded the base of the superstructure. As he edged closer, he realized that his suspicion was correct. It was *she*—Sally.

"Goddamit, Sally," he shouted in anger, bracing against the wind and snow which rasped at him like sharp, cutting icy fingers. He was furious at her, not only for obviously disobeying his order to stay in her cabin, but also for putting herself in such obvious and unnecessary danger. She was frozen with fear, unable to move. "I'm coming after you. Don't move! Stay right where you are. I'm coming to get you," he yelled, doubtful that she could hear him above the roar of the wind. "Just hang on." He could not tell from her expression

156

whether or not she had heard his words. Her features seemed paralyzed with terror.

Suddenly above them both he saw a great wall of water rising on the starboard side and knew that it was only a matter of seconds before it would come crashing down over the deck, sweeping all over the side in its wake. There was no time to inch his way along the rail. Letting go, he dived down the deck, grabbed the railing on either side of Sally and pinned her against the deck with his own body, praying he could just hold on. Sally simply stared at him, her eyes wide with fright.

As the ten-foot-high wall of angry water was about to smash down on them with all its fury, a near miracle occurred. A trough apparently opened on the port side away from the wave and the vessel simply rolled down into it, evading the peak force of the exploding mountain of icy water. Haverson closed his eyes, shook his head, gave a sigh of relief, and uttered a silent prayer.

As the ship righted itself once more, rolling over to its opposite side, a shudder reverberated through its hull. Foamy, white, waist-deep water swirled about the pair, engulfing the entire deck before it was gone again, as quickly as it had come, over the side.

Shivering, soaking wet, and cold down to her very bones, Sally, thoroughly shaken by the experience, suddenly collapsed in Haverson's arms.

"Maybe next time when I give you an order, you'll follow it," he reprimanded, shouting over the howling wind. Somehow this same woman who seemed so strong and defiant and angry on other occasions seemed now helpless and vulnerable, stirring his sympathies. Haverson took her limp body, which seemed surprisingly light, into his arms and headed back inside.

24

At dawn the following morning the storm suddenly abated, the seas calmed, and only a few scattered snow flurries dotted the air. In the distance layers of clouds were beginning to break up, and the wind velocity diminished considerably, although it was still strong enough to slow the ship. By the time breakfast chimes rang, the clouds had completely dispersed and the sky was a clear, brilliant blue, all traces of snow only a memory, the summer sun dazzlingly bright above a cloudless horizon.

Sally recovered quickly from her near disaster, and Haverson, apparently in a forgiving mood, consented to her request for an interview.

Because of the favorable change in the weather, Sally decided to conduct the interview out on the wings of the bridge where the wind tousled Haverson's blond hair and the bright sun highlighted his gaunt-boned face with its square jaw and deep-set light eyes. Secretly, Sally suspected that his dashing good looks were a definite factor in the high ratings her televised segments were receiving.

"I've had enough experience sailing this part of the globe to know that weather around here is the most fickle," he said. "This present clearing we're enjoying is temporary at best. In these seas you've got to learn to expect the unexpected."

"How would you evaluate the *Aquarius*'s performance thus far, Captain?" Sally asked, looking thoroughly absorbed and earnest.

"This ship is amazingly steady," Haverson replied. "She's been running a straight course before these heavy seas, persevering through the storms, taking each one in stride, not showing much sign of strain. Her average speed has declined somewhat since she entered the turbulent waters of the Southern ocean, but we anticipated that. Then, too, we've experienced thick fog, sometimes for days on end, and the ice pack, which drifts north in summer, has impeded our progress a little, too."

Suddenly, one day, Sally awoke and found that the ship seemed to have burst into an open sea free of both fog and ice floes. The transformation seemed almost incredible. Many of the crew wandering about the deck seemed as impressed as she was. Even the most experienced sailors were touched with awe. Deciding this was definitely material for a broadcast, she collared Maslov before her cameras.

"Could you tell us something about where we are?" she asked as the camera panned the lofty, snow-covered peaks rising in the distance. "After all that time at sea, this is the first land any of us has seen."

"We are now entering the Ross Sea," Maslov replied, amused by everyone's reaction to the first glimpses of the continent at the bottom of the globe. "The mountains you see are in an area known as Victoria Land, named, I believe, after the British queen."

"Yes, and we've begun to see wildlife native to Antarctica—seals, gannets, and penguins—basking on the ice floes or flying over the ship or swimming beside it." As she spoke, Sally directed the cameraman to get a shot of an enormous walrus as it climbed out of the icy, kelpy water onto a floating chunk of sea ice and exhaled a fine, misty spray beneath its curved ivory tusks.

The ship continued across the Ross Sea, southward past Possession and Franklin islands, until a smoking volcano was sighted. Maslov identified it as Mount Erebus and even pointed out the wreckage of the DC-10 on its slopes from the crash in 1979 in which a planeload of tourists lost their lives.

Sally saw to it that the television cameras caught the barrel-hulled Coast Guard icebreakers as they plowed channels through the dissolving pack ice. The scene served as a great backdrop for an impromptu interview with the ship's ranking officer.

"We've already had several giant T-5 tankers loaded with aviation diesel and automotive fuel call at McMurdo utilizing these sea lanes," the captain of a Coast Guard ship informed the KHOT viewers. "Of course, we'll have to widen the sea lanes considerably to accommodate a ship as large as the *Aquarius.*"

Prior to the vessel's arrival Haverson had notified Jim Donovan, the commanding officer of the naval support force, and was assured that the ship and its mission would receive the fullest support and cooperation.

At one time in their naval careers, Donovan and Haverson had been shipmates. They had remained good friends ever since. When Haverson had announced his resignation from the navy, Jim had been one of those who had written expressing his regrets. Haverson valued his fellow officer's support and loyalty and was counting on his help in the *Aquarius*'s mission.

As they crossed the Ross Sea, the crew became aware of icebergs for the first time, and Sally recorded the reaction on tape. She got some great first impressions from the men. Then she sought out Haverson.

"These are not relatively small, thin chunks of sea ice we've been plowing through for days," Haverson explained on camera, "but the huge masses of glacial ice originating from the Ross Ice Shelf, a sheer white wall of ice one hundred and eighty to two hundred feet high and as big in area as California. Some of the icebergs themselves are as large as Rhode Island or Connecticut. They're propelled through the water by subsurface currents. Only one-ninth of their volume is visible above the ocean surface. They move in much the same way a great ship does, plowing easily through the fields of pack ice."

"Are you picking out our iceberg?" Sally asked.

"No," he replied. "For now, we're only observing numbers—things like that."

"Well, there sure seem to be plenty to choose from," she said.

"It would be impossible to select an iceberg for towing simply by using one's eye," he went on. "We've got to know how they are inside and beneath the water—whether there are any cracks or defects—how tightly they are packed. Things like that . . ."

"How do you determine those factors, Captain?"

"From information we get from satellites," he answered. "We will utilize data gathered at the satellite tracking station at McMurdo."

"I see," Sally nodded, although her understanding was sketchy at best.

"This Ross Ice Shelf sits on the land at the south end of McMurdo between Ross Island and Victoria Land, but at its outer edge it actually floats on the sea," he explained. "Great chunks break off and float away. These are the flat-topped or 'tabular' icebergs, like the ones we've been seeing."

"They're so big they look like islands," Sally remarked.

"Some of the early explorers thought they *were* islands," Haverson said, going on to say that the converted super-tanker would travel up the lane carved in the sea ice until it proved unwise to go further because of the uncertainty of the depth of the water. "We'll anchor as close to McMurdo as possible and commute between ship and the base by Coast Guard cutter."

"What about the *Aquarius*'s helicopter?" she asked.

"Flying in the Antarctic can be very tricky," Haverson said. "Besides, Coast Guard boats can transport many more people ashore at a time. The helicopter would have to make quite a few trips back and forth."

Impatient to get off the ship and plant her feet on solid ground again, Sally joined the men on deck waiting to board one of the cutters Haverson mentioned which was pulling alongside the *Aquarius*. The wind was so cold it took her breath away. While they were waiting, MacFergus loaned her his binoculars.

"I'm sure you'll be wanting to do some broadcasts on it," he said. "It's a fascinating place, I hear."

Sally was surprised to see a crowd on shore watching *them* with binoculars. Obviously the arrival of the ship generated great excitement.

"They don't get many visitors down here, you know," MacFergus remarked.

In the distance, she noted the same volcano she had seen earlier from further out at sea. Instead of black smoke, Mount Erebus was now spewing forth a column of white steam, which the fierce wind quickly swept away.

The landing pier at McMurdo proved to be a great slab of ice covered with a layer of volcanic ash and dirt. Haverson, the first off the Coast Guard boat, was greeted by his old friend Jim Donovan, who escorted him to a fleet of heated trucks which were to convey the crew of the *Aquarius* to the base.

"Neal, great to see you again," Donovan said in a hearty,

jovial tone. He was a distinguished-looking man with prematurely gray hair and heavy black eyebrows. Years earlier when they had served together he had been tall and slender. Haverson could see that with time, he had put on weight. "That's quite a ship you've got for yourself. I'm not sure just how I'd classify it."

"Me either, Jim," Haverson said.

The military trucks bumped over the tidal crack that separated ice from land and proceeded onto a gray ash-and-lava road leading to a collection of sheetmetal quonset huts and burlap-and-board buildings seemingly scattered at random about a relatively small area. These structures were connected by slushy roadways, pipes, and power lines. Donovan took great pride in pointing out newly constructed buildings among the power station, hangar, clubs, mess halls, laboratories, satellite tracking station, dispensary, theater. Also rows of trucks, both wheeled and tracked, bulldozers, and other heavy-duty vehicles stood in readiness beside some of the buildings.

Towering fourteen thousand feet into the air, the massive volcanic cinder cone of Mount Erebus dominated the McMurdo site from all directions. As they drew closer, Sally, sharing a truck cab with Haverson and Donovan, observed a cross visible near the summit and in true reporter fashion asked about it.

"That cross was hauled up there by members of Scott's last expedition. They placed it on the mountain in memory of the explorer and those who died with him," Donovan explained. Very few women visited McMurdo and not many who did were as attractive and vicacious as Sally. Donovan wondered what her relationship to Haverson might be. Even though he had been married when the two officers had served together, Donovan had noted his friend's predilection for strong-minded, independent women.

"Nothing's really changed much," Haverson said, looking out at the base.

"We're living up to the saying that in the Antarctic everything is preserved for eternity," Donovan replied, referring to the fact that the extreme cold kept everything permanently frozen, providing little chance for decay. "This entire continent is in 'cold storage,' so to speak."

Building #165 housed the administrative offices, including that of the base commander, which Haverson had once occupied, and was the center of naval activity. At Sally's request,

Donovan·arranged a tour of the base for her and the rest of the crew but did not accompany them. When they were off, he lost no time in inviting Haverson to his office for a talk.

"Well, Neal, how does it feel to be back?" he asked when they were alone.

"A little strange," Haverson replied, looking over the quarters he once occupied. Donovan had made few changes. Only the photographs of the wife and children on the desk were different.

"Yes, I guess so," Donovan said, opening a bottle of Scotch he kept in a desk drawer and filling two glasses. "I want you to know that I think this mission of yours is damned exciting. And important."

"I think it is," Haverson agreed. "Otherwise, I guess I wouldn't have taken it on."

"I suppose not," Donovan said, "It must have been pretty hard—coming back here, I mean. Tell me, Neal, do you miss the navy?"

"Sure. Sometimes," Haverson admitted. "But I try not to think about it too much."

"I suppose if it hadn't been for that incident . . ."

"You mean Elizabeth Nagy's death?" Haverson said.

"Yes," Donovan replied. "If it hadn't been for her death, you might still be one of us?"

"Possibly," Haverson conceded.

"It was a tragic thing," Donovan lamented, shaking his neatly barbered head. "They say she was a brilliant scientist."

"Yes, she was."

"I see you have a woman in your current party," Donovan said. "What's her name?—Sally Brennan?"

"I didn't choose to have her aboard the *Aquarius*," Haverson said.

"She said that she's been giving your mission good TV coverage."

"That she has," Haverson nodded.

"Anyway, she's damned attractive."

"I suppose she is," Haverson responded indifferently.

"I also hear you've got that Russian defector in your crew," Donovan said. "I'm surprised you're working with Maslov. I understand that he gave you a pretty rough time when you were in charge here."

"He did," Haverson said. "But I needed him. He's working out okay."

"You're not worried about his loyalty?" Donovan asked.

"Sure I'm worried about it," Haverson readily admitted. "I'm worried as hell about it. The only thing I can do is keep an eye on him and believe that he's going to be loyal until there's evidence to the contrary."

"How do you get along with him personally?"

"Okay. No big problems so far."

"Good," Donovan smiled.

"You know, I've been trying to familiarize myself with your work in my free time, which as you know, there's a lot of around here. I admire what you've done, what you are trying to do."

"Thanks, Jim."

"I want you to know that everybody here is ready to cooperate fully with you in every way," Donovan continued.

"Just let me know what you need. You have all our personnel and equipment at your disposal."

"We're pretty well equipped for the job, but we can still use all the help we can get. I certainly appreciate your offer," Haverson said.

"As I told you, we're going to have to make a lot of use of the Satellite Tracking Station. It's important that we select the best iceberg possible for transport back to the States."

"I understand," Donovan replied.

After a short while Neal and Donovan decided to tour the Eklund Biological Center where Elizabeth Nagy had her laboratory. Her research involving krill was now being completed by one of her former students.

Looking over the tanks filled with the tiny crustaceans that Elizabeth Nagy had been studying so intently, believing there were the world's future source of protein, Haverson allowed himself to reminisce about the past, despite Donovan's presence, recalling the times he and the nun-scientist spent together during the seemingly endless darkness of the antarctic winter. Though someone else now occupied the laboratory, it still looked very much the way it did when Elizabeth Nagy was alive. As he stood there, he could almost see her bending over her microscope, jotting notes, sipping coffee, smiling in that special way as he entered. The one thing Neal Haverson remembered about Elizabeth's lab was the smell of brewing coffee—rich, dark, European coffee. For the personnel wintering over in the Antarctic, days and nights were no longer determined by the clock, but by whatever work they wished to accomplish. Elizabeth's work was studying the tiny krill in her tanks at various intervals. These observation periods were always accompanied by lots of coffee to help her and her assistant get through those long night-days. Her mother-house had been most reluctant to grant her permission to winter over in Antarctica amidst an almost exclusively male population. One of the strict conditions they imposed was that she be accompanied by another young nun who would serve as her lab assistant as well as chaperone. Unfortunately the lab assistant-sister had great difficulty adjusting to the perpetual night of winter and seemed to require inordinate amounts of sleep, frequently leaving Elizabeth unaccompanied in her laboratory.

Haverson remembered that last night. She was alone in the lab, carefully recording data in a ledger when he came in. He even recalled the pen and pad and a partially completed letter on her desk. Elizabeth was an inveterate letter-writer.

She looked distressed to see him. "Neal, I thought we agreed . . ." she said.

"Who else can I talk to at this hour?" he said, trying to sound lighthearted, although he was not feeling that way.

"I'm sorry, but I'm very busy. This data is crucial . . ."

"You always seem to be busy lately when I want to talk."

"Well, I have a lot to do." She made nervous gestures in the air.

"That's what you always say," he said. "What are you afraid of?"

"Nothing." She seemed flustered and at a loss for words. "Everything. Please go away."

"Why do you have to make it so difficult?"

"Because it is difficult," she said. "Now, please, Neal, I beg you, go away. Sister Mary Catharine might return any minute. It wouldn't be good if she found us alone again."

"Can't you understand that I want to be with you?"

"Can't you understand that it's an impossible situation?" she blurted back, her voice on the edge of tears. "You are a married man. Marriage is one of the sacraments. I am a nun. I have my vows. We just can't continue seeing one another as we have been. Please, Neal, if you have any consideration for me at all, go away," she pleaded, turning away from him and burying her face in her hands.

In spite of himself, Haverson was irresistibly attracted to her as a woman—her high, almost oriental cheekbones, her almond-shaped hazel eyes, her smooth olive complexion. He was also attracted by her gentleness, her honesty, her sensitivity, her faintly-accented soft voice, her intense femininity; but more than that, there was an elusive, mystical quality about her, an other-worldliness he couldn't explain but to which he was strongly drawn. Had he been raised a Catholic, perhaps he would have never considered her in such a way. She was the epitome of the madonna for a man whose upbringing had not included the madonna concept. And he felt sure that she was equally attracted to him, despite her denials.

"You know you don't mean that," he said.

"Yes, I do. Please go," she insisted.

"Look at me and say that," he challenged.

Instead she lowered her eyes to avoid his demanding gaze. He was quite correct. She did not mean it. In spite of her words she wanted him to stay. Desperately, she wanted him to stay. "Can't you see how wrong, how impossible it is?" she said.

"Elizabeth . . ." He clasped her shoulders and forced her to look at him. When she raised her face, he bent forward and planted his mouth firmly on hers. At first she resisted as he knew she would, but eventually she surrendered with an unexpected intensity and abandon, throwing her arms around his neck so tightly she nearly cut off his wind, returning the urgency of his kiss, pressing fervently, desperately against him.

Placing his hand on the doorknob, Haverson attempted to snap the lock. The gesture caused Elizabeth to stiffen and draw away from him.

"What are you doing?" she demanded.

"You don't want anyone coming in on us, do you?" he said.

As though suddenly coming to her senses from a wild, abandoned fantasy, the realization of forbidden dreams, she extricated herself from his embrace.

"Please!" she said, her face chilled with anguish. "You must go."

With a mixture of anger and disappointment and dashed expectations, he protested. "What? Go?"

"Please, Neal, you must."

"What was all that about—just a minute ago?"

"I'm sorry," she said, tears streaming down her cheeks. "It was a terrible mistake."

"You were teasing, weren't you?"

She looked at him with shock and indignation. "No. Of course not. I wasn't. I swear I wasn't."

"Then what's this?"

"You must understand. Please go away. I must be alone. If you have any regard for me at all, you will leave."

"All right. If that's the way you want it," he said quietly, taking the doorknob in his hand.

"It's simply the way it must be." She wiped her cheeks with a handkerchief.

"I could have sworn a couple of minutes ago you wanted something else. But maybe I was wrong." With that he left the lab and slammed the door on Elizabeth before her microscope, once more in tears.

As nearly as Haverson could put together the next twenty-four hours, Elizabeth Nagy had abruptly left her lab, apparently almost as soon as he had gone, signed out a vehicle from the motor pool, insisting that it was vital she collect krill samples at that time. She had driven out onto the ice—too far, as it turned out—crashed through and was sucked under the thin, frozen sheet where she drowned. Her departure and failure to keep in touch with the base at the required intervals had been reported to Haverson but he had been so involved at the time trying to calm the highly paranoid Yuri Maslov that he neglected to go out after her right away. When he did, he found her—a horrifying sight—a short distance from where the vehicle had broken through. He would reproach himself over and over for months afterward for not having gone in search of her sooner. The investigation into her death ultimately cleared him, but in his own mind Haverson still felt responsible, refusing to live with even the slightest inference that he had not fully lived up to his obligations as a naval officer.

When Haverson and Donovan returned to the base commander's office, he unlocked a desk drawer and produced a large, sealed manila envelope.

"Being in that lab reminded me of this," Donovan said, handing Haverson the envelope. "There's something inside that might interest you."

Puzzled, Haverson opened it and found a small book bound in red leather, a curiously romantic volume with gold-embossed, rococo decoration, more than likely a diary. Haverson was sure he had never seen it before and wondered why Donovan was giving it to him.

"Where did you get this?" he asked.

"After Dr. Nagy's death, nobody used her lab for a while. But you know how short space is around here. Somebody eventually took it over—one of her former students. This was found behind one of her fishtanks. I wasn't sure what to do with it. The investigation was closed. She had no living relatives in this country. I simply put it away in a drawer. Then, when you arrived, I began thinking about it again. I thought maybe you might want to have a look at it. I don't know, Neal ..." Donovan shrugged, somewhat embarrassed that he might be getting into a highly personal area.

Keeping a diary seemed a frivolous activity for a serious scientist like Elizabeth Nagy, at least in Haverson's judgment, but when he opened it, he recognized her handwriting at once. After reading a few sentences, he realized it was indeed a diary. Perhaps if it had turned up before the investigation, he mused, it might have answered a few nagging questions he had, especially about the exact frame of mind she was in before the tragedy.

"Thanks, Jim," Haverson said and slipped the small book into his pocket.

That night aboard the *Aquarius* Haverson lay on the sofa in his dayroom poring over the diary, anxious to learn as much as he could about Elizabeth's state of mind at the time of her death.

I have no other choice except to immerse myself in my work, which I love, and to remind myself of the religious vocation to which I have dedicated my life. And yet, try as I do, I find that I am still very human and subject to all the frailties and weaknesses of my fellow humans. At heart I am very much a woman with all of my female emotions intact. There remains inside me still the need, the desire—the strong desire—to respond to the opposite sex. I find that I am, alas, quite capable of the most fundamental kind of human love—that between a woman and a man. I have not had feelings of this intensity before, and they disturb me greatly because I cannot control them despite my almost constant prayers. Can it be that deep down I do not really want to be relieved of these feelings? No, it cannot be.

It is as though everything conspires to throw us together—the darkness, the silence, the loneliness, the isolation, the cold, our constant association, our mutual interests. What am I to do? I am happy and yet miserable at the same time. At times, my guilt and anguish are more than I can bear and death would seem a welcome release.

Thank God Yuri Maslov had burst upon the scene, despite the havoc he is causing around here. He helps to relieve the pressure on both Neal and me in a strange way. Yuri needs my support and my encouragement to help him carry out his daring political act. How odd it is that the weak are called upon to provide strength! Sometimes, for no apparent reason, he will suddenly turn on me in spite of the fact that I am his best friend and faithful supporter here. I wonder what prompts these odd changes in his attitude toward me. Can it be jealousy? Sometimes I think I can see jealousy in his expression when he comes upon Neal and me together. There is certainly a rare kind of intimacy, understanding, between this dashing naval officer and me that I know others must perceive—Yuri among them. My feelings for this erratic Russian are those of a mother for a confused and bewildered son. On the other hand, my feelings for Neal are quite different—those of a woman for a man. Is it this love—this impossible love that torments me and sometimes even makes death seem the only solution to my yearning?

One of Maslov's most irritating habits as far as Haverson was concerned was his total lack of concern for social amenities, such as knocking on a door and requesting permission to enter. Haverson had grown accustomed to Maslov's unannounced intrusions on his privacy, although he still didn't like them and never would. He had reproached him on a number of occasions, but Maslov was always so distracted by other concerns that reprimands had little effect on him. This time when the Russian burst in, he discovered Haverson with the diary.

Pointing to the small red leather volume, he asked, "What is that?"

"Why?" Haverson replied, realizing that Maslov was staring at the book as if he had seen a ghost.

"It looks like the diary Elizabeth Nagy used to write in every day," he said. "I remember because I used to be amused by this habit of hers. It seemed to be the kind of silly thing schoolgirls or heroines of Tolstoy novels do, not a scientist."

Examining the book more closely, he declared, "It *is* hers! I recognize the gold decoration. Where did you get it?"

"It was in her lab," Haverson replied, deliberately vague about the details.

Maslov scowled. "I think that perhaps you should not read it," he said.

Raising his eyebrows, Haverson said, "Oh? Really?"

"Yes," Maslov affirmed. "A diary is very private."

Haverson was amused at the Russian's conception of privacy, especially after just having burst into the room. "Yes, I suppose you're right," he agreed, closing the book, satisfied that he had found what he had been looking for. Namely that Elizabeth Nagy had been responsible for her own fate.

25

While Haverson, Maslov, and some of the others occupied themselves with selecting the iceberg, Sally was forced to do stories on seals, penguins, krill, and other aspects of Antarctica as well as occasional interviews with scientists working under the auspices of the National Science Foundation. Although she had requested permission to report on the iceberg selection process, Haverson was reluctant to let her do a segment on it yet.

"Things are too uncertain," he said. "I don't want to broadcast our uncertainties to the world. Try to understand."

Despite the sophisticated technical equipment and experienced personnel at the Satellite Tracking Station, Haverson could see that the selection of the appropriate iceberg was not going to be easy. Basically they were groping in the dark.

"Let's face it," he confided to Maslov as he looked over piles of computer printouts. Outside, beyond the windows of his office high in the *Aquarius*'s superstructure, the frigid antarctic winds howled incessantly. "We're pioneers—the first ones to tackle something like this. As far as picking the iceberg is concerned, all we can do is concentrate on those few factors we know something about. For example, we know just how big a chunk of ice we can expect the ship to pull. That's a starting point."

"You don't have to convince me, you know," Maslov replied. "I agree with you."

"I'd like to choose our iceberg, harness it to the ship and start north as soon as possible," Haverson said.

"There's plenty of time," Maslov assured him.

"Yeah, but I want to allow for trouble."

Maslov frowned. "What trouble?"

"There are bound to be problems," Haverson said.

"You worry too much," Maslov remarked. "If there are problems, we will solve them."

For a number of years the variation in the ice cover of Antarctica had been fully recorded by weather satellites circling the earth in a polar orbit and studied carefully. Each time a satellite passed over the Antarctic it released approximately nine hundred "scenes" as the images were called, which were picked up by the tracking station. By assembling the multitude of serial scenes, it was possible to put together a composite photo of the entire Antarctic continent.

"We've got to narrow it down to regions where the sea ice is thinnest and rapidly breaking up," Haverson said, looking over the current picture. "According to these satellite photos, the dissolution of the sea ice seems most advanced here in the part of the Ross Sea approximately one-hundred-eighty degrees longitude."

"The greatest cluster of icebergs seems to be either here off Cape Colbeck or in the area of the Thwaites Iceberg Tongue," Maslov observed.

"Icebergs in these areas tend to be tabular," Haverson said.

"What is 'tabular'?" Maslov asked. Although his English was superb, there was an occasional word he did not understand.

"That refers to icebergs that have flat tops and sharp, distinct edges—like a pane of glass," Haverson explained. "The ideal iceberg for our purposes should be like a giant shoebox—square on the ends and about twice as long as it is wide. And as dense as possible. Packed really solid without any cracks or crevasses. It should also be free from any contamination with brine."

"It's not going to be easy to find such an iceberg," Maslov said.

"We've just got to look hard," Haverson said. "That's all."

During the antarctic summer the sun provides twenty-four hours of continuous daylight. For visitors unaccustomed to this round-the-clock sunshine, insomnia—nicknamed the "Big Eye"—is a frequent problem. At first, Haverson suffered from sleeplessness but used the time to examine thousands of pictures of icebergs sent back by the polar satellites, making an evaluation of each.

Eventually the candidates were narrowed down to a few dozen and at that point, Haverson decided it was time to fly over the area in question for a closer, firsthand look.

In a navy helicopter loaned them by Donovan, Haverson and Maslov flew over the Thwaites Iceberg Tongue and, using an impulse radar system, attempted to detect cracks, crevasses, and brine infiltration in the various icebergs.

Always anxious for a good story, Sally was exceedingly curious about the iceberg selection process, but despite her repeated requests, Haverson refused to grant her permission to cover the work going on at the Satellite Tracking Station.

"Oh, come on," she protested. "I can't keep talking about penguins and antarctic microbes forever."

"She's right, you know," Maslov commented. She had deliberately approached Haverson in Maslov's presence, feeling certain from past experience that he would support her request.

"See? Yuri agrees with me," Sally said.

Haverson was unimpressed. "Yuri always agrees with you."

"It's his sense of what's right," she said.

"Look, I make the decisions around here and I say you can report on the iceberg selection when I say so and not before," Haverson declared. Turning to Maslov, he said, "Let's get back to business."

•

One evening when the sun was particularly brilliant despite the bitter, unrelenting cold and gusting winds, Haverson studied a photo and made his decision. "This is it," he said.

Maslov had to admit—at least on photographic evidence—that the iceberg in question was truly magnificent. He quickly compiled a data sheet on the iceberg with the aid of a computer and found that it was ideal in configuration and free of serious cracks, brine, and crevasses. "Yes, this is it," he agreed enthusiastically.

To confirm their opinion, they carried out more detailed studies, including MICRAD (Microwave Radiometry). The radiometric signals gave precise information about both the composition and the physical structure of the iceberg. When this MICRAD data was combined and checked against the impulse radar information, Haverson was convinced that he had indeed found the iceberg he was seeking.

When Sally got word that the iceberg had been selected, she was elated and made immediate plans to break the news on the air. To compensate for his earlier news ban, Haverson agreed to appear on-camera with her.

"Just how will the iceberg be attached, Captain?" Sally

asked in her crisp reporter's voice, shoving a microphone in front of Haverson.

"We had several different options," Haverson replied. "For example, we could put a large cable or network of cables around the iceberg so that the stress of the pull would be evenly distributed. It could also be pushed from behind. Many ways. We finally decided on an alternative method which involves implanting large, hooklike devices called 'bollards' into the top of the iceberg and attaching towing cables from ship to these bollards."

"Are there any serious drawbacks to this method?" she questioned.

"Well, yes," he conceded. "It does put stress on small localized areas where the bollards are implanted. That could conceivably be a problem."

Shortly after the interview, Haverson arranged with Donovan for navy helicopters and crewmen to airlift the bollards and other equipment and supplies from the ship to the iceberg so that the attachment process would begin. It was agreed that Maslov would supervise the implantation of the bollards atop the iceberg while Haverson would remain aboard the ship and coordinate activities from there.

Naturally Sally requested permission to record the process, but Haverson explained, "This is a tricky thing. It involves a lot of heavy equipment—cranes and big bores and complicated machinery. I don't want any more people than absolutely necessary on that iceberg. You and the camera crew will only be in the way. Besides, it could be dangerous. I don't want anybody getting hurt."

"Aye, aye, sir," Sally said, and walked away disappointed once again, regretting that Maslov was not around to plead her case.

Despite the subzero cold and the unceasing wind, the antarctic skies proved clear on the day the implanting was to begin, and the bollards, anchor posts, electric drills, and other equipment were airlifted from the deck of the *Aquarius* and flown across the Ross Sea to the area of the Thwaites Iceberg Tongue where the iceberg was floating unperturbed, shimmering silvery white in the summer sunlight.

When the navy chopper touched down on the flat surface of the vast block of ice, Maslov was the first one off. Bracing himself against the powerful, frigid wind, he surveyed it, scarcely believing its enormity. On paper he was well acquainted with its dimensions, but the reality of actually standing and viewing its expanse was extraordinary. As the icy wind raised flurries of snow from its surface, Maslov brushed off his goggles and strode about in giant, exhilarated steps, seeking the ideal location for implanting the trio of bollards. He and Haverson had decided that the bollards must be positioned a generous distance from the front end to allow for melting in transit and also to withstand a pull of more than two hundred tons without fracturing.

Once Maslov decided on and marked the locations of the bollards, navy men, together with some of the crew of the *Aquarius*, went to work boring holes more than eighteen feet deep, straight down into the frozen interior with the electrically heated bores. Anchorage tubes were then inserted, held fast deep within the ice by the water which quickly refroze around them. In such extreme, subzero cold, the refreezing process was almost instantaneous.

As a crane hoisted one of the anchorage tubes aloft, a group of men guided the electrically heated bore down into the ice nearby. Responding to what he thought was a hand signal from Maslov, the crane operator started to swing the arm around. A sudden blast of wind caused the huge steel tube to swing crazily from the end of the arm, and the operator temporarily lost control. Seeing the massive piece of steel swinging out of control, the men dived to the ground, but one young sailor wasn't fast enough. Before he could hit the ice with the others, the steel tubing struck him, sending him flying across the ice and into the nearby shaft. His terrified screams as he fell into the hole sent shivers far more intense than those of the antarctic cold through those who heard him. Efforts to cut off the current in the electric bore came too late. The young sailor was either electrocuted or burned to death. Maslov insisted on being lowered into the narrow shaft to retrieve the charred remains.

The death of the sailor spread a pall of gloom over the proceedings, temporarily depriving the project of much of its spirit. Haverson was profoundly upset, especially when Donovan was compelled to conduct an investigation to determine the exact cause of the accident, recalling painful memories of another such antarctic investigation which had nearly destroyed him.

"I'm sorry, Neal, but I don't have any choice," Donovan said.

"It's okay, Jim, I understand," Haverson replied.

To add to Haverson's anguish, the crane operator accused

Maslov of giving him a faulty hand signal, thereby causing him to lose control of the gigantic crane.

Seeking out Haverson, Sally found him alone in his office aboard the *Aquarius*, drapes drawn against the perpetual summer sunlight, a half-empty bottle of Scotch on his desk. It was the first time she had ever seen him unshaven, his eyes sunken and ringed by dark shadows.

"I have to report the accident," she informed him, her tone sympathetic. "Donovan gave me permission. The sailor's family has been notified."

"Come on, Sally," he protested, looking both angry and upset. "What are you doing this to me for?"

"I'm sorry," she apologized, "but it's an important news story."

"Is that the only thing you ever think of—an important news story?" he reproached. "Don't you realize the effect a story like this is going to have on the project?"

"Accidents happen. People understand that," she assured him.

"It gives this project one helluva black eye."

"Not really. It's a risky project. People will realize that and understand."

"The hell they will," he said, his temper flaring for a moment. "I know you don't give a damn. All you care about is getting your goddam story on the air."

Indignant, Sally replied, "Don't you dare say a thing like that."

"If you cared, you'd forget the story."

"I can't do that and conscientiously call myself a reporter," she said.

"Call yourself what you want, but get out of my office," he ordered.

Sally started for the door. "I thought I'd leave out what the crane operator said about Yuri," she said. "He's pretty upset, you know. You're not the only one. He's accusing the crane operator of trying to cover his ass."

"I wish I could believe that."

Sally looked stunned. "My God, you don't think that Yuri deliberately . . ."

Haverson cut her off. "At this point I don't know what the hell to think," he said, reaching for the Scotch. "About anything."

26

Sally reported the sailor's death and, although Haverson was somewhat irked with her for doing so, he was forced to admit to himself that he admired her courage and determination.

Carefully studying all weather information, Haverson decided that it was a good time to hitch the iceberg to the ship and get underway. Despite the fact that most of the crew were nursing hangovers from the last of many farewell parties at the base, he gave the order for the men to prepare to sail. They managed to pull themselves together, man their duty stations, and, in a reasonable length of time, were ready to go. After an orientation talk with his officers and a thorough inspection of the ship, Haverson was satisfied that everything aboard was in good working order. With assistance from the navy and Coast Guard, the *Aquarius* sailed down the channel carved in the sea ice and headed east across the Ross Sea to where the iceberg sat tethered and waiting.

"Remember, François, if too much force is applied too fast, one of two things will occur," he said. "Either the cable will snap, or the iceberg will be set in motion so fast it'll collide with the ship and cause serious damage. It's got to be nudged, rather than jerked or yanked. Is that clear?"

"You forget, *mon capitaine,* you are talking to a Frenchman," Gaspar said. "We are masters of subtlety."

Gaspar proved to be a man of his word. The ship's initial forward motion was so smooth as to be almost imperceptible. Observing through binoculars from the stern, Haverson watched the towing cable, a light but tough mixture of steel and polyester, slowly rise above the choppy water and grow taut. As it did so, the iceberg dipped forward, hesitated a moment and then righted itself again, gliding obediently behind the ship just as he hoped. Cheers resounded all around the ship, and Haverson breathed a sigh of relief—at least temporarily.

The voyage across the Ross Sea toward the Antarctic Circle proved tense and miserable because of the weather. The skies, initially clear for the hookup, turned quickly dark as gale-force winds arose and turbulent seas unmercifully assaulted the ship.

Despite the storms and rough seas, Haverson ordered continuous monitoring of the iceberg by the bank of complicated electronic instruments which measured such things as sea temperature, salinity, etc.

There were times when Haverson stood looking at the enormous block of ice through his binoculars when he could not believe that it was really there, that it was an illusion and not really captured, harnessed, and following obediently behind. His main worry now was to deliver the iceberg intact. Maslov nicknamed their iceberg "Snegoruschka" after the snow maiden heroine of the Russian fairy tale.

The return route along South America's west coast was longer by about two thousand miles, but Haverson was convinced that the swift and powerful Peruvian current would more than compensate for the increase in distance.

As the ship approached the southern tip of the South American continent, it entered an area known as the "Zone of Convergence," a region where the icy waters of the Antarctic converge with the warmer water of the Pacific, the colder water sinking beneath and setting up strong currents. There Haverson had to watch the water temperature and salinity readings of the iceberg's monitoring systems closely. The iceberg would be surrounded by warmer water, and he expected some degree of melting. The question was how much and how fast.

Despite the fact that the weather continued to be cold and miserable, the temperature monitors showed a marked warming trend in the water, a trend accelerating much faster than Haverson had anticipated. He and the crew knew before setting out that sooner or later the iceberg would have to be insulated. Haverson and Maslov had discussed the matter many times and looked into many different methods and materials.

Now looking over the data from the different monitoring systems at Haverson's suggestion, Maslov said, "I think we must insulate the iceberg at once. If we don't, there will be very much melting. Too much."

"I don't want to undertake something as difficult and complex as that until the weather's better and the ship's in calmer water," Haverson replied. "I didn't expect to encounter such a sharp warming trend quite so soon."

"You have to be ready for the unexpected," Maslov said. "That is the way with the sea."

Even while they were talking, a fierce storm, yet another in the series they had encountered steadily since leaving Antarctica, was buffeting the ship. "We've got to wait," Haverson said.

"There is no time," Maslov argued. "Too much melting is already taking place. You can see for yourself. If we don't insulate soon, there may be nothing left of Snegoruschka by the time we reach California."

"Don't you realize what's going on out there? The sea . . . the wind? . . ." Haverson said, worry in his voice. "I'm not ordering anyone to begin the insulation until I'm absolutely sure it's safe. I can't have men under my command risking their lives unnecessarily."

"Suppose I want to volunteer?" Maslov proposed.

"Thanks, but no one is going out to that iceberg until I say so," Haverson said, with a smile, throwing his arm around Maslov's shoulder. "And that includes you."

A few days later, the weather began to clear, and Maslov started checking the iceberg carefully, through his binoculars, at every opportunity. Earlier the almost one-mile span between it and the ship had been obscured by high waves, sea spray, and sleet.

"Look!" he said, finally, urging his binoculars on Haverson, who was standing beside him at the stern rail. "The waves have produced a notch. You know what that means, don't you?"

"It means there's a notch and nothing more." Haverson shrugged.

"According to what I have read, there is a very high incidence of cracks developing from such notches," Maslov said. "The notch comes first and then the crack follows."

"I've read those same things," Haverson replied, peering through the glasses. "But I'm not worried."

"You should be."

"Well, I'm not," Haverson repeated. "I see the notch you're talking about. It's not unexpected."

"It is obvious we must insulate," Maslov insisted. *"Now."*

Haverson was not convinced of Maslov's devotion to the mission, but he thought the Russian was being obsessive about the insulation. "A few days more, perhaps," he said and handed the glasses back to Maslov.

27

As Governor Kirkwood and his staff stepped out of the concealed VIP elevator at UCLA Medical Center, they were accosted by a white-haired, bespectacled, professorial-looking man. Instantly the governor's bodyguards reached for their weapons and moved between the chief executive and the intruder.

"Don't try to stop me," the man warned. "This is a democracy, not a police state. I am a citizen doing my duty. I'm here to present the governor with a petition against the Aquarius project."

The governor recognized Dr. Thurston Terhune at once and indicated to his bodyguards that there was nothing to fear. Reluctantly, the guards backed off.

"Professor Terhune, if you would call my office in Sacramento and set up an appointment," Kirkwood advised, "I'll be more than happy to see you and consider your petition."

Without giving Terhune a chance to respond, Kirkwood and his party hurried down the hospital corridor, stationing two guards behind to prevent any further incidents.

"You haven't heard the last of this, Governor!" Terhune called after them. "We'll stop the *Aquarius* yet!"

"How the hell did he get in here?" Kirkwood asked Drew Ramsdale. "I thought our route through this building was supposed to be cleared of all extraneous personnel? Thank God it was only Terhune and not some nut with a gun."

"I've made a note to speak to the head of hospital security about it," Ramsdale replied.

Kirkwood paused in front of Bonnie's door, apprehensive about entering the room. A few days earlier she had undergone the first in a series of reconstructive surgeries, and he did not know how it had gone. Each time he entered the room, he suffered for Bonnie, and today his concern was more acute than usual. Because she was a person who made her living appearing before the public, the doctors had decided to begin with her face. Kirkwood knew how important her appearance was to her and hoped the results would be good.

As the governor was trying to work up enough courage to enter, a nurse suddenly opened the door and announced that Bonnie was waiting anxiously to see him.

Leaving his retinue outside, Kirkwood stepped into the cheerful room. Bonnie was lying on a special frame that allowed her to be rotated at intervals so that no single area of her body bore the pressure of her weight for too long a time. Most of her body was covered with a special antibacterial cream and gauze dressings through which an array of tubes entered or exited. Since the surgery, her face had been totally bandaged except for her eyes, nostrils, and mouth. In one corner of the room the television flickered, the volume lowered almost to the point of inaudibility.

"Hi," Kirkwood said, softly closing the door behind him.

Indicating her right eye, she said, "Kiss me here."

"How are you feeling?" he asked, trying to conceal his anxiety and concern.

"Great," she answered with forced cheerfulness. "Really, I am. I think they must have me on some kind of uppers or something. I feel great."

"How'd the surgery go?"

"Fine," she responded. "At least that's what they tell me. My face has been bandaged since I woke up. I can't wait to see my retreads. You're coming to the unveiling, aren't you? It's in a few weeks. Oh, boy, that'll be something. A new face!"

"Bonnie," Kirkwood said, unable to take her forced joviality any longer, "you don't have to do this, you know. I don't give a damn what your new face looks like. That's not important. I'm not in love with you just for your face. I love you no matter what."

Relaxing a little, Bonnie asked, "Do you really mean that?"

"Of course I mean it."

"You're not just saying that to make me feel good?"

"Hell, no. I'm saying it because it's the way I feel," Kirkwood declared, biting his lip to hold back tears. "Jesus, Bonnie, how can you doubt me? You're worse than my political opponents. The one thing I love about you . . . about our relationship is the goddam honesty."

"This is getting pretty heavy," Bonnie remarked. "We'd better lighten it up a little. The doctors said it's bad for the operation if I cry. Can you imagine telling an actress that? My drama coaches would freak."

"I just wanted to make sure you know how I feel."

"I do," she said, "and I love you for it, Paul."

"I love you, too, goddam it."

"Say, you haven't heard about any good horse auctions lately, have you?" Bonnie asked.

"Good God, Why?"

"I've decided that I want to replace Pepper and Salty as soon as I can. Whenever my doctors say it's okay, I want to start riding again. I'm going to rebuild the ranch, too, exactly the way it was. I'm staying there. I'm not going to let any fire force me out. Rancho Bonita will rise again out of the ashes like that bird—what's it called?"

"You mean the phoenix?"

"Yeah. That's the one," she said. "Rancho Bonita will rise like the phoenix."

"I flew over the ranch the other day," Kirkwood said. "All that's left of the house is the fireplace we built last summer."

"With rocks from the creek bed," she reminisced.

"The creek was dry even then."

"It's drier now, I bet," she said. "Listen, I've been following that Aquarius project on KHOT. They're giving it great coverage. Sally Brennan's super. Last night she showed how they're hooking the iceberg to the ship. It was fantastic. It took my mind off my face for nearly fifteen minutes. That's a record. I was so proud whenever she mentioned your name, Paul. You know what? I think it's one of the most important things that has ever happened in this country—in the world, for that matter. I really mean it. I just hope that I'll be in shape to help celebrate when it arrives in California."

"You will be," he assured her.

"Do you really think so?" she asked anxiously, her eyes haunted by doubt.

"Sure," he said, squeezing her hand lightly. "That's *if* there's a celebration."

"Of course there's going to be," she said. "What are you talking about?"

"I haven't told you this before, Bonnie, but in order to get Prince Akbar to undewrite the project, I had to promise to turn over some of my mother's family land to him in exchange. It was supposed to be a secret, but when George Bashore was assaulted in London, a copy of the secret agreement was stolen. I've just been informed that the contents of that agreement have been leaked to Fred Olafsson."

"The Washington columnist?" she asked. "He'll print it. He prints anything."

"If the Aquarius Transfer is successful, I don't care if he does," Kirkwood replied. "Then, the people in this state aren't going to give a damn. If California gets water, I'll be forgiven."

"Forgiven?" she echoed. "You'll be president."

"Anyway, if Olafsson breaks the story—and he undoubtedly will—I'm prepared to deny it for a while and stall for time that way—you know, lots of accusations and denials flying back and forth and nothing substantiated. Whoever assaulted George in London is probably afraid to let the agreement itself surface. It'll all be rumor. I can hold off my critics for a while."

"Until the *Aquarius* arrives," Bonnie said.

"*If* the *Aquarius* arrives," he qualified.

28

"**Haverson is a madman.** A madman," Maslov said as he hunched over the chessboard contemplating his next move. "Now that we have a nice iceberg and are pulling it successfully, he seems quite satisfied. He thinks that it is perhaps enough. He doesn't seem to care that unless it is insulated, the iceberg will be very soon melted."

"Oh, I'm sure he cares," Sally said, advancing her bishop. There was no doubt in her mind that Haverson cared about the iceberg, probably more than just about anything else, except the safety of his ship and crew, which was undoubtedly why he had refused to insulate until the stormy weather abated and the vessel was in calmer waters.

"Still, I don't understand him," Maslov said.

"I agree that he is a hard man to figure out," she replied, wondering if perhaps Maslov was trying to sound her out about Haverson and his attitude toward the Russian. The two men were dedicated, thoroughly professional seamen who worked well together, and yet she could tell that Haverson still did not completely trust Maslov, and maybe never would. She could not help but think that Maslov, too, was aware of his suspicions and hurt and puzzled by them.

"For the ship he is doing a good job. A very good job," Maslov conceded. "But sometimes I worry very much."

"What about?" "Worry" seemed an odd word for Maslov to use in connection with his relationship to Haverson. The contrary seemed far more likely.

"I don't know how exactly to say it," Maslov replied. "Sometimes I feel that very deep inside, something is bothering him. I don't know why I say that; it is only a feeling I have. Sometimes he does things that are very strange."

"I think you could say that about any one of us," she said, hoping the vagueness of her comment would force Maslov to be more specific. "What exactly are you referring to?"

"The fact that he will not allow the iceberg to be insulated," Maslov answered. "And also because he seems not to be concerned about the notch that I am certain has developed and that I warned him about. A notch like that can sometimes precede a serious crack. Perhaps already there is a crack. I don't know. I cannot know for sure because he refuses to let me check it."

"Well, he must have his reasons," Sally replied, knowing perfectly well that Haverson would obviously be very concerned about the possibility of a developing crack. The fact that he wouldn't permit Maslov to check out the situation implied to her that Haverson did not trust Maslov and was taking no chances, an attitude she felt was silly. *She* certainly trusted him and saw nothing suspicious in his behavior or his concern for the iceberg. Worse than silly, she felt Haverson was being unjust. She was resolved to do all in her power to reassure Maslov—subtly, of course—that she had complete confidence in him. "What does he say?" she asked.

"To study the iceberg properly and obtain accurate data, I must make a trip to it," Maslov explained. "Haverson argues that the weather is too bad for our little helicopter to fly, that it is too dangerous."

"You find *that* strange?" Sally questioned, listening to the gale-force winds howling about the ship. For the moment both of them had lost interest in the chess game.

"Not just these things I have just told you," Maslov said. "But other things as well. Small things."

Sally was intrigued. "Like what?"

"For example, one night I saw him reading a diary which belonged to a woman who is now dead. Haverson is not a man to read a woman's diary."

"Why not?" she asked, sure that the diary to which Maslov referred had belonged to Elizabeth Nagy. Obviously the circumstances surrounding her death still concerned Haverson.

"Well, you know the kind of things women write in diaries," Maslov said. "Silly, stupid things. Romantic nonsense."

"Not necessarily," Sally said. "But what makes you think he has no interest in silly, romantic things?"

"He is a very serious man, a dedicated officer, an accomplished seaman. We are not concerned with such things," Maslov replied. "He was reading it to find out something."

"Find out what?" She knew that Maslov was trying to convey to her that Haverson was still troubled about the nun's death, perhaps voicing a few suspicions of his own.

"I don't know," Maslov said, indicating that he wished to drop the subject. "I am more worried about Snegoruschka. She is melting too fast. We could lose half, maybe more, before we reach California. They will call our mission a failure. Because I am a foreigner and a Russian, I will be the one they will blame most if we fail."

"Not necessarily," Sally said.

"If only he would let us put the insulation around Snegoruschka *now*," Maslov said. "Once that is done, the ship can sail in a very warm sea and, still, we will arrive in California with plenty of water."

"Well, one thing I can tell you for sure," Sally said. "It won't do any good for me to talk to him. He won't listen to me."

"He will not listen to anybody," Maslov replied.

"Captain Haverson only listens to those who outrank him," Sally remarked. "Like God."

Her humor was wasted on the Russian, who leaned across the chessboard, his eyes suddenly bright. "Why do we need his permission?" he said. "We can do certain things without him."

"You mean, insulate the iceberg?" she asked, amused by such an idea.

"Oh, no, not that," Maslov laughed. "That is a very complicated process. It requires many people all working together. For that we would have to have Haverson's cooperation. But I can at least check to see if a crack is forming in the iceberg. I need, maybe, only one person to help me." He glanced at her expectantly.

"Are you asking for a volunteer?" she said.

Maslov shrugged. "That is up to you."

"What's involved?"

"Very little," he answered. "For you."

Successive storms, one right on the heels of the other, and continued rough seas kept Haverson up and working most of the time. His presence was required all over the vessel, and he was able to get very little rest. Finally, he informed First Officer Alex MacFergus that he was going to bed to try and sleep a few hours. "I just need to clear my head," he said.

"You deserve a rest, sir," MacFergus said. "I'll look after the ship. Don't worry about a thing."

"If you should have any problems, Mac, as far as the technical side of the ship is concerned, call Maslov; he can handle anything along those lines. Just don't let him get carried away," Haverson warned before he headed to his quarters.

When Maslov found out that MacFergus was in charge of the ship for a while, he headed for Sally's quarters and knocked quietly on the door. When she opened it, he said, "Come, I need you."

Pulling on her red parka and heavy gloves for protection against the stinging cold, Sally followed Maslov down to the Main Deck. Fortunately, most of the crew was occupied elsewhere and no one was on deck. Sally wondered whether it was just a happy coincidence or whether Maslov had planned it that way. Stopping beside an enormous winch to which one of the towing cables was attached, Maslov quickly explained his plan.

Earlier, he had attached a seat resembling a ski-lift chair to the cable leading to the iceberg. By means of a pulley arrangement, the seat traveled along the line, controlled manually by the person in the seat. To Sally, it looked very much like the traditional highline used to transfer passengers from one ship to another at sea in emergencies. Despite the fact that she felt she understood what Maslov was going to attempt to do, she still did not see the reason for his enlisting her in his plan. It seemed that whatever he was going to do, he could have done without her.

"Watch me through these," he directed, handing her a pair of binoculars. "If it looks to you as if I need help, notify someone."

"All right," she agreed, a little apprehensive about accepting such a responsibility.

Without further comment Maslov made sure that a pack containing special electronic equipment with which he intended to study the iceberg was strapped tightly to his back. Then, he hopped up into the seat, rocked slightly from side to side, waved goodbye to Sally, and shoved off, sliding swiftly along the cable, over the stern, and then finally out above the churning water.

With the binoculars, Sally anxiously followed his progress as he moved rapidly along the cable, which, despite its strength, sagged slightly under his weight. Slowly it began to occur to her how dangerous such an undertaking was.

When Maslov arrived at the cable's midpoint, he was perilously close to the sea. Although she feared for his safety as he moved farther and farther from the ship, often teetering precariously in the swaying chair while powerful winds ripped across the tops of the towering waves, showering him with an icy mist, she also wished, with a true reporter's compulsion, that she could be filming this daring escapade.

Traversing the first half of the cable was relatively simple, since it was downhill. After reaching the midpoint, however, Maslov had to pull himself along the remaining half while dangling dangerously close to the water—so close, in fact, that the tops of the waves splashed over his legs, and he worried about the safety of the pack on his back. Pulling against gravity, rather than aided by it, as before, required considerable effort. Maslov tugged hard on the rope, anxious to get as high above the water as he could. Once the waves were no longer lapping at him, he could feel a little more secure. The vast block of ice was still nearly half a mile away and already it was beginning to seem like a long, hard—perhaps impossible—pull.

The rolling and pitching of the ship were transmitted to the cable as vibrations which set Maslov bobbing up and down like a yo-yo or swinging from side to side like a paperclip on a rubber band. With great effort he inched his way forward, proceeding far more slowly than he would have liked. Refusing to look anywhere but straight ahead, he, nevertheless, caught sight out of the corner of his eye of an enormous, freak wave rising directly to his starboard side, far higher than any so far. Grasping the line as tightly as he could, he braced for the onslaught. Higher and higher the gigantic wall of water rose, eventually curling over on itself and smashing down upon him in a raging, freezing, gray-green deluge.

From the deck of the ship, Sally watched the assault of the giant wave in horror and, when it subsided, saw that the cable was empty. Her heart pounding with fear, she hastily scanned the entire length of the mile-long towline but saw only the vacant seat, swinging from side to side as the cable reverberated from the impact of the waves. Maslov was nowhere in sight.

Despite a feeling of panic, Sally immediately raced to the Emergency Action Stations Switch, and pulled it. A high-pitched whistle signaled the presence of danger with a desperate urgency, sending chills through experienced seaman, and alerting the entire ship to the existence of an emergency situation.

In seconds, crewmen scurried to their appointed stations, including Haverson who, roused from sleep, had hurriedly pulled his parka over a T-shirt. He raced toward Sally, his open boots flapping against his ankles as he ran.

Nearly hysterical and clutching Haverson's sleeve as she ran to meet him, Sally pointed in the direction where Maslov had disappeared. "Yuri Maslov is out there!" she cried. "In the sea! Overboard!"

Haverson immediately shouted the order via his VHF transmitter to stop the ship and initiated "man overboard" procedures.

Grabbing Sally roughly by the shoulders, he shook her to control any potential hysteria. "Where is he?" he demanded as the others began to gather around in response to the emergency signal.

Just as she pointed toward the iceberg, Maslov suddenly bobbed into sight, a tiny red speck on the gray, turbulent sea. "There he is!" she cried.

"Okay, men," Haverson said. "We only have about three minutes to fish him out. So let's move and move fast!"

"Why only three minutes?" Sally asked anxiously.

"Because in water as cold as this, after three minutes, it's too late; he's a dead man," Haverson snapped. Hopping into a lifeboat with a half-dozen other crewmen, he ordered it lowered into the water at once. At the same time, pilot Greg Dunne hopped into the helicopter and prepared to assist in the rescue mission.

With its engines cut off, the ship could be stopped at will, but the iceberg, on the other hand, was under no such control. Although the ship was eventually halted, Snegoruschka continued forward, propelled by its own momentum and the strong Peruvian current.

As davits lowered the lifeboat into the sea, Haverson looked up and realized that the iceberg was rapidly approaching the ship. Fearing a possible collision, he ordered Gaspar, via the VHF transmitter, to turn the ship and at the same time alerted the crewmen in the lifeboat to keep out of the way of both ship and iceberg.

By necessity, Gaspar's turn was exceedingly sharp; the ship failed to follow the line of its bows and instead underwent a pronounced sideways motion, like a car skidding on ice, bringing the starboard side of the *Aquarius* at an acute angle to the rapidly nearing mass of ice.

"Jesus Christ! . . ." Haverson muttered.

Just as the words left his lips, a deafening roar thundered over the water and the iceberg struck. The great ship shuddered violently, rolling from side to side under the devastating impact.

"My God, the ship's been struck!" One of the men in the lifeboat gasped.

"Never mind the goddam ship!" Haverson shouted. "We've got a man overboard!"

A short distance from the lifeboat, Maslov suddenly bobbed into sight. Quickly Haverson ordered the duty life-ring tossed to him. Maslov, his arms flailing wildly in the thick red parka, struggled desperately to reach the life-ring. The helicopter hovered overhead, its spotlight trained on the thrashing Russian. Maslov almost leaped across the water in a frantic effort to reach the ring, and somehow he managed to latch onto it.

When Haverson saw that he had hold of it, he directed the men in the boat to pull him in as fast as possible.

"Hold on, Yuri!" he shouted.

When Maslov was pulled into the lifeboat, he was barely conscious, and by the time he was hauled aboard the iceberg-battered *Aquarius* he was out. Haverson ordered him stripped of all wet clothing and placed under the shower at once. "Start with cold water," he directed. "Gradually—very gradually—increase it to hot." Suddenly noticing the pack on Maslov's back, Haverson stared at it suspiciously. "Wait a minute," he cautioned the crewman who was about to unstrap it. "Don't touch that pack." The thought occurred to him that the pack might contain explosives with which Maslov had intended to blow up the iceberg. Although he was beginning to trust the Russian, Haverson was not about to take any chances. He knew from experience that just when you begin to trust someone all hell can break loose.

"We'd better see what's inside, sir, in case it's something that needs drying out," the crewman insisted.

"Don't touch it, I said," Haverson snapped.

"Yes, sir," the crewman responded and returned to the task of removing Maslov's clothes.

Finding Sally who looked pale and shaken, still totally

unnerved by the incident, he asked, "What the hell was Maslov doing when he fell overboard?"

"I think you'd better ask him that," Sally said, not wanting to make trouble for the Russian.

"I'm asking you."

"I'm sorry, but I don't know."

Irked by her lack of cooperation, Haverson grabbed her arm. "This is important," he said. "What was he doing?"

"He was going out to check the iceberg—for cracks," she said.

29

One of the crewmen with experience handling explosives gingerly opened Maslov's backpack and discovered it contained electronic equipment for studying the iceberg—just as Sally had claimed. Haverson felt embarrassed about his suspicion of Maslov and the way he had lost his temper with Sally. He began to wonder if he were being overly paranoid about the Russian. Absolutely nothing that had happened during the entire voyage could possibly justify his reactions. He apologized to Sally and promised himself he would relax a little. But the first order of business was to restore order and calm aboard the ship, and get a crew together to inspect for damage done to the vessel by the crash of the iceberg.

At present, the iceberg was resting dangerously close to the ship, and Haverson wanted to reestablish the original distance between the two as quickly as possible so that there was less chance of further damage.

When he had been assured that the Russian was feeling better, Haverson decided to pay a call on Maslov in the sickbay to discuss the report of the damage revealed by a team of SCUBA divers who went down under the vessel. Although he was angry with the Russian for his escapade, he respected him as designer of the ship and knew that Maslov knew far more about it than anyone else, at least from a structural standpoint.

When he entered the room, Haverson found Maslov propped against a pair of pillows, a nasal catheter taped to his nose supplying him with oxygen. Maslov looked pale and decidedly ill. Sally Brennan was perched on the side of the bed urging him to eat a bowl of soup.

"How are you feeling?" he asked.

"Fine," Maslov replied, launching immediately into a spasm of coughing. Sally put the bowl aside and handed him a wad of tissues.

"I didn't know your talents included nursing," Haverson said to her.

"I have a lot of talents you don't know anything about, Captain," she replied, still feeling cool toward him for the way he had lost his temper with her earlier.

"So I see," Haverson remarked.

"What's your diagnosis?" Haverson asked Maslov. The ship's doctor had sent a full report to his office, but he had been too busy assessing the reports of the damage to read it.

"Nothing. A cold," Maslov said.

"He has pneumonia," Sally said.

"No," Maslov objected between coughing spells. "I have no pneumonia." Looking expectantly at Haverson, he asked, "Have you inspected yet? Is there much damage to the ship?"

"That's what I came to talk to you about," Haverson replied. "One of our props was cracked in the collision."

"Is that all?" Maslov asked.

"That's enough," Haverson said.

"You see what a good, strong hull I designed?" Maslov said proudly.

"I wish you had designed better props," Haverson said.

"That's a helluva thing to say," Sally reproached, rising to the Russian's defense. The two of them seemed to have a mutual defense pact.

Ignoring her, Haverson addressed himself to Maslov. "We'll have to replace it. It's cracked clear through the hub. There's no way to repair it," he said.

Maslov's pale face brightened. "I'm glad I insisted that we have an extra one on board in case of trouble," he said.

"The problem is going to be changing propellers," Haverson continued. "It's going to be rough. I'm going to try and contact the Chilean authorities and see if they'll let us put into Valparaiso. It's a big port. They should have the equipment we need to do the job. I can't think of any other answer, can you?"

"I guess not," Maslov agreed. "The way I have designed it, the ship can run for a short while on three propellers, but not all the way to California, of course. The strain would be too much."

"The biggest problem, as I see it, is what the hell we're

going to do with the iceberg while we're in port," Haverson said. "The Valparaiso harbor certainly isn't deep enough to accommodate it and, even if it were, I'm sure the Chileans wouldn't let us bring it in."

Nodding his head, Maslov said, "It will have to be anchored at sea—somewhere off the Pacific shelf. The water is very deep there."

"You mean you're just going to leave it?" Sally asked, somewhat amazed at the decision.

"Just for a short time," Haverson said. "Just until we get the prop changed."

"There is no question now that it will have to be insulated," Maslov said.

"You're right," Haverson agreed.

Maslov sighed. "I have caused all this trouble," he said contritely. "I am sorry."

"Just don't cause any more," Haverson said. "And get well."

"Now we must concentrate our efforts on the repair," Maslov said. "As soon as I am well . . ."

"You just take it easy and don't worry about it," Sally cautioned. "There are plenty of other guys on this ship. They don't need you."

"But it must be done right," he insisted.

"It will be," Haverson assured him. "You can bet on that."

Eventually Maslov began to show signs of fatigue, and Sally suggested they withdraw and allow him to sleep.

As they walked down the corridor outside the sickbay, Sally asked, "Do you think I could persuade you to talk on camera about the collision and the damage?"

"Nope."

"Why not?"

"I'll talk, but only after the prop's successfully replaced and functioning," he said.

"But you will say a few words just in general now, won't you?" she persisted. She knew that once she got him in front of the camera he would be more expansive on the subject. Getting him there was going to be the hard part. The collision and damaged propeller were just too big and too exciting a story to be suppressed.

"You never give up, do you?"

"It's not a question of giving up . . ."

"A story is everything to you, isn't it?"

"Haven't we been through all this before?"

195

"Yeah, I guess we have," he conceded.

"Yuri's apology in there was sincere, you know," she said. "He feels genuinely bad about all this. He really does."

"He should," Haverson said. "God only knows how long it's going to take to install a new propeller—and that's *if* we can do it. We don't know if we can or not."

"And if you can't?" she asked.

"If we can't, we might as well throw in the towel and call it quits."

"That would be a real disaster," she said, worriedly biting her lip.

"Yeah. No more stories," Haverson said. "Then what the hell would you do?"

"Kill myself," Sally quipped, and the tension between them suddenly relaxed as they laughed.

30

When Haverson returned to the ship's sickbay, he was pleased to see that Maslov seemed to have improved considerably. The Russian's face had regained its normal color, his eyes were far more alert, and he no longer needed to receive oxygen through a nasal catheter. Sally was with him, just as before, sitting on the bed, this time contemplating the chessboard between them. Neither looked up when Haverson entered. He cleared his throat to get their attention.

"Well, Yuri, how're you feeling today?" he asked.

"Oh, fine, thank you," Maslov replied, glancing up only an instant before concentrating on the game once again.

"Excuse me for butting in, but I just thought you'd like to catch up on what's happening," Haverson said.

"And what is happening?" Maslov asked, his attention still focused on the chessboard.

"I got word from the Chilean harbor officials," he announced.

Maslov looked at him expectantly. "And?" he asked.

"We have permission to enter the Valparaiso harbor," he replied. "They assure me they can handle a ship our size."

"Very good," Maslov said.

"The next question is what to do with the iceberg," Haverson said.

Maslov shrugged as though the answer were very simple. "That's obvious," he said. "She must be insulated."

"I agree with you," Haverson said.

"At last," Sally sighed, smiling at both men.

"Some of the men are checking out the insulating equipment now," Haverson said. "I want to get underway as fast as possible."

As though to overcome his disbelief, Maslov asked, "You're planning to insulate *now?*"

"As soon as we can," Haverson affirmed.

Maslov moved the chessboard aside, shoved the covers off, and threw his legs over the edge, obviously preparing to get out of bed. But the exertion of such a sudden move sent him into a severe coughing spasm.

"What are you doing, Yuri?" Sally protested. "Get back under those covers. You just ruined the great move I had in mind."

"I must get out of bed," he insisted, gasping for breath between coughs. "I want to put on my clothes. I must supervise the insulation."

"You're in no shape to do that," Sally reminded him. "Besides, you know you're not allowed out of bed. The doctor wants you to rest."

"I have rested enough. I am tired of resting. I want to get to work," Maslov declared. "I am not made to stay in bed." Scooping up clothes from a nearby chair, he headed toward the bathroom and closed the door.

Turning to Haverson, Sally asked reproachfully, "What did you do that for?"

"Do what?" he retorted, slightly irritated by her earlier remarks and her interference in his relations with one of his officers.

"Getting Yuri all stirred up by talking about insulating the iceberg," she replied. "You know how gung ho he is."

"Sick or not, he's still Chief Engineer aboard this ship," Haverson said. "He has to be kept informed."

"Regardless of how it affects him?" she challenged.

"How he takes it is his problem. I can't do anything about that," he insisted.

"You don't give a damn about anybody, do you?" she said.

"Maybe the same thing could be said about you," he retorted, offended by her remark.

"You've said that already," she shot back. "Many times."

Feeling a need to defend himself, Haverson said, "If you want to know, I happen to care about a lot of people— specifically twenty million or more Californians who are right now without water. I also care about a billion or so more people on this planet who may find themselves in the same— or worse—predicament any day. If I didn't care about people, I wouldn't be here."

"Look, don't try and bullshit me," Sally said. "I happen to know why you took on this job."

Haverson cocked one eyebrow skeptically. "Oh, really?" he said. "And would you mind telling me?"

"Sure," she said. "For several reasons. First of all, it's one helluva ego trip."

"You're wrong about that, but go on," he encouraged. "This is interesting."

"Secondly, you wanted a challenge, to see if you still had the old stuff, to see if you could handle something like this—which, even you must admit, is a far cry from a cruise ship plying the 'dangerous' waters between L.A. and Acapulco." Sally felt like a bitch having it out with him this way, but she felt a need to retaliate for his insinuating she was a ruthless opportunist. She hated herself for what she was saying, but couldn't stop. "You wanted to restore your confidence in yourself."

Looking her squarely and angrily in the eye, he said, "What makes you think I ever lost it?"

Sally decided to ignore that and continued, "And thirdly, it gave you a chance to go back to Antarctica and see if you couldn't dig up something—anything—to prove to yourself, in your own mind, that your neglect wasn't responsible for the death of Elizabeth Nagy." Haverson's face paled, and Sally knew at once she had hit home with that remark. "I think you had a suspicion she might have felt an overwhelming guilt over her involvement with you and decided to end it all by driving off onto the ice, knowing how dangerous it was." Maslov's informing her about the diary had helped her conclude the last.

Haverson was just barely controlling his anger. With clenched fists, he said, "And how do you happen to know all this?"

"Jim Donovan told me," she replied.

"And what else did he tell you?"

Feeling a little remorseful for her attack, that she had been hitting too hard and too low, Sally said, "He said that you were one of the best officers he had ever served with. He told me it was a damned shame that you felt forced to resign over the incident. He felt the investigation had absolved you of the responsibility for her death. He said he didn't see why you couldn't accept their conclusions."

"You know everything, don't you?"

"What I don't know, I try to dig out," she replied. "It's my job."

"Now that we've pretty much covered me, let's talk about you," he said.

"Fair enough," she agreed, a little apprehensive.

"What about those letters you wormed your way aboard this ship with?"

"What about them?" she said, uneasy at the mention of the supposed letters.

"They're nonexistent, aren't they?"

Sally somehow welcomed the opportunity to come clean. She hated deception and those who practiced it, even when it was necessary—as in the case of the letters. "Not really," she admitted.

"You know, Sally," Haverson said, considerably more in control than a few moments earlier, "maybe you'd better put your own house in order before you start attacking other people and their motives." He headed for the door, suddenly recalling that Maslov had been in the bathroom for an excessively long time. It occurred to him that the Russian had overheard their heated exchange and was probably too embarrassed to come out. "Tell Maslov when he comes out that if he wants to see me, I'll be in my quarters."

Long before leaving California, Maslov and Haverson formulated a plan for insulating the iceberg which included polyurethane foam to be applied in large sheets by equipment especially designed for that purpose. The equipment had been tested experimentally on a small scale, but never at sea on a full-sized iceberg. No one, including Haverson, knew whether it would successfully envelop the entire gigantic block of ice in what amounted to one large plastic bag which would retain the melted water, resulting in little or no loss.

Ill or not, Maslov was determined to participate in the insulating process. When no one was watching, he snuck out of the sickbay, and doing his best to stifle his cough, joined Haverson on deck. He was surprised to learn that the insulation process was already in progress.

"What the hell are you doing here?" Haverson said. "Did the doc give you permission to leave sickbay?"

"Never mind," Maslov replied. "Lend me your binoculars."

Reluctantly, Haverson handed him the glasses, and Maslov trained them on the iceberg where the remote-controlled tractorlike vehicle equipped with special treads was dispensing the hot, foaming polyurethane, methodically coating the entire surface.

"This is the easy part," Haverson said. "We still have the sides and the bottom to go."

"How long do you think it will take to cover the whole thing?" Maslov asked. They had made some projected calculations at one time, but they were only theoretical.

"I don't know," Haverson replied. "Maybe forty-eight hours, if all goes well—maybe more, if we have problems."

Applying the insulation to the sides took considerably longer and was more difficult than the top, but eventually it was accomplished, leaving only the bottom.

"In many ways, the bottom will be by far the most difficult area to cover," Maslov said.

"Yes, but it's the most important," Haverson reminded him, "as far as a loss of water is concerned."

"Good! Now we will use the bathyscaph I have designed," Maslov said.

The bathyscaph was basically a two-man submarine weighing about five tons and launched from the *Aquarius* by special davits. Its purpose was to travel beneath the iceberg to make measurements, take samples, or apply the polyurethane foam to the undersurface as needed. Manning the underwater vessel was a difficult and possibly even dangerous job and full of uncertainties. It required two skillful men, one to drive the miniature sub and one to operate the insulating equipment. Originally, they planned that Haverson would drive the craft while Maslov supervised the application of the polyurethane but with the advent of the Russian's illness, the dispensing job was given to another crewman.

"I want to go down there," Maslov said. "I want to operate the equipment I designed. It's my right."

"I'm sorry, Yuri, but the doc would never permit it," Haverson replied.

"Please, I want to go," the Russian begged.

"Look, I've already interfered enough with your medical treatment...."

Maslov insisted, "It is my obligation to go. If it is a risk to my health, then I want to take it. I don't care. It's *my* life."

Without question the Russian knew far more about the operation of the sub and the equipment than any of the other men aboard the ship, and for that reason, Haverson would have felt more confident with him than anyone else.

"I'm not going to say either yes or no. That's between you and the doctor," Haverson said.

Beneath the gigantic block of ice, the sea was dark and murky, eerie and mysterious, but at the same time beautiful and strangely fascinating. Haverson was far too preoccupied driving the bathyscaph to rhapsodize about this forbidding realm more than two hundred-fifty meters deep. Maslov, sitting next to him, concentrated on operating the quirky and difficult machinery that applied the polyurethane foam to the bottom of the iceberg. There was little conversation between the two men. Haverson was glad to have Maslov aboard, even though he was there against medical advice.

The bathyscaph phase of the insulating process required long hours in the shimmering darkness beneath the iceberg. The chill of the icy waters eventually permeated the underwater vessel. Maslov began to feel the effects of the cold, but stubbornly said nothing, determined not to abandon the bathyscaph until the job was completed. After a while, he could no longer suppress the urge to cough, and soon was almost unable to stop coughing. Haverson offered to surface, but Maslov refused.

"No. We must finish," he insisted. "I will not give up until we have finished."

Despite the fact that he risked a serious relapse, Maslov forced himself to stick with the project until it was completed. When the bathyscaph was hoisted back aboard the *Aquarius*, Maslov emerged with a high fever, shaking chills, and violent cough. Sally, on hand for the return, rushed to his aid with a blanket and threw it around him, immediately hustling him off to the sickbay—but not before she got off a parting scowl at Neal Haverson.

Once the iceberg was successfully insulated, the next step was to anchor it to the ocean floor.

"The only feasible method seems to be the conventional drag embedment anchors," Haverson announced to his officers. "We'll take soundings to determine the depth of the ocean in the area and proceed from there."

Anchors attached to the towing bollards were dropped into the water in such a way that they formed a kind of tripod over the great bulk of the ice, giving it maximum stability. At the last moment, Haverson ordered Lew Corbin to install a radio beacon on the iceberg which would emit a signal to be constantly monitored aboard the ship. "Any interruption in the signal should be interpreted as a sign of trouble, Lew," he said. "Is that clear?"

"Yes, sir," Corbin replied.

Leaving the gigantic hunk of ice, now snugly insulated in its blanket of polyurethane and anchored firmly to the ocean floor, the crippled *Aquarius* headed toward Valparaiso.

From the bridge, Haverson watched with a certain wistfulness and concern as the majestic Snegoruschka bobbed peacefully, slowly disappearing in the gathering mist. He wondered if he would ever see it again.

31

Annalise lay face down on the massage table while Rico drizzled avocado oil onto her back and began to rub rather languidly.

"Harder!" she commanded. "Don't be afraid to do it hard. You know I like it hard. The harder the better."

"What will you give me to do it harder?" he asked slyly, his large hands continuing to knead her flesh.

"I take good care of you, don't I?" she replied. "What more do you want?"

"I will think of something," Rico earnestly promised.

"Yes, I can always count on you for that," she said. Despite the fact that he had been back from the Swiss clinic for quite a while, Rico's disposition had failed to improve very much. Occasionally there were flashes of the former playful, sensuous, eager-to-please Rico, but not often. His moods were so unrelievedly glum and petulant that Annalise seriously contemplated getting rid of him, but her basic need for him made her hope he would recover his sensual inclinations, and she inevitably postponed the decision, in favor of giving him yet another chance. In an attempt to amend for the terrible gaffe of presenting him the ostrich leather shoes when he was so upset about his own scarred skin, she showered him with gifts of all kinds—from Turkish hashish to silk shirts from Thailand. Unfortunately, so far, nothing seemed to please him. Once again she was becoming impatient with him.

"You know that box you keep in the safe?" he began, indicating the wall safe in the adjoining bedroom.

"I keep lots of boxes in my safe," she said. "Why?"

"No, I don't mean jewel boxes," he corrected. "I mean the

204

ordinary cardboard one, not velvet—very large, like a box for shoes."

At the mention of the 'box for shoes,' Annalise tensed slightly. "What about it?" she asked.

"What is in it?" he asked, slapping her shoulders to make her relax again.

"Shoes," she replied.

Skeptical of her answer, he asked, "Why do you keep shoes in a safe?"

"Because they're very special."

"I would like to see them."

"Maybe someday I'll let you," she teased.

"When?"

"Someday. If you're good," she said. "Now stop fooling around and rub harder."

As Rico moved to her lower back, Annalise moaned pleasurably. Her bliss was short-lived, however. They were interrupted by the telephone.

"Damn! Who the hell can that be?"

Rico stopped, wiped his oily hands on a towel, and presented her with the phone. It was Preston Farleigh from Washington.

"Well, I think I've finally convinced the Resource Protection Subcommittee to exempt the Import-Export Bank from the National Environmental Policy Act," he announced.

"Is that what you've interrupted my massage to tell me?" she replied.

"It's a very important development, Annalise," he said, sounding a little rebuffed. "Basically, it means we can go ahead on the Amazon project without filing an environmental impact report and waiting for the damned subcommittee to act on it. That way we can get started a lot sooner. You may not realize it, but I've won a very important victory for Hydrolliance. When I pointed out that American businesses are at a competitive disadvantage against foreign companies when they have to file such reports and wait—God knows how long—for action on them, that was the decisive blow. It wasn't easy, I can tell you. Some bastard on the Resource Protection Subcommittee kept reminding me of that nuclear power plant the Import-Export Bank financed for the government of Turkey that they built right on top an earthquake fault."

"Listen, Preston, I'm glad you called, actually," Annalise said, changing her tone a little to sound more amiable.

"There's another very important matter I ought to discuss with you."

"Oh? What's that?"

"I've just had some news about the *Aquarius*," she replied. "My informants tell me that the vessel has been damaged. They radioed for permission to put into Valparaiso, Chile for repairs. They're planning to leave the iceberg anchored at sea."

"You're kidding!" Farleigh exclaimed. "They really left the iceberg at sea? I don't believe it! What an opportunity! Have they provided any kind of security for it?"

"I doubt it."

His voice was full of excitement as he said, "Sounds like we're in luck."

"The fact that they've reached Chile with the damned thing is very bad for us," she said. "They've demonstrated that an iceberg can be transferred successfully that far."

"So what?" he retorted. "Chile is a long way from California."

"Shame on you, Preston," she chided. "You know perfectly well that Hydrolliance has a deal with Chile."

"What are you getting at?"

"Hydrolliance is involved in a survey to try and determine a way to bring water to the great Atacama desert in the north," she reminded him. "Don't you see? Chile could very well be influenced by all this iceberg business and withdraw from their agreement with us."

"How could they do that?" he said. "You have an agreement."

"We also have agreements with Bolivia, Peru, and Argentina—to say nothing of Brazil and the Amazon project," she said. "But the domino theory could apply. If Chile goes, we lose all the rest one by one. Those agreements mean nothing. They can always find a clause to get them out. That's why we've got to stop them in Chile."

Farleigh was silent for a few moments. "You know what we've got to do?" he proposed. "We've got to blow the goddam thing up right now—torpedo it. That's what we've got to do."

"The *Aquarius*?" she questioned.

"No. The iceberg," he replied. "It's a sitting duck, for chrissake."

"What good will that do?" Annalise said with a slightly exasperated sigh. "It could cause far more harm than good. Besides, they'd just go right back to Antarctica and get another one. There's still time. It isn't iced in yet. They've got plenty of fuel. As I've told you many times, we will sabotage

206

the project—and fatally—but only when the time is right. This is not the proper time. Right now everybody regards Kirkwood and Haverson and that bunch and their iceberg scheme as crazy and harebrained. I don't want to suddenly generate sympathy for them that might change that opinion. Secondly, it's also liable to point a finger in our direction. We can't afford to let Hydrolliance fall under that kind of suspicion. That's why I selected the aqueduct as our first target. It was least risky and could be attributed to the work of kooks—as it was. We've got to keep our hands clean throughout all this. Any violent acts have got to look like they're the work of radical crazies like the Sea Vigilantes and that Armistad girl. Hydrolliance's image is one of dignity and respect. I want to keep it that way—unblemished."

Forcing a note of levity into his voice, Farleigh said, "Hell, Annalise, you take the fun out of everything."

"This isn't fun, Preston," she reproached. "It's serious business—damned serious. Billions are at stake. The thing we've got to do now is get those Chileans we've been courting all these years to go to work for us."

"It's going to cost," he warned.

"It always does," she said. "But if that's what it takes, then I'm prepared to pay. In any case, I want the *Aquarius* harassed out of existence while it's in Chile. But more than that, I want the whole project discredited in the eyes of the world. And its backers as well. I think it's time we planted a few innuendoes in some of the more sensational publications about the land deal Kirkwood made with Akbar. Of course, we can't say too much, or it might point the finger of suspicion at us with regard to the attack on Kirkwood's attorney in London, and we can't afford that."

"What about Haverson's family? Have you decided to let up on them?"

"There's no point in bothering with them any more," Annalise replied. "The point of that harassment was to get him not to take command of the project as Kirkwood wanted."

"We obviously failed on that score," Farleigh remarked.

"Getting back to what I was saying," she continued, "the Aquarius transfer has got to be made to look like a bad thing—certainly nothing to favor over our Amazon project. But whatever's done, I want done as subtly and smoothly as possible. We've got two objectives, after all—to discredit Kirkwood and everyone connected with iceberg-hauling in general and to delay the ship as long as possible."

"Long enough for the iceberg to melt?" he asked.

"No, silly, it can't melt now," she said impatiently. "They've gone and insulated it. The reason I'm stressing the delay tactics is that if we keep them stalled until the Antarctic freezes up again, we're safe for at least another year. Californians will never wait that long for a solution to the drought. This iceberg business will be finished forever. Projects like our desalination plants and river rerouting will be shoo-ins. The people will be clamoring for them. Hydrolliance will be sitting pretty. Once we control the state's water supply, we'll control California. And that's just the first step—just the beginning of a master plan. A lot bigger things will follow. And you'll be part of it, Preston."

"The only thing I want is to see Paul Kirkwood finished forever," he said.

"There's no question about that," she assured him.

"I hope not," he said.

"Now, then, we must get to work on those Chileans," she said. "There's no time to waste."

Rico took the phone and replaced it for her. "I heard you speak of Chile," he said.

"Yes, I did."

Resuming the massage, his strong hands began kneading her tense flesh once again. "Chile is very near my country," he said.

"I know."

"I would like to go home again. Soon. I have much nostalgia for my country," he said wistfully, apparently forgetting his many scrapes with the Rio police.

"You'll go," she said.

"To Brazil?"

"Maybe somewhere even better than that."

"Where is better?" he challenged.

"You'll see."

"Do you have another job for me to do?" he asked anxiously, as though that might be the requirement for the trip.

"I might have," she said, resting her head on her folded arms as his hands moved slowly toward her neck.

Applying more force, he said, "I will do better this time."

"You'd better," she warned, her voice sounding half-choked but full of excitement and anticipation as his powerful fingers encircled her throat.

32

The entry of the *Aquarius* into the busy Valparaiso harbor was not entirely without incident. Pilot Gaspar followed the normal procedures, pulling the ship parallel to a jetty and then gently nursing it alongside the pier with the help of tugs and the vessel's engines. A minimum of motion was required, and the exact moves were extremely difficult to judge from the bridge, one hundred feet above the water and more than twenty times that distance from the bows of the ship. A man had to walk one hundred and fifty feet from port to starboard just to see what was happening on the other side. There had been some minor damage to the harbor—a few pilings knocked out from beneath a pier—as much the fault of the inexperienced Chilean tugs as the *Aquarius*, nothing Haverson considered serious. Initially the harbor officials were sympathetic and cooperative until the local media suddenly protested the presence of the *Aquarius*, citing the damage it had done. Attitudes seemed to change overnight; officials who had originally been friendly, became distant and cold.

"Something funny is going on," Haverson said to Maslov. "I don't like this sudden switch in attitude. I smell a rat." By the time the ship was berthed, the Russian had improved considerably; all that remained of his bout with pneumonia was a slight, raspy cough, which he tried to suppress. "I don't know who's behind it, but I don't like it. The only thing we can do is hope for enough cooperation to get the old propeller off and the new one in its place. Then we'll get the hell out of here as fast as we can." Haverson and Maslov decided that the cracked propeller had to be replaced. Any sort of repair would have been impossible. "And the sooner, the better as far as I'm concerned."

A huge crane would be required for the propeller exchange, and Haverson set about looking for one capable of doing the job. Valparaiso was Chile's leading port, a bustling, international city ringed with hills, its harbor jammed with all kinds of ships of nearly every nation. Haverson assumed that finding such a crane would not be difficult. In fact, he located several capable of doing the job, but when he inquired about their availability he was told that they were either in service to others or out of order. After a while, he began to be suspicious and finally in utter frustration, confronted a crane operator and, through an interpreter he had hired, demanded the use of his crane. When the operator refused, Haverson's temper flared and he began yelling at the man. Fortunately, his outburst was in English and came pouring forth too fast for the interpreter to keep up with.

"I don't believe a goddam word you're saying," Haverson shouted at the somewhat sheepish Chilean crane operator, as the interpreter stared at him in stunned dismay. "I think there's some kind of a plot going on around here and I'd like to know who's responsible. Did someone tell you not to let us use your crane?" He turned to the interpreter and indicated that he wished the last question translated.

"I am only following the orders of Señor Peña," was the crane operator's translated reply.

"Who the hell is Señor Peña?" Haverson demanded of the interpreter.

"He is the marine superintendent," the interpreter replied. "The man in charge of the harbor."

The crane operator showed Haverson a directive he had received from Peña's office stating that no aid was to be given the *Aquarius*, its captain, or its crew until all fines levied against the ship were paid.

Haverson was astonished. He knew nothing about any fines. "What the hell is this?" he said.

"He received it only yesterday," the interpreter explained.

"What 'fines' is this man Peña talking about?" Haverson questioned. "I don't know anything about any fines."

"I am sure Señor Peña will inform you very soon," the interpreter answered. "You must be patient, Captain."

The interpreter was indeed correct. A short time after Haverson returned to the ship, a group of Chilean officials boarded the *Aquarius* and presented him with a sheaf of official-looking documents.

Knowing that the papers obviously dealt with the "fines"

alluded to earlier, Haverson threw the papers contemptuously onto his desk. "You've got to tell me what they say," he said. "I don't read Spanish."

"Very well, Captain," the leader of the group said in careful English. "I shall be pleased to explain to you the contents. These papers describe the damage your ship has done to the harbor."

Haverson leafed through the many sheets and realized that the list of supposed "damages" was very long. "From the looks of things, there must have been a lot more damage than I saw," he said.

"Shall I read you the list?" the head official offered.

"I don't think I'm in the mood to listen at the moment," Haverson replied. "Just let me know what you expect me to do about this so-called damage."

"It's very clear," the official replied with an unctuous smile. "You must pay the fines."

"A lot of the damage is not our fault," Haverson asserted. "It was done by your own tugs."

"Some of the tugboats were also damaged," the official informed him. "You have been charged with those damages as well."

"It's not my fault your goddam tug operators are so inept," Haverson charged, his temper rising.

"I am sorry, Captain, but they do not agree with you," the official said.

"Who is this 'they' you keep referring to?" Haverson demanded.

"Those in charge of the port."

"Señor Peña?" he questioned, recalling the signature on the papers at the crane operator's.

"Yes. He is the superintendent."

"I'm going to pay a call on Señor Peña and see if something can't be done about this," Haverson declared angrily.

"Señor Peña will see you," the officer said, still smiling. "But that will change nothing."

Despite the harbor official's attempt to discourage him, Haverson called on Señor Francisco Peña in his office.

"Captain Haverson," Peña said, rising from behind his paper-strewn desk, a short, stout man with a thick, dark, carefully-shaped moustache. "In what may I serve you?"

Haverson waved the papers enumerating the fines which had been levied against the *Aquarius* and himself, as captain. "I want to talk about these," he said. "I want some kind of explanation."

Peña strolled around to the front of the desk. "It is all very simple," he said, affecting a casual air. "The law states that if a ship damages our harbor or any of its facilities, the owner and the captain are responsible. Fines are imposed both as punishment and to cover the cost to repair the damage."

"I had an interpreter go over this list of damages," he said. "Frankly, the whole thing is preposterous. These are just a lot of trumped-up charges," Haverson retorted. "What's more, I've checked into some of the alleged damages and found nothing. Some of these supposedly damaged facilities are intact. What little damage my ship actually did was minor. The rest is pure bullshit. There is no way I am going to pay these fines—or anybody else, for that matter. Do you want to know what I think? I think somebody has paid you to deliberately harass us."

"Captain, do you accuse me of corruption?" Peña said indignantly.

"If the shoe fits, wear it," Haverson snapped.

Puzzled by such an expression, Peña frowned. "I beg your pardon?" he said.

"I first started to smell a rat when I had trouble getting a crane," Haverson said.

"I can assure you, Captain, that there is no conspiracy to prevent you from securing the use of a crane for your repairs," Peña said. "If you feel I have treated you and your ship unfairly, you are free to take your case to higher authorities. I can only tell you that I am upholding the law. I do not make the laws, I only enforce them."

Feeling that any further exchange would be futile, Haverson stomped out of Peña's office and returned to the ship where he found, much to his amazement, that Maslov had secured a crane and was already preparing for the removal of the damaged propeller.

"How the hell did you get that?" Haverson asked, pointing to the crane. "And where?"

"There was no trouble," Maslov replied, going on to explain that the crane had come from the very same crane operator who had refused Haverson earlier.

Shaking his head, Haverson muttered, "Well, I'll be damned . . ."

Sally, who was standing nearby, chimed in, "Yuri always gets what he goes after."

Haverson was far more concerned with this latest, puzzling development. Apparently their opponents had decided to shift tactics; the order not to cooperate with the *Aquarius* and its crew had obviously been rescinded. Perhaps they planned to put more insidious obstacles in their path once the propeller was replaced, making the situation even more frustrating. In any case, Haverson felt ready for anything they had in mind.

Under Maslov's direction the damaged propeller was removed and the spare put in its place. It was a long, difficult, and complicated procedure, but the Russian's enthusiasm for the job made it seem easy.

One evening Haverson dropped into Maslov's quarters. "Well, Yuri, I suppose we'll be sailing soon?" he said.

"Oh, yes," Maslov assured him, adding with a frown the afterthought; "What about the fines?"

"What about them?" Haverson echoed indifferently.

"Did you get that Señor Peña to remove them?"

"Nope."

"Then how can we sail?"

"We're going to say to hell with everything and just go ahead and do it."

Maslov was still perplexed. "We can't do it without help. We will need tugs to tow us out of the harbor," he reminded Haverson.

"I have a feeling that somebody spread around a few bucks to cause us all this trouble in the first place," Haverson said.

"If you say so," Maslov reluctantly agreed.

"I *know* so," Haverson replied emphatically. "All right, then, we'll spread around a few bucks of our own and get ourselves out of here."

"I hope you are successful," Maslov said. "I have no desire to stay here a moment longer."

Much to Haverson's surprise, however, he found that most of the tugboat captains were resistant to bribes and refused his offer of cash to tow the *Aquarius* out to sea.

"We will be in great trouble if we help you," one captain said, eyeing the bills in Haverson's hand regretfully. "Once you pay the fines, however, we will be glad to be of service."

Just as he was becoming thoroughly discouraged, Haverson found, much to his surprise, that a few renegade tugboat captains were apparently willing to go along with him for cash. The only thing that Haverson did not like was that they insisted on their money in advance; the only assurance he had that they would cooperate and appear with their boats at the appointed hour was their word.

"I don't think you can trust them," Maslov warned.

"It's worth a try," Haverson replied. "If we do succeed in getting out of this harbor, there's nothing big enough in Chile to stop us."

On the scheduled departure day, Haverson was not really surprised when none of the contracted tugs appeared. "I guess I should have expected this," he said. "Damn!"

An hour or so later, an official car belonging to the harbor police pulled alongside the *Aquarius* and a bullhorn announced that Señor Peña was coming aboard.

Accompanied by what seemed like a platoon of armed police officers as well as customs and immigration officials, Peña greeted Haverson, a smug smile creasing his pudgy face. "Captain Haverson, I have a warrant for your arrest," he announced.

"Arrest?!" Haverson repeated.

"Yes," Peña affirmed. "For conspiring to break Chilean law. We cannot tolerate such a thing. Therefore, you are under arrest."

With that, Peña gave the signal, and two officers rushed forward and clapped Haverson into handcuffs.

33

When the harbor police dragged Haverson away, Sally was on the bridge interviewing Maslov about the replacement of the propeller. Glancing down, she was astounded to see the ship's captain in handcuffs. "Yuri! . . . Look ! . . ." she cried, almost speechless.

When Maslov realized what was happening, he, too, was stunned. "Come!" he said. "Let's go!" Dropping everything, they ran down the steps in rapid pursuit.

Grabbing one of the arresting officers by the sleeve of his uniform as he was about to start down the gangplank, Sally demanded, "Hey! What do you jerks think you're doing?"

"The captain is under arrest," the English-speaking official answered, removing her hand from his sleeve.

Undaunted, she protested, "You can't do that. He's the captain of this ship!"

"That, my dear señorita, is precisely why he has been arrested," the officer replied.

Furious, Maslov cursed them in Russian.

"But you can't do that!" Sally insisted.

"I am afraid we are doing exactly that," the officer said with a facetious smile.

Unable to restrain herself, Sally began to pound at him with her fists. Maslov, following her lead, yanked one of the arresting officers by the collar.

Fearing Sally and Maslov might be arrested too, Haverson said, "Don't fight them. It won't do any good. You'll only get yourselves in trouble. Save your efforts for those with the authority to do something about the situation. These guys are just stooges following the orders of somebody higher up."

"Who should we see?" Maslov asked.

"Try the American consulate first," Haverson replied. "Explain the situation to them."

Before he could give further instructions, the arresting officers shoved Haverson inside the police car and quickly drove away.

As she watched the vehicle disappear down the pier, Sally turned to Maslov in dismay. "My God, Yuri. . . ." she muttered.

"The bastards!" Maslov swore, clenching his fists and pounding on the rail in anger and frustration.

Later, over coffee in the wardroom with MacFergus and Gaspar, Sally and Maslov discussed what steps should be taken to obtain Haverson's release.

"Very simple," Maslov said. "We must do what he advised."

"You mean contact the American consul in Santiago?" Sally asked.

"It seems like a sensible step to me," MacFergus agreed, after considering a moment, and Gaspar nodded.

From the ship Sally attempted to reach the American consulate in Santiago but could not make contact. Acting on the radio operator's advice that it was often easier to get through to the United States than to a local foreign city, Sally took a chance and placed a call to Kirkwood in Sacramento.

In a matter of minutes, the governor of California was on the line. "Sally, what's up?" he asked anxiously.

"The Chilean police have arrested Haverson and hauled him off to jail," she related. "Just a little while ago."

"Well, I'm not surprised," Kirkwood said, sounding calm. "I've been expecting something like that. Our opponents have high-level connections everywhere. What kind of charges are they holding him on? Did they plant dope on him or something?"

"No. Nothing like that," Sally answered. "They fined the ship for damage it supposedly did. Then they accused him of trying to bribe the local tugboat captains to disobey the injunction against towing the ship out to sea without paying the fines."

"Bribery?" he said, sounding bemused. "Since when are our South American friends so sensitive about bribery? Well, Sally, I'll tell you what, I'm going to put through a couple of calls to some high-level people in Washington and see what I can do. It's going to be a power game—a contest between me and my opponents to see who has more friends in high places."

"I hope you do," Sally said.

"Even if *they* do, don't worry," Kirkwood assured her. "I still have a couple of aces up my sleeve—in case of emergency."

"This *is* an emergency," she said.

"We'll get Haverson out," he promised. "Somehow."

"I hope so," she said.

"Listen, is the iceberg okay?" he asked anxiously.

"As far as anybody knows."

"Hasn't anybody checked on it?"

"A radio beacon was attached to it before it was anchored at sea," she replied. "We're still picking up the signal okay."

"Good," he answered, sounding a little relieved. "Tell whoever is in charge to keep a very close check on it. Anchored at sea, unprotected, and unguarded, it's very vulnerable. Haverson's arrest just might be a red herring to deflect attention from the iceberg."

Sally contemplated a moment and then asked, "So they can blow it up?"

"Who knows what they might pull?" he replied. "The point is we've got to be ready for anything at any time."

Sally relayed Kirkwood's warning about the iceberg to MacFergus who was in charge in Haverson's absence. The Scottish First Officer made immediate plans to divide the crew into teams and assign them guard duty atop the iceberg. The guards would be housed in tents and on the lookout for possible trouble. Some of the other officers and crew objected to the plan, pointing out that it was impractical and also placed the men in great jeopardy in case there actually were plans afoot to blow up the great block of ice.

"Besides, it's too big for a couple of men to guard," Gaspar asserted.

After a few more minutes of debate, Maslov suddenly stood up. "I will go," he said. "I will stay out there. I'm not afraid. After all, I sailed around the Antarctic alone in a very small boat. I am not afraid to guard Snegoruschka."

"No," MacFergus objected. "Suppose something happens to you? What would we do for a Chief Engineer the rest of the voyage? No one else knows as much as you do about all this damned complicated electronic stuff on board here. As far as I'm concerned, you're indispensable."

"Nothing will happen," Maslov said. "I am afraid of nobody or nothing."

"That's not the point," MacFergus argued. "We can't take chances."

"Why not fly periodic reconnaissance missions over the area," Gaspar suggested.

"In the helicopter?" MacFergus asked.

"Yes," Gaspar nodded.

While the men debated how best to protect the iceberg, Sally decided to continue with her efforts to reach the American consulate in Santiago, but difficulties in transmission persisted, and she began to wonder if there had not been some kind of sabotage to the ship's communication system. When she finally did get through, the receptionist at the consulate kept assuming that she was calling about a friend who had been arrested on drug charges and advised her that the consul could do nothing in such cases. "All travelers must obey the law, señorita," she admonished in an officious voice.

"But you don't understand," Sally insisted. "This has nothing to do with drugs." Her words were futile; the receptionist had already disconnected her.

Annoyed and frustrated, Sally decided to take off for Santiago and try and see the consul in person. The Chilean capital was a relatively short distance from Valparaiso, and she hailed a cab to take her there.

Santiago was a flat, grayish city lying at the foot of the Andes, full of unbelievable noise and heavy traffic. The cab driver deposited her at the American consulate and eventually, through her persistence, she secured an appointment with a foreign service officer and explained the situation.

"It's odd that you've come here today, Miss Brennan," he remarked.

"Odd? How so?" she questioned.

"Well, you see, I've just received a call about Captain Haverson," he said.

Surprised, Sally asked, "From whom?"

"From an undersecretary of the Chilean navy," he answered with a genial smile. "It seems he's received word to see that Captain Haverson is released. Needless to say, he apologized profusely for the arrest."

Sally breathed a sigh of relief, although she couldn't help wondering how all this had come about. "Why the sudden change?" she asked.

"I'm not sure," the officer replied. "The Chilean official seemed a little reluctant to say. All that I could get out of him was that a certain Saudi Arabian prince has gotten involved in the matter. Just what he has to do with it, I'm not sure...."

Sally realized that the Saudi Arabian was Prince Akbar. More than likely he had threatened an oil embargo or a price hike or something and, thus, brought about the sudden reversal in Haverson's case.

"As I understand it," the foreign service officer continued, "the fines against the ship have been lowered considerably and bribery charges against Captain Haverson are going to be dismissed."

Sally could scarcely believe what she was hearing, and yet her experience as a reporter told her that it was not surprising at all. The name of the game was "expediency." Power and influence applied at sensitive levels made anything possible.

"I believe that the Saudi prince has guaranteed the payment of the fines so that the ship can sail immediately upon Haverson's return," the officer added.

"I'm sure Captain Haverson will be glad to know that," she said, rising to leave, her mission in Santiago concluded, an ironic smile flitting across her face. The war had ended without a single shot fired.

34

The morning following Haverson's release, a fleet of tugs appeared to assist the *Aquarius* out of the harbor. Obviously the ship would be leaving with the blessing of the Chilean port authorities.

When they reached the open sea, the tugs released the great ship, and Haverson gave the order to start the reactor. In a short time, the *Aquarius* got under way.

"From all indications, it looks like the new propeller is functioning smoothly," Haverson announced to his officers, looking pleased and relieved.

As the rugged Chilean coastline, with the snow-covered Andes looming in the background, disappeared in the haze of morning, the vast blue expanse of the Pacific spread before them once again.

When the iceberg was first sighted in the distance, bathed in white sunlight, floating majestically, wrapped in a coat of polyurethane, there was a great burst of excitement among the crew aboard the *Aquarius*. Hearing the commotion, Haverson grabbed his binoculars and scanned the horizon.

"There it is! Right where we left it," he said to MacFergus, breathing a sigh of relief. "And it's a damned good thing."

Haverson was anxious to check the iceberg with the various electronic sensing devices to learn whether or not any damage had been done while it was anchored at sea, buffeted by wind, waves, and current. How an iceberg would stand up to the constant stresses imposed on it by the hauling procedure was one of the great unknowns of the project. Haverson sent for Greg Dunne and asked that he and another crewman fly out to the mass of ice in the helicopter and check its integrity at close range using various instruments.

When Greg returned he turned over the data he had gathered to Haverson, who studied it carefully. Maslov soon joined him, equally curious to learn the condition of the iceberg.

"Remember the notch you pointed out?" Haverson asked. "Well, it's much larger now."

Maslov frowned. "You know what that means? . . ."

"It means there's an even greater possibility that a crack will form, a crack that could pass right through the whole iceberg and split it in two."

"How long do you think it will take for a crack to form?" Maslov questioned.

"I don't know," Haverson replied. "We'll just have to wait and see."

By using the helicopter once again, the cables were reattached to the ship, linking iceberg and vessel together once more. Although there were no navy men available this time for the operation and the *Aquarius*'s chopper was considerably smaller than those used in Antarctica, the hitching was accomplished in about the same time.

"This time we weren't hampered by subzero temperatures and those godawful polar winds," Haverson said to MacFergus, pleased with the crew's efficient work.

When all were satisfied that the iceberg was securely attached once again, the ship resumed its original northward route. The sight of the great chunk of ice trailing behind once more gave everyone on board a sense of joy and relief.

As the ship sailed further north toward the equator, the chill wind warmed and the days grew increasingly balmy. Afternoons were sunny and pleasant with the wind fresh across the Main Deck. Blessed with good weather and a sea that reflected its name "pacific," for a change, the *Aquarius* plied its course steadily northward.

For his part, Haverson was chiefly concerned with the possibility of a sizable crack developing beneath the notch now manifest in the iceberg, and he had it checked regularly.

"How is it doing?" Maslov asked anxiously.

"As far as we can tell, everything seems to be fairly stable—at least for the moment. If the notch is growing larger, it's doing so slowly," Haverson replied.

"What about melting and water loss?"

"The insulation seems to be doing a good job," Haverson said.

"Wonderful!" Maslov said with a smile.

All things considered, the present leg of the voyage seemed to be going smoothly, and the crew seemed content, happy to be away from Chile and on the high seas again. The only person on board with any complaints was Sally.

"In the news business, no news is definitely not good news," she said to one of the men working as her cameraman, after a succession of more or less uneventful days. In a desperate attempt to keep KHOT supplied with material, she had resorted to a series of interviews with various crewmen, talking to them about their individual jobs and their feeling about the project. She realized it was not terribly exciting stuff—at least in terms of what Ken Wilson wanted from her to keep his ratings up—but for the moment she had little choice. Sooner or later she felt, something would break, and from past experience she knew she probably would not have long to wait.

The ship skirted the northern reaches of Chile where the dry, desolate Atacama desert doubled for the moon in the astronaut training program. Just before the *Aquarius* officially entered Peruvian coastal waters, Haverson was warned by Governor Kirkwood to be on the lookout for trouble.

"We've gotten word that the Sea Vigilantes have taken off for Lima," the governor informed him. "Amy Armistad and Dr. Thurston Terhune are among them."

"Our old friends," Haverson remarked.

"They're expected to ally themselves with some of the local radical groups to cause trouble," Kirkwood went on. "I think it may be the big move we've been anticipating."

"We can take care of them," Haverson said confidently.

"Terhune's been coming out loud and strong against this project—writing articles galore, appearing all over television, speaking on college campuses, flooding my office with petitions—the whole gamut, you know. They're working hard to try and turn public sentiment against us."

"What about Amy Armistad? What's she up to? I thought she was supposed to be working for Senator Farleigh these days—his special advisor on ecological affairs or something like that?" Haverson asked.

"Officially she's on a fact-finding tour in Peru," Kirkwood said.

"I don't like the idea of those two down here," Haverson said. "There's already a lot of anti-American feeling in some parts of Latin America. We don't need that pair adding fuel to the fire. Some of the local radicals will jump on any excuse to stir up the people. The Sea Vigilantes might just provide them with what they're looking for."

Shortly after dawn, off the southwest coast of Peru near Arequipa, Haverson was alerted to the fact that a large fleet of fishing boats was strung out across the *Aquarius*'s course.

"They'll move when they see us bearing down on them," he said confidently.

But despite numerous warnings of various kinds from the large ship, the fishing fleet did not move, and as the *Aquarius* drew nearer, instead of scattering, the smaller vessels drew closer together, encircling the great vessel. When he saw what was happening, Haverson gave the order to prepare for trouble.

As it became clear that the larger vessel would be forced to halt, the lead Peruvian ship broke ranks from its sister ships and approached the *Aquarius*. As it drew alongside, its crew suddenly began unfurling banners bearing slogans in Spanish and English and marched around the deck chanting.

"ICEBERGS KILL FISH! AQUARIUS MENACES WORLD WEATHER! AQUARIUS GO BACK! SEA VIGILANTES PROTECT FISHING! LIFE NOT ICE!"

Recognizing the news value of the protest, Sally and her crew began filming at once. Leading the group of protesters was none other than Amy Armistad and Dr. Thurston Terhune. Amy shouted alternately in Spanish and English, probably to give her efforts wider appeal—considering most of the crew were undoubtedly Peruvians—while Terhune, far less fiery and vociferous by nature, stuck to his native tongue.

"What do we do, sir?" MacFergus asked, bewildered, indicating the protesters below.

"We have a couple of options," Haverson answered. "We could plow right through the whole fleet or . . ."

"Are you kidding?" Sally interrupted. "If you damage any of those boats with this ship, you'll get a worldwide black eye."

"The second option," Haverson went on, ignoring Sally for the moment, "is to talk to them and see if we can come to some kind of accord."

"From a P.R. standpoint, the latter would be a lot better," Sally said. "If the world could see the captain of the *Aquarius* actually sitting down at a conference table and talking in a civilized fashion to the leaders of the Sea Vigilantes, it would be a real coup. Wow!"

"I'm sure you're ready to report it all," he said.

"Of course," she replied.

"The trouble is these people don't talk," Haverson said. "They're only interested in screaming and shouting and raising hell."

"Offer them the chance and see what happens," Sally urged. "What have you got to lose?"

Haverson thought about it a minute and then grabbed the bullhorn and leaned over the rail directly above the lead vessel which was named the *Maria Graciela*.

When the crew of the fishing boat saw him preparing to address them, they chanted more loudly than ever, "*Aquarius* go back! Out of Peruvian waters! *Aquarius* go home!"

Ignoring their protests, Haverson shouted, "Attention, *Maria Graciela!* Attention *Maria Graciela!*"

Eventually the chanting subsided. "We want to invite you to come aboard and air your grievances," he said.

Taking charge, Amy Armistad leaped on a crate, took up a bullhorn of her own and shouted back, "There's nothing to talk about!"

"No, nothing!" Terhune echoed through a second bullhorn. Always the proper academic, he wore a rumpled blue cord suit and striped tie, even on a grubby fishing boat.

"*Aquarius*, take your iceberg back where you got it!" Amy yelled. "The world doesn't want it!"

"Yes, take it back!" Terhune repeated.

"We are willing to make reasonable concessions if you are willing to talk. Nothing can be lost by having a dialogue," Haverson offered. "Are you willing or not?"

"*Aquarius* go back!" Amy replied. "There's nothing to talk about."

This time, though, instead of automatically taking up Amy's cant and rhetoric, Terhune took her aside and seemed to be trying to explain something to her. Impatiently, Amy listened, eventually nodding her head in somewhat reluctant agreement.

Placing the bullhorn over his mouth once again, Terhune shouted, "All right, *Aquarius*, we'll meet with you!"

Haverson made arrangements with the crew to prepare for the visitors. He wanted to create a relaxed, comfortable atmosphere, yet maintain strong security at the same time.

The moment Amy Armistad and Terhune stepped aboard, the aging climatologist insisted on inspecting the nuclear reactor before he would agree to sit down and confer. As he was doing so—under Haverson's vigilant eye—he made several disparaging remarks, but pronounced the ship essentially safe from radioactive contamination and finally settled into one of the upholstered chairs in the ship's library. Amy Armistad's voluptuous good looks excited considerable interest among the crew, although they were a bit put off by her strident militancy. In addition to Haverson, Maslov, MacFergus, and Gaspar also attended the conference. Sally, as a representative of the media, requested and received permission from both sides to record the proceedings on tape, which she would edit later. At first Amy was reluctant to give her permission for the taping until Sally finally persuaded her by promising her a solo interview when the conference was over, saying that she would need to review the material discussed in the conference in order to formulate questions for the interview.

At the head of the table Haverson indicated that it was time to get down to business. Quickly he performed the round of introductions, although it was probably not necessary; most of the participants knew one another, either directly or indirectly.

Turning to Amy, Haverson said, "Would you like to speak first, Miss Armistad?"

"Are you patronizing me because I happen to be a woman?" she challenged.

"No, not at all," Haverson replied, wanting to add that in spite of her aggressiveness, one could not easily overlook the fact that she was a woman and an attractive one.

"Good," she said. "What it all boils down to is that we of the Sea Vigilantes think the Aquarius project is dangerous and we intend to stop it."

"I've gathered that," Haverson replied. "Would you mind telling us why you object so strenuously? And please be specific."

In response to the question, Terhune spoke up. "That's very easy, Captain. As you've heard me point out many times before, we're opposed to the Aquarius Transfer because hauling icebergs around might very well alter the climate of certain regions—and perhaps the entire earth—in a detrimental way. As you surely must realize, the air around the iceberg becomes cooled considerably. As this air sinks and

225

passes over the adjacent land it causes a condensation of water vapor in the air which could easily produce heavy fogs, rains, and other potential hazards in areas unprepared to deal with such conditions."

"*What* other hazards, Doctor?" Maslov questioned. "Would you explain, please?"

"Sudden, abrupt condensation could produce gigantic rainstorms with subsequent flooding, possible tropical storms, hurricanes, tidal waves. Weather is a precarious thing; balances are very delicate. If they're upset, all kinds of catastrophes can occur. There is no end to the possible dangers and detrimental effects," the elderly scientist warned, shaking his finger at the group.

"Dr. Terhune, do you seriously believe that an iceberg the size of the one behind this ship is capable of producing any of the disasters you just ticked off?" Haverson questioned.

"I think there's little doubt that it's bound to affect the weather conditions to some degree," Terhune assured him. "Even a small change can sometimes precipitate a major catastrophe."

At that moment Amy decided it was time to enter into the discussion. "Besides all that stuff about the weather, there's the fish," she said. "The iceberg is not only chiling the air, it is also chilling the water around it and driving the fish away from their customary locations. This single iceberg, which you are now towing, has already chased the anchovies away from their usual grounds and ruined the fishing for the men in the boats now surrounding this ship. That's why these humble Peruvian fishermen have so willingly agreed to join us in our protest. There's not a man out there in those boats who's seen a single anchovy since you started up the Peruvian coast. Peru has the biggest share of the world's fishing catch—ten percent. Fishing is a major industry in this country. A lot of poor people will starve because of what you're doing, but we're not going to let that happen. We are determined to see that the *Aquarius* proceeds no further. In other words, Captain Haverson, we intend to stop you no matter what it takes," she declared, banging her fist on the table so hard a glass ashtray bounced to the floor and shattered.

35

The confrontation between the representatives of the *Aquarius* and the leaders of the Sea Vigilantes continued until dusk with little progress toward bringing the two sides to an understanding, since Amy Armistad and Thurston Terhune demanded that the *Aquarius* abandon the project at once.

"We intend to deliver this iceberg to the citizens of California as promised," Haverson asserted. "That's not going to change."

"Okay, okay," Amy said impatiently, hopping out of her chair and tossing her dark hair from side to side. "We've given you a chance to talk and explain your side of things, but we don't buy anything you're saying. We didn't come here to deliver an ultimatum, but you give us no alternative. All I'm going to say is that if you try and proceed any further north with this iceberg, we cannot promise that your voyage will be safe from possible interference by the Sea Vigilantes."

MacFergus—never one to beat around the bush—asked her, "Are you threatening us, miss?"

"If that's how you choose to take it," Amy snapped.

"But I thought, *mademoiselle*, that the Sea Vigilantes were supposed to be against violence?" Gaspar said.

"We are," she responded. "However, if violence is committed against us or against the seas of the world, we will be forced to retaliate in kind in order to defend ourselves and our ideals. We consider your insistence on continuing north with the iceberg an act of violence—violence against the earth's weather systems, violence against the sea, violence against the Peruvian fishing industry and the Peruvian people, violence against all life. . . ."

227

"To say nothing of the threat of this nuclear-powered ship and the ever-present danger *it* presents," Terhune interrupted.

"I'm sorry to disagree with you," Haverson said, retaining his composure despite the grueling session. "But we look on this project as humanitarian, one which can only benefit the world at large."

In spite of the unresolved disagreement and, at times, the outright animosity directed at him personally, Haverson decided to invite Amy and Terhune to remain on board for dinner when the chimes at seven sounded as a goodwill gesture.

"No. No thank you," Terhune responded. "We couldn't do that. Besides, I'm a strict vegetarian."

"Our cook does marvels with vegetables," Gaspar said.

Getting Terhune's attention by taking hold of his sleeve, Amy whispered something in the elderly academician's ear.

"Well, all right," the climatologist conceded. "We'll stay."

"Fine," Haverson replied and rising, led the way to the dining room.

Dabbing politely at the corners of his mouth with a napkin at the close of the meal, Terhune said, "Well, I must say, this dinner has been a delight."

"Perhaps you'd like to join me in my quarters for an after-dinner drink?" Haverson suggested.

"All right, Captain, we'll join you," Amy said, flashing a surprisingly flirtatious smile.

Amy's sudden change in attitude did not escape Sally's attention. As they were filing out of the dining room, she whispered to Maslov, "Haverson had better watch his step."

Conversation in the dayroom of Haverson's quarters was on a far more civil plane than in the conference room. At times, Amy and Terhune almost seemed willing to listen to the group's explanations. Outside, Haverson could hear the wind stirring and knew the sea was getting rough, although such changes were scarcely noticeable aboard a ship as large as the *Aquarius*. The Peruvian fishing vessels, however, would weather a storm badly—even a relatively small storm.

Maslov was most concerned about the change in the weather, and quietly expressed some anxiety regarding the iceberg to Haverson, who assured him that Snegoruschka could take it.

The leaders of the Sea Vigilantes seemed to enjoy the relative luxury of the *Aquarius* and were in no hurry to leave, especially when the alternative was the rigors and discomforts of a small Peruvian fishing boat in a storm. When Haverson invited them to join the crew in the ship's cinema for the screening of a recent film, they accepted.

As time passed the wind began to howl, waves splashed across the deck, and rain began to fall in torrents. When the movie was over, Haverson extended the pair an invitation to spend the night. "We can put you up on board if you like," he offered.

Both Amy and Terhune accepted eagerly, almost as if it were exactly what they were hoping for.

"Frankly, I'm getting a little sick of that 'fish' smell on the *Maria Graciela*," Terhune remarked. "To say nothing of the primitive accommodations and facilities."

Haverson directed one of the crew to conduct them to guest quarters on the Upper Bridge Deck.

During the night the storm increased its fury, causing the ship to pitch and roll excessively. Although they had endured far worse storms earlier in the voyage, Maslov began to fret about the iceberg.

"Go to bed and don't worry about it," Haverson advised a little impatiently. "The only thing we can do—as I see it—is to hope and pray that if there is a defect, it doesn't get any bigger before we reach California."

"The danger is that the crack might divide the iceberg in two," Maslov said. "The force of such a split will tear the insulation."

"I don't expect the insulation to keep it together. It wasn't designed to do that, just to prevent water loss by evaporation," Haverson said.

"But if it does split in two . . ." Maslov persisted.

"Then we'll haul both halves," Haverson replied. "Now go to bed."

Reluctantly, Maslov left and headed for his cabin.

Later in the night as the fierce wind howled against the windows of his quarters high above the Main Deck, Haverson was awakened by someone pounding on the door. Maslov, he thought, coming to air his anxieties about the iceberg once again. He got out of bed clad only in his undershorts. When he opened the door, he was surprised to find, not Yuri Maslov, but Amy Armistad, barefoot, wrapped in a blanket.

"Yes? What is it?" he asked, standing behind the partially opened door.

"Oh, Captain Haverson, I'm sorry to bother you," she said

in a soft, childish tone that contrasted dramatically with the fiery, hostile radical shrillness of earlier in the day. "I've been lying in bed listening to the wind and the sea pounding against the ship and the rain beating against the windows and I got scared. I went to Dr. Terhune's cabin, but I couldn't wake him, so I came here. It seemed like the logical thing to do. You *are* the captain. You know the most about what's going on. Please, may I come in?"

Before he could plead for a moment or two to slip into his trousers, she was inside. Plopping down on the sofa in the dayroom, she said, "Oh, I feel so terrible. . . ."

"You mean seasick?"

"I guess," she nodded. "I don't know, because I've never been seasick before. Mostly, I think I'm just scared."

"I'd better take you down to the sickbay and let the ship's doctor have a look at you," Haverson suggested.

Amy raised her hand in protest. "Please, just let me sit here a minute," she pleaded. "Go ahead and do whatever you were doing before I disturbed you."

"I was sleeping," he replied, observing that her complexion was not the usual greenish hue of one who was seasick. He began to wonder what kind of game she might be playing with him.

"Then go back to sleep," she said. Without any encouragement, she stretched out on the sofa exposing one entire leg and a generous portion of both breasts as she hugged the blanket around her.

A few moments later the ship apparently plunged down the trough of a large wave and under the impact, vibrated badly. "My God!" Amy gasped. "What happened?"

"Nothing," he reassured her. "The ship's just shaking a little, that's all."

"Nothing to you maybe," she said. "You're experienced." Reaching out, she suddenly clutched his hand.

Haverson was attracted to her; she managed to seem both sensual and vulnerable at the moment, but he remained wary of her motives. He realized that her appeal was heightened by the fact that he had been away from home and Ingrid a long time. Struggling against the rapidly rising desire inside him as he gazed at her voluptuous body, he said, "I think we'd better get you down to sickbay pretty quick."

"No!" she protested, squeezing his hand. "Please, give me a minute." With a sudden, unexpected jerk, she pulled him down on the sofa with her, at the same time tossing aside the

230

blanket, exposing her nakedness. Wrapping both legs and arms around him, she planted her mouth firmly on his, probing deeply with her tongue.

"Hey, what is this?" Haverson said in a half-choked voice. She had such a tight grip around his neck that he found it difficult to speak.

"You really turn me on. The whole time I was sitting across the table from you today I could hardly keep my mind on our discussions," she confessed breathlessly. "Couldn't you tell?"

"No," he replied.

"Well, I think you're terrific," she declared, and, as she spoke, she slipped her hand inside the elastic waistband of his undershorts. Haverson made a token gesture of resistance, although considerations other than his conscience told him he ought to resist more.

Tugging desperately at his shorts, she attempted to slide them down over his hips, at the same time thrusting against him in a highly suggestive, rhythmic frenzy. Haverson could scarcely believe what was happening.

"Take me!" she whispered hoarsely, half biting his ear. "Take me. I need you. I want you. I want to feel you inside me. Deep inside. Deep, deep, deep. Oh, please, hurry! Don't make me wait. Do it! Do it now!"

Sure that Amy had more in mind than just a casual romp in the hay, Haverson decided to try and extricate himself from her embrace, but she held him locked between her surprisingly strong arms and legs. "Hey, Amy, cool it," he protested. "Are you nuts or something? What the hell are you trying to do? What is all this?"

At that moment there was a loud knocking at the door, and Haverson thought he had unraveled her plot. Someone—most likely Terhune—was to catch them in the act and threaten blackmail unless certain concessions were made.

But Amy said, "Don't answer it."

"Neal, get up!" It was Maslov's voice shouting from the other side of the door.

"Tell him to go away," she demanded in a harsh whisper.

"I can't do that," Haverson said. He was beginning to get angry with her.

"Neal, are you in there?" Maslov shouted, continuing to pound on the door.

"Listen, Amy, I'm going to get up and answer that door," Haverson informed her, roughly detaching her arm from around his neck.

Amy's eyes narrowed viciously and her voice took on a hard, threatening edge. "If you open that door, I'll scream rape!"

Furious, Haverson took her by the hair, yanked her to her feet, and threw the cast-off blanket at her. "Put this around you," he ordered.

Ignoring the fact that she continued to stand defiantly naked in the center of the dayroom, he jumped into his pants. "Just a minute, Yuri," he called out. Then turning to Amy, he said, "In about ten seconds I'm going to open that door. You have a choice—you can either be naked when Yuri Maslov comes in here, or you can cover yourself. I leave it up to you."

"How are you going to explain it?" she challenged.

"Right now I'm not concerned about explanations," he said and started toward the door. Reluctantly, Amy enveloped herself in the blanket once again and curled up seductively in a corner of the sofa.

Maslov was out of breath when Haverson opened the door. "Neal, you've got to come quick," he said, scarcely noticing Amy.

"What's wrong?" Haverson asked anxiously, knowing from the Russian's expression that it must be something serious.

"The cable," Maslov replied, pointing toward the stern of the ship. "They're trying to cut it."

"Who is?" Haverson asked.

"The people in those boats all around us," Maslov replied.

"Don't listen to him. He's crazy," Amy interjected. "Why would those poor fishermen want to cut your cable, for chrissake?"

Ignoring her, Haverson grabbed a pair of .45s from the drawer of his desk and handed one to Maslov. Locking Amy inside his quarters despite her screams of protest, he and Maslov raced down the steps to the Main Deck, pushed the Emergency Action Stations Switch, setting off the alarm, and dashed to a lifeboat where they were quickly joined by several other crewmen.

"What's up, Captain?" one of the men asked.

"Never mind, just get in," Haverson said, giving the order to lower the boat at once.

When the lifeboat hit the water, Haverson himself manned the motor and, despite the rough sea, howling wind, and driving rain, traveled at top speed, using the towing cable overhead as a guide through the storm-lashed darkness. As they approached the *Maria Graciela* it was suddenly apparent to Haverson what was happening. While Amy had been using her diversionary tactics on him, other members of the Sea Vigilantes were at work on the towing cable.

"I hope we get there before they do too much damage," Haverson said.

"The cable's tough," Maslov said. "It can take a lot."

"Everything has its limits," Haverson replied.

Maslov had gotten up during the night to check how the iceberg was weathering the storm and noted a persistent shower of bright sparks at one point along the line through his binoculars. In view of the threats and past antics of the Sea Vigilantes, it was not difficult for him to conclude what was happening.

Aboard the Peruvian fishing boat the saboteurs were so intent on their work, despite the raging storm, that they failed to notice the lifeboat as it drew alongside. The cable, swaying in the wind, wet and slippery from the rain, was proving an unruly target. There were four of them involved in the attack on the line, two Americans and two Peruvians. One of the Americans stood on a shaky ladder applying the acetylene torch to the cable, while the other three braced the ladder and supplied the light for the job, a small battery-operated lantern whose beam, on the wildly bobbing boat, was erratic at best.

As Haverson and Maslov, .45s in hand, climbed aboard the fishing vessel, Haverson fired a warning shot in the air. Instantly all four saboteurs whirled around, including the man on the ladder.

"Drop that torch and put your hands in the air," Haverson shouted. "High."

The American on the ladder heaved the acetylene torch at Haverson, who ducked in time to hear it go whizzing over his head, crashing to the deck in a shower of sparks. One of the Peruvians started to make a move toward Maslov, and the Russian fired a shot, grazing the man's jacket, forcing him to back off. Ordering Maslov to cover the quartet, Haverson summoned some of the other crewmen from the lifeboat and instructed them to search the saboteurs for possible weapons and bind their hands behind them.

When the four were bound, Haverson ordered them into the lifeboat, nudging them with the barrel of his .45. There was little resistance; they knew Haverson meant business.

233

36

Kirkwood was surprised when he entered Bonnie's hospital room and found a screen around her bed. "Bonnie?" he called out tentatively.

"Just a minute," she replied from the opposite side of the screen, her usually strong voice sounding slightly nervous.

"What's the screen for?" he asked.

"They're changing my dressings," she said.

"I can't wait to get a look at you," he said. "Do you realize how long it's been since I had a look at your face?"

"Don't remind me," she replied.

From the far side of the screen, the nurse addressed Bonnie. "Well, I think that's it for today. Let's move this screen out of the way so the governor . . ."

"No!" Bonnie cried out in panic. "Not yet."

The nurse seemed puzzled. "Why not?"

"I need it just a minute or two longer."

"What for?" the nurse said.

"Yes, what for?" Kirkwood echoed.

"Give me one more minute," she insisted. "I'm sorry, Paul, but I need a little more time to get my head together. I told you how I always get nervous and sick and throw up before I start a picture. Remember? Well, I feel the same way now, like it's the same thing—new picture, new face."

"Come on, Bonnie, you don't have to worry with me," he said.

In an attempt to calm herself, she said, "Listen, tell me about the *Aquarius*. What's been happening? Wasn't that business in Peru awful? Imagine those guys trying to cut the cable! I couldn't believe it. And that Amy Armistad. . . . You

234

know what I think? I think she's a phony. I really don't think she believes all that stuff she's been saying."

"That doesn't stop her from saying it," Kirkwood said.

"She's got a big mouth on her," Bonnie said.

"Listen, Bonnie," Kirkwood said, his voice sounding impatient. "What in the hell are you doing back there?"

"Nothing," she replied. "I told you—I'm just trying to get my head together."

The nurse, too, was impatient with Bonnie. "I think we can safely take the screen away now," she said and started to fold it.

"No!" Bonnie cried out with such urgency that the nurse stopped trying to close the screen.

"Goddam it, Bonnie, let her take it away," Kirkwood demanded sternly.

"No!" Bonnie cried again.

"I'm going to turn her over to you, Governor," the nurse said resignedly and left the room.

When they were alone, Kirkwood took hold of the screen. "You've hidden from me long enough," he said.

"No! Not yet!" Bonnie pleaded, sounding desperate.

"Now!" Kirkwood declared and shoved the screen away.

Bonnie let out a shriek and attempted to cover her face with her hands, but Kirkwood seized her wrists and firmly but gently, pulled them away, forcing her to expose her recently reconstructed face to him for the first time.

There were a few moments of stunned silence as each stared at the other, Bonnie, suspensefully awaiting Kirkwood's reaction, Kirkwood apprehensive about what his reaction might be and how it might affect her.

"Well . . . what do you think?" she asked.

The skin was red and crusted and still puffy, but that did not obscure the fact that the surgeons had obviously done a good job.

"How do I look?" she asked.

"What difference does it make? Your face wasn't the only thing I fell in love with, you know," Kirkwood reminded her.

Bonnie would not be put off. "I look awful, don't I?"

"You look great."

"I do not," she said. "You're lying."

"You look great, I tell you," he repeated. "But even if you didn't, I'd still love you." Looking her straight in the eye, he said, "I want us to get married."

"Married? Us?" Bonnie was truly flabbergasted.

"Sure. Why not?"

"I already tried it once and it didn't work out," she said. "Besides, you're only saying that because you feel sorry for me."

"Come on, Bonnie," he reproached. "Enough of that stuff."

"You can't marry me. You've got all you can handle just being governor."

"I can handle that, you, and a lot more," he said confidently.

"You're going to run for president," she said. "How's it going to look—me up there on the platform with this face?"

"It's going to look terrific," he assured her.

"Suppose you win?"

"I intend to."

"Then, I'd be the First Lady?"

"Right."

"I'd be the first First Lady with a reconstructed face," she mused.

"Hardly," he said, holding her close.

37

Despite Amy's protests of innocence, Haverson exerted authority as ship's captain and placed her under arrest too, ordering her detained aboard the ship together with the four captured saboteurs. Terhune, on the other hand, presented a somewhat different problem. Haverson found it difficult not to believe the elderly scientist when he professed to know nothing of the plot to sever the cable and even seemed dismayed by it, but he felt obliged for security reasons to take him into custody as well.

"I swear to you, neither Miss Armistad nor I knew anything about a plot to cut the cable," he said. "I demand that you release us at once!"

"You might be right about yourself, Dr. Terhune," Haverson admitted, "but I'm not so sure about your cohort."

"I have always found Amy to be a truthful young lady. If she says the others formulated those plans in our absence, then I believe her," Terhune staunchly declared.

"You must have known that the acetylene torch was aboard the fishing boat," Haverson pointed out. "What did you think it was going to be used for?"

"I never notice tools and things like that—especially aboard a boat," Terhune said, dismissing the question. "And neither does Amy. Even if we did, we would undoubtedly assume it to be part of the normal equipment—to make repairs and such."

Haverson declined to argue and ordered the crewmen to see that the professor and Amy were confined to their cabins under house arrest until further notice.

"You can't do this to us!" Terhune protested.

"I'm sorry, Professor, but I have to," Haverson replied, convinced that the Sea Vigilantes would make no further attempts to sabotage the ship while six of their comrades were detained aboard.

Later that night, Haverson notified the fishing fleet, which had been more or less dispersed by the storm, that the *Aquarius* intended to start up again and anyone who tried to interfere did so at grave risk. Following the stern warning, he gave the order to start the reactor; the great ship would resume its journey northward.

Although the cable-cutting incident would provide KHOT viewers with some excitement, Sally was aware that she would have to come up with further exciting or controversial stories in order to maintain the momentum her Aquarius series had created. She sensed that Amy's current plight might prove interesting, but doubted that Haverson would permit her to interview the girl. Sally did not care much for Amy and suspected that her almost fanatical opposition to the Aquarius project arose from selfish or opportunistic motives, but putting her personal feelings aside, she decided to try and spend some time with her, probing for a story, perhaps in the process uncovering the *real* Amy Armistad.

Sally wanted to talk over the situation with Maslov first and try and determine from him how Haverson might feel about letting her interview Amy. Locating him in the radar room, she found that he was absorbed in other matters at the moment.

"This is not good," he declared, shaking his head as he examined a profusion of charts and graphs, all of which meant little to Sally. "Not good at all. Our findings indicate without question that there is a definite crack now developing in the iceberg—just as I predicted."

"Are you certain?" Sally asked.

Referring to the mass of technical information around him, he said, "There is every indication. And yet, I cannot make Haverson aware of the seriousness of the situation. I cannot make him see that we must be prepared for the possibility that the iceberg may split in two. He makes jokes and refuses to take my warning seriously." Looking up from the piles of papers in front of him, he added, "I think he is too distracted by that Amy Armistad."

"I don't think he likes her very much," Sally remarked.

Raising a dark eyebrow skeptically, Maslov said, "Doesn't he?"

"I don't think so," Sally replied, wondering whether Maslov

was implying that there was something going on between the captain of the *Aquarius* and one of his fiercest opponents. "Do you?"

"Tell me this, Sally, do you know where Amy was while her comrades were trying to cut the cable?" he asked.

"She was right here, on board the *Aquarius*," Sally replied.

"Yes, but do you know where *exactly?*" he persisted, giving emphasis to the word "exactly."

"In her cabin, I assume. Why?"

"She was not in her cabin, but Haverson's."

Surprised, Sally said, "But it was the middle of the night."

"Nevertheless, that's where I found her when I knocked on Haverson's door," Maslov revealed. "When I entered, she was there, covered only by a blanket—and not very well covered."

"Really?" Sally said. The story came as a real shock, although she tried to hide her reaction. She also knew it was true; Maslov was neither a gossip nor a liar.

"I don't speculate on what was happening," he said. "That is their business."

Sally had been around long enough not to be shocked by any amorous pairing of individuals, no matter how unlikely. By painful experience she had learned that, in certain situations, anything goes. In addition, she was aware that despite Amy's quirky political bent, she was an attractive, sexy woman who made no effort to conceal her generous physical assets, even when spouting the most radical rhetoric. Yet, in spite of herself, Sally was stunned, scarcely able to believe that a man she had come to regard as highly principled would actually succumb to Amy's seductiveness. That certainly must have been how it was; she assumed Amy had come on to Haverson. The more she contemplated Maslov's story, the more indignant she became. Haverson had never shown any romantic interest in her, yet had apparently succumbed easily to Amy. The more she thought about it, the more determined she was to interview Amy and get her side of the story.

At this point she decided to go directly to Haverson himself. "I can see you're busy, Yuri," Sally said. "I'll talk to you later." And, leaving the Russian to fret over a possible crack in the iceberg, she headed straight up to the captain's quarters.

Haverson looked at her curiously as he admitted her to his office. "What's up?" he asked.

Trying to sound as genial as possible, she said, "I'd like your permission to do an interview."

239

Looking puzzled by her request, he said, "I gave you blanket permission as far as the crew is concerned."

"It isn't the crew I want to talk to," she said.

"Who is it then?"

"Amy Armistad."

Sally couldn't detect any obvious emotional reaction on his part. Haverson considered her request a moment, then asked, "Why Amy?".

"I think she's interesting," Sally replied, "Don't you?"

He nodded noncommittally, conceding, "Possibly."

"I understand she's confined to her cabin."

"That's right."

"Will somebody let me in?"

"I suppose I could arrange that."

A bit curtly she said, "Thanks," and started for the door, heading straight to Amy's cabin.

Amy, sullen and petulant, angry at being locked up, proved a somewhat disappointing interview. No matter what tactics Sally employed, she could get her to reveal very little. Since Haverson would allow no one else except Sally in the cabin with Amy, she had had to set up the camera and sound equipment on her own while Amy watched her suspiciously.

"This is the interview I promised you," Sally said brightly. "Remember?"

When the tape started to roll, Sally had to listen to diatribes against the political system in general and against the Aquarius project in particular.

"Amy, I was just wondering," Sally interrupted cautiously, about to touch on what she knew might be a delicate area. "There is the matter of airfare for you and the Sea Vigilantes and the costs of staying in Lima and preparing for the protest. As we both know, it's certainly not cheap and probably runs into a considerable amount of money. Am I right?"

"Yeah," Amy conceded grudgingly.

"I'm wondering where this money comes from."

"It comes from ordinary citizens who are concerned about the world's oceans and the vital part they play in our lives, our survival," Amy replied.

"Would you care to name a couple of your most generous supporters?" Sally asked.

"I don't feel that's my place," Amy snapped, annoyed by the question. "People don't contribute to the Sea Vigilantes for self-glorification. It's not your usual charity."

"But you are obviously an official spokesperson for the Sea Vigilantes," Sally reminded her.

"Yes, but only on matters of direct concern to the welfare of this planet," Amy said. "Anything else I consider irrelevant and superfluous and a waste of time."

"Then you decline to discuss who the Sea Vigilantes' most vigorous supporters are?" Sally persisted.

"I do because if their names were publicized, they might be subjected to all kinds of harassment," Amy asserted. "There are a lot of powerful forces in the United States who would like to stifle us. My imprisonment aboard this ship is a perfect example of what I mean. I am a political prisoner being held in violation of my rights."

Cagily, Sally asked, "Has anything else happened which you feel might also be a violation of sorts—anything between you and Captain Haverson, for example?" She held her breath, scarcely believing she had had the courage to ask such a leading question. Uneasily, she waited for Amy's answer.

"Yes, as a matter of fact there is," Amy answered. "Haverson harassed me because of my sex."

"Would you care to elaborate, Amy?" Sally prodded.

"Your captain invited me to his cabin under the pretext of wishing to discuss our differences further," she said. "When I arrived, he proceeded to try and force himself on me—physically."

"Could you be more specific?" Sally asked.

Amy looked at her askance. "Come on, Sally, you're a woman, a media person," Amy chided. "I don't have to spell it out for you, do I? I'm sure you've been hit on—you know, subjected to the same kind of sexist harassment—many times yourself."

"I suppose I have," Sally admitted; Amy was right on that point. They discussed the problem of unwanted sexual overtures for a while, but, as far as Sally was concerned, the interview was over. She had learned what she had come to find out. She packed up her gear and prepared to leave, thanking Amy for her cooperation. Amy looked a little surprised that the interview had ended so abruptly, but she said nothing.

Later, as Sally looked over the part of the interview she had taped, she found it disappointing and realized she had been far too absorbed in her own personal concerns regarding Amy's relationship with Haverson to do a truly objective job

241

of reporting. If the segment were to succeed and generate the kind of excitement she had been striving for in the series, she would need additional material to augment the session with Amy. The only possible story she knew which had elements of suspense and was, therefore, a "grabber" was the supposed crack Maslov insisted was developing in the iceberg.

When she quizzed Maslov about it, he declined to discuss the matter on camera, claiming that the evidence was not sufficiently conclusive to make a statement. Her personal guess was that Haverson had warned him about talking to her about it. Because of his reluctance, she was forced to go before the camera herself and tell what she had learned of the situation from Maslov, hoping that she could present the facts in a way which was both credible and interesting and would keep the KHOT viewers tuning in for further developments. That was, after all, what was expected of her. When the segment was wrapped up, she stepped behind the camera, turned it off, and scarcely gave the matter a second thought, except to hope that it would help to liven what she considered a rather lackluster segment.

During the next few days, things were uneventful aboard the *Aquarius*. The prisoners did their share of complaining and protesting, but no one paid much attention. Sally discovered, much to her dismay, that her feelings of hostility toward Haverson, based on what Amy had told her, unconsciously surfaced from time to time in spite of her attempts to suppress them.

One evening at dinner, Gaspar commented to those around the table—Haverson, Maslov, MacFergus, and Sally—that the leg of lamb was roasted to perfection. "Even in France we could do no better," he declared.

"I understand one of our prisoners didn't think so much of our lamb," MacFergus said.

"You're referring to Amy, no doubt?" Sally asked.

"Of course," MacFergus confirmed. "She threw her whole tray at the poor mess steward."

"She trashed all the furniture in the cabin," Haverson said. "I had it removed. Now it's just her and four walls."

"Where's she sleeping?" Sally asked.

"On the floor one would imagine," Gaspar said.

"On the floor?!" Sally repeated, surprised at Haverson's harshness.

"Why not?" Haverson said. "That's good enough for her."

"And if it's not, you can always share your bunk with her," Sally said caustically. "Again."

At her final word, the table fell awkwardly silent. The four men stared at her. Embarrassed, Sally rose, excused herself in a mumble, and ran to her cabin.

In her quarters, Sally tried to convince herself that she had acted out of indignation and nothing more. Haverson's attitude toward Amy was contemptible, an insult to all women. But later, after giving the matter a lot of thought, she reluctantly conceded that she might be slightly jealous, an admission that did not come easily.

After the dinner incident, Haverson summoned Sally to his office, and when she arrived, she could see from his expression that he was obviously angry about something.

"Sit down," he said rather gruffly, indicating a chair next to his desk. "I've just had a message from Governor Kirkwood. It seems that station KHOT broadcast the news that the iceberg the *Aquarius* is towing has a serious crack in it and is in danger of splitting in two."

"Yes. That's what Yuri told me," Sally readily admitted.

"That's beside the point," Haverson snapped. "There is no way in hell we want that bit of speculation relayed to the whole world—especially right now. That's all it is, you know—mere speculation. Frankly, I don't happen to agree completely with Maslov's interpretation of the data. In any case, I thought we had the understanding when you forced your way on board this ship that before you transmitted any stories back to the States, they would have my approval. I gave you permission to interview Amy Armistad, not to pass along idle and irresponsible rumors."

"I'm sorry," Sally apologized. "I didn't realize it was such a sensitive issue. I also didn't know it was a secret. I've heard the possibility of a crack in the iceberg discussed openly around the ship for days."

"That still doesn't give you the right to broadcast it without permission."

"I said I'm sorry."

Suddenly the angry tone in his voice seemed to be replaced by weariness. "You know, Sally, I've tried to be understanding. I've even tried to be forgiving, but this time you've gone too far."

"I didn't mean to indicate that . . ."

"I know you didn't mean to. You never *mean* to," he interrupted. "But I'll tell you what I'm going to do. As soon as

243

we reach Mexico, I'm going to have you removed from this ship."

Sally was stunned. "What?!" she gasped. By this time she had felt—at least in her own mind—that she was a part of things, thoroughly accepted by Haverson and the crew. The thought of being expelled from the ship seemed inconceivable. She could tolerate his dallying with Amy Armistad, even his earlier harassment, but she could not accept the thought of being sent off the *Aquarius*, especially for what she considered a minor infraction. "You don't really *mean* that, do you?"

"I'm afraid I do," he said. There was no compassion in his voice.

That same night it wasn't Amy Armistad who came to Haverson's quarters but Sally Brennan, a little more substantially attired—a coat over her nightgown—than the radical protester had been. Agonizing over Haverson's decree, she had been unable to sleep and finally arrived at the conclusion that it was better to try and appeal to him directly than to cry helplessly into her pillow. She knew from past experience that he was an extremely stubborn man, but she felt compelled to make a direct appeal anyway. He had had dinner and drinks in the wardroom with some of his officers and time to cool off. There could be no harm in trying again.

In order to rouse him, she had had to knock loudly and persistently on his door. Possibly because of his experience with Amy, he was hesitant about opening the door immediately without identifying the caller.

"Who is it?" he asked.

"It's me—Sally," she answered.

"What is it?"

"Please . . . I'd like to talk to you."

"I'll see you in the morning," he said brusquely.

"No," she insisted. "I have to talk to you now."

Wearily, he opened the door and invited her in. He had on a pair of trousers and an unbuttoned shirt, obviously put on in great haste. "Look, Sally," he began, "if you've come here to plead with me to change my mind about putting you off the ship, it isn't going to do any good. You're just wasting your time."

"That isn't why I've come," she lied. "I just came to ask you a simple question."

"What is it?"

"Why the hell do you have such unshakable animosity

toward me?" she demanded. "Okay. I admit that I inveigled my way aboard and not under the best of circumstances, but I've tried my best to make amends. I really have. I made a simple mistake—an innocent mistake—and you're practically crucifying me for it. I don't think it's fair."

"I said we weren't going to discuss my decision," he reminded her.

Unable to restrain herself, Sally clenched her fists in frustration. "You're like a goddam robot that's programmed a certain way and can't be changed. Shit!" she exclaimed.

"Maybe I am," he conceded indifferently.

"Not only that," she said, tears of rage and frustration welling in her eyes, "you're one of the coldest men I've ever known. You're devoid of all feelings. Were you like this with Amy? I'll bet you weren't."

Haverson glared at her. "What the hell are you bringing *her* into this for?"

"I heard all about it," Sally shot back. "From Yuri. *And* from Amy herself."

"I'm not going to talk about it now," he said. "Besides, it's none of your business anyway."

"You know what? I'll bet you're even like this with Ingrid," she speculated.

Bristling, Haverson warned, "Keep my wife out of this. Ingrid doesn't need your help."

"How do you know what any woman needs?" she shot back.

Grabbing her by the arm, Haverson dragged her toward the door.

Sally fought back, venting her hurt and frustration by pummeling him with her fists until he forcibly restrained her by seizing her wrists and holding them tight.

"Let me go!" she cried, struggling against him.

"No. Not until you promise to behave."

Eventually exhausted and subdued, and knowing she was no match for his strength, Sally murmured, "Okay, okay, I promise."

Haverson released her, but instead of leaving, Sally crumpled into a nearby chair and buried her face in her hands, crying softly.

Haverson was astonished, realizing for the first time how really vulnerable she was. These were not crocodile tears. Placing his hand sympathetically on her shoulder, he said, "Look, I'm sorry if I upset you."

Unexpectedly she placed her own hand on top of his and

squeezed it tight, a gesture he interpreted as forgiveness. For several moments they remained very still, neither moving. Then without a word, Haverson swept her up in his arms and carried her to the bedroom. Sally offered no resistance.

The first time their lovemaking was not slow and languorous and filled with the small sensual nuances of confident lovers, but instead was frenzied, intense, fumbling, and out of control. They were so overwhelmed by tension, desire, and sheer physical attraction that they consumed one another like a pair of raging, opposing fires driven by the winds of a passion that had been too long denied. The first time resembled a contest or match or bout. The second, which followed a short time later, was lovemaking in its truest form. Both Haverson and Sally savored one another as an orchardman savors the first ripe peach for which he has waited impatiently throughout a sluggish summer, or an eager vintner the first sip of wine after an interminable decade of aging. They ascended to the peak slowly, lovingly, in careful but accelerating steps, and when they reached it, it proved to be every bit as magnificent as they had dreamed.

"Wow! My God! I can't believe it!" Sally exclaimed, sitting up in bed and shaking the tangled mass of blond hair out of her eyes. Tiny beads of perspiration dotted her upper lip, and as she lovingly stroked Haverson's chest, she saw that it, too, was veined with heavy rivulets of sweat.

"Neither can I," he said, slightly breathless, his heart still pounding in his chest.

"Hey, how the hell did we ever end up in bed together?" Sally said, laughing.

"Now I wonder how we took so long," Haverson said, smiling and shaking his head. "You're not sorry, are you?"

"Sorry?" she repeated. "Hell, no. What would I be sorry about?"

Looking a bit sheepish, Haverson said, "Well, we haven't been exactly the best of friends."

"Well, we are now," she said. "If we're not, we'd better be."

Caressing her arm, he said, "I'm sorry I've been so rough on you. I really am."

Sally shrugged. "I can take it."

"Yeah. And you can dish it out, too, on occasion."

"I consider that a compliment," Sally said, tossing back the covers and preparing to get out of bed.

"Where are you going?" he asked.

"I thought I'd better leave. It's pretty late," she replied. "I don't want to start any trouble."

"Since when?" he chided.

"I mean, domestically," she explained.

"Let me worry about that," he said. "Get back under the covers. I want you next to me. All night."

"Whatever you say, sir," Sally said, doing as he requested. "You're the captain of this ship."

Haverson slid his arm under her bare shoulders and held her close. "That's a lot better."

"You know," Sally said, "I hate to bring this up right now, but I feel I have to. Ingrid's a nice lady. I wouldn't want to see her hurt. Once we get back to California, this is all over. You know that, don't you?"

Raising his head from the pillow, Haverson gazed at her. "If that's the way you want it."

"That's the way I want it," she assured him.

Haverson realized he had never met a woman quite like Sally before. "You know, we've spent months together, and I'm just now realizing I hardly know you. I mean, I hardly know anything about you."

"After tonight I'd say you know a lot," she quipped.

"I'm serious," he insisted. "I mean about your personal life. You never talk about that. It's always business, the job."

"Like a man, right?" she said. "What do you want to know?"

Haverson concentrated a moment. "Well, first of all, is there a guy in your life back in L.A. or what?"

"There was," she replied. "For a while. Three years to be exact."

"Then what happened?"

"Oh, men are kind of like cars for me. After three years I start hankering for a new model. They lose their charm or luster or something. I don't know. It's not my ideal, you understand, not the way I really want to do things. It's just the way it works out. I really don't think a long term thing would work for me. I wish it would, but I don't think it's going to happen. That's why I'm so heavy into my career. It gives me the only stability I have," she said.

Haverson contemplated what she said a few moments

247

before replying. "That explains a lot," he said. "What you just said—about your career."

"Does it make it any easier for you to forgive me?"

Squeezing her tight, he covered her face, neck, and shoulders with kisses. "What's there to forgive?" he said just before they made love a third time.

38

Accustomed to rising early, Haverson stirred first, shortly before dawn, and gently nudged Sally, who lay beside him, one arm across his chest. She opened her eyes tentatively, closed them again, and with a groan of protest rolled over onto her side.

"You're missing a great dawn," he said, his lips brushing her smooth shoulder.

"It's too early to get up," Sally mumbled sleepily and, reaching out, tried to prevent him from getting out of bed.

"Seriously, Sally, we have to get up," he urged. "I don't think it would be a good idea for the whole ship to find out you spent the night here. There are enough rumors going around already."

Sally reluctantly slipped out of the warm bed and searched for her nightgown, which had been carelessly tossed aside during their lovemaking. "Where the hell is it?" she wondered aloud.

Haverson retrieved the filmy gown from beneath the bed and handed it to her. Sally slipped it over her head and reached for her coat, draped over the back of a chair. Regretfully, Haverson watched her dress, sorry their night together was over.

Silently, Sally slipped out the door and down the passageway leading from Haverson's quarters to her own. As she turned a corner, she nearly collided with Maslov who was surprised to see her up and about at that hour of the morning.

"Sally! . . ." he said. "Good morning."

"Oh, good morning, Yuri," she replied sheepishly, feeling more than a little ridiculous running around in her nightgown just outside Haverson's suite.

"I'm surprised to see you here," he remarked, looking at her quizzically.

"I'm surprised to see you, too," she said.

Looking grave, Maslov shook his head. "The latest data show that the notch in the iceberg is definitely growing larger," he announced. "I was coming to inform Haverson. We must do something before it is too late. But what are you doing here so early? It is not usual for you to be awake at this hour."

"No, it isn't," she was forced to agree. "I was having trouble sleeping. You know that Haverson is upset with me for reporting the possible crack, don't you?"

Maslov nodded. "I have heard."

"I feel terrible about it," she said.

"You mustn't," he advised.

"I was so upset I couldn't sleep," she continued. "So I decided to have a talk with Haverson about it."

"He was awake?" Maslov asked.

"His light was on, so I thought he was," she said. "Actually I woke him." Sally was annoyed with herself for the awkward way she was groping for an acceptable explanation. From his expression she was certain Maslov didn't believe a word she was saying anyway.

"And then you talked?' he asked.

"Yes."

"What did he say?"

She shrugged. "Oh, nothing much."

"Sally, why do you lie to me?" he asked her pointblank.

"I'm not lying," she protested, knowing how unconvincing she must sound.

"You insult me when you say that," he said. "I know very well you spent the night with Haverson. I went to your cabin several times to see if you wanted to play chess. You were not in. I could find you nowhere else on the ship. Finally, when it became very late, I decided to give up looking for you. I'm glad you found something more interesting than a mere chess game."

"Now, just a minute, Yuri. . . ." she said indignantly.

"It is not necessary to explain or apologize—or lie—any further," he said and brushed hastily past her, disappearing around the corner.

A few hours after the spectacular dawn, Haverson was informed that reports from the weather satellite indicated that a tropical storm was forming off the west coast of Mexico. The chance of its developing into a full-blown hurricane was good. From the bridge Haverson surveyed the horizon. All around the ship great mountains of clouds rose out of the dark, murky sea, their tops brushing a pale, eerie sky. He didn't like the look of it—the stillness, the uneasy calm, and on the ship's intercom warned the crew to prepare for possible trouble. Over coffee Haverson discussed the impending storm with Maslov, wondering what, if any, course of action they might take if it struck along their course.

"If a tropical storm comes, we just have to hope that Snegoruschka doesn't split," Maslov said. "Don't forget, I warned you of her condition many times. Now we will just have to take our chances."

A little annoyed by the Russian's resigned indifference, which was not at all characteristic, Haverson said, "Sure, you *warned* me. But, damn it, Yuri, you haven't offered any solution either. Every goddam day you keep telling me that a possible crack is developing and a lot of other crap, but you don't tell me what the hell to do about it. I don't want to hear problems, I want to hear solutions."

"There is no solution," Maslov replied, trying not to react to Haverson's obvious irritation. "There is only a small amount of experimental data."

"Based on work *I* did," Haverson said.

"None of it gives the answer," Maslov replied. "Don't forget, we are the first to actually try something like this. When the answers are known, we will be the first to supply them. We are the experimenters. This entire mission is one big experiment."

"Don't you think I know that?" Haverson replied impatiently. He felt the Russian was being unnecessarily difficult and he was fast becoming exasperated with him. "What I expect from you are some ideas, some suggestions of where to begin at least."

"The only suggestion I have is to reverse the iceberg and tow it from the opposite end," Maslov said. "With the waves hitting it from another direction, perhaps that will prevent further erosion."

"Reverse the iceberg?" Haverson repeated as if to verify what he had just heard. "Yuri, do you have any idea what that entails?"

"Of course," Maslov snapped. "That is why I have said nothing before. That is all I can offer. Many things are

251

difficult and entail much work. We cannot always have things the way we want them."

Haverson considered Maslov's suggestion about reversing the iceberg and was forced to agree that it did, indeed, appear to be the only feasible solution at present. Such a maneuver, of course, would be very difficult, but the suggestion seemed sound. In order for the iceberg to be reversed, the bollards would have to be removed and reimplanted at the opposite end. The bollard implantation had not been easy in Antarctica, even with the help of ample and skilled navy personnel and equipment; off the hurricane-threatened coast of Mexico, it would be an entirely different, but equally difficult, situation. Even if the reversal were successful, there was no guarantee that the iceberg would not crack in two anyway. It was a difficult dilemma. Haverson had no desire to let success slip through his fingers when it was so close at hand. At best, whatever he did or didn't do would be a gamble.

Confirming the weather forecasters' worst fears, the tropical storm picked up speed and power and evolved into a full-fledged hurricane named Victor. By the time the hurricane reached the vicinity of the *Aquarius*, its winds had reached one hundred ten miles an hour. Just before it struck, there was a sunset of incomparable beauty and grandeur, the sky streaked with vivid strokes of green, scarlet, and violet. To Sally the brilliantly colored display was awesome and inspiring, while Haverson found it ominous and ordered all doors and hatches battened down. Sally was sent packing to her quarters and all unnecessary traffic prohibited on deck. Crewmen were withdrawn from hazardous areas. By this time Haverson had great confidence in the *Aquarius*, although he was aware that the two greatest dangers to supertankers were "turning turtle"—that is, flipping over—and snapping in two because of their great length. After the safety of the ship and crew, his greatest concern was the iceberg and whether or not it could withstand the onslaught of the storm.

Hurricane Victor struck during the night with a ferocity that stunned even the most seasoned crewman. Torrential rains, driven by cyclonic winds averaging well over one hundred twenty knots, slashed across the faces of those men whose urgent duties exposed them to the wrath of the storm. With incredible fury it roared across the deck, pinning men helplessly to bulkheads, flinging them heedlessly about, leaving them senseless. The maniacal winds swirled furiously around and around the eye of the storm and goaded its more-than-willing cohort, the vengeful sea, into a lethal partnership. Together, the two seemed bent on destroying the hapless *Aquarius*. Taking it by its great bow, they flung it around in an arc of nearly sixty degrees, pressing it over on its side into the valley of a giant trough. Over and over the bow plunged into one abyss after the other and lay at the foot of waves forty-five to sixty feet high which came crashing over its deck. As the ship fell repeatedly into the bottom of the troughs, the impact jarred every plate, strained every rivet, and tested every seam. Relentlessly, gigantic wave after wave smashed across the deck, some of the larger ones destroying the lifeboats and sweeping the shattered pieces of fiberglass over the side in their wake. Fortunately the helicopter was secured in its hangar. Every experienced hand on board wondered how much punishment the great ship could take before crumbling beneath the fury of the storm. No one, not even Haverson or Maslov, even dared to think of the iceberg.

At last Hurricane Victor subsided almost as abruptly as it had appeared. The swirling masses of dense, threatening clouds drifted quickly out of sight, moving onward, preparing to wreak their havoc elsewhere. Breathing a collective sigh of relief, the crew of the *Aquarius* surveyed the damage left in the wake of the storm. Needless to say, the ship was in a shambles. In the dining room, tables were smashed and chairs overturned, plates and utensils scattered about. In the cabins and crews' quarters, lockers were sprung, the contents spilled about, bunks askew, belongings everywhere. In the innocent calm which followed the storm, as though the latter had never occurred, the crew set about to put the ship in order.

When Haverson saw that things were once again under control, he turned his attention to the iceberg, hardly daring to contemplate what he might find as he raised his binoculars. Bringing the great white block of ice into focus, he realized that, although the insulation was ripped and generally torn away, the iceberg itself seemed miraculously to be intact. At least it had not split in two as Maslov had feared. Haverson, although not a religious man, lowered his binoculars and gave a silent prayer of thanks. If the ice had been able to survive the wrath of the hurricane, it could probably survive anything. Chances seemed favorable that it might actually arrive in California—and in reasonably good shape. As soon as possible he would follow Maslov's advice and arrange for the bollards to be replaced and the iceberg reversed. From now on he was taking no chances.

Dropping in on Maslov to inform him of his decision, Haverson found the Russian sprawled in his bed, his belongings still strewn about from the hurricane. He had observed that the Chief Engineer was conspicuously absent during the clean-up operations but gave it little thought, assuming he was preoccupied with the iceberg monitoring equipment. To see his quarters in such disarray was jarring and certainly uncharacteristic. Among the general shambles Haverson noted, with some dismay, several empty bottles of vodka.

His opening the door had apparently not aroused Maslov. "Yuri," Haverson called out. "Are you awake?"

After he repeated his name several more times in a louder voice, Maslov finally stirred. Raising his head, he opened his bloodshot and bleary eyes, looked at Haverson and mumbled something in Russian.

"English," Haverson demanded.

"You want English? I talk to you in English." Reaching for one of the empty bottles, he heaved it at Haverson, shouting, "You bastard!" Striking the wall, the bottle smashed to bits and showered the stunned captain with a hail of flying glass.

39

Although Haverson was puzzled by Maslov's open display of anger, he had no time to dwell on the reasons for it. Instead, his energies were concentrated on preparing to reverse the iceberg.

"I'm hoping that if we can get it turned around and put the towing stress on the other end, we can prevent it from splitting," he confided to MacFergus.

The First Officer considered a moment. "It's not going to be easy, sir," he said.

"I know that," Haverson agreed.

"I understand that Maslov's in no shape to count on?" MacFergus said, looking to Haverson for confirmation or denial.

"Not until he sobers up."

"And if he doesn't, sir?"

"Then we'll just have to proceed without him," Haverson said. "Nobody's indispensable around here."

Later that day, Haverson called a conference in order to outline the planned reversal. On his way to the ship's library where the conference would be held, he encountered Sally.

"Hi," she smiled. "Have you seen Maslov?"

"Yes. Why?" he asked, wondering what she was leading up to.

Looking worried and anxious, she said, "Then you know?"

"Know what?"

"That he's absolutely smashed," she replied. "I've never seen anybody so drunk. I mean, he's really wild. And his cabin—it's unbelievable! You should see it—glass all over the place . . ."

"I know," Haverson said. "I was there a little earlier."

"I don't understand it. It's not like Yuri. What's happened to him?" she questioned.

He put a hand on her shoulders, he said, "I'm sorry, Sally, but I just don't have time now to go into it. I have an important meeting with the ship's officers."

"Important meeting?" she repeated, the romantic interlude of the previous night had not dulled her reportorial instincts. "Anything I should know about?"

"If you don't, you soon will."

"Are you going to tell me?"

"In good time."

"Don't keep me waiting too long," she said. "There's nothing worse than stale news."

"I'll keep it fresh for you," he said, brushing her lips lightly as though apologizing for his brusqueness, and continued on his way.

While Haverson was in conference, Sally decided to go back to Maslov's quarters. Armed with a broom, dustpan, and trash can, she entered as quietly as possible, trying not to disturb the sleeping Russian. As she was cleaning up the broken glass, she contemplated the Chief Engineer and his present state. It had not taken her long to realize that he was temperamental, perhaps even somewhat eccentric, but this new wrinkle—getting roaring drunk apparently alone— seemed out of character.

When she emptied a dustpan full of broken glass into a metal trash container, Maslov suddenly sat up, aware from the loud clatter that someone was in the room. He called out something in Russian which Sally assumed was the equivalent of "Who's there?" and then, as if realizing, despite his state, that his intruder might not understand the Slavic tongue, he shouted in English, "Who's there?"

"It's me—Sally," she replied.

"Sally? he repeated groggily, looking puzzled. "What are you doing?" His voice was thick, his speech somewhat slurred.

"Doing?" she repeated. "I'm trying to clean up this mess."

"Leave it," he said. "Leave it."

"I can't do that, Yuri. Look . . ."

"Leave it, I said," he repeated sternly.

"But there's broken glass all over the floor," she pointed out. "I can't just leave it. You could get cut or something."

"So?" he muttered, groaning as he shifted positions in bed. Laying her hand sympathetically on his forehead, she noted that it was damp with perspiration, although the quarters felt cool.

"I am still very drunk," he groaned, shaking his head in dismay. "Still very drunk."

"You're not drunk; you're hung over," she corrected.

"All right 'hung over,' " he conceded. "Whatever you want."

"Why did you do it?" she asked. "I mean, why did you get drunk alone?"

Rolling away from her, as though embarrassed by the question, he pressed his unshaven face into the pillow. "Do you have to ask?" he said.

"I'm certainly no mind reader, if that's what you mean," she retorted, beginning to suspect from the way he was behaving that it might have something to do with the fact that she had spent the night with Haverson. After all, he had seen her coming out of his cabin.

"In Russia if you have pain, you take a little vodka," he said.

"And you have pain?"

"A little."

"Where?"

Maslov shrugged. "What does it matter?"

"I'm sorry," she said softly, touching his cheek with the tips of her fingers.

Attempting to shift the focus of his complaints from the emotional to the physical, he moaned, "Ah, what a terrible headache I have. And my stomach hurts very much also."

"Do you want me to get you some aspirin?" she offered. "And maybe some Alka-Seltzer?"

"Yes," he nodded. "Please, get me something."

When Greg Dunne set the helicopter down atop the iceberg, Haverson could see at once that the hurricane had all but denuded the vast chunk of ice of its layer of insulation that had taken so much time and effort to apply. Bracing himself on the slippery surface against the fierce wind whipping the loose flaps of polyurethane about his legs, he said, "Greg, will you look at this?"

"Not much left of the insulation, is there, sir?" Dunne observed.

"We'll have to replace it as soon as possible," Haverson said. "With this hot sun beating down, we'll lose a lot of water fast if we don't. But first, we've got to get it reversed. If it splits before we get it turned around and reinsulated, we're in big trouble. Big, big trouble."

Haverson decided to use the original techniques employed in Antarctica for repositioning the bollards. The ice surrounding each bollard would be melted electrically, the bollard extracted, transferred to the opposite end of the iceberg and reimplanted in a new socket. The operation would be complicated and difficult and require all available manpower aboard the *Aquarius*. In addition, it was dangerous. Haverson was determined to prevent any such accident as had occurred in Antarctica when the young sailor had been killed.

Once the operation got underway, the two-seater helicopter made a score of runs, shuttling the crew from ship to iceberg, leaving only the most essential members aboard the vessel.

In the subzero antarctic temperatures, once the holes were drilled, the melted water immediately and solidly refroze around the base of each bollard, but in the tropical climate off Mexico's west coast, chemical additives would be necessary.

With Haverson and the other officers pushing hard, the operation progressed rapidly. While one work crew was extracting the first bollard, another was preparing its new site at the opposite end of the iceberg and a third group readied equipment with which to apply the new insulation. Haverson wanted insulation applied around it immediately, the moment a bollard was securely in place, to speed the refreezing process.

Maslov's absence was quickly noticed by the men. It was most unusual for the Russian Chief Engineer not to be involved in such activity, offering leadership, giving suggestions, coming up with all kinds of advice.

"Where's Yuri?" one of the men attempting to master the insulating equipment asked.

"Yeah, where the hell is that mad Russian when we need him?" his partner added.

"The Chief Engineer is under the weather," Haverson said, hoping such an explanation would end their inquiries.

While most of the men labored atop the iceberg, Sally attempted to help Maslov shake his hangover by feeding him strong coffee, aspirin, and B-vitamins. Eventually he recovered sufficiently to realize that an important operation was in progress—and without him.

"You must help me, Sally," he pleaded, anxious to become

258

a part of things as fast as possible. "Perhaps some tomato juice? . . ."

A little later, somewhat uncertainly, Maslov rose from his bunk, and made his way down to the main deck.

Watching the activity atop Snegoruschka, he suddenly pounded his fists against the rail. "That's where I must be!" he declared in frustration, pointing to the iceberg. "I was so stupid. So stupid."

As he and Sally monitored the distant activity they were interrupted by Lew Corbin, the radio operator, who burst upon them, looking pale and shaken.

"What is it?" Maslov asked, alarmed by the young man's appearance. "What's the matter?"

"On the radar screen," Corbin began in a quavery voice. "We've picked up another ship. It's on a no-bearing drift, rapidly closing range. Relative bearing is 0-5-7 off the starboard bow. If it continues its present course, there's a good possibility we could collide at approximately fifteen forty-three hours, sir."

"Impossible," Maslov scoffed. "They must have picked us up on their radar."

"From the looks of things, sir, their radar's probably been knocked out by the hurricane," the young radio operator answered. "They've made no move to alter their course."

Maslov was so stunned by the information that he started to give the man orders in Russian before he caught himself and switched to English. "Notify them on the emergency radio frequency," he commanded.

"We've been trying, sir," Lew Corbin said.

"And?" Maslov said expectantly.

"No response, sir."

Maslov was stunned. "What?! How can that be?"

"Apparently the storm must have knocked out their radio also, sir."

Shaking his head, Maslov said, "I can't believe this."

Without further exchange, Maslov headed to the radio room to see for himself exactly what the situation was. Although the day was bright and sunny, the room was dark and close, blinds drawn across the ports to shut out all external light. The only illumination in the room came from the various dials and screens of the banked communication equipment.

Standing before the pale and ghostly radar screen, Maslov observed a large white dot gliding silently, ominously across the series of range markers, obviously heading, just as Corbin had said, in their direction.

"My God!" he groaned.

"What do we do now, sir?" the radio operator asked.

"Nothing," Maslov replied, adding, "We sit and wait—for a miracle."

40

Despite the alluring and elegantly conspicuous mahogany bar, Preston Farleigh could not recall ever having seen Annalise Rudd take a drink in her office. She dispensed liquor to others quite freely, but she only sipped Perrier with a twist of lemon herself. This evening, however, was different. She went to the cabinet, filled a tumbler with gin, and promptly downed it.

"What's the occasion?" Farleigh asked, still unwinding from his last minute trip from Washington in response to an urgent summons from Annalise.

"Tonight, dear Preston," she announced with a twisted smile, "we are celebrating."

"Celebrating what?" he asked.

"Victory," she said. "Victory at last."

"Don't you think you're being a little premature?" he asked. "After all, the Amazon deal isn't closed yet, although I admit that—thanks to my efforts, if I may be so immodest—it does look like it's in the bag."

"That's not what I'm talking about," Annalise said. "To hell with the Amazon project—that's the least of my concerns at the moment. Besides, even without your help Rudd International has enough influence in high places in South America to get it through. I'm not worried about that."

"Your friends in Chile didn't do a very good job of holding Captain Haverson," Farleigh pointed out.

"That Saudi Arabian Akbar got into the act," Annalise replied. "He blackmailed them into releasing Haverson by threatening to interrupt oil supplies."

"You still haven't told me what victory we are celebrating," Farleigh reminded her.

"We, my dear accomplice, are celebrating the end of that dismal and irritating *Aquarius*," she said. Glancing at the diamond-studded Piaget around her slender wrist, she continued, "If my watch is correct—and it'd better be at the price I paid for it—in only a matter of minutes it will be all over. That ship and its ridiculous iceberg will be blown to bits. Nothing will be left to show for all of Kirkwood's machinations except a lot of little ice-cubes floating around the Pacific and maybe a sliver or two of steel." Annalise smiled and took another swallow of gin. "Too bad, isn't it?" she mused. "The whole thing is finished—kaput."

"Bad?" he questioned.

"Yes. Just when they were so close to home, too. Defeat snatched from the jaws of victory, so to speak," she sighed. "And then there's the matter of that great, big, and useless aqueduct waiting off Point Mugu to bring water to thirsty Californians. It was so considerate of Gabriel Rincon to reconstruct it after my little Rico played his dirty tricks. You do recall the name 'Rincon,' don't you?" she asked slyly. " 'Tony *Rincon*'?"

Uncomfortable at the mention of the name, Farleigh snapped, "Yes, of course I do."

"If it weren't for the poor departed Tony Rincon, you might not have your Senate seat today," she said. "Just imagine. . . ."

"I'm not so sure I wouldn't," he said defensively.

"Before his death in that unfortunate plane crash, the polls showed you didn't have a prayer, Preston dear," she chided. "You know that as well as I do. How convenient that Tony Rincon decided to take that small private plane to his rally. And how convenient that it just happened to crash in the Tehachapi Mountains. What would we ever do without Rico?"

Farleigh drummed nervously on the arms of his chair. "It was an accident," he insisted. "Small planes crash every day. I thought we agreed not to talk about it anymore?"

"You and *I* did," she said.

Somewhat alarmed, Farleigh said, "What about Rico? I thought you said he could be trusted? You're supposed to have him under your thumb."

"Lately he's been getting a little unruly."

"We can't have that."

"No, we can't," she agreed.

"What do you plan to do?"

"For the moment—nothing."

"He was the one who sneaked into that hangar the night before. . . ." Farleigh said anxiously.

"For the time being, I think we can count on Rico to keep his mouth shut—as long as I keep him entertained and regaled with gifts. In any case, we won't belabor that issue today." Changing the subject, she continued, "I suppose you know that Paul Kirkwood had a big celebration planned for the arrival of the *Aquarius?*"

"I figured he would," Farleigh said. "That bastard will squeeze every bit of publicity he can out of anything."

"You can't blame him, Preston. You'd do the same thing," she said. "You've *done* the same thing."

Farleigh bristled slightly. "So what?" he retorted.

She didn't want to launch into an argument and spoil the elation she was feeling, Annalise said, "I hear that the big surprise was that Bonnie Breit was going to sing at the ceremonies."

"What?! Impossible," Farleigh said, almost choking on his drink. "I heard she was disfigured beyond recognition in the fire."

"My dear Preston," Annalise said, "you underestimate the skills of our modern plastic and reconstructive surgeons. They can do miracles these days. I know. I understand that no one's seen her except Kirkwood and the staff at UCLA. If he decided to have her participate in the program, she must look all right. Naturally it will be her first public appearance since the Malibu fire. What a shame it will all be spoiled."

"If we can backtrack a moment, Annalise," Farleigh said, "just *how* do you plan to blow the *Aquarius* and its iceberg to bits? And why didn't you tell me before this?" he asked, somewhat miffed.

"Because I didn't want any leaks," she replied. "I have to have these offices checked every day to see if they're bugged. You have no idea how often the service uncovers things—and in the most unlikely places. I feel secure about what is discussed within these walls. In Washington, I feel no such security. You know what Washington is like. I don't have to tell you about the bugging that goes on there." Annalise paused a moment. "Besides, there is the matter of Sarajane. . . ." she added.

"Why are you bringing my wife into this?" he asked somewhat indignantly.

"She *does* have a certain reputation, you know."

"Reputation?" he challenged.

"For not keeping her mouth shut when she should."

"Only when she drinks," he said. "Sarajane has been on the wagon for months."

Annalise raised one of her finely shaped eyebrows. *"Has* she?" she questioned, sounding highly dubious.

"I should know, I'm her husband."

"Husbands are the last to know anything."

Farleigh bristled. "Now just a minute. . . ."

"Don't get huffy. I don't mean any offense. I'm just stating facts."

"I'm not so sure you've got your facts straight."

"Please, let's not argue tonight, all right?" she said, patting his hand and forcing an affable smile. "Don't you want to hear *how* I'm planning to do in the *Aquarius?*"

"Of course," he answered quietly.

"One of Rudd International's largest carriers of LNG is programmed to collide with it," she disclosed. "In fact, at this very moment, it's on its collision course."

Farleigh was stunned. The plan sounded far too bold and chancy for his taste. "What about the crew? There could be serious charges—homicide. . . ." he said anxiously.

"No one's going to know. It'll look like one of those freak accidents that seem to happen so often at sea. I have it all carefully worked out," she explained. "The ship is operated strictly by remote control—you know, instruments. There will be no casualties. Thank God for computer technology. I gave orders for the crew to be evacuated because of supposed damage to the ship from the hurricane which passed through the area recently. You may have heard about it?"

"Yes, of course," Farleigh said, his hand shaking as he raised his glass to his lips.

Annalise returned to the bar and poured herself another tumbler of gin. "Come on, Preston, drink up and stop being so nervous," she said. "Enjoy."

Standing atop the iceberg, which was slippery from the melting water, Haverson, confident that the first two bollards were firmly implanted and ready for the reattachment of the towing cables, was about to give the order to remove the final bollard. Routinely surveying the distant horizon with his binoculars, he was stunned to see what appeared to be a ship heading straight in their direction.

"What the hell!" he muttered to himself, certain it must be some bizarre kind of mirage, perhaps a result of the interplay between the cold from the ice and the heat from the sun. Passing the binoculars to MacFergus, who was nearby, he pointed in the direction of the oncoming ship and instructed him to take a look.

Equally filled with disbelief, the Scotsman turned and stared at Haverson. "What do you make of it, sir?" he asked.

"I don't know, but somehow I think I smell a rat," Haverson said. "A big rat. How about you?"

"What do we do?" MacFergus asked anxiously.

"The first thing we do is stay cool," Haverson advised. "We can't panic—at least not yet. I'm going to get in touch with Lew Corbin and make sure the proper signals that indicate to passing ships that we're towing are plainly visible on the mast. If the other vessel continues to pursue its present course, we'll blow the warning signals. If that fails, well, there's little else we can do except sound the alarm and put out the word over the intercom to prepare for a collision."

Haverson had difficulty accurately estimating how fast the oncoming ship was traveling, but even if it were coming at a slow speed, there was little to do. So far, none of the men on the iceberg had seen the approaching vessel, engrossed as they were shifting bollards and reapplying insulation. His first move was to inform helicopter pilot Greg Dunne that he wanted to fly back to the ship.

From the deck of the *Aquarius* Sally watched apprehensively as the strange ship drew ever closer, silent and malevolent, like the ghost ships of the horror movies and tales from her childhood. Despite her anxiety, her journalistic instincts remained intact. Setting up a camera, she began to record what could very well be impending disaster, resulting in not only the demise of the ship, but her own as well.

The moment the helicopter touched down on deck, Maslov ran to meet it. Flinging open the door of the aircraft, he pointed in the direction of the strange ship and shouted, "Do you see? Do you see it?"

"Hell, yes, we see it!" Haverson snapped.

"What are we going to do?" the Russian asked anxiously, finding it difficult to project his voice over the roar of the rotary blades. "We must do something quickly."

"We're sure as hell not going to sit here like sitting ducks," Haverson replied. "The way things are, we can't do much about our ship. We can't go anywhere to get out of the way.

265

The only thing we can do is try to do something about this other ship."

"Of course," Maslov concurred, adding, "but what? That is the problem."

Haverson gazed at Maslov as he considered the options. There seemed to be only one course of action and that was to board it and actually try and change its direction. In order to do that he would need expert help, someone who had a vast knowledge about the workings of all kinds of ships. The logical choice was Maslov. It was a crucial decision. Haverson would essentially be putting the lives of the crew, the ship, the mission, everything on the line.

"Come on, Maslov, get in," he said. "We'll talk on the way. We don't have a second to waste."

Eagerly Maslov climbed aboard the aircraft, squeezing next to Haverson, and slammed the door as they took off.

On deck Sally aimed her camera at the ascending helicopter as it rose into the sky and headed toward the oncoming ship.

The helicopter hovered above the mysterious tanker whose basic structure consisted of a series of five spherical tanks set into the hull with a multilevel superstructure at the stern.

"It looks like an LNG tanker," Haverson remarked.

"Do you think it's full?" Maslov asked.

"It seems to be riding very high in the water," Haverson replied. "So probably, yes."

"How much gas do you think she's carrying?" Maslov asked.

"Maybe seventy-five thousand cubic meters," Haverson speculated.

"You know what's weird, sir?" Greg Dunne asked. "She's got no flags or nothing—no identification."

"What do you expect?" Haverson said. "This is no ordinary ship. This is a death bomb, for chrissake."

"How fast do you think she's traveling?" Dunne asked.

"Maybe fifteen knots," Haverson guessed. "Which doesn't give us much time. She'll be on top of us before we know it. Whatever we do, we've got to do fast."

"There's no use trying to contact her," Maslov said, remembering earlier futile efforts aboard the *Aquarius*. "Everything's apparently dead, knocked out by the storm."

"More likely nobody's aboard and she's being run by remote control from some place far away," Haverson said in an ominous tone.

"Sir, you don't think ... she's been sent deliberately to blow us up?" Dunne asked hesitantly.

"Hell, yes!" Haverson snapped. "Do you think you can land this chopper on that baby?" he asked, referring to the LNG tanker below. The spherical tanks filled with the highly volatile gas under tremendous pressure and very low temperature obliterated most of the usual deck space.

"Yes, sir," the pilot answered and descended at once. Selecting an area just forward of the superstructure, Dunne deftly set the chopper down.

"Come on, Yuri, let's go," Haverson urged, tugging at Maslov's sleeve. As they scrambled out of the helicopter, he directed Dunne to be ready to take off fast when they returned.

With their combined knowledge of all types of ships, Haverson and Maslov located the pilothouse quickly and found it empty, just as suspected. The old-fashioned wheel was replaced by a single steel lever firmly locked into position. In spite of their efforts, it refused to budge.

"Well, there's only one thing to do in a case like this and that's to play pirate," Haverson said.

" 'Pirate'?" Maslov repeated, puzzled. "What is that?"

Discussing the general plan of the ship, eerie and ghostlike without a crew, the two men descended deep into the hull, their footsteps echoing hollowly, hoping to locate the shaft alley.

"If we can put a few well chosen pins into the proper place, we can deflect the rudder and cause this ship to swerve away from the *Aquarius*," Haverson explained.

"Let's go," Maslov nodded in agreement.

Locating the shaft alley, they sized up the situation from a navigational standpoint, found some pins of the sort they required, and tried to figure out the most strategic points at which to place them.

"Here's hoping we're successful," Haverson said as he inserted the first pin, hoping it would force the mechanisms to act contrary to electronic signals from the remote control base. "If we're not, it could be the end of everything—us included."

"They say that the explosion of a tanker this size loaded with LNG is equivalent to a hydrogen bomb," Maslov said as he prepared to insert a second pin.

From the creaking and groaning, obvious signs of strain, they were fairly certain that the rudder was being successfully deflected to some degree, but more was necessary.

Maslov inserted several additional pins as Haverson glanced at his watch.

"Come on, Yuri, we'd better get out of here," he urged. Based on rough calculations of how long it would take the LNG tanker to reach the *Aquarius,* he knew that there was little time to spare if the ship were set to blow up the moment the two vessels came into contact.

Racing up to the deck, they jumped into the helicopter and Dunne immediately took off.

"Hey! You did it!" the young pilot said, excitedly. "You guys did it! The damned ship is turning. Look at it! She's turning!"

"Just get us away from this mother as fast as you can," Haverson said.

"I still don't understand what 'pirates' means?" Maslov persisted.

"When pirates attacked a ship and wanted to get control of it, they had special wedges they used to drive between the rudder and the ship."

"Ah! Just like we did," Maslov said with a grin.

From five thousand feet up they watched the tanker continue on its altered course. Just as Haverson was about to express doubts to Maslov and Dunne that the tanker had been set to blow up, a series of soft "pops" came from it, which he was certain represented the rupture of the LNG-filled tanks. Following the pops, a large, milky-white cloud began to form, resembling a patch of very dense fog.

"Hey! Look at that!" Dunne exclaimed.

"That cloud's due to the supercold gas converting the normal moisture in the air into ice crystals," Haverson explained, as the cloud spread out, forming a gigantic white umbrella.

Suddenly there was a flash so blinding, even at five thousand feet, that neither Haverson, Dunne, nor Maslov could see anything for several minutes.

"Hiroshima!" Dunne cried.

Seconds after the flash, the sound of the blast, which was louder than anything any of the men had ever experienced before, occurred. The concussion rocked the aircraft.

"Hold it steady, Greg!" Haverson shouted, fearing the pilot might lose control from the impact.

"I am. I am," Dunne replied.

The air quickly cleared—as it would not have in a nuclear

blast. And below, where only moments before the gigantic LNG tanker was plying its way through the water, there was nothing.

The LNG blast rocked the *Aquarius* harder than the biggest waves of the worst antarctic storms, breaking a few of the armored windows and knocking a few hatches off the hinges. All in all, however, no one was seriously injured and the damage to the ship was minimal. The iceberg, too, seemed to come through all right. Many of the men on its surface at the time of the explosion were knocked off their feet by the concussion, but none fell into the surrounding sea. Everyone recovered rapidly.

Later, when things were once again under control, Maslov stopped by Haverson's cabin and attempted to apologize for his drunken outburst. "I don't know what was wrong with me," he said. "I must have been crazy."

"Look, Yuri, I don't want to waste time with apologies now," Haverson said brusquely. "I want to check out our baby back there and find out how she came through that concussion from the blast. I know she looks all right, but it's what's going on inside that block of ice that concerns me."

"I will look into it right away," Maslov said.

"And don't come back unless the answer is that she's okay and is going to make it to Point Mugu," Haverson added with an exaggerated scowl.

As soon as Maslov left, Haverson resumed trying to learn the identity of the LNG tanker, convinced that the *Aquarius* and all aboard had been its intended victims.

Maslov reported to Haverson that the crack over which they had agonized so long had been definitely aggravated by the tremendous force of the blast, and now extended deep into the mammoth block of ice.

"It's my belief," Maslov said, "that the force of the sea, as it rushes past, will exert sufficient pressure on the sides to keep it together once we get it reversed."

"Which is what we were doing when we were so rudely interrupted," Haverson remarked. "Will you stake your reputation on your theory about the sea keeping it together?"

"I will," the Russian answered.

Surprisingly it was none other than Sally who contributed the most useful information in uncovering the identity of the

LNG tanker. She had successfully recorded it from its approach to the final explosion, and she turned over the tape to Haverson, who, in turn, notified Kirkwood of its existence. Kirkwood requested a copy at once and in a relatively short time sent back word that the identity of the mysterious supertanker had been uncovered. The governor agreed that it was part of a plot to demolish their undertaking and assured them that steps were being taken by the appropriate agencies against the company involved.

"Well, Sal, it looks like it's in the governor's hands now," Haverson said. "All we have to do is arrive at Point Mugu with the ship, ourselves, and Snegoruschka in one piece."

41

When Annalise's agents warned her that the authorities had gotten wind of the plot against the *Aquarius* and might close in at any moment, she made hasty plans to escape. A private jet would whisk her away to her father's heavily guarded ranch near Asunción, Paraguay. Rushing about her elegant townhouse, she gathered up jewelry and other valuables. Rico would remain behind, unaware that a generously paid assassin was lurking in the shadowy garden behind the house waiting for a signal from Annalise—the raising of a blind in the master bedroom—to blow the boy's head off with a high-powered rifle. Annalise had few regrets about having arranged her paramour's impending execution. She accepted it as inevitable. Rico simply knew too much and could no longer be trusted to keep his mouth shut. Besides, he had become a bore. As for Preston Farleigh, she knew that he would have to be taken care of as well, but in a different fashion. If things got hot—and she was certain they would—there was no telling what desperate measures he might stoop to. Unlike Rico, Farleigh had some measure of power, and she could not risk his using it against her.

As she was scooping her priceless collection of imperial Chinese jade from the safe behind a panel in the dining room into a Vuitton bag, Rico entered unexpectedly.

Puzzled by her frenetic activity, he asked, "What are you doing?"

"I have decided to have my jewelry appraised, that's all," she said. "To see how much it has appreciated."

Rico was not fooled by such an explanation. "There is trouble, isn't there?" he said.

"Yes," she admitted, deciding there could be little harm in

271

his knowing anything at this point. As soon as she raised that bedroom blind, it would be all over for him anyway.

"You are running away," he observed.

"Not exactly," she replied. "I'm just leaving for a while, that's all."

"And me?"

"I'll send for you in a few days," she said. "As soon as I get settled."

"Where are you going?" he asked.

"I'm not sure."

"I don't believe you."

"I haven't made up my mind yet."

"You are not telling the truth," he accused.

"Look, Rico, I don't want to discuss it now," she said. "Go up to my bedroom and watch TV."

In spite of herself, Annalise still could not shake a certain sentimental attachment she had for the boy. Since she had hired the assassin, she had been trying to convince herself that she was tired of Rico, that he was an inept bungler, a risk, a detriment, that his death would be no great loss. At the moment she had far more important things to think about than the fate of one Brazilian street waif.

Against Jeremiah Gaines's advice, she had used Rudd International stock as collateral in the highly speculative Neptunus Limited deal. After a legal decision against the company nullified its claim to manganese nodules on the ocean floor, the lenders were demanding their money. A lesser person might have been devastated by the recent chain of events, but Annalise was strong and still felt very much in control. When she reached Paraguay, she would be safe. Her father had enormous influence in that country, a haven for ex-Nazis. She knew that she could never be extradited to face charges in the United States and she had enough personal assets to live luxuriously for the rest of her life. And as for sex—well, Paraguay was close to Brazil. There would be plenty of Ricos.

At the moment her chief concern was getting the present Rico back to the bedroom. Perhaps if she were to go first, he would follow, especially if she offered the right lure.

"Where are you going?" he asked, trailing at her heels.

"There are some things in the wall safe in the master bedroom I need," she replied.

"You won't send for me," he pouted, folding his slender arms across his smooth chest. "I know you won't."

"Yes, I will," she said unconvincingly. "Please, Rico, sit down on the bed and watch television and don't bother me now."

"How will I live without you?" Rico continued, ignoring her pleas.

"You'll have nothing to worry about," she assured him. "I have arranged with Jeremiah Gaines to see that you continue to get your allowance while I'm gone," she said. She had done no such thing. In fact, a short while earlier, an officer of the company had phoned to report that Jeremiah Gaines had been taken to the hospital, the victim of a massive heart attack, and was not expected to live. The shock of the impending collapse of the Rudd International empire had been too much for the old man.

As Annalise twirled the dial on the wall safe, Rico paced nervously back and forth across the room. "Why can't I go with you?" he persisted.

"Because you can't," she said. "Now go lie down and smoke your hash pipe and drink your liqueur and watch TV like I asked you to. I have no time to argue."

"You will take me!" he said, stomping his foot. "You will!"

"I told you," she said, swinging open the round steel door. "You will stay here until I send for you."

Flinging himself to the floor, he pounded his fists into the thick white carpet in a childish tantrum. "I want to go! I want to go!" he wailed.

"Stop it, Rico," she demanded. "Stop it this minute, damn it."

"No! No! I don't want you to go without me," he cried, violently kicking a gilded Louis XIV antique chair.

She decided that another approach might be more effective and switched to a more persuasive tone. "If you stop this hysterical outburst, I'll give you a very special present."

The ruse worked; he halted his tantrum and sat up. Eyeing her suspiciously, he asked, "What is it?"

"You'll see," she said with a sly smile, abandoning her diamonds for the moment. From deep within the safe she removed the ordinary shoebox by which he had been fascinated for so long. Rico's eyes grew wide with desire as she held it teasingly in front of him.

"Let me have it!" he begged, reaching out for it. "Please let me see what is inside. You promised, remember?"

"No, not yet," she said, keeping the box beyond his grasp. "First you must promise me something."

"What?"

"Actually several things," she replied. "First you must promise to get up off the floor and stop these tantrums and that you'll stop making a silly scene over my going away."

"Is that all?"

"No. I want you to go lie down on the bed."

"What else?"

"There's a phone call I want you to make."

Rico frowned. "A phone call?" he repeated. He was stunned by such a request. It was something she had never asked of him before. "You know I don't speak English very well on the telephone."

"Don't worry," she assured him. "This time you'll do fine. I'll tell you exactly what to say—every word."

Coached by Annalise, Rico made the phone call informing no less an agency than the FBI that the crash of Tony Rincon's private plane had been no accident.

"If you will investigate better the wreckage," he advised, "you will find evidence of sabotage. The person who benefited most from Tony Rincon's death is Senator Preston Farleigh. He is the one responsible."

Listening to Rico repeating these incriminating accusations in his heavily accented English, Annalise smiled triumphantly. This bit of information leaked to the FBI would fix Farleigh for good. She had no regrets. She had, in fact, nothing except contempt for him. Besides, like Rico, he had outlived his usefulness. At best the relationship had been expedient, and now it was over.

When Rico replaced the receiver, Annalise delivered the box into his eager hands. Quickly removing the lid, he parted the layers of tissue paper. Inside were nestled the most elegant and beautiful pair of shoes he had ever seen. Caressing the leather, he found it incredibly soft and supple, deep ivory in color, yet almost translucent.

"I have never seen shoes like these before," he gasped, handling them delicately as though his fingertips might damage the leather.

"No, I don't suppose you have," she agreed, placing her hand on the pull-cord of the blind, preparing to raise it. He couldn't have been more advantageously positioned for the gunman outside. Within seconds Rico would be dead. Suddenly Annalise began to have second thoughts. The least she could do for him would be to allow him to die in the shoes. "Don't just stand there staring, put them on," she urged.

"Oh, I could not," he protested, awe in his voice as he gazed at the shoes.

"Of course you can, silly," she chided. "Now, put them on."

"They are too beautiful for the feet."

"Go on, put them on."

Shaking his head, he said, "No, no. . . ."

Shoving him down onto the bed, Annalise yanked off his shoes and prepared to replace them with the new ones. As she began to slip the new shoe over his foot, Rico suddenly stiffened, and bolted upright.

"What's wrong?" she asked. "Too tight?"

"No."

"What then?"

"There is a mark," he pointed out, looking deeply distressed. "Near the toe."

"I don't see anything. . . ."

Suddenly snatching the shoe in question out of her hand, he snapped on the bedside lamp and examined it in a stronger light. Near the toe there was a definite blemish, rather bluish in color. Inspecting it closer, he saw that the blue marks were a row of numbers deeply tattooed into the leather.

"That is a—how do you say?—tattoo," Rico said.

"So it is," Annalise admitted.

"This is not leather," he said.

"It's the finest," she insisted.

"It is . . . human skin!" Rico gasped, hardly able to get the words out.

"I said, it's the finest leather," Annalise repeated nonchalantly. "A gift from my dear father. A memento of the camps. His greatest regret was that the Nazis didn't run everything as efficiently as they did the death camps."

"Monster!" Rico gasped, pointing a finger accusingly at Annalise. "You are a monster!"

"What are you talking about?" she asked nervously. She had never seen such shock and revulsion on Rico's face before and it frightened her. Quickly she reached for the pull-cord on the blind, but before she had a chance to raise it, he sprang off the bed at her and seized her by the throat. "Monster!" he cried again and again. The pressure of his strong hands around her neck provoked only terror and dread and none of the erotic sensations she had expressed on previous occasions. This time as the veins in her neck bulged and pulsated against the increasing pressure of his fingers, she struggled

275

to free herself but could not. Her strength was ebbing too fast.

"Monster!" Rico was still shrieking as his fingers locked tightly beneath her purple, swollen face, her tongue protruding, thick and limp.

42

During the final leg of the voyage, tensions ran high. As the ship drew nearer its destination, concern for the iceberg mounted. Despite the fracture through its middle, the reversal proved successful in keeping it together. The crew of the great ship had worked hard, experienced more hazards and adventure, both natural and man-made, on this voyage than many seamen do in a lifetime, and they were glad that the end was near, anxious to set foot on land and be reunited with families and loved ones once again.

The morning the *Aquarius* neared Santa Monica, Haverson announced over the intercom that if all went well, they would reach their ultimate destination in a few hours. Raucous cheering and shouting greeted the news. Bottles were opened, passed around, and emptied. Songs were sung; impromptu dances danced.

"I can't believe it!" Sally exclaimed, making preparations to tape the ship's arrival.

"It does seem pretty incredible," Haverson admitted. As they stood at the rail he slipped his arm around her and held her close. "Even to me. I can't believe it. Do you realize how many men never live to see their dreams fulfilled?"

"What about women?" Sally reminded him. "Not many of us get that chance either. Look what I had to resort to in order to make this voyage."

Haverson looked at her quizzically, wondering if she were serious or not. "You mean this was your dream, too?"

"One," she said, "of many. I'm still working on the rest."

According to plans formulated before the ship's departure, the *Aquarius* was anchored in the deep waters off Point

Mugu, the iceberg detached, and nudged into place adjoining the floating aqueduct so that appropriate connections between iceberg and aqueduct could be made. The insulation was removed from a portion of its surface and special photovoltaic cells which concentrated the sun's heat were trained on the exposed ice. The heat generated by these solar energy cells melted the ice, and the resulting water flowed into the aqueduct which would, in turn, carry it to shore and into the existing California water system. It was all relatively simple and quite efficient.

In Sacramento Kirkwood's staff was jubilant and planned a gala program to celebrate the delivery of this first antarctic iceberg. As the governor's press representative, it was Wally Weisswasser's job to see that the event received maximum attention from the media.

"Look at this," Weisswasser said, letting loose a flurry of pink telephone message slips. His desk was piled high with telegrams and letters. "Everybody wants to get into the act. Scientists, sports figures, entertainers, politicians. Everybody wants to be a part of the program. The tough part is choosing."

"Let's face it, Wally, it *is* an incredible accomplishment," Kirkwood said.

"I'll say one thing, if nothing else, this iceberg has really turned around our standing in the polls," Drew Ramsdale commented, sifting through the latest public opinion surveys. "We've zoomed from the bottom to the top in a matter of hours. From the way people are responding to the polls, it looks as if we can do no wrong."

"Good," Kirkwood said, slapping his chief aide on the back. "That's what we want, isn't it?"

On the day of the ceremony, officially proclaimed "Aquarius Day" by the governor, Paul Kirkwood stepped proudly to the red, white, and blue draped speaker's rostrum. Flanked by United States and California flags and looking both dapper and triumphant, he faced the assembled crowds and flashed the broad, friendly smile that had served him so well in many political campaigns.

"My good friends, fellow Californians, and fellow Americans," he began, aware of the national television coverage of the occasion. A stiff breeze off the ocean tousled his dark hair. Nature had been kind to Aquarius Day, providing exceptionally clear air. Offshore, in the distance, the *Aquarius* as well as the gleaming, bluish white mound of south pole ice were clearly visible. "Today is indeed a proud and significant day in the history of our state. There is nothing more gratifying to those of us in public life than to see a promise fulfilled. As I stand here before you gazing out over this blue Pacific, I am reminded that a promise made to the people of California has been kept. At last I have been able to bring water to our beleaguered state. Captain Neal Haverson and the outstanding and gallant crew of the *Aquarius* are to be applauded." He paused, turning to acknowledge Haverson's presence on the platform. The crowd cheered and applauded. Ingrid, seated beside her husband, smiled and squeezed his hand. Haverson, unaccustomed to such public praise, blushed slightly. "Those daring and enterprising men have proven that we do indeed possess the technology to bring water in the form of frozen icebergs from Antarctica, not only to California, but to all the arid areas of the earth. I am proud that our state has taken the lead in expanding the horizons of the world with regard to that most precious and least appreciated of all resources, water. We are no longer dependent on the caprices of local weather to provide us with the water on which our lives so vitally depend. Yes, my friends, the long, dry siege is over at last. Drought has been conquered. Man's ingenuity and resourcefulness have once again triumphed. Thanks to Almighty God, California has and will continue to have . . . water."

With those words, Kirkwood stepped down from the rostrum and walked over to a symbolic valve connected to the floating aqueduct and turned it. Instantly sparkling clear water appeared. Holding a glass beneath a spigot, he filled it, raised the glass high and toasted the crowd. "To your health, Californians, America!" As he drank, a deafening roar went up. Kirkwood knew from that overwhelming acclaim that no matter what was said about the Akbar land deal, he was home safe. That most powerful of forces, public opinion, was on his side.

The program was concluded on a startling and triumphant note of an entirely different kind—the combined brainchild of Kirkwood and Weisswasser. From a sleek, dark limousine parked behind the speakers' platform, Bonnie Breit emerged wearing a long-sleeved, high-necked gown of pale turquoise, nicely offsetting her auburn hair. The plastic surgeons had concentrated on restoring her face so that she could resume her career as soon as possible and their efforts had been most successful. Although she still faced many more operations in the future, Bonnie considered herself fortunate to be able to greet the public once again, even in her present condition. When her adoring fans realized she was about to make an appearance, they went into a state of near hysteria, screaming, "Bonnie! Bonnie! We love you, Bonnie!"

Surrounded by a special contingent of bodyguards, Bonnie made her way up the steps, with only minimal assistance. On the platform she was greeted with a warm kiss from Paul Kirkwood, which brought forth a riot of excited squeals from the crowd.

Stepping confidently before the microphone, Bonnie thanked her fans for their loyal support throughout the long recuperation. Then, in a slightly quavery voice, overcome with emotion, she began to sing, *"This land is your land, this land is my land. . . ."*

43

The strangulation of Annalise Rudd by her teenaged
Brazilian paramour and the concomitant collapse of the vast
Rudd International empire usurped considerable attention
from the Aquarius story in the media. Sally Brennan's superb
coverage kept the success of the Aquarius Transfer mission a
major news story. KHOT's ratings had risen to new heights
on the basis of the Aquarius series, and Ken Wilson was
anxious to keep them high. In all kinds of subtle—and not so
subtle—ways he tried to induce Sally to stay on, well aware
of her value as a personality and the fact that her contract
was about to expire. At one time it had seemed that her job at
the station was the very center of her life, but since her
return from Antarctica, she was no longer so certain. Among
his inducements were a prestigious parking space right next
to the entrance, an unlimited expense account, an opportunity to anchor the nightly news coupled with the option of
doing stories of her own choosing, as well as a substantial
increase in salary. Sally had not escaped the attention of
executives of the three major networks in New York, and
several attractive offers were said to be in the works for her.
For her part, Sally was taking things in stride, listening to
all offers but making no commitments to anyone, steadfastly
refusing to give even the slightest hint as to what her
ultimate decision might be.

"I think I might like to help with Paul Kirkwood's campaign if he is nominated for the presidency—and I'm sure he
will be," she said casually over coffee to Ken Wilson. "Maybe
that way I could get myself a position on the White House
staff. That might be interesting. I could be press secretary or
something. I might even wind up with a cabinet post. It's

possible. At this point, the only thing I know for sure is that I'm going on a vacation."

"Good. You need one. You've earned a rest after the great job you've done," Wilson said. "Go with my blessing. But you'll have some kind of an answer for me when you get back, won't you?"

"Possibly, Ken," she said with an enigmatic smile.

Sally's vacation took her to Washington, D.C., certainly not a likely place for a reporter to relax and unwind and get away from things, but Sally had learned that Haverson was going to be there.

"Well, now what, Captain?" she had asked after the Aquarius Day ceremonies as the two of them stood on the high rocks at Point Mugu gazing wistfully at Snegoruschka shrinking slowly as she relinquished her precious water to drought-stricken California. Ingrid and their two daughters had remained behind to chat with Bonnie Breit and the governor.

"Home for a while, I guess," he responded.

"Ingrid will like that."

"Yeah, I suppose."

"And then?"

"I'm going to Washington to try to clear my name with the navy—for my own personal satisfaction, if nothing else," he said. "I think the diary will help. It shows what was going through Elizabeth Nagy's head the day she died."

"Well, good luck," Sally smiled.

"Thanks. Good luck to you, too." After an awkward pause and a cautionary look around, he suddenly took her in his arms.

Back at her Marina del Rey condominium, Sally found herself restless, nagged by the feeling that there were still some loose ends in her relationship with Haverson which needed to be tied up. Learning he had left for Washington after only a few days at home, she decided that the nation's capital might be a good place to do just that. Washington offered the kind of anonymity she was seeking.

The moment she arrived she got in touch with Haverson, who was surprised to hear from her.

"I hope I haven't done something stupid by coming here," she said, wondering if she had been too impulsive.

"Let's talk about it over dinner tonight," he said.

As they faced one another across a quiet table at the Prime Rib, a waiter in black tie served them.

"Have you seen the latest polls?" he asked. "Kirkwood has pulled way ahead of all the other presidential hopefuls. In fact, there's nobody even close—pretty good when you think how low his popularity was a little while ago."

"I don't think there's any doubt he'll get the nomination," Sally said.

"He gets things done and that's what counts," Haverson said. "This country could use a few more individuals like him."

"You ought to run for something," Sally proposed. "I'm serious."

"Politics isn't for me," he said. "Whatever I do, it'll have to be something connected with ships and the sea. It's in my blood."

"For sure," Sally agreed, having observed this love first-hand aboard the *Aquarius*.

"You still haven't told me what you're doing in Washington," he said. "I thought that when we said goodbye at Point Mugu that was going to be it."

"I came to see you," she admitted with her characteristic candor. "You see, I'm not much for one-night stands."

Reaching across the table, he took her hand and gazed at her with a glint of sly humor in his eye. "Want to make it two?" he asked.

"Sure. Why not?" she replied.

Just as they settled comfortably between the sheets in the bed of Haverson's hotel room and into one another's arms, the phone on the nightstand rang.

"Damn!" Haverson swore as he reached across Sally and picked up the receiver. She rolled onto her stomach and covered her head with the pillow to muffle the conversation.

When he hung up, he nudged her excitedly. "Want to hear something that'll knock your socks off?" he said.

"I'm not wearing any," she replied. "I'm not wearing anything."

"That was Kirkwood," Haverson went on. "Preston Farleigh has just been arrested."

Stunned, she bolted upright. "Preston Farleigh, the senator? Our senator? What the hell for?" she asked.

"Remember Tony Rincon, the candidate killed in a plane crash just before the election?"

"Sure. It was a big story."

"Well, it seems that an anonymous tipster informed the

authorities that Farleigh had Rincon's plane sabotaged. They investigated the wreckage and found the tip was correct," he said.

"That Brazilian kid who strangled Annalise Rudd claimed she put him up to it."

"The FBI said the caller sounded suspiciously similar to that same kid," Haverson said. "He also claims he's the one who shot a bullet through my kids' bedroom window and hit my oldest girl with a drugged dart—among other things."

"Wow, this is all pretty heavy stuff," Sally remarked. "It seems hard to imagine a man like Senator Farleigh in prison."

"When he comes out he'll write a book and go on talk shows and become rich and famous like all the Watergate boys," Haverson commented. "Speaking of prison, what's happening with Amy Armistad? I expect to get subpoenaed any day on that case."

"You mean you don't know?"

"I'm not in the news business," he said. "Once the *Aquarius* was anchored, I turned her and her cohorts over to the authorities. And gladly."

"You know they let Dr. Terhune go, don't you?" she said. "They said he was clean with respect to any involvement in the conspiracy."

"Poor Terhune," Haverson mused. "He was so obviously being used by those people."

"Getting back to Amy, her lawyers are trying to plea bargain, offering her services to a legal clinic for the poor," Sally said. "It looks like she might get off easy."

"American justice," he said with a cynical sigh and, reaching out, pulled Sally toward him once again.

The single night Washington idyll, both Haverson and Sally agreed, would be the end of their affair.

"Let's not prolong it," she said. "We'll think of it as a summer romance—as if we had met at a Club Med or something—and now it's fall."

"Whatever you say," he said, as they stood beneath a canopy of delicate cherry blossoms near the Capitol.

"We'll keep in touch," she said, snuggling close to him. "And we'll be friends."

"I hope so," he replied. "And if you ever need anything . . ."

"I know," she said. "Just whistle."

Circling her with his arms, he felt her softness and warmth against him, sad that it was probably the final time. He knew

Sally was right. Anything more involved or complicated was out of the question. They were both mature enough to realize that they had responded to specific needs at a certain time and place. Now, those needs no longer existed, at least not in the same way or with the same urgency. Each of them was free to pursue his or her own destiny without any complications. Perhaps if circumstances were different . . .

The success of the Aquarius mission made Haverson much sought-after. Although he had become somewhat of an international celebrity, at home he had to share the limelight with his wife and daughters. Cathy had just been elected captain of the cheerleaders, Jill had won two blue ribbons in the latest horse show, and Ingrid had decided to go after her master's degree in special education. She was glad to have him at home, even though she knew it would not be for long, despite his intentions and whatever promises he made. Offers poured in from many sources. After thinking things through, he decided to sign with Prince Akbar and initiate a program transporting antarctic icebergs to Saudi Arabia, a new challenge he accepted with enthusiasm. Others offered more in the way of remuneration or benefits, but Haverson felt he owed a debt of gratitude to the Arabian magnate for his support of the project. His contract with the prince did, however, allow him to act as consultant to other firms planning to import antarctic water to such arid locations as southwest Africa, Australia, and western China.

"The crew had a lot to do with the success of the project," he said to Ingrid as they talked over his future. "I'd like to hire as many of the men as want to sign on with me. Ironically, the one man I want most turned me down. Yuri has chosen to return to Maine and have another go at writing his autobiography."

"At least that's what he says," Ingrid remarked, somewhat skeptical.

Leaving Washington, Sally, having learned from Haverson about Maslov, headed, rather impulsively, to Maine where she sought the Russian out much in the same way Haverson had originally and found him in a new cabin hideaway not far from the one which had been destroyed by fire.

"Call off those damned dogs, will you, Yuri?" she shouted above the noisy barking of the Dobermans, Russlan and Ludmilla.

Maslov was shocked to see her. And extremely happy. "Sally! ..." he said.

Instead of writing, he had been spending his days at his drawing board, trying to improve the design of future iceberg hauling ships, utilizing data he had compiled while aboard the *Aquarius*. Proudly, he showed her his work, though she understood little of the highly technical matters he was trying to explain.

"I want to design the perfect ship," he said. "The *Aquarius* was just a crude beginning."

Sipping the Russian tea and warming her hands with the glass at the same time, she asked, "Have you been playing much chess these days?"

"Not much," he said. "I have lacked partners."

"Well, you don't anymore," she said. "At least not for a while. Go get the chessboard."

GREAT ADVENTURES IN READING

☐ **FREE FALL IN CRIMSON**   14441 $2.95
by John D. MacDonald
Travis McGee comes close to losing his status as a living legend when he agrees to track down the killers who brutally murdered an ailing millionaire.

☐ **THE PAGAN LAND**   14446 $2.95
by Thomas Marriott
The story of a bold journey through the wilderness of nineteenth century South Africa in search of a homeland and of love.

☐ **CAPTIVE OF DESIRE**   14448 $2.75
by Becky Lee Weyrich
Even in the arms of the king, young Zephromae's cries are for her childhood sweetheart, Alexander. But Alexander can no longer protect her from the sly priest, the lust-mad prince, or the bitter queen.

☐ **MARRAKESH**   14443 $2.50
by Graham Diamond
Magic and miracles, satanic evil and everlasting love. This is an exotic adventure even more enchanting than the Arabian Nights.

☐ **BRAGG #1: BRAGG'S HUNCH**   14449 $2.25
by Jack Lynch
The first book in a new action series. Bragg finds himself in the middle of a deadly crossfire when he is hired to investigate who's been threatening the life of an ex-hood.

Buy them at your local bookstore or use this handy coupon for ordering.

COLUMBIA BOOK SERVICE, CBS Inc.
32275 Mally Road, P.O. Box FB, Madison Heights, MI 48071

Please send me the books I have checked above. Orders for less than 5 books must include 75¢ for the first book and 25¢ for each additional book to cover postage and handling. Orders for 5 books or more postage is FREE. Send check or money order only. Allow 3-4 weeks for delivery.

Cost $_____   Name_____

Sales tax*_____   Address_____

Postage _____   City_____

Total $_____   State_____ Zip_____

*The government requires us to collect sales tax in all states except AK, DE, MT, NH and OR.

Prices and availability subject to change without notice.   **8239**